An]
of England

Clive S. Johnson

Daisy Bank

Lancashire… "in this so unbridled and badde an handfull of England"

Ferdinando Stanley, Lord Strange, 1583

ISBN: 1799147983
ISBN13: 978-1799147985

4.5.1

CONTENTS

1   A Matter of Seconds   1

2   An Assuredly Grateful England   4

3   Recourse to Proof   12

4   Articulo Mortis   21

5   Fateful Comings and Goings   28

6   Last Straw   35

7   Out of an Affray   44

8   Newparke   54

9   Stolen Days   59

10   A Prospective New Companion   70

11   Silent Running   80

12   A View of the Mountain   87

13   A Paradox   97

14   Distractions   103

15   A Dawn Start   114

16   South, to Brereton   122

17   The Yellow-Haired Man   126

18   Choice of the Righteous   138

19   Misfits   144

20   What of Staffordshire?   152

21   Chance of a Rare Wisdom   162

22	Cocking a Snook	172
23	A Different Mountain	179
24	Consolatione Philosophiae	189
25	Setting Wheels in Motion	193
26	An Arresting Thought	198
27	Hope Dashed	207
28	"Butterfly Attack"	212
29	An Innocent Spy	217
30	Audience with the Queen	226
31	St. James's, Clerkenwell	235
32	A Rock and a Hard Place	245
33	Of the Heart, Not the Head	251
34	Hope Springs Eternal	256
35	A Letter in Evidence	262
36	Stir-Crazy	268
37	An Ill Wind	277
38	In the Dark	282
39	Salutary Reflection	289
40	Palm Sunday	295
41	A Weeping Wound	303
42	The Superior Weapon	309
43	Good Friday	315
44	Holy Saturday	320
45	The Colour of Rusty Iron	326

46 Black-Swathed Gentlemen   332

47 "Image of Waxe"   339

48 A Different Perspective   348

49 On Eagle's Wings   354

50 The Lesser of Two Evils   362

51 A Stalwart Companion   369

52 For a Graceful Child's Day   378

53 Bit of a Long Shot   387

54 A Lancashire Renaissance   393

Historical Notes   403

About the Author   425

1   A MATTER OF SECONDS

Something caught Dr Peter Buchanan's attention out of the corner of his eye. He looked up from his armchair, every muscle tensing.

Striding purposefully from the far corner of his lamp-lit lounge, towards the sofa across from him, came the figure of a man. Neither transparent nor wholly solid, the apparition ignored Peter, even when he shot to his feet, spilling papers to the floor.

By the time he'd noticed the man's strange clothing, the lower half of his body was already passing through the upright cushions of the sofa, his sights seemingly fixed on the alcove beside the fireplace. Peter had got no further than his mouth dropping open when the man silently vanished through the wall, the whole event over in a matter of seconds.

A shiver ran down Peter's spine, his stomach feeling strangely light, his mouth remaining open as he slowly sank back into the armchair.

"What the..." but then he noticed the medical

reports and paperwork scattered on the floor at his feet. He gathered them up and sat back, then again stared at the empty alcove.

"My God," he barely breathed out into the apartment's now noticeably cold silence, a shiver returning to his back. "That can't have happened. It just can't have," and his rational doctor's mind quickly dismissed it as him having just nodded off for a moment.

"It must've been. I must've dreamt it, for there's certainly no such things as ghosts." But even in his own ears, his subsequent sharp laugh sounded feeble.

That, more than the apparent apparition itself, worried him the most: was the strain of his life as a hospital doctor becoming too much? Despite how much he loved it. Despite the purpose it gave to his life. Despite it having been all he'd ever wanted to do since childhood. Had his single-minded dedication brought him, at only thirty-one, to this? To seeing things? Things that just couldn't be there.

Not for the first time in his life, he missed having someone close in whom he could confide.

"I wonder where you are now, Sophie, where in the world you might be." For a moment, his apartment dissolved to a view through the woods, down to the glitter of a river as it swept by where she sat on its bank. The reflected light dappled her freckled face and glinted from her long lashes as she bent forward, towards what only she could see in the water.

Slowly, the image faded and he shook his head, looking down at last at the gathered notes in his hand. He put them back in order and searched through for the blood results he'd been checking.

"At the moment, my clinic tomorrow morning's far more important, and I've still a lot to get through," and with that, he finally dismissed the whole event. Before long, he'd once more become wholly engrossed in the plight of his patients, everything else, for their sakes, studiously put behind him.

It was late for Peter when he eventually got to bed, by then content he'd done enough preparation. But only as he drifted off did the strange experience come back to haunt him, yet this time as nothing more than a fleeting thought before he sank into sleep.

2 AN ASSUREDLY GRATEFUL ENGLAND

The harbour was a riot of activity, goods being carried back and forth, men shouting, children running amok amongst it all. A high sun shone down strongly on Peter's back, warming the close-fitting jacket he wore. He was making his way through the throng towards three men standing by the edge of the quay, one of whom stepped forward to meet him.

Only now did their clothing surprise him, as too did the forest of masts and rigging that rose up beyond the quay, and only then did he wonder where he was.

"William Stanley?" the man quietly and guardedly enquired, leaning in a little closer, to which Peter's head seemed to nod of its own accord. "My master has sent strict instructions that thou art to refrain from addressing him by name, nor by his title. For the timbers of a ship have more ears than the bricks and stones of many a house. Be that understood?"

Again, Peter's head nodded, and a vague memory of having before seen the style of clothing the man wore now drifted briefly into his thoughts.

"If thou wouldst follow me," and the man led Peter toward the other two, still waiting by the quayside.

A scabbard briefly swung out from his escort's side as he silently took them all from the quayside and down some stone steps to a waiting rowing boat. The craft was crammed with rough-looking men, three a side and each seemingly ready at his shipped oar.

When Peter was taken aboard, he noticed he too seemed to be wearing the same thick leggings, a short fold of unfamiliar clothing at his hip briefly snagging on a rowlock as he stepped across.

Soon, they were through the placid waters of the busy harbour and out into the glistening swell of the open sea, a sailing ship at anchor directly ahead bathed in bright sunlight. At the bottom edge of his vision, drawing his attention from the hypnotic action of the rowers before him, Peter noticed his leggings were now darkened by his own shadow.

We're travelling north, away from the coast, he reasoned to himself. So, wherever we are, it must be a port on the north coast of somewhere. But everyone's speech had been so hard to get his ear around that he'd been unable to place what language had been in use by the labourers ashore, and all those in the boat remained resolutely silent.

Once alongside the sailing ship, drawn up tight against its rigging-hung hull, Peter was soon clambering up the rungs towards the rail. Hands helped him over and onto the deck, where more sailors dallied here and there, keeping their distance, half an eye on their guest. Those who'd helped him aboard drew away themselves at a look from Peter's escort.

"The captain's cabin," the man stated as he nodded astern.

Again, with none of his own volition, Peter pitched his way down the gently rolling deck and climbed a broad and steep ladder, up to a higher deck from which rose another huge mast. Going astern, he went in beneath a smaller deck above and fumbled his way down a dark passageway, drawn to its end by the dim light of an open doorway.

He stopped at its threshold, staring into a cramped cabin lit only by a long and low, gently bowed window across the extent of its far wall. Within lay a bunk upon one side, a chest of shallow drawers at the other, and a trunk in one corner. A narrow table took up much of the remaining space, a small bench on each side. At its head and facing Peter stood a chair, now occupied by a darkly silhouetted figure.

"Come, come into the light," it cautiously commanded in a light but masculine voice, and Peter stepped into the cabin. "Ah, my good sir, 'tis a relief to see my secretary has delivered me the right man," and he laughed, but without much mirth.

The unfamiliarity of his own voice, when it came, startled Peter: "My most esteemed... Er, *sir*, God give you good day."

"I'm hoping so, sir, though I don't take kindly to being ashipboard, although our crossing was slight—or so I was assured. If it would please you, sir, sit down here, beside me, so we may hold our words the privier." The man opened a delicate hand out across the corner of the table, towards the far end of one of the benches, to which Peter went and sat.

Closer now, and in the silence that ensued, Peter could just make out the man's long and narrow face, made the more so by his sharply pointed beard. His sallow complexion and heavily bagged doleful eyes, though, could hardly be seen from within the shadow cast by the light from the window behind him. Only his light-brown and swept-back hair caught its light directly. It set aglow a shimmering halo about the man's head.

"And to what, good sir," William's voice said, for Peter had now come to accept it as not his own, "may I ascribe your most courteous summons?" The man shuffled a little closer, resting his cultured hand confidently on the table top.

"I trust your travels within these our neighbouring countries are affording you a good measure of pleasure? And perhaps some illumination and a wider education?"

"Indeed, sir, they are. Though I must say: I find their papist ways somewhat of an affront that's at times hard to swallow, now I'm more...cheek-by-jowl with them."

"It seems to me that your being discharged from your service to Her Majesty's embassy at the French King Henri's court has delivered you some...some greater freedom, shall we say? In where your feet may take you, and to what knowing others there may have of your person and rank."

"A most welcome benefit, that I can't deny."

"And where, I wonder, will your coming days find those feet taking you, eh, William? What's likely to be there for the younger son of an earl that may arrest his interests? Can there be much to satisfy and thereby sate an astute mind such as yours?" He leant closer, across the corner of the table, his voice now barely audible.

"Eh, William Stanley, the *second* son of the fourth Earl of Derby? What prospect will there be then for you? And when, it has to be remembered, any attainments and ennoblement will still be forbidden you. And merely upon the whim of so cruel a mistress as time herself. Upon her fickle ordering of your own and your brother's births."

The man sat back, steepling his fingers against his narrow mouth, his shadowy eyes clearly attempting to read William's features. William himself shifted on the bench but finally straightened his back and cleared his throat.

"Where, sir, are you driving with this?" at which a smile slowly spread across the man's face.

"There's a matter, William, that I have close to my own interests, the purpose of which I need not go into. But one that my own eyes—beyond any intelligence I may know of—tell me is to our mutual gain." Again, he drew closer, his voice dropping even lower.

"You have a distant kinsman, a namesake who's at large in these parts. One whose interests now clearly lie with King Philip of Spain and Pope Sixtus of Rome."

"Do you mean the soldier, Sir William Stanley? My traitorous cousin?" William barked, at which the man clasped his arm and drew him nearer, keeping his voice this time to an emphatic whisper.

"Your brother, the cultured Lord Strange, he who has strongest claim of all in England to accession to the throne, has but two daughters as yet. Hence, he offers no direct heir to your father's earldom other than himself."

"His claim to the throne? His inheritance of the earldom afore me? What're you suggesting, sir?"

"If your brother, Ferdinando, the good Lord Strange, were to be discovered actively pursuing his claim to the throne, and if the Catholics abroad were found to be helping him, well, what could then unfold, eh?"

"But my brother's no Catholic. He does clear and regular observance unto the Protestant Church."

"He does, indeed he does, as a mummer from his own company of players might enact his learned part in one of their plays. But none can vouch for what may truly be in Lord Strange's heart—except, perhaps, his own blood brother. And perhaps said brother might, upon one day soon and when in easy discourse with a distant cousin, impart such *secret knowledge* unto that said distant cousin."

"Whether it be true in word or not," William mumbled, to which the man sat back, again steepling his fingers.

"I know there's no love lost between the two of you. That you've long been at odds with each other. That your confluence has always and only ever could be but oil within water. So, I see no true hindrance to such a dissembling?"

"But—"

"And as for your brother's likely agreeing to any such papist proposal: I know what's been said of him abroad. That 'though he were of no religion, should he find friends to decide a nearer estate to the throne, then it may be that he could be thus persuaded'. But, consider this: he's clearly unsure about his faith; he's also hardly cunning in politics; nor does he have experience in war. So, it strikes me he'd be the least right choice to rule England. Unmasking his plans would, therefore, be a most rightful conclusion, would it not?"

William remained still and silent for a long time, Peter all the while fervently wishing he could hear the man's thoughts. Eventually, though, William did stir himself.

"I need to think more upon the matter."

"You have, sir, until the tide turns in less than an hour. I've not Queen's passport to leave England for today's task and so cannot stay longer."

At William's further silence, the man suggested they could take bread and meat to fill that time, but William sat up straight, his hands firmly gripping the edge of the table.

"And no finger will point out my part in this?"

"No record is to be writ down of any of this matter, I assure you, sir. I, too, on my own part, have no desire of such. It must wholly be seen as but the papists abroad and your brother, Ferdinando's, own doing."

"Very well, *sir*, then you can have my answer forthwith. I will indeed seek out my cousin Sir William Stanley and gain his confidence, as you so wish. Whereupon, I will also endeavour to convince him that my brother would, with all certainty, look more than kindly upon any such advance on the part of his papist friends." But William then sighed, heavily, and slowly shook his head. "And when such discourse does finally bear fruit, may God, in His gracious clemency, grant me forgiveness of my fraternal sin."

"Rest assured, William, for by your deed a grateful England will long offer God its honouring prayers for such," and the man placed a firm hand on William's arm. A reassuring smile now shone full from his features, until a sustained and almighty screech filled the cabin and all abruptly fell into darkness.

Peter groaned and slipped his arm out from beneath his duvet, his fingers groping around on the bedside table for his alarm clock. Silence briefly filled his ears, until he shot bolt upright in bed, a startled look on his face.

"What the Hell?" came hissing, this time in his own voice, from between his dry lips.

3   RECOURSE TO PROOF

"**G**ood evening, Derek. Welcome. Come in, come in. Glad to see you found it okay." Peter drew wide the front door to his ground floor apartment for his biomedical scientist colleague to step in. "Here, let me take your coat," and when he'd closed the door behind him, Peter hung the man's jacket up on a row of hooks just inside the short hallway.

"No problems getting here, I hope?" Peter asked, to which Derek grinned, pushing his slender fingers through his greying Irish locks.

"No. Your instructions were spot on. But when you said you were out in the countryside, I never thought you meant *this* far out. Must take you an age to get in to the hospital."

"Oh, it's not too bad, not at the times I tend to travel to and from Preston. But go on through to the kitchen; I'll get you a drink. Coffee all right?" and he held his arm out towards the only open door along the hallway.

"You wouldn't have a whisky to hand, would you? I've just come from this week's clinical governance meeting and I could do with a damned good stiffener. Doctor Gupta should be shot. At least if she put in a bit more preparation beforehand it might help," at which Peter shot Derek a sympathetic laugh as he followed him into the sizeable kitchen.

Seeing the room over his colleague's shoulder granted Peter an oddly salutary glimpse of how it must have looked to the few visitors he'd ever had. He now wondered if the largely bare countertops and lack of clutter might not impart something of a spartan look. The room's only evidence of industry was a bubbling Cona machine beside a rather lonely-looking electric toaster.

"Yes, she is a bit scatty," Peter offered, "but she's a damned good dermatologist. As for a whisky, would you mind if we steered clear of alcohol? I'd rather we kept clear heads this evening."

Derek was now standing at the kitchen's tall and deeply recessed window, looking out into the courtyard carpark, until he turned a questioning look at Peter.

"I've got to say: your invite sounded a bit...well, a bit mysterious."

"I can't tell you how grateful I felt when you said you'd come. But first off, can I tempt you with that coffee I promised?" Derek nodded and returned to the view outside.

"When you said 'Apartment'," Derek then said, "I thought it'd be a lot smaller. You know, in a modern block or something. Definitely not this," and he turned and looked up at the high and heavily moulded ceiling, at its broad and ornate cornice.

As Peter took down a couple of mugs from a cupboard and began filling them from the Cona, he explained that the place had once been part of the east wing of a stately home called Lathom House.

"It was occupied by the military during World War One, then became a school for a few years before eventually being demolished. They kept part of the east wing, though—what you can see here— and converted it into flats, as they called them back in the nineteen-twenties. Milk and sugar?"

"It certainly explains the open aspect, that it does. Oh, and yes…just milk, thanks." Peter whitened both coffees and passed Derek his.

"Let's go through to the lounge, shall we? It's more comfortable in there, and where I can better explain why I've asked you here this evening."

Derek's brows lofted, but Peter only forced a thin smile onto his lips as he led Derek out of the kitchen, across the hallway and in through the door to the lounge.

Just as lofty but even larger, the clearly expensively decorated room boasted a broad fireplace, a sumptuous three-piece suite and two tall and deeply recessed windows. Their heavy and thickly lined curtains were tied back into matching fabric loops. Here and there, against the walls, stood expensive reproduction antique furniture, while the classically but opulently patterned carpet lay hidden in places beneath thick Persian rugs. To Peter, though, even after all his years living here, it still embodied an anodyne appearance. The kind so carefully fostered by the interior designers employed by upmarket redevelopers.

Peter sat in an armchair facing away from the windows, a large coffee table between himself and where Derek sat, at one end of the sofa opposite. From his perch on its seat's edge, Derek carefully placed his coffee on a coaster on the occasional table beside him.

"So," Derek said over the pedestrian tick-tock of a mock-Victorian longcase clock, "which family used to own this now largely demolished stately home? Lathom house, I think you said."

From a shelf beneath the coffee table, Peter drew out a recently well-thumbed potted-history of the property. One that had come with the apartment's sales pack, back when he'd bought it in two-thousand-and-three, seven years earlier. He scanned down to a now familiar paragraph.

"'Edward Bootle-Wilbraham, the third Earl of Lathom and fourth Baron of Skelmersdale' it says here, and 'built between seventeen twenty-five and forty by a Sir Thomas Bootle, MP for Liverpool'. Apparently, he commissioned Giacomo Leoni— whoever he was—to rebuild it in the Palladian style. Supposedly as the 'finest house in the county of Lancashire'."

"It must have got into a right state to have ended up being pulled down."

"It wasn't the first time. Did you know there was a castle here once, or hereabouts, also called Lathom House?"

"A castle? Of course, now I remember. Wasn't it involved in the Civil War? I'm sure I recall something about it from my childhood days growing up in Westhead. I think it was our Junior School teacher who told us about it being besieged and holding out for months, under the command of the lady of the house."

"That I can well imagine. Seems it was quite a formidable and substantial fortification, from what little there is about it in here," and Peter flicked the leaflet he held, his gaze casting down to pick out more reminders of its nuggets of knowledge.

"The castle was the seat of the Stanley family, home of the Earls of Derby, going way back to when they built it in the fifteenth century. Though it's reckoned to have replaced a much earlier wooden structure."

"I also remember us being told," Derek said, "that it's why you come across so many Stanley Arms and Eagle and Child pubs in Lancashire."

"Eagle and Child?"

"Ah, that one's to do with some story spun by an ancestor of the Stanleys who didn't have a male heir. To explain away a bastard boy of his that he wanted his lady wife to adopt."

When Peter only looked blankly back, Derek went on to explain that his own local pub's landlord had once told him the fabled story. That a great eagle had been seen to fly onto the Earl's estate, a child clasped in its claws. When the lady, out for her regular morning walk and knowing of the reported sighting, came across an abandoned child, she agreed it must have been the one brought by the eagle, and was, therefore, a "most auspicious omen".

"As such, or so the story goes, she readily adopted the mite. Face-saving strategy on both sides, if you ask me," Derek concluded, laughing heartily.

"Well, having the myth in the family history, it

was added at some point to the Stanley coat of arms." Peter stood and passed the potted history and its illustration to Derek.

"There, at the very top," he said as he lit the table lamp beside Derek, and another on a mock-Georgian cabinet beside the fireplace, before sitting back down.

"So," Derek exclaimed, that's where the design on the pub signs comes from. Well, I never. We learn something new every day." But as he leant forward to pass the notes back to Peter, his eyes narrowed. "But I don't suppose it's this place's history you really wanted to discuss."

"No," Peter said, a little distantly. "Not entirely. But the thing is: I need your utmost discretion before I can say anything. Your word that it won't go any further than the two of us." Derek cocked his head.

"It's not illegal, is it? Or unprofessional? Nothing the hospital would baulk at or find inappropriate for one of their senior biomedical scientists to be involved in?" Peter found a grim smile seeping onto his face.

"No, nothing like that, Derek, I assure you. Although, were it to get out, it could affect my standing amongst my peers and my reputation with my patients for being a safe pair of hands."

"Just your reputation? And it's nothing…nothing sexual in any way?"

Peter had to laugh. "No, nothing like that, but a newly promoted specialty doctor, especially an ambitious one, has to be seen to be as…well, as sane as a judge is sober."

Derek sat silently for some time, the stare of his blue eyes held unwaveringly on Peter, as though seeking an answer there. Finally, he sat forward and took a deep breath.

"Very well, Peter, you have my word. Do you want to shake hands on it?"

Peter shook his head. "Your word's more than enough for me," then he himself sat silently, staring back at Derek, wondering how best to broach the subject that had brought them here this evening. Finally, he plumped for the direct approach.

"Do you believe in ghosts, Derek?" The man's features flickered with a hint of incredulity, which eased Peter's concerns a little.

"No, not in the least," he finally and quite emphatically stated.

"Good. I thought not, and neither do I...even now. You see, Derek, over the years we've known each other, you've always struck me as the pragmatic sort. Down to Earth and no nonsense. Which is why I asked you in particular here this evening. To help me out with this little problem I have."

"Plumbing," Derek declared. "Old houses usually have bad plumbing. Hence any knocks and weird—"

"No, it's not your ears I need, Derek, I assure you, but your eyes. Cold, calculating, impartial, and objective eyes."

"You've seen something? Here? Seen a...a *ghost*? and disdain dripped from the word, although Derek did then twist in his seat, to cast a dismissive look over his shoulder.

"Five weeks ago, at just after ten o'clock on the Tuesday night," at which Peter glanced at his watch, "I was sitting just where I am now, going through some patients' notes for my clinic the next morning. I caught sight of something out of the corner of my eye and looked up, straight at a man who was walking through this very room, eventually passing through the sofa you're sitting on."

"A man? And where did he go?"

"Straight through that alcove wall," at which Peter pointed, immediately taking Derek's gaze that same way, a gaze he only slowly returned to Peter. His face had by now become etched with a frown, his eyes narrowed.

Peter lifted his mug to his dry lips and gulped down a mouthful of its now bitter and rapidly cooling coffee.

"The thing is," he said, trying to lighten his voice, "the 'ghost' wasn't like they're depicted on the TV or in films. Not quite see-through, nor entirely solid. But I could clearly see what he was wearing: the sort of outfit you see in Shakespearean plays."

"Doublet and hose," Derek quietly said.

"Whatever, but I could also see his face, almost as plain as day: a full and pointed beard, a broad-set square face and rather melancholy eyes beneath thick, wide-set eyebrows."

The retelling brought back some of the strangeness Peter remembered having felt at the time: the lightness in his chest, the prickling of the hairs on his arms and at the nape of his neck, and he shivered.

"The weirdest part, though, was the dream I had that very same night."

"A dream? What sort of dream?"

"What sort, eh?" and Peter thought hard for how best to describe it, how best to impart the impact it had had on him that night; and at its memory every night since. At last, he again held Derek in his unwavering gaze.

"A most vivid and disturbingly real-seeming

dream, Derek, that's what it was," and again he looked at his watch. "One I'd better press on and quickly describe."

And Peter did just that, all the time trying to read Derek's rather implacable expression. But at its conclusion, Derek only sniffed in disgust.

"Bit of a shit, wasn't he?" he said.

"Hmm?"

"That William Stanley you dreamt you were: bit of a shit; prepared to finger his brother, Ferdinando, for the sake of gaining an earldom. But then, I suppose they were all at it back in those days. Harsher times and all that, eh?"

"Yes," Peter said, stretching out the word, his mind elsewhere. "But the thing is…the ghost I saw on that occasion wasn't the last."

"You've seen it again? Here?"

"Here, yes, but not the same one. Same type of clothing, same path through this lounge, but without the dream afterwards."

"Tuesday night, you say," and Derek looked at his own watch. "And just after ten," at which he stood up, abruptly, and moved away from the sofa, staring at the far corner of the lounge.

"Every Tuesday night since, Derek, the same man has passed through this room. A bit more solid each time. If you see him too, then, whatever he is, he must be real. Then I'll know I'm not going mad."

This time they both checked their watches, both stared briefly at each other. Then Peter also got to his feet, and together, they swung their expectant gazes towards the far corner of the room.

4   ARTICULO MORTIS

Derek's lapse into an Irish-accented "B'jesus" gave Peter all the confirmation he needed for relief to flood through him, a wild and unexpected impulse close on its heels.

Before he knew it, he was standing at the end of the sofa, its length lying between him and the obliviously closing ghost. Wild-eyed but determined, he stared into the apparition's seemingly distressed and fast-looming face, until it and his own collided.

A fizz of pain bleached brightly across Peter's vision. Then he was being swept along over cobbles, beneath a hot sun within a bright-blue blazing sky, towards a huge stone parapet wall. An arched way through its high-soaring gatehouse loomed ever larger.

He yelped, its immediate echo coming painfully back from close beside his mind, then, in a trice, cool darkness enveloped him.

Breathless and stunned, this time the echoes that startled him came from his own hurrying footsteps as they urged him out from the darkness and into a broad bailey. At the far side, the rising bulk of a many-storeyed tower reached up to touch the sky.

Despite his shock, from within his sense of cramped confinement Peter ineffectually fought to master his limbs. He also tried to wrench his gaze away from a large entranceway ahead, only managing to claw desperately at his peripheral vision, frantically trying to see where he was.

It revealed soaring elevations of a close-jostled hotchpotch of castellated and window-filled walls and turrets and lesser towers, stretching away to both sides. Now it was all his vision held. Soon, only a flight of steps passing beneath him in a blur, then the close press of a vestibule, the hollow sounds of his footsteps on its darkly-lit stone-flagged floor. A moment later and the shock of his footsteps echoed within a dim but lofty hall as bowed heads flashed by. In a further blur, their stride took him swiftly up broad wooden steps to a precipitous gallery, where at long last he was brought to a walk.

His mind in a whirl, Peter was carried into a long passageway. Doors ran along one side, one open, and there, before its threshold and damp from his exertion, he finally came to an involuntary but welcome halt.

Too dumbstruck to say a thing, he took a deep and steadying breath as he stared into a large bedchamber, light slanting in through two partially shuttered windows at its far side.

Figures stood in groups of two or three between the spills of light, most dressed in what Derek had described as doublet and hose, one or two in black robes. All, though, at various distances, faced in towards a huge fourposter bed. Its hangings were drawn back, revealing a man lying beneath its coverlet, his head propped against a mound of pillows. Sitting before the heat of a fireplace beside it but bent forward, an elderly woman rested her elbows upon its mattress, her hands clasped before her face, as though in silent prayer.

From within the hushed room, a tall, grey-haired man, close by the doorway, glanced Peter's way, a thin taut smile momentarily interrupting his sombre expression. He stepped nearer as Peter entered, his smile becoming one of sympathy.

"Ferdinando, my dear nephew," he said, quietly. "I'm glad my messenger reached you and you're here so soon."

"Is he..." came unbidden from Peter's mouth, then a shock of realisation stilled his thoughts.

"Fear not. My brother Henry still lives, though he's weakened greatly since the palsy struck him this morning."

"But I—"

"An hour, no more, from when you left his side."

"I should have stayed, despite his protestations," and Ferdinando—for Peter now knew himself to be within this someone else—stepped further into the chamber. Those between himself and the bed respectfully drew back at his passing.

Of course, Peter rationalised, this is just another vivid dream, like the one I had before. And of course, Ferdinando; now I remember. So, all I need do is wait until I wake up, and at this, relief washed over him as he came to stand quietly beside the seated woman.

From there, he gazed down upon the bedbound man's worryingly ashen face, at his closed eyes, at his slack mouth through which his shallow breaths barely rasped.

"Father?" Ferdinando hardly breathed, at which the woman faltered in her prayers and briefly looked up. She stiffly got to her feet. But nothing more than further rasps came from between the old man's blue lips as the woman briefly nodded at Ferdinando. She backed away from the chair, where he slowly sat and again proffered "Father?".

Only when he'd leant his elbows on the mattress and lowered his mouth to his father's ear did Ferdinando's repeated salutation evoke a flickering of the old man's eyes, although they remained lightly closed.

"Ah…be it," he could hardly be heard to say, "be it you, my own William? Come home at last? Just in time to—" but he choked back phlegm, coughing awhile until his head once more lay heavy against the pillows.

At his father's sigh and laboured breathing, Ferdinando's gaze took Peter's to those closest, to their lowered faces and respectful expressions. Their hands were clasped before them, some held low but others raised in supplication. One in particular of the latter held Ferdinando's interest for a moment: a tall and rosy-cheeked man in a robe, a black book clasped between his raised and long-fingered hands. His eyes, though, refused to meet Ferdinando's gaze.

Then his father more strongly uttered "Ferdinando?", his eyes open when Ferdinando again looked down at him.

"Aye," the old man drew out, "bless'd am I, 'tis so. 'Tis my eldest and most favoured son; I see that now.

Come, heir of mine, come closer, for I wish to speak with you in confidence; now my end's almost upon me."

As Ferdinando leant forward, bringing them both nearer, Peter was sure he felt a nudge at his disembodied ribs, something wriggling close against his awareness. He wondered if he had indeed been knocked out and was only now vaguely aware of Derek trying to rouse him. But when the dying Henry's suddenly stronger voice reached Ferdinando's ears, Peter couldn't help but listen.

"Take great care, my son, as we've hitherto discussed. Attend your best to our good Sovereign Lady, Queen Elizabeth. Give her all right cause to look upon you most kindly. You're the only solace left me from my marriage to your God-forsaken mother, by the…by the right of succession her own line gave you. And may the good Lord Himself judge…judge my estranged Lady Margaret when her own time justly comes."

Henry's eyes closed, the effort of talking clearly too much. He did, though, have strength enough to take Ferdinando's hand in his own, albeit weakly. But after a while, he appeared to rally.

"The only solace left to me by she who had, in the words of those who accused her, a 'womanish curiosity in prying into the queen's future, who foolishly consulted with wizards and cunning men to predict her passing'." He spluttered to a halt and gulped in air for a moment.

"And by it," he laboured on, "did naught but risk her head, and every worldly thing of mine. Ah, but from one such as her to…to one who's been but my mainstay."

He tried to smile and turn his head, to look past

Ferdinando, but to no avail. His head only fell against the pillows as he once more strained to draw in breath.

With great effort, he presently continued, "Ensure my last written wishes for Jane and her bastard offspring by my own seed all come to pass. Promise me that, my son. She's given me much succour and been lack of wont to complain."

At his faltering grip of Ferdinando's hand, his son promised him it would come to pass, which seemed to ease the old man.

Some time passed before Henry stirred again, but when he did, he drew his son close to his words.

"Watch for your greatest enemy…" faintly slipped from between his lips. "He who…who seeks the very same exalted seat, but 'pon far flimsier claim." But this last barely drifted out upon his faltering breath, followed only by silence.

Ferdinando held his own breath for a while, expectantly, then, clearly disappointed, drew away from his father. Henry wetly coughed, further words barely slipping from his now slate-blue lips.

"Much the prideful lord is he, 'twas clear… No, no, 'tis my stillness, now so close before my God, that grants me such clearer sight. That lets me see his arrogant threat. That tells me at last what drives his words to seduce her regal regard."

Ferdinando, his ear now close to his father's once more stilled lips, stared towards the corner where the praying woman, presumably Henry's longstanding mistress, Jane, had earlier retired. She seemed not to notice, her gaze intent only upon the unmoving countenance of the man she loved.

Peter noticed another, younger woman beside her, a

comforting arm about the distraught Jane's shoulders, a concerned but loving gaze directed purposely straight into his and Ferdinando's shared eyes.

"Protect yourself from him," Henry now whispered, but loud enough to startle Ferdinando. "From his besmirching your good name," to which his son quietly asked of whom he spoke, but the old man only mumbled an incoherent reply.

Ferdinando again slowly leant away from his father, watching his flickering eyelids and twitching lips as his own shoulders slumped and he took a settling breath.

Then, to both Ferdinando and Peter's surprise, the old man uttered nothing more than the name "Robert Devereux".

"The Earl of Essex?" Ferdinando quietly queried, but all the old man could bring himself to do was offer the slightest of nods. His rasping breaths then once more filled the silence, a silence that soon seemed to settle about the bedchamber like a winter's frost.

5   FATEFUL COMINGS AND GOINGS

Not long after Ferdinando had relinquished his seat to Jane and her litany of prayers, the seeming frost finally turned to ice at Earl Henry's last rasping breath. It rendered the bedchamber frozen for what, to Peter, seemed an eternity, until the late Earl's body spasmed and sucked in a huge last gulp of air. Thereafter, he lay as still as the stones of the castle about him.

Men soon stepped forward, listening at his chest and open mouth, peering into his staring eyes, feeling and pressing. Quietly, they conferred, each head shaking in turn, then one of the doctors gently closed the departed Earl's eyes.

They withdrew, one granting a further but discrete shake of his head to the tall black-robed man with the rosy cheeks as they filed past him. Clearly a priest of some kind, he then spoke out a solemn prayer for all to hear. During this, Jane stifled her sobs against the dead Earl's chest, her hands fisted into the coverlet of his deathbed.

Peter felt fingers slip into Ferdinando's hand, felt a close warmth, then the woman who'd been comforting Jane pressed herself nearer. Her breath came close at Ferdinando's ear, soft and consoling.

"My dearly beloved," she said, in a low and private voice, "my heart embraces you, my husband. Such sadness, but truly he was a good and righteous man. So, must ere long be well received by our Father in Heaven." When the prayer being intoned came to an end, the room filled with Amens.

Not once had Ferdinando lifted his gaze from his dead father's peaceful face, but he did squeeze his wife's hand, reassuringly. The priest, though, now stood before them, a nod to each before his gaze rested on Ferdinando.

"My Lord Strange, soon to be the next Earl of Derby, I and Lancashire, and indeed the whole of England, will do great condolence upon the death of your father. I'm sure he'll be with our Holy Father in Heaven afore long. I will pray for his soul, and also your own good self and your family's most noble fortunes. May all bear the sorrow of this day in the surety of God's good grace."

"My most excellent Lord Bishop of Chester, your gracious thoughts and God's own mercy do ease my grief, for which I give thanks. You were always and ever a stout and loyal good friend to my father, for which I will ever be grateful. He never failed to cherish you in his thoughts, and in his words and deeds."

Although the exchange proved brief, so began many more. Each only further served to confuse Peter with their weight of names, titles and often, he suspected, veiled meanings. Amongst them were clearly family members, those whose presence came from love or duty, and those others whose purpose was no more than to bear witness to the passing of a great lord. But with each consoling conclusion, the bedchamber's press of people lessened, until only Ferdinando and his wife remained, now standing together beside the late Earl.

"He'll be sadly missed by all," Ferdinando's good lady proffered. "On my own behalf no less than by so many others. This sorrowful Tuesday, here at Lathom House on the twenty-fifth of September, will ever be remembered. No less so than by the Queen herself, who'll be most sorely disquieted, and to whom I must write before this day is out."

"There's no need, Alice. All due obituarii have already been prepared. Now only awaiting a date, and my signature and seal."

"But I know she'd dearly wish to be apprised of my own heart and mind on this so sad an occasion," Alice offered, only for Ferdinando to turn his attention to the doorway. A grey-haired figure now stood there in the gloom.

"Enter, Uncle Ned. Worry not, we can mourn anon," he softly called. "Is there something amiss I need to address that brings you back so soon?"

As Edward stepped into the bedchamber, he assured Ferdinando that it was but a trifle, although something for which much more delay would bring it a portion of urgency.

"One of the Hesketh family called upon you at Newparke," he went on to explain, "and was sent on here, unawares, he says, of the Earl's ill-health. He, one Richard Hesketh, is now at the inner bailey gate."

"*Richard* Hesketh knew not?" and Ferdinando took Edward a little removed from his father's body, and so away from Alice. "You do mean the Rufford Richard, don't you? I wonder why he didn't—"

"No, Ferdinando; the Aughton Richard. The one who went abroad after the slaughter of Mr. Howghton at Lea Hall. He's been returned from Hamburg these seventeen days and wishes to present his passport and deliver letters he carries."

"But why didn't he present them at his earliest opportunity? Shortly after landing on these shores. And what possible letters... No. No, this isn't the time. Dismiss him to attend me at Newparke tomorrow, two hours after noon. He may present to me then," and a curt nod from Edward saw him withdraw.

When he rejoined his wife, Ferdinando only stared through her for a while, until she had to ask, "Something other than sorrow distracts you, my lord?"

"Hmm? Oh, only why, on this day of all days, this Richard Hesketh should seek my endorsement of his passport. Knowing nothing of my father's decline, why didn't he come here first, to my father's higher authority?" But Ferdinando chastised himself and apologised to Alice, urging them to return to paying homage to his father.

Only after they'd prayed that his soul should soon pass into the Kingdom of Heaven, and given thanks over his body for the good his life had bestowed upon them and their friends, family and retainers, did they then recite the Lord's Prayer together. A final bow to Earl Henry's now empty vessel, and they retired from the chamber and went out into the passage.

Edward awaited them there, a retinue of servants

lined up along the wall vanishing back into the gloom behind him. "May your father's body be prepared now, my lord?" he asked, and at Ferdinando's nod, he signalled the servants to go into the chamber, following them in himself.

"And Thine is the kingdom and the power, and the glory for ever," Ferdinando recited, clearly reflecting on the final lines of their last prayer.

Alice lifted his hand to her heart, holding it there as a ward against his sorrow. "But remember:" she said, trying to lighten her voice, "give us this day our daily bread. It's almost noon and time you took some yourself, my husband, before time itself becomes too short in the days ahead of you."

He smiled and declared "Amen", then, hand in hand, they returned the way Peter had come into this world of theirs, those few but long-seeming and largely confusing hours before. It helped, though, that Peter at last seemed to be getting his ear attuned to their old way of speaking, thereby making more sense of it all.

But as they descended the steps into the busy hall below, thought of the late Earl's body set Peter to worrying about his own. Although it was no doubt in Derek's excellent care, the length of time that had now elapsed didn't bode well. He needed to wake up, and wake up soon; the sooner, the better.

"Shit," he spat from within what now seemed more his imprisoned mind than a dream. "If I don't wake, what the fuck's going to become of me?" to which something shifted, there at the edge of his mind, something that quickly froze.

Before they could reach the hall's high table, set

before a large and blazing fireplace, Alice stopped them amidst the helter-skelter of servants hurrying back and forth from the kitchens. Intrigue, and certainly the look on Alice's face, for the moment washed away Peter's growing mountain of worries.

"Whilst I have your ear, my husband," she said, drawing near, and Peter looked at her properly for the first time. "I hope your father's last words to you were a comfort," at which her dark and rounded eyebrows rose up her broad forehead. They reached towards her mass of black curls that stood proud beneath the high line of her elaborately decorated headdress.

At the feel of Ferdinando's eyes narrowing, Peter more closely studied the round face of the countess-to-be, her dark eyes now holding her husband knowingly in their gaze. He noted the applied rose of her well-fleshed cheeks, her small round chin and narrow mouth, a hint that she tasted lemons seemingly on the enhanced flush of its now expectant lips' pout.

Then she inclined that head of hers a little, and Ferdinando glanced aside, assuring himself of the privacy of their words. "Nay, but more to the contrary, Alice, although here's not the place. Other than to say my father was clearly most vexed."

"Vexed, Ferdinando? But by whom or what?"

"By one of the Court," and he lowered his voice still further. "By one Earl of Essex, to be precise. One with whom, on more than one occasion, I've had misguided dealings."

"Ah, it doesn't surprise me, not in the least, for many a lady's confessed to me that the man has a smooth tongue but a rough mind. You must tell me more, but later, my love, when we're abed."

"Very well; later, then; but for now, where are our daughters?" and Ferdinando ran his gaze about the crowded hall. "I hope they got to say their farewells to their grandfather before he departed them."

Alice assured him they'd been to see his father shortly after he'd left that morning, which clearly eased Ferdinando.

"They're taking their meal in their own chambers," she told him as he escorted her to the high table, "for want of privacy in their sadness."

Once she'd been seated, Ferdinando took his place beside her, at which everyone else took theirs, upon benches drawn up along their own and two long tables set out below.

Then her words "when we're abed" struck Peter, and struck him forcibly: unless this dream-of-sorts ended soon, he was likely to find himself a voyeur during one of their most intimate of shared moments.

Had his heart been his to call his own, it would have sunk to his undeniably borrowed boots. Especially when he thought of what else his imprisoned senses might yet come to witness.

6   LAST STRAW

For Peter, much of the remainder of his seeming dream's day proved little more than a whirlwind of unfathomable tasks, all punctuated by the hourly toll of a clock somewhere within the castle bounds. Esoteric discussions followed one after another, interspersed with long-winded documents and tall piles of letters. But from all this, Peter did at least discover to which year's September he'd been transported: 1593.

Seeing those numbers being scratched out by Ferdinando's quill made Peter's dream seem just too disturbingly real. He was thankful, though, that he was here in mind only and not in body, for he now knew he'd not have lasted five minutes. Not left to his own anachronistic devices. The past, he conceded, was very much an alien world.

He saw little of Alice. Ferdinando, in company of his uncle Edward, principally dealt with a tall stick of a man whom he'd greeted as Michael Doughtie, seemingly a kind of personal secretary. There were others, some of whom appeared to be the late Earl's own servants, but who now seemed to be in Ferdinando's service.

He'd kept himself largely secluded in one room, in which much of the paperwork resided, or to where it would be brought by others. The confines of its walls, largely hidden behind shelves of books, held cabinets and chests crammed into the space left by a table and two stools. These stood before a single window, its shutters thrown back to admit the late September sunlight and its lingering warmth.

The shadows cast had begun to lengthen when the Bishop of Chester appeared in the open doorway, his tentative knock on the doorjamb lifting Ferdinando's gaze. Edward had earlier gone upon an errand elsewhere, leaving only Michael with Ferdinando. He'd been standing at his lord's side, pointing out details in a document. Now, he stood aside and folded his hands before him as he lowered his head in deference.

"Ah, my Good Bishop Chaderton," Ferdinando said, standing to greet him. "Please, come in," and he nodded at Michael, who respectfully withdrew. "If you'd care to take a seat," and Ferdinando indicated the stool across the table from him.

The Bishop settled himself down, carefully arranging his robes before regarding Ferdinando with a keen eye as he too then sat back down.

"I hope you're faring well, my good Lord Strange, and trust you're content in the knowledge that your honoured father's soul will soon be joined with those of his who've gone before him unto Heaven's everlasting glory."

Peter thought the Bishop's tone signalled an impending "But", which Ferdinando must also have heard, for he replied: "My mind's at peace on this, my lord, for I know him to have been loyal in his service to the Almighty, as indeed am I."

"Indeed so," the Bishop allowed, "to the Almighty Himself, perhaps. But in regard to His body, the Church, then I'd suggest your father's service went only as far as expressing intent. And on that thorny subject, may I now remind you of letters you wrote to me some ten years ago? Letters in which, I seem to remember, you complained of your father's duty unto that very same Church."

When Ferdinando refused to answer, the Bishop went on: "If memory serves me right, your words were 'I am through with my father'. And the following year: 'So doubt I not but your lordship will proceed to frame some better reformation in this so unbridled and bad an handfull of England, for I myself am otherwise willing to give the first blow'."

"Aye, I remember such. But I was much less experienced then, poorer in wisdom of the ways of this county. At that time, I failed to grasp the mountain of papistry that I now know afflicts Lancashire. That affords it such a perilous climb to overthrow."

The Bishop spat a harsh laugh, but he did smile. "Your now more seasoned view carries much truth, I vouch. A view it seems Our Sovereign Lady also shares, and hence the leniency she's shown to your father. A leniency, I may make to mention, for his affording her great military as well as diplomatic service."

Ferdinando absently played with a pen knife that lay close by his hand upon the table as he held the

Bishop's gaze. Again, Peter wished he could eavesdrop on his thoughts, but the only clue afforded him was a tensing of Ferdinando's stomach.

"I assure you, my Lord Bishop, and you may also assure Lord Burghley, and his son, Secretary Cecil, that I will, in time, conquer that mountain. Provided Her Majesty sees fit to award me the position of Lord-Lieutenant of Lancashire and Cheshire, of course, as has until now been the custom."

"I hear Secretary Cecil's so inclined, although I don't know about William, his father; or the Queen, for that matter. Without it, though, your authority in this would be greatly diminished, so I'd imagine custom must prevail. May I assure you that, however I can, I'm prepared to offer you my support in your petition."

"You would have, by it, my lord, my utmost gratitude. And thereby, in the fullness of time, a county unencumbered by recusants."

With a flick of his robes to free his legs for standing, the Bishop rose, bringing Ferdinando to his own feet.

"I intend," the Bishop then said as he groaned himself straight, "to be at your disposal these coming three days, the most my duties will afford; if you'd indulge me my presence here, of course. Your father said he was to be laid to rest in the Stanley chapel in the church of Ormskirk, in company of his forebears. So, if I may be of any assistance in such ecclesiastical matters..."

Ferdinando explained that all was in hand, but that the Bishop's very presence should help promote better haste with the clergy there. Although, he admitted, it would do little to hasten the arrival of the many nobles and their retinues he'd yet to invite.

"In which case, Lord Strange, I'll delay you no further." The Bishop nodded and turned to leave, but as he did so, he paused, adding his caution that, "Your standing at the Court, my lord, would be greatly served by an improved reporting of cases brought against your recusant Lancashire neighbours. Keep well in mind that our Sovereign Lady does not long take kindly to words that are left to outlive their promised deeds," at which he swept out and was gone.

Lowering himself slowly to his stool, Ferdinando stared at the now empty doorway, clearly deep in thought. It left Peter even more convinced that his host's religious leanings were indeed widely mistrusted. He thought back to Henry's deathbed warning to Ferdinando, and to his own dream of having been Ferdinando's brother, William, aboard that ship.

Could it have been the Earl of Essex who'd sat waiting in the captain's cabin, who'd then set William against his own brother? And if so, why? What bad blood could there be between the two?

As Ferdinando finally stirred and called out for Michael, Peter berated himself for not having been more attentive during his History lessons at school. As it was, all he could do was await Ferdinando's promised talk with Alice, later, once they were in bed together. Peter's heart sank again at the thought of his dream lasting that long, and of his subsequent role as an unseen gooseberry.

As it turned out, Peter needn't have worried. Both Alice and Ferdinando wore thick nightshirts and loose sleeping caps when they came to retire. For despite the shutters having long been barred, they held out little of the chill Autumn night air. And it seemed the size of the bedchamber proved too much for the hearth's blazing log fire to remove much of its edge.

Ferdinando lamented to Alice that his duties had not yet allowed him to console his daughters, especially at their bedtime, but she assured him they were bearing their loss more than well enough. And so, it wasn't long before the two were beneath the bedsheets, close tight together for their mutual warmth.

Peter tried his best to ignore their tender caresses and mingled breath as they lay there for some time, warming their limbs. The only relief to the darkness came by the light of the fire's flames, flickering across the drawn bedcurtains. And when Ferdinando closed his eyes, the only sound was the draw of the chimney and the occasional crunch of settling embers. No distant hum of a cityscape, no close by neighbour's overly loud stereo, just black silence beyond the chamber.

It seemed to Peter that Ferdinando had fallen asleep. It left him to wonder, if he didn't wake from this dream, how he was going to suffer a long night of imprisonment within Ferdinando's mind without his own recourse to slumber. But then Ferdinando shifted, slipped his arm from around Alice and lay more on his back. He opened his eyes, allowing Peter faintly to discern a starry pattern painted on the underside of the bed's canopy.

"So," Alice mumbled against Ferdinando's chest, "what intrigues rest between the handsome Earl of Essex, and of course, your more than handsome but soon to be equally ennobled self?"

Ferdinando let out a soft breath before asking, "What do you know of the Essex adherents?" Alice drew her face away from his side, as though trying to see his features in the dark.

"I know them to be a London gathering of those with a like mind for poetry and plays, like the Wilton House adherents. And I do believe Anthony and Francis Bacon and Fulke Greville are members, along with much of Essex's family and friends. But…what has this to do with you?"

"Well, some years ago, when in London, I too would attend their gatherings. As an occasional member, you understand."

"You never said."

"I'm sure I must have."

"I'm sure you didn't."

"Well, it matters not, for it wasn't long before I forewent my visits altogether. You see, I found their interest in poetry and plays went beyond any merit such works may have possessed in their own right. Their aim seemed to be to make popular a particular kind, and for a singular purpose."

"Knowing the Earl of Essex's reputation, I can well imagine what that might be."

"No, Alice, something far more devious. They choose only those that best engender a popular belief in the old ways, derived from a rather selective reading of the teachings of Tacitus: that powerful positions should be granted by right of nobility, not merit. Ways that, were they to return, Heaven forefend, would put a stop to men of a more lowly status being appointed to high government positions."

"Like Robert Cecil, the Queen's Secretary of State?"

"Indeed. A role Essex would more than likely be granted himself. After all, it's common knowledge he coverts the position, and he *is* close to the Queen."

"Ah, Cecil and Essex; and therein lies a barely-hidden bone of dissension."

"Indeed, and their enmity has established two opposing factions. But, more's the shame, the dangerous game it engages them in often brings England to little more than an impotent stalemate."

"So, why your father's warning?"

"I think, Alice, it's because of a last straw."

"A last straw? I don't understand."

"A well-guarded belief of theirs came by chance to my ear. I learnt that some of them regard the Queen's frequent failures to side with Essex on many of his proposals as an…well, as an indictment of her treachery."

"Queen Elizabeth a *traitor* to England? Because she favours merit over nobility? And knowing Essex's reputation as a warmonger, words above the wielding of swords?" Peter felt her shift in the bed, as though angling herself to stare through the darkness at Ferdinando.

"It is so, my dear. And as my own views set me squarely with Secretary Cecil and hence the Queen, and thereby apart from Essex, my very reason for withdrawing from his adherents. I could never be persuaded to condone such dated, and I believe, wholly destructive beliefs."

Alice remained silent for a while, only her breathing giving away her place in the darkness. Then she quietly said, "And you told… No, even you wouldn't be *so* foolish. But you told all this to her closest advisor, Secretary Cecil, didn't you?"

"In confidence, yes. It only seemed fair, for both Cecils have always dealt favourably with our family. And I'm far more in accord with his views."

"And this eventually got back to Essex, didn't it?"

"I…" Ferdinando now barely whispered. "I do believe it may very well have done so."

"One of the most powerful men in England, a favourite of the Queen herself, her secret lover's own son, and you told the one man who was bound to use that knowledge against him?"

When he didn't answer, she fumed, "You may soon become the fifth Earl of Derby, my husband, but it doesn't mean you're not a complete ass," and she huffed herself down beside him, clearly exasperated.

7   OUT OF AN AFFRAY

The sounds of footsteps on wooden floorboards and the dull clunk of earthenware met Peter's awareness, then Ferdinando opened his eyes.

Their surroundings were coldly lit, as though by dawn light that had barely crept into the chamber, faintly lifting a pattern of entwined briars from the cloth of the bedcurtains. Against the sound of water being poured, Peter realised, with considerable relief, that he too must have slept as Ferdinando did. What was more, it was as though his night's sleep had brokered a deal with his fears, as though something had bartered for him a measure of contentment. Then that something seemed to stir beside his mind, a warmth that hurriedly disentangled itself.

Reaching out a hand, Ferdinando discovered the space beside him to be empty. Alice must already have been up and about, Peter thought. Then her voice came softly in response to an even quieter enquiry, at which Ferdinando stirred himself and slipped from the bed.

His good lady wife was already dressed, a young woman standing behind her now making adjustments to the collar of her bodice. Ferdinando stretched his arms above his head, groaning all the while, then scratched at his chest through the fabric of his nightgown.

"Did you sleep well, my dear?" he sought, to which Alice shot him a glare.

"When I finally managed to put your 'last straw' from my mind, yes, Ferdinando, I did. But now, you see, your question's only brought it back to the surface," and Alice tugged savagely at her sleeves, to straighten them. The girl at her back lowered her eyes, her fingers hastily withdrawn from Alice's neckline but left poised to continue.

"I'll go and dress, then," Ferdinando hastened to announce and quickly withdrew to another room.

Afterwards, Peter expected him to go down for breakfast, but Ferdinando went straight to the small office, there soon embroiled in checking documents with Edward and Michael, and issuing commands for all manner of preparations.

And so, the morning passed much as the previous afternoon, until they drew nearer midday and Michael reminded Ferdinando about his promise to receive Richard Hesketh at Newparke. He also made mention that it was nearly time to eat, which seemed to lighten Ferdinando's distinctly dour mood.

The great hall was quite full when they presently went down, Alice there to meet Ferdinando and so be escorted to her place at the high table. As he did so, she informed him that their daughters had once again chosen to eat apart from the household. Ferdinando promised he'd visit them later in the day.

Once both were seated, their napkins on their shoulders, everyone else took their places on benches to each side, and along both sides of two lower tables. Bishop Chaderton seated himself beside Ferdinando, his greeting cordial enough.

But then a rich aroma of something spiced and sugared began to fill the air as bowls were brought from the kitchens and placed on the tables. With them came platters of boiled meats, custards, tarts, fritters, and fruit, white bread for the high table, rough brown for the rest.

Ferdinando washed his hands in water poured from a ewer by a boy who came suddenly to his side, caught in a bowl held beneath by another, and dried on a towel handed to him by a third. He then removed a spoon and a knife from an ornamental case he carried about his person, laying them on the white linen tablecloth.

At this, a young lad wielding two knives approached and delicately cut the meat into slices, from which Ferdinando helped himself. As he began to eat, the hall came alive with conversation and some laughter, enough noise of eating to mask Ferdinando's subsequent words to the Bishop.

"There's one of my retainers," he said to him between mouthfuls, "who wishes to present his passport, having recently returned to this country. I wondered if you might wish to accompany me to Newparke, where he's to arrive this afternoon. I thought the short ride on such a temperate day might be to your liking. And I must admit, I've some unease about the whole affair."

"Unease?" the Bishop said, raising an eyebrow. "And why should that be, my Lord Strange? Is there, perhaps, bad blood between you?"

"No, not at all, but he's a suspected recusant, abroad these past three years, having left under something of a dark cloud. If you'd do me the honour of riding with me, I can tell you more on the way," to which the Bishop acquiesced, his curiosity clearly piqued.

A little later in their meal, Ferdinando signalled for Edward to attend him, asking the same of him, and if he'd arrange for horses to be got ready and waiting in the inner bailey.

"I'd like to be there before Hesketh should arrive at two o'clock," he went on to explain.

They'd only been at their meal for little over an hour before Ferdinando rose, washed his hands again and excused himself and the Bishop to Alice. They and Edward then made their way out to the entranceway, where three horses awaited, and on which they were each soon mounted.

Other than his confusing dash into the castle at his shocked arrival, this presented the first opportunity Peter had had to get a proper feel for Lathom House from the outside. It looked nothing like its namesake apartment block, nothing at all.

In their statelier pace towards a massive and encircling fortified wall, Peter had time to appreciate how the whole place appeared so solidly imposing. Not only the wall but also the house itself, a mass of soaring gables and castellated towers, all studded with tall but narrow windows. And rearing high above it all, over Ferdinando, the Bishop and Edward's heads, rose a huge tower that stood a little apart from the house.

The sort of place, Peter for some reason thought, lofty enough for an eagle's roost, and then he remembered Derek's telling of the Stanley myth of the eagle and child. A longing to be home in his own time now crept upon him, but then the clop of the horses' hooves rang out loudly in Ferdinando's ears as they passed into the shade beneath the wall's gatehouse arch.

Peter drew in a sharp mental breath when they emerged into the sunlight on the other side, for before him now, beyond a further bailey, ran yet another wall, this one more massive still. Punctuated by towers, it curved away to both sides, clearly encircling the house and its inner wall. Their party of three rode on at a shallow slant towards it, another but larger and this time twin-towered gatehouse within its sweep presently coming into view. Ferdinando, for some reason, then glanced back at the house.

"My God," Peter gasped to himself, "but I never really appreciated the wealth and power the Stanleys commanded, not until seeing all this. No wonder William was so keen to inherit the earldom."

As Ferdinando brought his gaze back to the gatehouse, to which they were now drawing near, Peter was sure he'd heard a sharp but close intake of breath in response to his voiced thoughts. He listened more intently within his mind, but Ferdinando and the Bishop's casual conversation impinged too much.

Once through this second gatehouse and across its long drawbridge, over a surprisingly broad moat, they followed a rough, stone-bedded track up a grassed incline and into some woods. Here, within its confidential confines, Ferdinando began to tell the Bishop about Richard Hesketh.

"It's been said that he was at the Lea Hall affray in eighty-nine, when Thomas Howghton was slaughtered that night."

"Ah, that," the Bishop said. "What a waste of a life that wholly unnecessary tumult brought with it, and over the rightful possession of some cattle. Of course, I know of the enmity that's long simmered between the Langton and Howghton families. So, it was no surprise to me that such an otherwise easily resolved argument could bring it to the boil so violently."

"Actually, a waste of two lives: a lowly Richard Bawdwen also went unto his maker that night."

"That may be so, but it took your father two years to try to convene a lawful court, which he couldn't in the end manage. And so, not one of those charged with murder against Thomas Howghton, especially the troublesome Baron of Newton, was ever brought to justice by him."

"Indeed," Edward hastened to add, "but Henry did try, most assiduously, and in the end had to petition Lord Burghley to intervene. Before it became a ceaseless and most dangerous quarrel."

"At least the Baron of Newton was eventually brought before the Star Chamber," Ferdinando said, "though he was fortunate to have frumgild substituted for the death penalty that he certainly deserved."

Edward barked a laugh. "That he paid that recompense to Thomas Howghton's widow last year came as something of a surprise, I must admit, given the debts the man has. It's believed he had to mortgage

Walton Hall yet further still to meet the commitment."

"And this Richard Hesketh, was he one of the dozen-or-so from both sides who were arrested?" the Bishop enquired, clearly now more intrigued about their forthcoming meeting with the man.

"No, he wasn't apprehended," Ferdinando told him, "and none could be found willing enough to place him there with any certainty. But it was his immediately going over the sea, to safety in Prague, or so I heard, that compounded his complicity in my own eyes. And indeed, I have to say, in the eyes of many others."

"Yet he's back now," the Bishop said, more to himself.

"Well, the matter's been settled in law, and so it is at an end. Something with which, given the passage of time, he must now be acquainted. And I, for one, have no intention of opening old wounds. I've enough on my shoulders as it is."

"Perhaps that's why Hesketh's returned, then, believing he can again live openly in Lancashire."

"Well, we'll find out soon enough, for I can now see Newparke's chimneys." Ferdinando pointed through the gaps between the trees before flicking his reins at a peppering of flies that had been bothering his horse's neck.

The woodland track took them down a short slope and out into a meadow, across which Newparke was revealed in all its seemingly pristine perfection. Even Peter recognised it as a walled, moated and recently built black and white timber-framed house, though the timber was of a pale honey colour. Peter wondered if it would blacken with age.

Here, no gatehouse guarded its entrance, only a large plain wooden gate that hung invitingly open. They'd gone in before figures appeared: a man from the front door of the house and two lads from around its corner at one end.

"Welcome, Lord Strange," the man said as they neared. "Most distressed, my lord, at hearing the unkind tidings. Hope Lady Alice ain't faring too badly with it all, my lord."

Ferdinando thanked him for asking after them as he dismounted, handing his horse's reins to one of the lads.

"The Hesketh gentleman ain't 'ere yet, my lord, it being a while afore the agreed hour."

"We'll be in the solar, Simon," Ferdinando told the man as he invited the Bishop across the threshold, Edward following him in. "When he does arrive, keep him to the great hall and send word to me. Oh, and have some wine sent up before he gets here," and with a deep bow, Simon was off into the depths of the house.

Peter could smell the aroma of new timber on the air Ferdinando breathed as he led the Bishop and Edward down a short passage and to a broad flight of steps, up which they went to a gallery and a passageway beyond. Now away from the front of the house, here small windows admitted light from an inner courtyard. But before long, Peter realised he'd become completely lost in what seemed a warren of a place. Finally, they arrived at the door to a large and airy room, into which Ferdinando led the others.

An expanse of leaded lights filled much of the wall opposite a broad brick chimneybreast, in whose stone fireplace a peat fire sweetly smoked and smouldered. Between the two ran a dark-wood table and its benches, to one of which Edward went and sat. Ferdinando and the Bishop stood at the window, each looking out onto a recently planted garden.

"You say it's meant one day to be decorative?" the Bishop said, angling his puzzled gaze this way and that through the small windowpanes. "You clearly reckon its promised prettiness will be worth the loss of herbs for the pot, poultice and potion." Peter could feel Ferdinando grinning broadly as he, too, stared down at the arrangement of saplings, barely grown bushes and swards of scythe-swept grasses.

"Judge me my seeming folly, in your own eyes at least, my Lord Bishop, once those eyes have drunk of its matured balm in the years to come. Say then if it doesn't move you to value it far above any number of draughts of tonical potions."

The Bishop's brow creased as he turned his narrowed gaze back onto Ferdinando, but a rap at the door forestalled any further words.

"Come," Ferdinando called out, and a young man hurried in with a tray of glass goblets and a flagon. No doubt, Peter thought, of the finest wine. As the lad laid them out on the table, he informed Ferdinando that he'd been told to say that Richard Hesketh had arrived early, and now awaited his lordship's pleasure in the great hall. But just then, Simon himself pressingly sought permission to enter. He gave Ferdinando a peremptory nod as he came to stand before him.

"My lord, Mister Hesketh has just informed me that he comes by way of a letter of introduction from Thomas Langton, Lord of Walton," which letter he promptly placed in Ferdinando's hand.

"The Baron of Newton, eh? Well, speak of the Devil," and Ferdinando stared down at the letter, reading its scrawled address and noting the red seal on its reverse.

"So," he noted, "Richard Hesketh returns to the very hothead whose stirring up of an affray forced him abroad in the first place, and who it would seem has some part to play now. But what? I wonder," and he went and sat opposite Edward and took out his knife, sliding its blade beneath the seal and so freeing the letter to fold open in his hand.

For the life of him, Peter could decipher nothing intelligible in the long body of scrawled and scratched script, despite how long Ferdinando sat reading it. Eventually, Ferdinando looked up, seeking out his uncle's face as he put the letter down on the table.

"My good Sir Edward, but would you mind attending the man on my behalf? Excuse my absence against my persistent sorrow at my father's death. Have him entrust his passport and letters, if he will, to your own safe hands. So I may receive and consider them in private."

At Edward's nod, and as he left the room, Ferdinando took a gulp of his wine. His eyes narrowed as he stared off into the distance and as he drew the baron's letter closer beside him.

It seemed to Peter that only he noticed, out of the corner of his host's vision, that the Bishop, still standing at the window, had also narrowed his eyes. Through them, though, he stared at Ferdinando as his hand rose to his own immaculately trimmed beard, which he then proceeded to stroke most thoughtfully.

8   NEWPARKE

It was a little while before Edward returned and laid a single letter and a rather battered, red-ribbon-bound passport on the table beside the Baron of Newton's letter. Ferdinando stared at them all before picking up the passport.

Written on the back of the many-times-folded document, neatly enough for Peter to read with ease, was written "License for travel for Richard Heskett, Esq.". Ferdinando pulled at the red ribbon's bowknot, which at first resisted before finally submitting and falling away. Once unfolded and laid out before him, Ferdinando bent over the large sheet's ornately scripted contents.

Peter soon became lost in its dense wording, the whole seeming nothing more than one long, convoluted sentence. Ferdinando, though, seemed content enough, only murmuring his approval before turning his attention to the unopened letter.

He stared at it for a moment before returning to

the Baron of Newton letter, running his finger along its scrawl. Where his finger stopped and tapped, Peter distinctly read the word "letters"; in the plural. After a "Hmm" to himself, Ferdinando then picked up the unopened letter along with his knife.

"Hesketh said he'd been given the one you're about to open," Edward broke the silence by saying, "whilst staying at the White Lion in Islington, on his way here from Canterbury. Given to him by a lad called John Waterworth, sent there by your father's man in London. And indeed, I can see the address is clearly in Mister Hickman's hand; I know it well."

"And the seal's also a Stanley one," Ferdinando noted before he carefully cut it from the paper, unfolding the letter into his hand. Presently, he cast it aside, so it lay on top of the Baron's letter on the table.

"This is only news of those who've recently died in London; blast the plague that's blighting them there. We can read it properly later, Uncle. But, my Lord Chaderton, I note there are some names there that may interest your good self."

He pushed this latest letter across the table towards the Bishop. Whilst the man stepped over and took it up, Ferdinando quietly folded the Baron's now exposed letter and slipped it into his doublet.

"Well, all seems in order," Ferdinando announced as he refolded and secured the passport. "If you'd return this to Hesketh," at which he held the document out to Edward. "And you can inform him I'm satisfied he may remain in Lancashire." But when his uncle took hold of it, Ferdinando hesitated to release it.

"I am, however," Ferdinando went on to say,

"somewhat intrigued by Hesketh's coming here with the Baron of Newton's introduction." As he let go of the passport, he turned his attention to the Bishop. "Perhaps I should make a start on that great Lancashire mountain. Eh, my Lord Bishop of Chester?" The Bishop's gaze broke away from the letter he was still reading, his face now a little wan.

"Mountain?"

"The mountain that's been built in this handful of England by the likes of the Baron of Newton."

"Ah, yes. Indeed. That Catholic mountain."

"But there's too much still to do if I'm to be ready to leave for the Court come Tuesday, as I've already announced. My late father's papers are far from being put in order yet, and the sooner, the better. I also have the relief of my late father's earldom to consider. Her Majesty certainly won't take kindly to my delaying attending her in this matter."

"No. No, not at all."

"But my giving Hesketh leave to remain in Lancashire puts him somewhat in my debt, which he might see to repaying from the coffers of his knowledge regarding the Baron."

"Indeed. Indeed so," but the Bishop's attention was clearly more invested in the letter in his hand.

"Did you, by any chance," Ferdinando now directed more softly at Edward, "make mention that we're not alone?" and he glanced towards the once more distracted Bishop.

Edward, too, looked that same way, then nodded.

"In which case," Ferdinando said, even more softly, "instruct Hesketh to return here tomorrow, at the same time. Tell him to be ready to stay until I can find the time to see him. Two days at the most."

Edward shot his own glance at the Bishop before meeting Ferdinando's eyes and again nodding. He then slipped quietly from the room, leaving Ferdinando to its silence.

Presently, a distant clock rang out a single chime, and Ferdinando gave a polite cough, dragging the Bishop from the letter.

"This is proving a harsh plague," the poor man said, his face now almost ashen.

"I am sorry. I know some of those mentioned were close to you."

"Cherish your good fortune, my Lord Strange, that none was to you, if I'm not mistaken," but just then, Edward came back into the room.

"All done?" Ferdinando sought, and when Edward affirmed it was, he bade them drink down their wine and called out for Simon. The man soon rushed in, bowing to them each before being sent on his way to have the horses made ready for their return to Lathom House.

The Bishop said not a word on their way back, Ferdinando and Edward clearly keeping their own silence in respect for his losses. After a while, and as they came out from the woods, the castle of Lathom House suddenly dominated the view. On the track down the grassed slope, though, Ferdinando's horse stumbled on its loose stones.

He jerked himself upright in the stirrups, keeping his balance and taking his weight from his horse's back. It soon regained its footing, but by the time they'd entered through the outer gatehouse and into the first bailey, the horse had begun to favour a leg.

"Looks like his off fore," Edward suggested, at which Ferdinando dismounted and inspected the offending limb.

"There's some heat in the fetlock," he told them as he consoled the beast, stroking its muzzle then patting its neck. "You go on ahead; I'll walk him the rest of the way, then I'll go see my daughters and join you later, Uncle Ted. I've neglected them for far too long as it is," at which the others nodded and went on at a walk.

His horse now hobbling beside him, Ferdinando slowly fell behind, the two of them alone as they approached the inner bailey gatehouse. A horse-groom came rushing out, taking the reins from Ferdinando.

"See it gets bathed with plenty of cold water," he ordered as he patted his horse's lame leg, then he left the two behind and hurried towards the gatehouse.

A cloud must have slid over the sun, obscuring it, for everything went very dim, the air about Peter seeming too close. Then something jostled past him and a sharp pain shot across his brow.

"Well?" Derek said, from where he stood beyond the far end of the sofa. "Did you feel anything?"

9   STOLEN DAYS

"**Y**ou did say yourself," Derek said, somewhat shakily into his tumbler of whiskey, "that I wouldn't believe what you were about to tell me." He snatched a quick nip before shuffling to the edge of the sofa. "But I have to say, now you have, it would have beggared my belief if…if it wasn't for having seen that…that…that ghost myself."

At Derek's wide-eyed stare and now pallid features, Peter averted his eyes and rested his neck against the back of his armchair, finally staring up at the ceiling. His own shot of whiskey slopped unsteadily in his uncertain grip. Despite how crazy it sounded, he knew what he'd experienced. And even now, back safe in his own home, he was even more convinced it had been real.

"But then," Derek said in a carefully measured way, as though calming his nerves, and it drew Peter to look along his nose at his colleague, "you aren't showing any of the classic symptoms of psychosis.

And I've never before known you to behave in anything other than a rigorously sane way. So..."

Lifting his head, Peter stared at Derek. "So? So, you're saying you...you believe me?"

"I'm not saying I do, and I'm not saying I don't... damn it, now look what you're doing, bringing out the Irish in me." He drew in a long breath. "I know what I think I saw, and that's already more than enough to get my simple head around, never mind what you say you then..."

Derek's face turned deadly serious. "Well, what I find the hardest to believe about that is that it all took place in just a matter of seconds. That just doesn't make sense. The ghost, or whatever it was," at which he took another sip of his whiskey, "passed straight through you, and then your face went blank for a moment. But you broke out of it almost immediately, although you did then look as though... Shit, but I was going to say 'you'd seen a ghost'. And then, to top it all, you started gabbling away at me, ten to the dozen, until I got you to calm down. Even then, you still insisted on recounting a frankly unbelievable tale. You can see how it looks from my side, surely?"

"But... But how do you explain how I knew so much about what happened back then when I know bugger all about history."

"Is what you told me right, though? I don't know enough myself to say," but Derek then let out a sharp breath as he glanced at his watch. "Damn, just look at the time; it's nearly midnight. I'll have to get off. Work tomorrow, and didn't you say you had a clinic all morning?"

"Oh, shit. Yes, of course, it's still Tuesday here, isn't it?"

Derek stood up, downed the last of his whiskey and placed the tumbler on the coffee table.

"Look, Peter, I may not know much more than you, but Beryl, my wife, has a bit of an interest in history. Well, she seems to read a fair bit about it, and I sometimes go along with her to National Trust properties and the like. If she's still up when I get in, I'll see if she'd be into listening to your tale. Give you an idea of how accurate it might be. That sort of thing."

"Er, well, I'm not so sure about that."

"Don't worry; her word's as good as mine, if that's what's worrying you."

The thought of someone else being involved didn't sit easily with Peter, especially someone he'd never met. Eventually, though, when Derek made a point of checking his watch again, Peter stood up and nodded.

"In strictest confidence?" he asked, which Derek assured him it would be. "And all you'll tell her is that it was just a couple of vivid dreams I've had? Nothing about ghosts?" and although Derek hesitated, he again agreed.

"Very well, then. I should be finished by about one tomorrow. Give me a call in my office and let me know, either way. I'm just doing an afternoon admin session, and I'll hang around till you do. And…thanks for everything, Derek. I really appreciate it."

***

His car's GPS took Peter straight to the address Derek had given him over the phone for his home in Longton, a small village not far southwest of Preston. Pausing only to confirm the house name on the gatepost, he pulled into the moderately long drive of a large 1960's detached house within a copse of mature trees. As he parked beside an electric-blue Range Rover with heavily tinted windows, he noticed his dash clock showed a quarter to three—a quarter of an hour early.

He glanced at the imposing entrance, unsure whether he should wait or not, but then its door swung open and a woman with long, expensive blonde hair, probably in her early-forties, stepped out. She'd almost reached his car by the time he'd grabbed his notepad and was out, pressing the lock button on his key fob. An inquisitive smile cut through the woman's carefully made-up face.

"Doctor Buchanan?"

"Mrs Jameson?"

"Call me Beryl," and she reached out her hand.

"Peter," and they shook. "It's good of you to see me, and at such short notice. I hope I'm not too early."

"A little. My lunch with the girls finished earlier than usual, though, so, as you can see, I'm here now. Come on in," and she led him to the house and in through its entrance.

"You've a lovely place here," Peter commented as Beryl closed the front door behind them and they stepped into a not particularly large but certainly grand-looking entrance hall.

"Derek's never been keen on it. Says it's too ostentatious. Can I offer you a coffee or a tea?"

"A tea would be fine, thanks."

They were soon down the side of the hall's rather showy staircase and through into a spacious and fully equipped modern kitchen. Unlike Peter's own, this one looked well used, clean and unblemished but littered with evidence of a hectic lifestyle.

"You're down in Westhead, aren't you?" Beryl asked as she began preparing the tea.

"Not far from it."

"Lovely village. Where Derek was born, and where he'd love to live again: a small, unobtrusive cottage within staggering distance of the pub. Do you take milk? Sugar? Oh, and do sit down."

"Just a touch of milk, please. So… So, why Longton and this house?" and Peter sat on a stool at the kitchen's central island.

"This is where *I* was born."

"You don't often find that: someone who's lived in the same house all their life."

"Both my parents died before I could fly the nest. Dad owned a large regional housebuilding and property development company, so he couldn't really live in anything less; part of the image, and all that."

The kettle boiled and Beryl filled the teapot, stirring it a few times before popping on its lid. After she'd got some cups out, she sat on a stool beside Peter, reaching across to her handbag that sat on the counter.

"So," she said, taking out a packet of cigarettes and a lighter, "recurring dreams set in the past, Derek said," and she pulled an ashtray nearer.

"Oh, right. Yes. It was fortunate you weren't working today, though," Peter said, probing a little. "In which case, taking advantage of that, and that you're the history expert, I'd like to ask you a few questions about them, whilst it's all still fresh in my mind."

"I haven't worked for some time now, Peter," and Beryl cocked her head and grinned. "The only job

I've ever had was doing the books for my first husband's business…where Derck worked before starting at the hospital. That's how we met…Derek and me. He was instrumental in helping Tom, my husband then, to make a success of it. So we sort of lived in and out of each other's pockets for a good few years. But then, when Tom died suddenly in two-thousand-and-one—"

"Oh, I am sorry. I didn't know."

"It was quite sudden, and him only twenty-eight, but it left me in a right state," and she lit her cigarette, blowing smoke across the kitchen. "Derek was so supportive. I don't think I could have got through it without him. And without knowing it, we became even closer friends, then… Well, then we seemed to be an item. So, after a couple of years, he ended up marrying a rather wealthy widow," at which Beryl smiled.

"A wealthy… Oh, I see. Right."

"Are you married yourself, Peter? No wedding ring?"

As she got up to pour their teas, Peter glanced down at his left hand, then at the surprisingly modest diamond on Beryl's own. "Er, no. No, I'm not married. I suppose the right girl just never came along."

"They don't tend to, Peter. You have to go out and look for them," and she grinned as she stirred milk into their teas and placed the cups down on the counter, then sat beside him again.

"You're probably right, but I've never had much time to socialise, not really."

"Not socialise? You've not taken vows or anything, have you?"

"Ha, no. Well, not exactly," and for some reason

a feeling he'd had during his last dream came over him, one that seemed to quell the shyness he always seemed to suffer around women.

"Well, it's…it's like this, Beryl," he surprised himself by saying. "From being a youngster, I've only ever wanted to be a doctor, or something in that field; a lifelong obsession, you could say. But I was never one of those kids who shone, neither at school nor university. You know, who sailed through all their exams with flying colours. I've had to work hard for everything I've achieved, so damned hard that… Well, I suppose almost everything else just got squeezed out. A couple of girlfriends at university, but nothing that lasted, certainly nothing since I qualified."

"Well, from what Derek tells me, all that hard work's clearly paid off. He assures me you're one of the best specialty doctors in the trust."

"Only 'one of'? Damn! That means I need to work even harder, then," and they both laughed, which was when Peter realised he now felt relaxed in Beryl's company. It brought him to recall his lying in bed beside Alice, their limbs entwined; well, Ferdinando's and hers, at which he coughed, politely.

"But… But as to why I'm here; my dreams," he hurriedly went on to say. "I was wondering if you could tell me how genuine they might be, you know, in terms of historical accuracy. It's just that they felt so vivid and real at the time…as they still do."

"You can try me."

"Okay, then," and Peter referred to his notepad. "This is just something I quickly checked with Doctor Google before having to leave the hospital to come here—"

"Doctor Google?"

"Hmm? Oh, it's what we doctors say when we resort to checking medical facts on the internet. Now, in my last dream I dreamt about Earl Henry Stanley's death, dreamt it happened on the twenty-fifth of September, fifteen-ninety-three. Which, bizarrely, I found out was the exact date he did indeed die. Weird, eh?"

"The fifteen hundreds? That's a bit early for me; and don't tell Derek, but my interest in history doesn't often get much further than Regency romances. I've a bit of a weakness for bodice rippers."

"Oh, right. But Derek said—"

"He would. He doesn't really take much notice of what I read, and I suppose with the covers looking a bit historical—if you ignore the tacky embracing couples."

"No *sixteenth century* bodice rippers, then?"

"Sorry. I prefer the elegance of the Regency period. But if you managed to dream the right date for the earl's death, then that does sound awfully interesting. And even if I can't help much, I'd still love to hear more, and you never know."

Peter hadn't wanted to tell her everything of his dreams, just to see if she knew whether any of the events might be true. However, Beryl's easy-going manner seemed not just to tease it from him but to draw the full story out, although he still stayed clear of any mention of ghosts.

"Wow," she said when he'd finished. "And you dreamt all that?"

"Dreamt? Well, it's my only explanation, really, although none of it felt much like your usual dream state. And one of the many odd things about the last one was that it happened yesterday, Tuesday, the same day of the week as in my dream."

"You dreamt this yesterday?"

"Yes. Why?"

"What? When Derek was with you?"

"Ah..."

"I'm sorry, Peter, but I do actually know what happened. Derek couldn't keep it to himself, I'm afraid. And you didn't really expect him to, did you? Not when it freaked him out like it did. He's always prided himself on being the rational scientist, so you can imagine the state he was in when he got home."

"I suppose so, yes. I can see that now. A bit unfair of me to expect otherwise, really."

"So, not quite a straightforward dream, then?"

"No. Not quite."

"And this happened on the same day of the week but ten days apart."

"Ten days?"

"You said the earl died on the twenty-fifth of September, but you dreamt it yesterday, the fifth of October; ten days, which reminds me."

"Of what?"

"Well, I don't only read Regency romances. A few have been set a bit earlier, so I know about the riots they had in the mid-eighteenth century. When they cried out 'Give us back our eleven days' in protest," and Beryl aped an angry Georgian protestor, waving her fist in the air.

"You've lost me."

"When England went from the old Julian calendar to the new Gregorian one, that we still use today."

Peter only stared dumbly back at her, so she went

on to explain that the two calendars had started out in step back in the first century, but, being of slightly different year lengths, they'd steadily drifted apart. The old Julian calendar, she told him, had fallen eleven days behind when the new one came in.

"So, you see, they woke up one morning and the calendar had jumped eleven days into the future, days they felt had been stolen from them. It must have been a nightmare for the bookkeepers of the time."

"But the difference in my dream was only ten days, not eleven."

"Just a minute," and Beryl again rummaged in her bag, this time producing her mobile phone.

"Right," she said, calling up its calculator function. "Let's say it was the year seventeen-fifty when they changed over, when the difference had become eleven days. So, eleven divided by seventeen-fifty," and she tapped in the numbers, "times fifteen-ninety-three, and…voila."

She held her phone out to Peter, and there on its calculator's display was ten-point-zero-one. "Ten-and-a-bit days," she said, triumphantly. "I did say I'd done the accounting for Tom's business, didn't I?"

Peter stared first at her phone, then at her. "Are you saying yesterday was the same date it would have been in the earl's time, if they'd been using our calendar back then?" and she nodded, still smiling triumphantly.

"But… But when I had each dream, it was just after ten in our evening, yet I arrived both at the harbour and at Lathom House sometime in their morning—about twelve hours behind."

"That I can't explain," Beryl admitted.

"So, when Ferdinando arrived back with his lame

horse, mid-afternoon on the Wednesday, today, that's…that's yet to happen. Twelve hours off, when his ghost for this latest event should therefore come through my lounge at about…about three or four o'clock in the early hours of tomorrow morning. Because the two times, ours now and Ferdinando's back then, must be in step. They have to be, given the otherwise unlikely coincidence of the dates."

"Er, well, as daft as it sounds, I can't fault your reasoning."

"Thanks, Beryl. You don't realise how much of a help that's been. It really has," and he gulped down the dregs of his tea. "But for now, I'm going to have to love you and leave you, I'm afraid. I've a few things to arrange before the afternoon's out, most importantly: finding someone to stand in for me tomorrow. Because I honestly don't think I'm going to get enough sleep tonight, not to get me through two NHS management meetings in the morning.

10 A PROSPECTIVE NEW COMPANION

That evening, the Sainsbury's Gourmet Meal for One packaging had just thumped into the bottom of the waste bin when the front doorbell sounded, making Peter jump. He glanced at the clock on the kitchen wall: almost nine-thirty.

"Who the…" and his gaze darted around the room, checking it was tidy.

"Hi, Peter," the caller said when he'd got to the apartment's front door and opened it.

"Beryl? What're you doing here?"

"I'm sorry I couldn't warn you I was coming, but your mobile number went straight to answerphone. And when we looked your landline up in the book, you weren't listed."

"Er, no, I wouldn't be; I'm… I'm ex-directory. And the battery ran flat on my mobile; it's charging now. Is Derek not with you?" and he peered past her into the darkness but could see no one.

"Nope. Just me, I'm afraid."

"Well, er, do come in, then, won't you?" and he stepped aside to make room. "Sorry, but you were the last person I expected, especially at this hour. Thought it might be a neighbour, although that's just as unlikely. Here, let me take your coat. Is everything all right?"

"Thanks; yes, and again, sorry for how late it is," and she slipped out of her sheepskin coat, which Peter hung up. Underneath, she wore a simple black sweater and a pair of dark-grey jeans.

"Come through to the kitchen; I was just about to make myself a coffee. Can I do you one?" and Beryl was soon perched on a stool as Peter fussed around her in the kitchen.

"I'm sorry to turn up like this, but it was just—"

"How did you know where to find me?"

"Derek still had your address and the instructions you gave him for getting here."

"Oh, yes; of course."

"He'd have come himself if he hadn't been going straight out to get the train to Birmingham; he's at a conference tomorrow and Friday. Presenting a paper, so there was no way he could get out of it. Hence why it's me."

"But why would either of you feel the need to—"

"It was only after you'd left this afternoon that it dawned on me what you intended doing tonight. The thing is, the last time, you had Derek here, and I hated the idea of you...well, going off again but this time with no one being here for you."

"Ah," and Peter froze, staring at her for a moment, before setting their coffees down on the counter beside her. "So, do I take it you…you really do believe—"

"That you've somehow travelled back in time? Yes, Peter, I think we both do now, however crazy it sounds."

"Now?"

"After you left I did a bit of searching on the internet. I can show you on your own PC if you'd like."

"Er, well, I have one—my NHS laptop—but we're too far from the exchange here for internet access."

"Ah, that's a shame, for I found some interesting stuff. Did you know Lathom House stood close by here somewhere?" to which Peter nodded. "And that the fourth earl, Henry Stanley, really did have a common-law wife called Jane Halsall, just like you said? And that he had a whole other family with her? And all that time, his real wife was under house arrest for—"

"Consulting with wizards to predict the Queen's death?"

Beryl nodded, enthusiastically. "And the other things I remembered you telling me, they all stacked up, as well."

"That's great, Beryl. It really is. But I'm not sure if I'm relieved or not at hearing it. I have to say: it's made it all feel that bit scarier."

"Which was why I was so worried about you; why we both were. I mean, it's real. It wasn't just a dream. It looks like you really did go back in time."

Peter, not knowing what to say, quickly became tongue-tied, but then Beryl asked, "The thing I'd really like to know, though, is what made you go over and stand in the way of a ghost, of all things. It's not what anyone else would do, I'm sure," which was exactly what Peter had already asked himself.

"Er, well, arrogance, Beryl. Straightforward

arrogance. Like Derek, I don't believe in ghosts, so when I saw it I suddenly felt overwhelmingly annoyed, as though its very presence challenged all my beliefs. So much so that I just wanted to confront it, head-on; prove it to be nothing more than an illusion."

"But it wasn't, was it, Peter?" and she placed her hand on his arm, at which he promptly stood and picked up his mug.

"I have to say, Beryl: it's really good of you; it is, but I'm sure I'll be all right. It's going to be a long night, and I can't expect you to stay for it all."

"But we're adamant I do, both Derek and myself. I've nothing on tomorrow, and Derek would have done the same for you himself if he'd been able to."

"Well...I don't know."

"Please, Peter. I wouldn't be able to sleep anyway, not wondering how you were doing."

Peter held his breath, but then let it out as a long sigh. "All right; if you're absolutely sure?"

"I am. Absolutely."

"Okay, then, seeing you're that sure. In which case, can I suggest we take our coffees through to the lounge? It's more comfortable in there, especially as we've quite a few hours to kill before—well, if I really am right about this new time of my next visitation— before my beliefs are once again challenged."

Once in the lounge, Beryl was clearly keen to tell Peter everything she'd learnt from her internet searches, but he politely forestalled her.

"I feel it just wouldn't be the same knowing too much beforehand, like taking a peek at the last page of a good novel. And there's something about it that... Well, that feels safe somehow. A sort of enveloping reassurance…a connection…a…" but although Peter dug deep, trying to pin down what he really meant, whatever it was continually slipped from his grasp. "It's as though I'm drawn to going back," was the best he could do.

Beryl was clearly disappointed, but then suggested it might at least be a good idea to make a record of what had happened so far.

Peter thought it a great idea and went and brought in his laptop, powering it up and creating a blank Word document for her to use. He placed the machine on the coffee table before her, before where this good-looking woman's husband had sat the previous night.

A glance at his watch told Peter it had just turned ten-thirty—still plenty of time to pass, which Peter soon set about filling. His recounting of his dreams this time had the advantage of a considered pace and a slightly better knowledge in Beryl against which it could all be sounded out.

She tapped away with ease, occasionally seeking clarification or a fuller description, but all the while, Peter kept a keen eye on the time.

It was after one in the morning when Beryl finally dragged from him all he could recall. The diversion seemed to have paid off, killing time whilst keeping them both engaged and awake. As Beryl typed on, head down, finishing off her notes, Peter regarded her more closely. Then, when she at last lifted the laptop from her lap and placed it on the coffee table, Peter asked her, "Do *you* believe in ghosts, Beryl?"

Her hand, now placing the mouse down beside the laptop, hovered for a moment, stilled as she stared across at Peter, then she finally put it down.

"I could do with a smoke. Is there anywhere outside we can go? I don't want to smell out your apartment."

Peter nodded, then showed her to his bedroom, excusing it as the only way out into his small back yard. Although the day had been warm, the October night had a distinct chill to it when he opened the French windows and they stepped outside.

The night-time view from there was hardly inspiring: a waist-high brick wall marked out the empty flagged yard, beyond it the occasional lit window in the rear walls that looked down upon the central court car park they surrounded. The sky, though, made up for it, its cloudless black dome smeared and speckled and sparkling with stars. And the night air hung as still and as silent as Peter remembered it had beyond Ferdinando and Alice's firelit bedchamber.

For a moment, though, it all vanished behind the glow of Beryl's lighter. She drew in a long breath, expelling it as a soft and satisfied shush of faint grey smoke from between her glistening lips.

"My gran did," she quietly said, her eyes lifting to the stars. "Although my parents would then quite affectionately say that she'd always been a bit fey. I was still quite young when she passed on, but the way she mentioned seeing them in that everyday way of hers stuck with me. So, no, Peter, you've no need to worry when yours turns up."

"If."

"Okay, if. But *if* it does, are you really prepared to go with it again? Back into the past?"

"I have to, Beryl. I've got to know what happens

to them all, especially Ferdinando."

"But we could still find out by doing some more online research. That'd be a far safer option."

"I know. Don't think I haven't thought of that, but, as I said before, there's something about it all that's drawing me there. It's a kind of...I don't know, excitement; the excitement of an unsolved mystery, I suppose. So, I'm loath to shatter it all by knowing in advance what happens," at which Peter checked his watch: twenty-past-one—still plenty of time.

After a short while of silence between them, Beryl exclaimed, "Bloody hell, but it's cold out here," and stubbed out her cigarette on the sole of her shoe. "Is there somewhere I can put this?"

When they again came to sit in the lounge, Peter in his armchair, Beryl now comfortably resting back on the sofa, two fresh cups of coffee on the table between them, Peter made a confession.

"This may sound really strange, Beryl, but when I'm there, I get the strong feeling I belong somehow. As though I'm sharing in something, something with a real purpose."

"A purpose?"

But Peter could see it no more clearly than that, and before long their conversation fell into a lull as the time slowly ticked by. He got up and turned on the stereo, choosing a soft night-time music station, then sat back down.

As he got himself comfortable in his armchair, an unusual urge to tell Beryl all about himself for some reason crept over him. But, despite finding her company surprisingly easy, he couldn't in the end bring himself to start.

It was his own involuntary jerk that stirred Peter, that made him realise he'd been asleep. Beryl sat slumped to one side on the sofa opposite, her eyes closed. He snatched his wristwatch close to his sleep-blurred vision.

"Shit," he hissed, and Beryl made a few grumbling sounds before her own eyes shot open.

"What? Where the—"

"It's twenty-to-three, Beryl. Bloody Hell, I hope I've not missed it," and he stared into the far corner of the room. Nothing lay there but shadows.

Beryl had leant forward, reaching for what would have long been her cold coffee, but Peter was already fully awake, sensing a cold stillness to the air. He slowly got to his feet, his eyes still locked on the corner of the lounge.

When he felt Beryl's gaze join his, the air somehow went electric, then Ferdinando's ethereal form strode out of the wall and towards the sofa.

Without a word, Peter rushed to the end of it, turning just in time to face Ferdinando's determined approach. This time his ghostly figure glanced along the rear of the sofa, his gaze clearly set beyond Peter. To the inner bailey gatehouse and his intended visit to his daughters, Peter now remembered, and then they collided.

More prepared this time, after the flash of blinding light, Peter registered his mind jostling into a confined space. He felt a nudge and a push, then a stillness as the inner bailey gate of Lathom House splashed across his vision.

Ferdinando carried him through its shaded passage and out into the bailey, the imposing sight of the house once again taking Peter's breath away.

Soon, they were in through its entrance, past house servants in the great hall and up the staircase to the upper gallery. Once into the long passageway, though, Ferdinando hurried past the late Earl's bedchamber and on to a narrow rising flight of curved stone steps. At the top, he turned into a much shorter and lower passage, where he came to a halt at the first of two doors.

Here he paused, his ear angled towards the heavy wood of the door, the sound of female voices drifting through it from within, then he gently knocked. The voices stopped.

"Come," one of them called out, and Ferdinando lifted the latch and stepped into a long chamber.

A wooden screen split the room in two, a girl of twelve or thirteen years standing in the part nearest. Her expectant gaze broke into a broad smile and she seemed to relax a little. Then another girl, maybe ten years of age, stepped around the end of the screen, her face, too, lighting up with delight.

"Father?" she cried out and ran towards him, quickly wrapping herself about his waist and legs as the older girl less hurriedly joined them.

"How are you faring, Anne?" he directed at the elder, "and you, Frances?" he angled down at the younger. "I hope your hearts are both bearing well the sorrow of our shared loss?"

Before either could answer, footsteps scampered from behind the screen and a girl of about five or six rushed to fling her arms about both Ferdinando and Frances. Her face was clearly stained by tears, a face she hurriedly buried into the hose of his legs.

"Now, now, now," Ferdinando soothed as he reassuringly stroked both the embracing girls' backs. But he held his eyes on Anne, now standing before him. "How are you all, my most cherished daughters?" at which Peter's mind froze for a moment.

"*Three* daughters," he exclaimed, confused, and as Anne began to answer her father, Peter's mind was dragged elsewhere.

"But the Earl of Essex said just the two," he spoke out in surprise into the close confines of his mind. "That Ferdinando had only the *two* daughters, and therefore no sons to stand between William and the earldom. So, that must mean—"

"For faz sake," an intimately close and startling voice growled. "What the Hell are you talking about, and who are—" but at that, this new but grown woman's voice fell silent. And all the while, as Peter recoiled in shock, Ferdinando and his three grieving daughters obliviously carried on their own quiet and consoling discourse.

11   SILENT RUNNING

For some time, Peter remained stunned. That comforting sense of being cocooned in Ferdinando's mind had deserted him. Now he felt exposed and vulnerable, prey to any vicissitudes that might come his way. That woman's voice, whoever it had been, had come worryingly close from right beside his mind, of that he was certain.

Neither Ferdinando nor the girls had heard it. They couldn't have done, for their concerns had remained solely with each other, as Peter only distantly registered was still the case. Tentatively, he felt around the edges of his awareness, fearful of what he might find.

There was definitely a closeness there, a constraint he'd noted before but had always dismissed; but now he couldn't. Something—or someone—was pressing against him, and when he stilled himself as best he could, it seemed that whatever it was occasionally shifted or stirred. But however carefully he tried, he couldn't seem to disengage himself, to put even a hair's breadth between them.

What had caused her to speak out when she did? Peter wondered. Only now did he recall her exact words: "What the Hell are you talking about?". Talking? and Peter struggled with the very idea of being able to do such a thing without recourse to a physical mouth.

He recalled it had been his surprise at seeing a third daughter that had made him… Yes, of course, that had made him cry out in his mind. Not a quiet thought but a loud internal voice; the former what the woman could plainly not hear, the latter that she clearly had. He took a moment to think, silent thoughts that carried no words, a conclusion on their coattails.

"Are you there?" he now voiced. Despite his trepidation, he had to acknowledge that his choice of words could have been better. Their definite ring of a séance threatened a nervous laugh.

He waited, still but attentive, aware that Ferdinando and the girls had seated themselves on a long highbacked bench facing the partially opened shutter of a window opposite. He could feel the heat of a fire at Ferdinando's back, heard the voices of the girls as they quietly talked about their late grandfather. But the woman's voice remained stubbornly absent.

He now recalled that her tone had been one more of exasperation than of surprise, as though she'd already been aware of his presence. So, there must have been something in what he'd said that had prompted her to speak out when she did, not simply the surprise of his voice.

Then it came back to him: it had been his shipboard experience of William's meeting with the Earl of Essex that had prompted his voiced thoughts. Not only that, but that first dream in which it had happened had clearly been just that: a sleeping dream. And it had, he suspected, therefore been entirely his own, shared with no one else, clearly unlike this and his previous one.

So, whatever it was he'd said about that meeting, it must have been something the woman hadn't known, something that had intrigued her. If so, then whatever it was clearly carried enough weight to unsettle her, some value of some sort in her own eyes. Enough perhaps to be to Peter's advantage now. Enough, maybe, to keep him safe.

"I know you can hear me," he tried again, the words pushing Ferdinando and his daughters' own into the background. "I know you're here beside me, here in Ferdinando's mind," but still nothing came back from the woman.

"If you want to know what was said between Ferdinando's brother, William, and the Earl of Essex, then you're going to have to make yourself known to me. You're going to have to speak again."

Ferdinando had by now reluctantly got to his feet, his daughters once again clinging to him. The youngest, the five or six-year-old, must have been unknown to Essex for him to have mentioned only the two. Or, it now dawned on Peter, she hadn't been born at the time, which seemed far more likely. And if that was the case, then what Peter had experienced in that genuine dream of his had to have taken place in the past. Some five or six years before this, Ferdinando's present.

Finally, taking his leave of his daughters and promising to see them again before the day was out, Ferdinando left the chamber and returned down the spiral staircase. He was just passing the late Earl's bedchamber when the woman's voice at last rang out in Peter's mind once more.

"A few questions first," she spoke out clearly but tersely.

"Ah, so you are there. Well, I'm all ears," he assured her as Ferdinando went out onto the high gallery and started down the steps.

"Okay. First one: how did you get here?"

"How did you?"

"Cut the crap. There'll be no talking between us until you've fully answered *all* my questions, geddit?"

"Er, yes, I think so. In which case, to answer your first, it would seem I got aboard what appears to have been a ghost train; an express, considering the speed it got me here."

This left only silence between them, until Ferdinando had turned into a passageway that led off from the great hall. When her voice eventually came, this time it did so with a slightly lighter tone.

"So, funny guy, eh? But where did you get on this…*express*?" and Peter now knew she was from a time after the invention of the railways, which aligned with her modern although slightly foreign-sounding language.

"In my lounge, why?"

"See-this, *I'm* asking the questions. So, where was your… Just a minute; what year were you in before you *climbed aboard*?"

"Year?"

"Yah, year."

"Er, twenty-ten."

"Oh, poo; real poo bad," and that rather bittersweet silence returned, persisting all the way to the small office where Ferdinando found his uncle Edward and his secretary, Michael, both already busy at work.

"You still there?" Peter asked.

"Quick ground rule," she barked back. "When I say 'Quiet running', there'll be no talking between us until I say otherwise. Geddit?"

"Why?" in response to which came a long pause.

"More important things to do," she eventually snapped back. "So," and this time her bark came in no uncertain terms, "*silent running*."

"And you'll say when we can talk again?"

"Shush."

Edward had already relinquished his seat at the table to Ferdinando, a large document now spread out before him. It lay surrounded by piles of others, from which sprouted long leather bookmarks. He leant nearer, running his finger along the document's scrawled text.

Michael, now standing at Ferdinando's elbow, began explaining something using such archaic terms that it all went straight over Peter's head. As it had on all such previous occasions, he acknowledged, and again it took him back to all those obscure medical terms he'd had to master at university.

He wondered if this might not explain the woman's need for their period of *silent running*.

Perhaps these documents were the "more important things" to which she'd alluded. If so, what could she possibly be looking for and why? And could this be the root of that sense of purpose he'd initially found so alluring?

That slightly foreign sound to the woman's voice brought to mind a previous comment he'd made to himself: how he'd come to find the past an alien land. Wouldn't the future likely be just as alien, the voices sounding just as foreign? Foreign lands stretching out in both directions, into the past and the future, he concluded. He then resolved, at some point, to ask the woman her own year of departure.

The chance didn't come until much later, when Ferdinando had completed his day's work and was sitting down at the high table. Beside him sat Alice and this time his three daughters.

Peter had heard nothing at all from the woman and had assumed that she too had been hard at her own work, whatever that might really have been. But now away from those documents, Peter saw no reason for their continued silent running.

"You haven't forgotten about me, have you?"

"I haven't said we can talk yet, so keep quiet. I'm still busy."

"Busy doing what? There's nothing going on but people sitting down to eat."

Somehow, Peter could sense the woman's shortening temper, but despite it, he persisted: "So, when can we get to talk again?"

"Oh, daggit," the woman's voice spat. "You're the most infuriating..." For a moment the space around them seemed to fizz, but then the effect slowly dissipated. "I'm an historian and trained mnemonist, busy committing today's observations to memory. I have to do this before Ferdinando takes us both into sleep."

"What? You mean I'm stuck here until tomorrow?"

"Well, you were last time, and you weathered that well enough."

"Ah, so you *were* there then. I thought so."

"See-this, in what's left of today, I'll only just have enough time to get everything committed. And if I don't, it'll be too late when we wake in the morning; I'll have forgotten stuff by then. And anyway, your...your impossible presence here means I've got something I need to get straight with you—something I now realise is Earth-shaggingly important. So fricking huge, when I think about it, that we can't risk talking to each other until I have."

"That... That sounds ominous. You sure you can't just give me a hint now?"

"I'll need some clear-head time for pre-thought before I can lay it on you. And no, you're just going to have trust me. Then, after we've got it straight between us, I'm going to have to be really careful what I say to you, for all our sakes—if I say anything at all. So, silent running until tomorrow, yah?"

"But—"

"Yah?"

"Okay; *yah*, for crying out loud."

12   A VIEW OF THE MOUNTAIN

The discomfort Peter had felt that very first night Ferdinando had retired to bed with Alice had, the night before, been heightened further. That he now knew there was a woman beside him in his mind meant he'd had to face the possibility of being embroiled in some kind of bizarre foursome. It had, fortunately, been avoided when Ferdinando found his wife in bed before him, already fast asleep.

Their host had soon lain there so still and quiet that Peter had begun to wonder if he'd fallen asleep, leaving Peter himself awake. He'd just been considering speaking out to the woman, to find out if she, too, had remained awake, when the next thing he knew dawn light was seeping into the chamber and Ferdinando was stirring.

As on that first morning Peter had arisen with him, Alice was already out of bed, although on this occasion nowhere to be seen. Once dressed, Ferdinando made his way down to the great hall but was intercepted by Edward, in the company of another but younger man.

"Good morning, my lord," Edward greeted him. "I trust you slept well?"

"Passable, Uncle, but the nights are drawing in and my bed was noticeably colder last night."

He now faced the rather rotund and rosy-faced man beside Edward. "And to what do I owe Mister Farington's presence this rather grey morning? And who I trust is also well?" to which the man respectfully nodded.

"If you remember, Ferdinando," Edward replied, "we were to address the Woodvale land near Parbold today. William, here, was instrumental in settling the matter of the agreement between your father and Mister Richard Howghton."

"Ah, indeed," Ferdinando enthused, "and we affirmed we'd ride out there to survey it. To see exactly what my father chose to commit such a princely portion of my forthcoming estate to buying. In which case, perhaps you'd arrange for horses. I've been cooped up in that office for far too long. A good ride out will put that to rights, I'm sure."

"Of course, Ferdinando, provided you're prepared to leave Sir Thomas Gerard kicking his heels when he arrives here presently."

"What? Oh, yes, although I...I thought his visit, to bring us his mock sympathy and his feigned honouring of my late father, was this afternoon."

"Nay, my lord, but at ten o'clock. And we couldn't get back from Woodvale by then, I'm afraid."

"Ah, no, I suppose not. Well, let's at least refresh our minds on the matter in the meantime," at which

Ferdinando carried on through the great hall and into the passage that led to the office. Before long they'd joined Michael there, once more setting to, delving into, for Peter, the mounds of indigestible documents.

For the most part it seemed they were just going over old ground, if this time checking it all against William's notes. Peter reckoned there couldn't, therefore, be much here to keep his mysterious female companion occupied, and so ventured to speak with her. She quickly answered, but only to say she wasn't ready yet, and despite his persistence, he heard no more from her.

Sometime later, a youth appeared at the open door, to announce the arrival of Ferdinando's visitors and to inform him they'd been shown to the solar. Ferdinando shot a brief look at his uncle, the man resignedly lofting his brow.

"Well," Ferdinando said, putting down the paper he'd been holding, "I think we've got to grips with this contract, although I still consider it an oppressive sum for such a rather inconsiderable parcel of land. But we shall see, shall we not, Uncle Ted? Now, though, I suppose I shouldn't keep Sir Thomas waiting. I take it my father's already been laid out in the chapel?"

"He has, Ferdinando, all as is due and proper. I'm told Jane has been at his side much of the time since, her vigil unstinting, even in sleep."

"Have her retire before Sir Thomas arrives to honour him," at which Edward nodded, knowingly.

The solar lay in half-light when Ferdinando entered alone. Two men stood close by the fireplace, its embers throwing out a dull red light. They turned to face him, each bowing as he approached. Once they'd straightened, Ferdinando briefly nodded to the taller of the two.

The man opened his empty sword hand to his side. "My Lord Strange, I'm grateful for your indulgence."

"You're most welcome, Sir Thomas. I trust your journey here proved uneventful?"

"It did, my lord. The weather and the roads have both been kind to us. But on the sad cause of our calling upon you, my lord, I would like to assure you that I and all mine do great condolence upon the reported death of your honoured father. His passing is a dearly felt loss to us all."

"You have my gratitude for your kind words, Sir Thomas. And yes, my father died this Tuesday gone. It's good to know he was held close in so many hearts."

"So, so; and only the other week, the Earl of Essex and myself were lauding his inestimable prowess."

"Indeed? I'm warmed to hear it."

"A fine example to us all. He managed to sow so much where so few of the nobility have, over these gathering poorer years, been inclined to reap far less. It's been much remarked upon. It would seem he's truly set the Stanley ship of fortune on a safer course of late, one I'd imagine will sail hereupon by the self-same heading."

When Ferdinando failed to respond, Sir Thomas turned to the man at his side. "This, my lord, is Joseph Althorp, my attorney-in-fact," to whom Ferdinando curtly nodded. "We're upon various matters of business in Preston, where he's to act upon my behalf. But, if it be not too much of an imposition, he too wishes to take the opportunity of honouring your late father."

"By all means," Ferdinando allowed, although Peter detected a tension in his voice. "You'll appreciate, I'm sure, the burden of preparation that's now my due. So, if I may invite you to attend my late father straightaway and afterwards forgive me my quitting you before you take some refreshment?" which appeared to be to Sir Thomas's satisfaction.

After their wordless passage through the castle, they came to a short flight of stone steps, at the foot of which stood an arched doorway into a dimly lit chamber. The air within felt chill upon Ferdinando's skin, stilled in a seeming eternal silence. The unadorned walls of what was clearly a simple chapel held within them four tall and un-flickering candles. Each stood at the corner of a long table, upon which rested the resplendently dressed body of the late Earl.

Both Sir Thomas and his companion stepped closer to the dead Henry's peaceful countenance, upon which they peered down inquisitively for a moment. Then a quick glance and an almost imperceptible nod to each other and they both straightened before bowing their heads in prayer.

A good few hours after Sir Thomas's visit, and having taken their midday meal in the great hall, the four men—Ferdinando, Edward, Michael, and William—rode out of the castle through the outer bailey gatehouse. The weeks of pleasantly warm and dry weather had finally given way to a grey and overcast day, a cooler hint carried on its air of the delayed Autumn that should soon to be upon them.

As they turned east along a track that skirted the outer wall and its moat, Michael and William fell respectfully behind Ferdinando and his uncle. Edward then asked how Sir Thomas's visit had gone.

"His and his witness's minds are at somewhat better ease, I imagine," Ferdinando quietly said. "Now they've irrefutably confirmed one less of Secretary Cecil's allies dwells upon this Earth."

"And by it, I've no doubt, the Earl of Essex will soon rest that little bit easier himself, once delivered of the affirming news."

"That I'm sure of. The good Sir Thomas clearly has an eye to what he sees as his best interests."

"Although the man does share a fondness for falconry with Secretary Cecil himself."

"Aye. A shrewd foot in both camps, I reckon. The man's no fool, Uncle, unlike Essex."

"No, but a fool can be the more dangerous foe, and so must not be so lightly dismissed. But then, fortunately, Secretary Cecil is plainly no more the fool himself."

"Indeed not, to our better fortune, I trust."

From behind them, William called out that a rider was fast approaching down the track from Newparke, at which Ferdinando drew his horse to a halt and turned. Seeing he'd gained their attention, the distant rider now urgently waved as his horse dropped from its gallop and into a less hurried trot.

"Looks like Simon's son," Edward noted. "I hope nothing's untoward at Newparke."

When the young rider finally joined them, he bowed to Ferdinando and Edward from where he remained in his seat. "My Lord Strange," he said, a little breathlessly, "father's sent me to say that Mister Hesketh's arrived."

"Hesketh? Ah, yes," and Ferdinando clearly paused for thought. "Tell your father I may see the gentleman later, if time and…" He looked up at the sky's darker grey stain to the west, beyond the woods on the hilltop that way. "And if the weather so allows. Make sure he's adequate board and, if I don't get to visit today, a decent enough bed." At his dismissal, the lad turned his horse and walked it leisurely back the way they'd come.

No more mention was made, neither by Ferdinando nor his uncle, of Richard Hesketh as they walked their own horses on beside the castle's moat. Where Peter could see no more need now for the mystery woman to forgo speaking to him, and so tried to engage her.

"On the way back," she told him. "When I know how long we'll have. Can't afford to have our next talk cut short," after which she could be drawn to say no more.

The track they followed soon diverged from the steady curve of the wall. It took them gently down into woods, and within whose breathless embrace they continued to descend, until they came to a shallow forded beck. Having crossed, they steadily climbed through the continued woodland, the track now weaving along contours and around ancient trees and outcrops of weathered rock. Eventually, it took them beside a large clearing cut into strips. Figures were dotted about within each, all bent to their tasks, none noticing, in their back-breaking labours, the party's passing.

And so, the afternoon wore on, their horses forging eastwards along track after track, some deeply rutted from the passage of cartwheels, most scuffed only by hooves and feet. Much of the land lay hidden beneath woodland and forested cover, and where not, lay largely earth-brown and furrowed.

When they finally came out from the woodland, a gently sloping patchwork of narrow fields opened out before them, a jagged line of trees at their bottom clearly marking the course of a river. Beyond rose yet more fields, until meeting a low mounded ridge upon the near horizon. To the south of this sprawled a dense forest, stretching away into the distance.

Edward brought them to a halt and pointed. "That broad mound, up to which the ridge rises, is High Moor; the near side of which is largely Stanley land, as is the forest to the south. We also have strips along both sides of the River Douglas, below us here, almost down to Parbold," at which he now pointed. A cluster of buildings could just be seen a little way further down the valley to the north.

"Both parcels of which are clearly fruitful, from the accounts I've seen," Ferdinando supplied. "Sheep from upon high, rabbit from the lower land and fish from the river."

"And between the two sits the parcel Richard Howghton has agreed to sell us; across there, where you can just make out the new fencing we've put up. Although I'm told it's lately been broken down in places. It seems the local families think they've a right to trap rabbits and graze their livestock there. They consider it common land, Ferdinando, a belief Richard Howghton's neglect has only gone to foster. More's the shame on him, for it's got particularly rich soil."

William deferentially cleared his throat. "More

importantly, my Lord Strange, the completion of the purchase would make your two sufficiently good parcels into one very productive one, the whole lot more easily accessed. Especially by river, my lord. And why Richard Howghton knew to hold out for a higher price."

"But," Edward added, "with land prices currently as low as they are compared with rents, that higher price still isn't really that great. We reckon the cost of purchase could be recovered in eight years."

"Less, I'm sure," Ferdinando asserted, "if the surplus to our estate's needs were to be sold on locally, or some of the land set aside for rental income."

"Ah, the very suspicion that's feeding the flames of so much recent unrest hereabouts. And hence the damage to our fences. In your retainers' eyes, they see our possession as an act of theft, the stealing of long held common land, its use until now theirs for the taking."

"Well, we'll see. Unless they can prove their case at assize against the deeds Richard Howghton assures us he holds, then they'll soon have to pay for such privilege. They're now *my* retainers, not I theirs, so let them complain."

"You do know that many of the families here are suspected of being recusants, or with strong Catholic sympathies, don't you, Ferdinando?"

"Ah, so here we are; at the foothills of that very mountain, eh?" and Ferdinando stared at the land in question for some time.

Presently, he announced, "I've decided: as soon as the estate's legally in my hands, we'll complete on the purchase and make good the fences once more."

At that, Ferdinando defiantly sniffed the air and spurred his horse about, leading the way back along the track.

"Right, then," the woman's voice said, startling Peter. "We've enough time now."

"What?"

"For that talk we need to have."

"Oh, right. Yes. That. So, what was it you needed to tell me? And by the way, what's your name? I can't keep thinking of you as 'That woman in my head'."

"No names; no pack drill."

"Eh?"

"You'll understand, once I've convinced you that the laws of physics make time travel completely impossible."

"You what? But what the hell's this if it isn't just that?"

"Well? Are you sitting comfortably?"

"Am I what?"

"Then I'll begin..."

13   A PARADOX

Now he was getting used to the dichotomy of his internal and external worlds, Peter found he could take in more of their surroundings whilst the nameless woman talked. This new ability, though, soon fell by the wayside.

"What do you know about quantum physics?" she asked, and Peter's mind at first went blank. Then he remembered an old Horizon television programme about the subject, but one he could now barely recall.

"Not much, I have to admit," he finally confessed.

"No, me neither, which is why I've found the prospect of this conversation a slip demanding. You see, all I've got to go on is a foundation course I had to complete before getting this job. And all that really left me with were its bullet points."

"Bullet points?"

"Yah, the first one being that time travel's impossible"

"But it isn't; we're here, in the sixteenth century!"

"Don't get ahead of me; this is hard enough as it is. Have you heard of the Grandfather Paradox? It was known about in twenty-ten, I'm pretty sure."

"Never heard of it."

"Well, then. Here goes: if time travel were possible, it says—actually going back and being there, so you can affect things and pass on info and the like—you could go back to before you were born, find your own parents and then kill them both."

"Sounds a bit of a pointless thing to do, never mind the criminality of it."

"No, you're missing the point. It's more than that. In doing so you'd be creating a paradox, which is another way of saying: if, after the killing, you could never have been born, then how could you go back and perform the killing in the first place?"

"I don't know. How could you?"

"That's just it: you can't. It'd be a paradox. It wouldn't make sense in the real physical world."

"But who'd want to do such a self-defeating thing, anyway?"

"It doesn't matter whether you would or you wouldn't. The fact that you *could* is all that matters, and what makes a nonsense of the whole idea of time travel. If it could happen, then all sorts of other impossible stuff could also happen, the fabric of the universe falling apart before it'd even got started."

Peter now recalled that he'd had a similar feeling at the end of that Horizon programme. As he tried to get to grips with it all, he noticed they were now in sight of the fields of toiling figures they'd passed on the way out.

"So, what's all that that's around us, then? Some

sort of illusion?"

"Nah, that's all real. That's our past and Ferdinando's very real present."

"Go on, then, how?"

"This is how it was described to us on that course I mentioned: imagine you're on a coastal clifftop, looking out towards a ship on the horizon."

"Okay."

"Now imagine that that ship's something in the past, that the miles of sea between you and it are the centuries spanning back to, say, Ferdinando's time. The ship appears to be just a small, distant feature on the horizon, doesn't it? But then imagine you've got a telescope, and when you look through it, you can see all that's going on aboard, all in fine detail."

"What, like I'm doing now? Seeing what Ferdinando's up to? But I'm experiencing this in the here-and-now, not just seeing it from a distance."

"True, but only through Ferdinando's senses, not directly with your own. It's like watching the ship's helmsman through the telescope; you can't physically influence which course he steers. You can't even tell him which way to go, because he can't hear you. And that's because you're not physically there, aboard that ship. It's just your senses that have been taken nearer. You're still back on the cliff, just looking through a telescope, seeing far back to that distant helmsman's time. And so, you see, just as you can't influence anything in his world, you can't therefore create a paradox between it and yours. You get that?"

"Ah, right. Yes, I think I actually do. So, what's the telescope thing we're using?"

"That I can't tell you."

"Why?"

"Because."

"Because what?"

"Because…*you* came along and looked through it."

"Me? Is this where you reveal why you were so freaked out and wouldn't talk to me?"

"'Freaked out'? How quaint, but yes. But haven't you worked it out for yourself yet?"

"Er…"

"Worked out that you've just gone and broken a frigging fundamental law of physics? Driven a bar-steward express train through it all?"

"I have? But how?"

The woman paused for a moment. "What's your name?"

"Mine? Er, Peter."

"Well, Peter, *you* are someone in *my* past, geddit? And by the very definition of time travel, I might not be able to affect you physically, but we are exchanging information. I'm communicating with someone from my own past, for Dei's sake. I could tell you, for instance, who my own parents are and where they lived in your time, then it'd be quite feasible for me to…well, just suddenly no longer exist; to never have existed."

"But I'd never do such a… Hang on; so, time travel really is possible, after all? Is that what you're saying? That, despite hypothetical paradoxes, we've…we've already proved it in actuality by my hearing what you're saying. By telling you my name."

"As I said earlier, I only did the physics foundation course. But it strikes me, if we're not really, really careful, we could end up unravelling the frigging universe. Or at least the one I'm currently quite happy to call home."

"Shit. I mean… No, it can't be true. Can it? Really?"

They'd reached the ford across the beck in the woods, where it now seemed much darker than Peter would have expected, as though dusk had stolen a march on them. Then Ferdinando groaned as he looked up through the canopy.

"Damn the weather," he cursed. "And so near," at which Peter felt raindrops splattering against the Earl's cloak, which he'd now gathered closer. "Trot on," he told them, then spurred his horse up the track, the sound of hooves clattering on its stones.

"I can't see how it's not real," the woman finally said as the horses carried their party steadily up through the woods, "but either way, we just can't take the risk. Not with what's at stake."

"I suppose I now understand why you can't afford to tell me your name, but would you mind if I called you Sophie? I think I need some sort of handle on you. Would that be okay?"

"I can't see it'd do any harm. So, yes, if you wish."

"In which case, Sophie, I'm really sorry for boarding your ghost train like I did. I just never realised what an horrendous problem it would cause."

"No, I don't suppose you could have. But we're stuck with it for a while."

"A while? Like how long?"

"Er, well…a few weeks."

"A few weeks!" then the skies opened, heavy droplets of rain thudding down through the canopy, chilling Ferdinando's face as each man wrapped himself more closely into his cloak. And so, they pressed on towards Lathom House, now barely visible through the stair rods slanting against them as they burst out at a gallop from the woods.

14 DISTRACTIONS

Their party swept into the great hall, where sodden cloaks were swiftly swapped for dry blankets by a solicitude of servants. Then stools were brought close to the fire, on which they sat and presently steamed. Only then did Ferdinando cast an eye across the hall to one of the lower tables there. He found the Bishop and half a dozen clerics standing by it, awaiting his pleasure.

"Ah, my good Bishop Chaderton and The Reverend Mister Ambrose, how is it with you?" Ferdinando called over, at which each cleric bowed low. "If you'd allow me time to get some dry clothes onto this currently drenched body of mine, then perhaps I may attend to your needs. Have you been waiting long? And do, pray, be seated."

"The dear reverend, here, has, somewhat," the Bishop gently censured as he sat down.

"It's of no great matter, my Lord Strange," the reverend was quick to say. "It's but my calling to serve upon others at their own leave," but Peter detected a certain tetchiness in the dour-looking man's answer.

"Better you were delayed here, Mister Ambrose, in the warm and dry, I vouch, than being caught out in this foul weather on an otherwise timely return."

This the vicar resignedly conceded with a slow nod as he and the others sat down. Meanwhile, one of the servants had pulled off Ferdinando's boot, emptying water from it onto the hearthstone.

"Richard and his brethren," the Bishop went on to say, "have need to address the matter of the order of service and seating in Ormskirk church for the funeral, my Lord Strange. They're particularly considerate of the numbers to be expected. All at your own leisure, of course, my lord." And so, at this, the table of men waited upon the now most powerful man in Lancashire whilst he retired to be dried off and dressed afresh.

The remainder of the day filled with the steady arrival of more local personages, each seeking to offer their sympathies. By then, Alice had joined Ferdinando, and between them they bore the growing press of condolences for, and obsequious recollections of, the late Earl with shared fortitude.

The early evening meal, therefore, proved to be a packed affair as those near enough to get home afterwards in the evening light took advantage of Lord Strange's hospitality.

Throughout it all, Peter deferred to Sophie's need to listen to what conversations Ferdinando had an ear to, even he finding the gossip increasingly of more interest.

Slowly, the lives of those around him were

becoming more real and immediate, the beginning of a sense of belonging to this alien world steadily settling within him. So, when, quite late on, Ferdinando was at last dressed in his nightgown and entered his and Alice's candlelit bedchamber, Peter's reticence at his covert intrusion had greatly diminished.

Alice was kneeling on a cushion, in prayer beside the bed, her hands lightly pressed together before her closed eyes. Ferdinando went and stood with his back to the fire, where its dully glowing peat threw out far more heat than the brightly burning logs had done at Peter's previous visit. Rocking on his heels, Ferdinando stared up at the moulded ceiling, as though deep in thought, until Alice called out and a servant girl hurried in.

With practiced actions, the lass took down a warming pan from where it hung beside the fireplace, filled it with embers from the hearth and swiftly carried it across to the bed. There, she swept the pan slowly back and forth between the linen bedsheets before returning the pan to the hearth and retiring from the chamber.

At the creak and groan of the bed ropes, Ferdinando went to join his wife as she got in between the sheets, her voice now coming partially muffled from beneath them.

"Oh, this is most comfortable," she purred, then looked up at him. "Do you still think you'll be ready to leave for the Court on Tuesday, Ferdy?"

"I'm hoping so," he said as he climbed in beside her, snuffing out the bedside candle. Then he released the bedcurtains and slid down into the welcoming warmth of the sheets.

"I'm glad we broke the back of much of it yesterday," he said, "for today's proved quite hectic. I never realised how much would be involved in arranging... Oh, damn it."

"What's wrong, Ferdy?"

"It's just I forgot all about Richard Hesketh. Well, I'll have to see how tomorrow fares, but it's not looking good, not by how today's gone. I can't believe it's almost Friday; the week's passed so quickly."

"What I can't understand, husband, is that, with all you have on, why you invited him back? And what does the man hope to profit by it?"

"I suspect he's a private letter for me, one he didn't feel he could entrust to Uncle Edward's hands, and particularly not into the Bishop's presence."

"Well, surely it could've waited until you were back? What's only going to be two or three weeks at the most."

"That Hesketh's willing to bide his time at Newparke upon my uncertain pleasure speaks of some urgency in his own eyes, or of some importance. My own suspicions are that it's an intrigue of the Baron of Newton's. You know what a fickle man he can be, likely more so now his fortunes are waning. It's why I'm keen to nip whatever this madness of his might be in the bud."

"The Baron of Newton?"

"Hesketh came with the man's introduction, so has clearly been in company with him, likely at Walton Hall since his return to Lancashire. Which, given that most of the Heskeths I've met these past couple of days have been unaware of his return, seems most likely the case."

"Hmm, the Baron," Alice mused to herself. "Myself, I'd entertain nothing that carried even a hint of that man's name. And anyway, I'll be surprised if you do find the time to get to Newparke before Tuesday."

"You're probably right, my dear," and now warmer, Ferdinando turned onto his side and snuggled up against her.

"If Richard Hesketh's errand is that urgent," Alice said, pressing her backside against him and lifting his hand to her breast, "and you're still adamant you wish to see him, then maybe you should arrange to meet on your way south. At least then you'll be free of all these pressing demands. You're staying first with Sir William Brereton at Brereton Hall, aren't you?"

"Yes. I added a message to that effect on the obituari he was sent. And I think you're right, as always, my love. If time doesn't present itself tomorrow, I'll send for Simon and pass instructions through him to Hesketh. If his reasons for wishing to see me are important enough, he'll be prepared to travel down to the County of Chester. If not, then he can attend me after I've returned."

"Poor Sir William. My heart's with him. I hope he's coping better now. It must be nearly six months since Margaret's death, and forty-four is too young an age to be parted from your wife."

Ferdinando's hand now softly kneaded Alice's breast, his warm breath closely favouring her neck. She murmured, appreciatively, which brought a reaction from Ferdinando that Peter had been dreading.

"Sophie?" he urgently asked, trying to ignore what his borrowed senses were now telling him—*their* borrowed senses, which only went to heighten his dread.

"I'm trying to avoid talking with you, Peter, but then," she said, a hint of amusement in her voice, "this is probably going to be your first time, isn't it?"

"I think you could have put it better, but yes."

"Don't worry. There's a technique," which seemed to Peter an even poorer choice of words. "It's a case of distraction, having something completely objective but fascinating to contemplate. I tend to go through checking the mnemonic records I've made. In fact, it should be easier with the two of... Ah, well, but then we do have to consider our paradox problem, don't we?"

Ferdinando and Alice's increasing intimacy would have made it hard for Peter to concentrate on what Sophie was saying, had it not been for the weight that had entered her voice.

"What... What problem's that, then?" he managed to say.

"That the more engrossing any conversation becomes, the greater the risk I'll reveal something I shouldn't."

"Are you doing this on purpose?"

"What?"

"You are, aren't you?"

"What I meant was revealing anything about your future...about my present...or anything in between." By now, the ropes supporting the feather mattress beneath them had begun to groan in a rather disconcertingly rhythmic manner. Peter fought hard to keep his mind on Sophie's words.

"But surely you can..." he attempted, "can tell me stuff I could have known about from my own time, can't you?" but by now, both man and wife had become a little more exuberant, challenging Peter's train of thought. "There's a...a lot I don't...don't understand, and... For God's sake, Sophie; this isn't at all easy."

"The problem is, Peter, I can't always be certain what historical knowledge came to light after your time. Any seemingly insignificant detail could end up having a butterfly effect, you know."

Peter had been trying his best to follow Sophie's words, which wasn't proving easy, but the wholly unexpected reference to butterflies finally seemed to do the trick.

"Butterfly effect?" he said. "Is this another bullet point from your foundation course?"

"It's part of chaos theory and describes the sensitive dependence on initial conditions in which a small change in one state of a deterministic nonlinear system can result in large differences in a later state."

"Run that by me again," but then a muffled moan came from Alice as Ferdinando groaned. He was just tensing and letting out a protracted sigh when Sophie laughed in Peter's mind.

"I'd learnt that off by heart, you know," and this time she tittered. "It just says that a seemingly insignificant change at the outset can end up causing a massive one later, that's all. That the flapping of a butterfly's wings in your own English garden could ultimately be the cause of a typhoon in China. See? I could let slip something that seems inconsequential at the time but that could then end up... Well, making a humongous difference."

"Hey, well done, Sophie," Peter gasped in relief against the sound of Ferdinando and Alice's subsiding breaths. "An excellently executed distraction, I must say," but then something else struck him. "It's just the thought of being here for…what? You said a few weeks. That's ages to go without someone to talk to, even if only occasionally."

"Well, yes, you can always talk to me, but you might only get a 'Yes' or 'No' in answer. Maybe not even that. Otherwise, I think you're just going to have to keep your own company for much of the time."

Peter had just begun to contemplate this untenable prospect when he seemed to black out. The next thing he knew, Ferdinando was opening his eyes to dawn light as he stretched out groggily in the bed. Alice's arm lay warmly across his chest, her slowly caressing fingers marking her own awakening.

"Did you sleep well, my beloved?" she sleepily purred.

"Never better, my cherished wife. Last night was—"

Her fingers raced from his chest to his lips, sealing them.

"Let's pray, Ferdy, that your seed takes as it has thrice before, but this time that it favours us with a boychild. Then all will be well with our world," and she lifted her head and graced him with a smile.

The day ahead of Ferdinando took a similar course to the previous one, although at mid-morning Bishop Chaderton, wrapped up against the persistent rain, took his leave of Lathom House. Peter got the impression that Ferdinando not only felt relief at the man's ecclesiastical absence but also sadness at the loss of his excellent conversation. His company at times during the previous days, particularly at dinner and their evening meals, appeared to Peter to have been something Ferdinando had largely enjoyed.

About the middle of the afternoon, quite by chance, Ferdinando came across Alice and the girls. They were on their way out to enjoy a walk in the fresh air, now the rain had ceased. She reminded him about Richard Hesketh, asking if he'd made any decision as yet regarding seeing the man. He'd had to admit he'd once again forgotten, promising to send for Simon without delay.

An hour or so later, and with just the two of them in the solar, Newparke's steadfast keeper presented himself to Ferdinando. There, he was charged with conveying Ferdinando's apologies to Richard Hesketh.

"Tell him I've been too saddened still at my father's death, and too weighed down by all it's laid upon my shoulders, to return to Newparke. He may, though, if he so wishes, attend me at Brereton Hall on the Tuesday evening, where I'll be staying the night. If this isn't convenient, then he'll have to delay any matters he may have with me until my return from the Court."

"Very well, my lord; you may consider it done," Simon avowed, bowing to Ferdinando before clearing his throat and adding, "I gave the gentleman and his man the Bower Room, my lord, where I'm sure their unavoidable tarrying was passed most comfortably."

"Is that so, Simon?"

"Indeed, my lord, although visits to the linen store did require utmost caution not to disturb them through its thin dividing wall."

"Very considerate of you, Simon."

"Mind you, my lord, after compensating their

waiting upon your pleasure with some of your passable wine, as you so instructed, I doubt their loosened tongues gave much leave to hear aught beyond their stridently hushed voices."

"I would imagine not, Simon, and I trust they didn't disturb the household too much."

"Bearable, my lord, if somewhat enlightening. It seems they went, at their first coming into Lancashire, direct to the Baron of Newton at Walton Hall. Where I do believe they intend returning."

"You made mention of Hesketh's man. Is anything known about him?"

"Oh, begging your pardon, my lord. He's one Richard Baylye, trumpeter, who, according to my son's disarming chatter with the man, served with one Francis More, himself Trumpeter to the Earl of Essex."

"A man of The Earl of Essex's livery, eh? Interesting, if not a little worrying."

"I must say, though, that he does seem to be an innocent soul in himself. Told my lad he'd been in Sluys in the Low Countries but had been left there by his master. He then came over into England a little before Michaelmas, being at an inn in Canterbury called "The Bell", where he first met Richard Hesketh."

"And it was there, I imagine, Hesketh offered to employ him?"

"The following day, it seems, my lord, when they met again upon foot, both travelling towards London."

"And so, he came with him as his favoured man into Lancashire."

"Baylye contended it to be a good offer, considering he was destitute, and so yes," but Simon silently regarded Ferdinando for a moment, his head to one side. "What worth my own opinion may be, my lord, but I do see an innocent in the trumpeter. It seems he plays no more part than paid soak to Hesketh's dribble of self-regard."

"And Hesketh himself?" Simon's mouth drew to a thin line awhile, then he grinned from one side of it.

"I think his self-regard, my lord, comes of finding his feet do not quite touch the bottom, and that the river he finds himself cast into is too broad to climb out upon one bank or the other. I'd say, my lord, he's trying to convince himself that he was once taught how to swim," at which Ferdinando barked a laugh, but soon sobered.

"Has he made any mention of a burden he may have for me? And if so, then from whom it comes?"

"No, my lord, he hasn't, though his satchel never leaves his side. As though it be a babe-in-arms."

"A babe-in-arms, eh? And one possibly delivered of one of the most desperate hothead Catholics in this papist county. One whose wife is known to be fair mad in the head from her beliefs taken whole from Rome."

As Simon silently looked on, Ferdinando quietly mused to himself: "Perhaps Alice's suggestion carries some wisdom, some she'd not realised it held. Sir William is, after all, a vouchsafe Protestant, and his hall at Brereton is upon the flat plane of the avowed Protestant county of Chester. Safer ground, it would seem to me, upon which to confront any possible threat from this county of Lancashire's stubbornly Catholic mountain."

15   A DAWN START

On the Tuesday of Ferdinando's departure, some of the Lathom household had unusually taken a small meal in the great hall before dawn. Afterwards, Alice had drawn Ferdinando to a halt as they'd passed through the vestibule, on their way out by the main entrance. In their brief privacy, she kissed him tenderly on the lips.

"Take good care of yourself, my husband. I hope the roads and weather are kind to you."

"I will, my dearest. At least the weather's being so at the moment," he noted, glancing through the open doorway, out into the inner bailey.

"You'll ensure Mister Hickman at our London property gets my letters to pass on to those we know who've lost close ones in that terrible plague of theirs? And you'll look to keeping free of its pestilence yourself? Oh, and don't forget to pass on my kindest and most loyal regards to Her Majesty. And my letter to her, of course."

"Yes, Alice, I will," and he patted his doublet beneath his thick cloak. "And I'm sure Her Majesty misses your company, so a letter should sweeten her usually trying manner."

"I've mentioned in it that I've found the most wonderful brooch for her, which I'll send on as soon as I've taken receipt. I know it'll enchant her and look most fetching."

"Worry not. I'll make sure your letter's delivered, and into her own hand. And in which case, if I've now eased all your particulars, can I finally get off on my journey? Seeing dawn's almost upon us."

"Hmm. Well, perhaps your memory will indeed end up surprising me," and she gave him a lame grin. "And before I forget, if you get a chance, see if you can find me some dried figs at the Autumn fair in Windsor. Oh, and I take it you won't be asking the Queen for her permission to visit your mother, to inform her yourself of your father's death?"

"Certainly not. I've no intention of darkening that woman's doorstep, especially not so close to plague-infested London. She can rot there in Clerkenwell without the dubious pleasure of my own company. She's been sent her own obituari. That'll have to suffice. And anyway, father would've been firmly set against the idea."

"Well, he'd have been right. Better not to rake over old coals, especially not with Her Majesty. I fear it wouldn't fare well for your own prospects. And remember, don't make a show of pressing her to bestow the lieutenancy on you—not at this visit, anyway. Rely on Secretary Cecil for that. He knows how best to nurture the Queen's thinking."

A servant hurried past, giving them cause to pause. Once he'd clattered his booted feet down the steps and out of earshot outside, Ferdinando drew a little closer to Alice.

"Do you remember me telling you about that 'last straw'?" he cautiously asked.

"Could I ever forget? Sometimes, Ferdy, you don't seem to have the sense you were born with."

"In which case, what would I do without you?"

"Perhaps you ought to remember that in future, before being so reckless."

"Ah, indeed. And to which matter, in his praise of wisdom, perhaps Thomas Blennerhassett should've ascribed *you* as the 'new Minerva', not our own Sovereign Lady."

"Flattery, Ferdinando, will not expunge my knowing of, nor should assuage your own guilt for, such a foolish act," and she let out a short breath of exasperation. "And so? What of the straw, then?"

Ferdinando now went on to explain the conclusion he'd come to regarding what he'd learnt of Hesketh's man, and of his worries that the Baron of Newton may secretly have shifted his allegiance to the Earl of Essex.

"I fear Essex is hoping to catch me in a trap of some kind," he revealed, "as, of course, he's been suspected of doing with others who've displeased him."

"In that case, husband, take even greater care, especially as you pass through his own preferred county of Staffordshire. Essex may have been confined to the Court since his ignominious recall last year, but it seems his fruitless campaign in aid of Henri of France at the siege of Rouen did little to mar his standing with the Queen. Nor his popularity within the country. I hear his influence at Her Majesty's ear is still great. I should, therefore, have no need to warn you about crossing him again."

"Indeed not, Alice. You can trust me on that," but the look on her face implied she didn't, not entirely.

"You, my treasured husband, have a fine mind and a virtuous soul, but an unthinking tongue. Mark my words: let it not trip you up again," and before he could answer, she leant closer and again kissed him. The clatter of yet more feet soon broke them apart, a pair of which belonged to Edward.

"Are you ready, Ferdinando?" he asked. "You don't want to be wasting the daylight, not with the long miles there are between here and Brereton," and he smiled, congenially.

As they stepped outside, they were met by a long but ragged line of horses and their attendants, snaking away along the front of the house. Most, and certainly all the horses, were livered under the Stanley banner, but only the horses laboured beneath panniers and rolls. Perhaps some fifteen or twenty, each was attended by one or two men, most checking and rechecking both burdens and tack.

A fine but strong-looking dapple-grey stallion was held by a horse-groom at the column's head, its attentive eye glistening towards Ferdinando. Behind it stood two bays, Michael Doughtie unyieldingly upright astride one, William Farington roundly slouching upon the other.

Once Ferdinando had mounted, he asked a rather puffed-up man standing to one side if all had been made ready to move off. The man nodded and called down the line.

"At your pleasure, my lord," he eventually returned, and Ferdinando looked across at Edward and Alice, both still standing in the entranceway. The breaking dawn light set them like ghosts against the dark interior behind them, but Ferdinando held his gaze on the seeming spectre that was his wife.

"Fare thee well, my lady, and adieu," he called, to which she nodded.

Ferdinando then spurred his horse into a steady walk, leading the clatter of hooves on the stone-packed path towards the inner gatehouse. From there they wound their way on to the outer one, and by which way they'd soon left the castle behind.

Under his breath, Ferdinando noted, "Once more from this handful of England I ride, but upon such occasion as should, before ere long, see me return as the new Earl of Derby."

He smiled and patted his horse's neck, then settled deep into his seat as the new day's sun broke a sliver of its golden light from beyond the forested ridge to the far southeast. Along the track towards which his fine mount now confidently carried him.

Peter began to enjoy the leisurely pace and the absence of frenetic activity. He took in such simple pleasures as the ethereal drifts of mist that rose from the dew-laden grass into the sharp but steadily more sun-warmed air. He was just marvelling at how still the world seemed at this unearthly hour, how it accentuated the occasional call of a bird, when Sophie's words in Peter's mind shattered it all.

"End of silent running," she informed him. "Plenty of time now for you to tell me what that meeting between the Earl of Essex and Ferdinando's brother, William, was all about."

"Ah, that. I did wonder if you'd forgotten."

"Forgotten? For faz sake, Peter, I am a mnemonist, for crying out loud."

"Of course you are. Silly me."

"I wanted to wait until we'd a good long uninterrupted period in which to discuss it. It seems to me, Peter, you've an unusual tale to tell, one that can't possibly fit neatly into what I know of how things work."

"Things?"

"Time travel things."

"Hmm. Well, you know more about that than me. And I don't suppose you'll be prepared to reveal a great deal more of it to someone from your past."

"No, but you might hold something that could greatly help us in your future. You see, I'm damned sure we haven't... Well, that we haven't...targeted Ferdinando's brother, William. Nor, for that matter, the Earl of Essex, not as yet."

"Targeted?" but Sophie fell silent for a while, until Ferdinando's column of men and horses had turned onto a track that ran beside the woods. Even at this early hour, people were already about, carrying hoes and forks upon their shoulders, but stopping and respectfully bowing their heads at Ferdinando's passing.

"The technicians," Sophie carefully said at last, "had been...been probing for Ferdinando, trying to get a fix. So, I suppose they could have hit upon either William or the Earl of Essex in the process. Although William was known to be rarely at Lathom, and never at the period we're now in."

"It was earlier, Sophie, much earlier. Something like six or seven years ago, depending on how old Ferdinando's youngest is."

"Lady Elizabeth? Well, she'll be seven years, four months and twenty-one days next April the… Er, let's just say she's getting on for being seven, presently."

"I wasn't far wrong in my guess, then. So, it'd make the meeting I dreamt about sometime in fifteen eighty-seven."

"The year Mary Queen of Scots was executed."

"If you say so."

"A dream, you say? What? Like this one?"

"Not really, no. It was whilst I was in bed, asleep. It started out as a normal dream, but I soon realised there was something unusual about it." Peter went on to tell her about the ghost of William he'd seen, and how he'd come to have such a strange dream afterwards, and what had happened during it.

Other than occasionally seeking clarification, Sophie remained silent throughout, deafeningly so once Peter had finished his recounting.

"It must have happened on the Continental coast," she finally and pensively said. "Probably France, given William was there at that time. But for Essex to travel there so covertly meant he was serious about getting Ferdinando embroiled in a plot to take the English throne from Elizabeth. No doubt another one of his provocateur exercises, to push up his esteem in Elizabeth's eyes at his own uncovering of it. And to get one over on Secretary Cecil, of course."

"And to threaten Ferdinando's life in the process."

"But only as an added boon, Peter. The real

battle's between his and Cecil's factions at Court. Essex wants to be top-dog, the most powerful person in England after Elizabeth. There are even historical hints that he'd at least half an eye on the throne himself, despite his weak claim."

"It sounds like Essex's involvement's all new to you, then."

"In the Hesketh Plot? Not quite, but it's the most solid evidence I've yet come across that he was. There's always been a suspicion but nothing concrete, nothing as promising as your dream," and Sophie sounded quite excited. "Although our scientists are going to have to get their thinking caps on, to work out how such a weird thing as your dream could ever have happened."

By now, the morning had fully broken into a promising day, the sun rising into an almost cloudless sky, leaving just a smear of grey along the southwestern horizon. Before them rolled the awakened fields, woods and forests of Lancashire, through which Ferdinando's party steadily pressed on towards Brereton. To where, Peter was already convinced, a trap of Essex's making would all too shortly be sprung.

16   SOUTH, TO BRERETON

The tracks and roads Ferdinando's column of horses took during the morning varied greatly in their state, although the Friday's heavy rain and a subsequent wet weekend had left no signs of flooding. Peter reasoned that the summer must have been largely hot and dry, the rain having therefore quickly run off the hard ground. Certainly, this Tuesday morning seemed to be extending that summer, for it had become sunny and surprisingly warm for the second day in October.

In the various conversations along their largely deserted and often desolate way, he recognised only a few of the place names. The first of these was when St. Helin's Chapel was mentioned, some three hours into their journey. He took the small church, and its hamlet they passed through, to be what would one day grow to become the town of St. Helens.

But it wasn't until Warrington, and their meal at the Barley Mow Inn at about ten o'clock, that Peter at last knew with certainty where they were. It could well have been anywhere, though, for what resemblance the large hamlet held for the town it would eventually become.

Its streets and market square were the busiest they'd yet encountered, more so when they left the inn shortly before noon and filed out of the hamlet.

They crossed over a bridge at its southern limit, beneath which flowed a broad river. William Farington, at this point, made mention to Ferdinando of a portion of contested land in the Stanley estate that lay not far down the "Marsh Flow" from there. Peter took this to mean the River Mersey, now flowing beneath them. And so, he thought to himself, we at last leave the county of Lancashire behind and enter into Cheshire.

Peter had assumed, therefore, that Brereton Hall wouldn't be that far off. But despite the considerably better maintained roads, their eventual arrival at its estate's gatehouse saw the sun dipping away to lend the scene an early evening light.

Now weary from his long day in the saddle, when they were stopped and challenged Ferdinando rose slightly in his stirrups, to relieve the numbness in his backside. They were soon warmly welcomed and invited through onto a long driveway bordered by saplings.

Beyond these, on either side, parkland stretched away into the distance. Here and there, a copse or lone tree stood proud. After some minutes, an ancient stand of elms appeared ahead, and rising from within it, a tower with pinnacles at each corner marked the half-hidden presence of a church.

At the northern edge of these elms and still some

way off, glimpsed through mature trees now beside the driveway, the frontage of a large house could occasionally be seen. Its central doorway appeared to be flanked by towers that reached well above the roofline, each surmounted by a copper-coloured cupola that reminded Peter of those on the Tower of London.

When they eventually came before the house, approaching it along a last straight stretch of the driveway, the magnificence of the building finally made itself most wondrously apparent. High gables at either end marked two wings that stretched away behind the three-storey house. But it was those copper-topped towers that drew the eye. That led its gaze down from an arched bridge between them, just below their cupolas, down to a rise of stone steps leading up to a large ogee-arched entrance set between their bases. And there, standing within the maw of its deeply recessed doorway, stood a small group of waiting figures.

As Ferdinando drew nearer, Peter saw they were a man and a teenage girl, both flanked by a handful of servants. Others were emerging from one end of the house, clearly a number of stable-lads amongst them.

Ferdinando said nothing as he drew his horse to a halt at the foot of the steps. Nor did he speak as he stiffly dismounted, handed his horse to an awaiting horse-groom and stiffly strode up the steps towards the man.

He stopped close before him, the two holding each other's gazes for a moment. Then the man briefly nodded. "Ferdinando."

"William, my dearly beloved friend. It's good to see you again," and they clasped each other's arms for a few silent heartbeats before Ferdinando looked down at the girl. "And Lady Mary," he said, disengaging from William and bowing solemnly. "The delight in beholding you does so greatly please my eyes, my prettiest thing."

The girl's sad-eyed face had coloured by the time she'd thrown herself into Ferdinando's offered embrace. But the strain expressed in it soon softened as he patted her back most affectionately.

"I suppose I should have addressed you in a right proper manner," Sir William said over her head. "Now you're to become the new Earl of Derby." He awaited no answer, straightaway inviting Ferdinando across the threshold of his imposing property.

Ferdinando turned to his mounted entourage, the horses now all drawn up along the driveway behind his grey stallion. He dismissed them to attend to the horses, then to make good of their own needs by the leave of Sir William's servants. At this, he removed his sword and handed it to the servant nearest Sir William. Then he offered the way ahead of him to Mary, following her into the house, her father coming in behind them.

17   THE YELLOW-HAIRED MAN

The room Mary led them to contained a large table in what struck Peter as more like a modern dining room. The table boasted a generous glass of wine and a pewter plate at its head, facing a tall leaded-light window. Cold meats and pies, along with a platter of bread and a bowl of fruit, lay arranged around them, towards which Sir William stretched out his arm in invitation.

Peter noticed Mary cast a keen eye over the supper, as though confirming all was as she'd ordered. Then she forced a smile to her face.

"Please, my lord, but do take of something to eat; you must be hungry after your long journey. Father and I ate a little earlier, not knowing what hour you'd arrive."

Her smile faltered slightly, but she lifted her head a little higher. "I must say, it's a joy to see you so well, my lord. But sad it is for it to be upon such an occasion." All the time, her gaze never left Ferdinando's eyes, as though through them she hoped to see into his heart.

"I cannot truly know of the weight of your recent loss, Mary, not from my father's death, for he and I were not as close as you were to your beloved mother. But I see a strength and a fortitude within you that would delight her. Virtues she would praise and in which she'd be truly uplifted." Mary lowered her gaze and clasped her hands before her.

"Thank you for your kind words, my lord, but sometimes such a charge seems entirely beyond me," at which her father tenderly placed his hands on her arms. A tear slipped from Mary's eye.

"You must be strong, Mary, strong for your infant brother, John, and for your grieving father." When Ferdinando raised his gaze to William, Peter saw the muscles of the man's face tightened against his own tears.

Mary eventually nodded. "I will leave you to your meal, my lord, and to my father's company. I'm sure you have much to discuss," at which she made to hurry from the room but stopped at the door when Ferdinando spoke again.

"But listen well, Mary," he now said a little more sternly. "Despite my forthcoming elevation, I'm still the old Ferdinando. So, no more of 'my lord', do you hear?"

She glanced over her shoulder, her face lighting up at Ferdinando's broad smile, a face now more alike to a thirteen-year-old's. Then she nodded again, this time resolutely, and finally slipped from the room, softly closing the door behind her.

Her father stared after her. "My daughter, Ferdinando, is truly my pillar of strength. I honestly don't know what I'd have done without her."

"She's had to grow up so quickly, William. It's a

shame, I know, but then, she's so alike her mother. And as Margaret was your strength before, so too will Mary be. You'll see." William slowly nodded, then looked down at the table, his eyes seeming somehow hollow.

"Please, Ferdinando, sit yourself down and eat. You must be famished." But as Ferdinando did so, William seemed to gather his wits about him and asked, "And are you truly that sanguine about your father's death?"

Ferdinando helped himself to bread and meat, and looked across at William, now seated at the table.

"My father had many virtues, William, all of which gained my utmost respect. But he was a man of the old times, when now a new world beckons England unto its truly wondrous future."

"You mean: a man still secretly of the old religion?"

"Nay, more than that, William. Although I see the passing of so much unyielding dogma clearing a firmer path ahead. Which reminds me: one Richard Hesketh hasn't yet presented himself here, has he?"

"The Aughton one who went abroad? He who kept company with my brother-in-law at Walton Hall, until that unfortunate Lea affair?"

"The very one."

"No. But is he back in England and meant to be joining you here?"

"He's been back these past few weeks, and yes, he's supposed to be." Ferdinando gazed out through the leaded lights and onto the driveway. "But then, perhaps not, now we're losing the daylight. He's likely thought better of it." But just then, three riders came into sight, approaching along the driveway.

"Ah, I see I may have been wrong. Tell me:" and Ferdinando pointed through the window, "is one of those not a yellow-haired man? For, if it is, then that'll undoubtedly be Hesketh." William went to the window and stared out.

"It would appear so, and if I'm not mistaken, the man ahead of him is Thomas Langton, the very brother-in-law I spoke of."

"The Baron of Newton? Why on Earth would he be—"

"After Margaret died, her sister Elizabeth—the Baron's wife, you'll remember—stayed here for a number of weeks. To help me through my grief and to give comfort and care to Mary and my poor mite, John."

Ferdinando stared at William. "I didn't know. You never said at the funeral."

"I didn't know at the time. Elizabeth has an unbending fervour when a notion takes hold of her. She invited herself. But I must say: her presence here proved invaluable, particularly the constant support she gave my distraught daughter."

"A recusant's support? You surprise me, William."

"Her unshakeable belief that Margaret's soul looked down benevolently from Heaven upon Mary's sorrow proved a sobering salve to the poor girl's distress. I cannot deny it. A fiction, as we both well know, I could never have delivered so convincingly myself."

"Indeed not, William; I see that now. The truth of the matter isn't something so readily accepted by one of such tender years. But your visitors are nearly at your door, my friend. So, if I may ask for some privacy when I come to speak with Hesketh? He's been trying to present himself since my father's death, so I'd like to find out what it is he's after. And I'd better do it this evening, seeing I need to press on south tomorrow."

"You get on with your meal, Ferdinando. Leave it with me," and William went off to receive his unexpected guests.

Not long after Ferdinando had finished his supper, William returned and took him up the grand staircase to a more comfortable, firelit chamber. Once again alone, Ferdinando stood before the window, a glass of William's best wine in his hand, and stared out at the descending darkness. He gazed up at the reveal of stars now spreading across the sky.

A tentative knock came at the door, at which he called "Come".

Out of the blue, startling Peter, Sophie commanded "Silent running" as a tall and stoutly built, blond-haired man entered the room, his face clearly well-kissed by the sun. His hands soon busied themselves wringing a hat they held as he walked over and knelt on one knee before Ferdinando. When he rose at command, his eyes didn't quite meet his lord's.

"My good Lord Strange," he said, clearly nervous, "I trust I find your most esteemed self as well as events of late might allow?"

"Thank you, Mister Hesketh. You haven't changed much since last I saw you. One of your father's feasts if memory serves me right."

"Yuletide of eighty-eight, my lord," and the man noticeably relaxed. "I remember it well. And as for myself: perhaps a little more weatherworn now, my lord."

"Indeed, perhaps a little, and I'm bearing the death of my father well enough."

"I'm heartened to hear it, my lord. And most grateful you're now able to grant me my attendance. Your good uncle, Sir Edward, assured me, at your returning of my passport, that you and England were content to have my presence once again upon these shores; for which, my lord, I will ever be in your debt."

"Undeniably so. And to which end, Mister Hesketh, perhaps you'd care to explain why you've clearly been so keen to speak with me beyond any matters of that passport?"

Hesketh shifted from foot to foot, his hat suffering yet further still at the wringing of his hands. Eventually, he revealed he'd a message of some importance, but one from special friends of his lordship who'd sworn it would, in all fidelity and secrecy, only be heard, not seen, by none other than himself.

"Special friends?" Ferdinando sought.

"If I may, my lord," and Hesketh retreated to the door and opened it, clearly checking for any eavesdropper. Quietly closing it again, he returned to Ferdinando.

"I desire your leave to utter it unto you, my lord. That is, withal, that I gain your solemn promise of security to myself. That at least I incur no danger for my travail and goodwill."

Ferdinando waved his hand before him, in way of assurance.

"In which case, my lord, I must also receive promise of fidelity and secrecy on your part, to which I will swear my own to our mutual trust. For my message is regarding the common good of all Christendom, especially of our own country, and in particular yourself." Silence settled between them for a while, and as Ferdinando gazed upon him, Hesketh's brow began to glisten.

At long last, Ferdinando solemnly swore to uphold their proposed accord. Hesketh let out a clearly long-held breath, before he, too, swore his own part.

"I'll listen to your message, Mister Hesketh, but cannot promise aught till I've heard it all. Do you accept this proviso?"

Hesketh nodded sharply, then, as though seeking a firmer promise, named to Ferdinando one Sir William Stanley, who had sent him. When this failed to stir Ferdinando, Hesketh added, "There is another of greater authority than he, my lord." At Ferdinando's continued silence, Hesketh asked, in something of a final tone, "Are you thereby content to hear my message now, my lord?"

Again, Ferdinando kept his own counsel, at which Hesketh's brow glistened the more in the candlelight. As a bead of sweat trickled down to the man's eyebrows, Ferdinando finally declared that he would indeed now hear of what else Sir William Stanley and "another of greater authority" would have him hear.

This time, Richard Hesketh's sigh was plain to hear.

"Thank you, my lord," he almost choked himself saying, then drew a deep breath. "As you're willing to hear me, I must now declare unto your lordship that divers ways have been proposed, and some attempted, for the reformation of our country. Hitherto, none has prevailed. But for a number of years now, a certain plot has been proposed, and lately resolved upon. It's felt to be in good time, my lord, although, through great affection and diligence on the part of those abroad who wish to support you, there's a desire that their offer doesn't prove prejudicial to your lordship's right and title."

Hesketh finally had to draw a kerchief from his doublet to mop his brow.

"Of this matter being resolved, there is some good hope," he went on to say, "in that your lordship might know what friends and help you may have here in England to such end. Until that's known, though, all assistance from abroad is to be stayed, pursuant upon such English support being affirmed by you. Then, if you can show you're capable of the good they wish of you—above all others in the world—and you so agree, then I'm to say that I'm here to offer you all their endeavours, their services and their assistance in your advancement. And by it, my lord, the advancement of the Catholic faith and religion in England."

Although Ferdinando had remained stock-still throughout Hesketh's long and clearly well-rehearsed speech, Peter felt him clench his hands behind his back, his mouth now so tightly clamped closed that his teeth had begun to ache.

"And so," Ferdinando managed to say, "by 'capable of the good they wish of you', you mean what, exactly?"

Hesketh swallowed hard. "We would make you king, but you would have to be capable, my lord, of...of being a Catholic. That you will bind yourself to restoring, advancing and perpetually maintaining the Catholic religion in our country."

"To be an avowed Catholic, you say? Not just to show leniency unto them?"

"It is, my lord, an absolute necessity, by the law of God and the Church, and also the particular laws of our realm. The King must keep and maintain the Catholic faith, swearing to do the same at his coronation, else he cannot be lawfully crowned."

"And if, once crowned, I were to renege upon such swearing?"

"You would be…be deposed, my lord. Removed of any aid of Sir William Stanley and others, and so have all English Catholics against you," and Peter couldn't help but think of that great mountain of such they'd only recently left behind in Lancashire.

"And if I were to accept the offer you carry from those abroad, how would my decision be conveyed to them?"

"You're to send one of credit, my lord, of your own choosing. One who could declare your full mind and sincere meaning. And by that person, signify what help you require, and when. And thus, it will, by God's good help, be so provided. I'm to assure you that some four- or five-thousand could be got ready within seven or eight months."

"Four- or five-thousand, eh?" and Ferdinando cupped his chin in his hand, clearly thinking it through carefully. But then he interrupted those thoughts by saying, "Pray, Mister Hesketh, but do be seated," and he nodded towards two wooden chairs that faced each other across the front of the hearth.

"So," he said, once he'd sat down and Hesketh was following his lead, "from where would such a sizeable army be drawn?" Hesketh licked his lips and looked off to one side of Ferdinando, as though seeing a script in his mind's eye.

"You're not to fear strangers, my lord. Firstly, the King of Spain does not, in his offer of aid, seek to hold any of England to himself. Secondly, neither the Pope nor Cardinal Allen would agree to such, if there be any other remedy. Thirdly, the King of Spain himself does acknowledge that though he might invade and conquer this realm, yet he can never possess it in peace. He understands that our nation is most impatient of foreign government of any kind, being a very populous island, being of very great spirits, being for art, skill in warfare and government, and inferior to none.

"And as for the Pope, he holds that it's better for Christendom to have many Christian Catholic Kings than one too great a monarch over all. And remember, my lord, that Cardinal Allen is a true Englishman, as are those who depend upon him, and all of whom do daily prayer in the hope of your lordship's conversion."

"A time of my own choosing, you say?"

"Indeed, my lord, but you're counselled to choose a time near at hand, whilst Queen Elizabeth still lives. Otherwise, the King of Scots would likely intervene upon his own claim to the throne. At the present, Cardinal Allen and Sir William Stanley are able to assist, and the Pope is willing; but perhaps another one would not be so inclined. Also, the state of France is such now that it will not hinder but rather further such a plot, for fear of what Spain could do to that nation after Queen Elizabeth's death." And at that, it seemed to Peter that Hesketh had finally run out of steam.

"Is there any more of your message?" Ferdinando

then asked. When Hesketh assured him there was not, Ferdinando steepled his fingers before his face and closely regarded the sweating man before him. He sat like this for some time, but then drew back and inhaled deeply.

"I cannot give you my answer as yet," he told Hesketh, authority now lacing his words. "I must think on the consequences any decision of mine may invoke. I'm sure you understand. This offer is deeply serious."

"Of course, my lord," Hesketh meekly replied.

"I'm away to the Court tomorrow, upon matters I can't delay, but I'll reach a resolve—in part at least—before this night is out. Have you eaten yet, Richard?" and the man again audibly exhaled, this time his whole body seeming to relax.

"Er, no, my lord. I came from Aughton this morning and only had time for a noon-hour meal."

"Then convey my request to Sir William, here, that you be provided with something. We cannot have you starving, now can we?" and Ferdinando waved his hand to dismiss the man.

When Hesketh had retreated as far as the door, Ferdinando stopped him by asking, "And did the Baron of Newton come with you from Aughton?"

"No, my lord," Hesketh said, lifting his gaze to Ferdinando. "We met on the road, my lord."

"Did you, indeed. And does the Baron know of your purpose in seeing me?"

"No, my lord. The Baron of Newton is ignorant of my intent. I believe he was on his way here to visit Sir William, his brother-in-law. Upon family business, he said."

"Very well, Richard. I'll call you back later this

evening. In the meantime, enjoy what food Sir William's kitchens can conjure up at this late hour," and again, Ferdinando dismissed him with a wave.

Still stiff from his day's ride, Ferdinando pushed himself to his feet and went over to the window, from where he stared out into the blackness of the night.

"Oh, dearest Alice," he softly said to himself, "my own 'New Minerva', how I do so sorely miss your sound advice. I should have made time to see this damned man whilst still at Lathom. Tell me, somehow, my cherished wife, what should I do now for the best," and from somewhere close beyond the window came the haunting hoot of an owl.

18 CHOICE OF THE RIGHTEOUS

"It's infuriating," Peter blurted out, in the hope Sophie would acknowledge him.

"What is?" she batted back, much to Peter's relief.

"This not being able to hear Ferdinando's thoughts." By now, the man had returned to his seat by the fire, staring into its crackling logs.

"Ah, that. Yes. I've never got used to it myself," she admitted. "And what's more frustrating: some people's actions belie their thoughts, especially those in positions of power, like our host. Don't forget, he's been brought up in an environment of intrigue and mistrust. And he's a clever man, adept at playing his cards close to his chest."

"Well, he wasn't too clever when he crossed the Earl of Essex, now, was he?"

"There's clever, and there's common-sense."

"Hmm, I suppose so. But it looks as though I was right about that first dream I had."

"Maybe."

"Maybe? But here's a plot to put Ferdinando on the throne, one instigated by the Catholic traitor Sir William Stanley himself, who Essex told Ferdinando's brother to contact. And, as Hesketh's just revealed, it's now not only Sir William Stanley but 'another of greater authority than he'. Seems an open and shut case to me; definitely Essex's trap."

"Okay, so, if we assume you're right, what's Essex likely to be doing right now, then?"

"Essex? Er, well... I suppose he'll have to be following how his trap's panning out. After all, if what you said about him doing this is so he can thwart it and hence look good in the Queen's eyes, then he's going to have to know when to strike and have the evidence to back up his claims."

"Exactly, and well done. Yes, he'll almost certainly have his spies shadowing Hesketh's movements. They're likely holed up somewhere near at hand, in an inn or a barn. Waiting for first light so they can slip over here and watch the gatehouse."

"I don't suppose following the movements of a well-built blond-haired man's proving that onerous. He's the first I've seen so far who's not been slight and dark-haired. No wonder he had to go abroad after the Lea affair; stands out like a sore thumb."

"You're right, and I know how he feels; I'm the same with my black, tightly-curled..."

"You know, I've been meaning to ask you for a while what you look—"

"Well, don't, and forget I told you that."

"What? About your hair? Why... Ah, right; I'm with you. 'No names; no pack drill'?"

"You've got it. And I'm going to have to be more

careful. But then, at least I'm still here, so that little slip can't have been too serious."

"You know, I've been thinking about this whole paradox idea, and it strikes me that—" but a knock came at the door, and as Ferdinando called out "Come", Sophie barked "Silent running".

William came into the room and joined Ferdinando by the fire. "Your retainer," he said, sitting in the chair opposite, "had that distinct look of a mouse who's narrowly escaped the cat's claws." At first, Ferdinando only stared at him, then he cocked his head to one side.

"William, if I may impose, but why did the Baron of Newton come to visit you today? Unexpectedly and at such a late hour."

"Well, he said he'd been to visit our mutual father-in-law, Sir John, at Rocksavage, only to find him away for the night elsewhere. Said his Elizabeth would have severely scolded him if he'd not taken the opportunity to travel on here, seeing he was down this way. She clearly frets about how we're all faring. I think Margaret's death has hit her hard. She and Elizabeth were such close sisters."

"This is quite a distance further to travel, though, when he could so easily have awaited Sir John at Rocksavage itself."

"You know, Ferdinando, you do look somewhat grey and drawn. I trust Hesketh's not brought you an overly vexing matter. And I hope it's not another mess of my brother-in-law's doing."

"No, not his, but I'm sure he has some part in it."

"Well, whatever it might be, if possible, I'd appreciate it if you could see your way to showing some leniency towards him. For all her faults, Elizabeth's a good soul at heart, and she's suffered so much from his rash actions and imprudent investments. For all her popish foibles, and in duty to Margaret's memory, I'd like to see her less put upon in future."

When Ferdinando returned to staring into the fire, William studied his friend's face for a moment. "Is it anything I can help you with? Not that I'm prying."

"No, my friend. Nothing I'd wish to draw you into. You could, though, ask Hesketh to attend me again, after which I must get to bed. It's been a long and tiring day."

A little later, and once more alone with Richard Hesketh, Ferdinando had by now clearly found a smile to grace his lips. He asked after the meal Sir William's kitchens had provided, and how Hesketh's journey from over the sea had gone. And whether he was more content, now he was received back into his own country. Eventually, though, he brought their thoughts to the matter in hand.

"I promised to give you an answer, in part at least, before we were to retire this evening, and so this is that part: I've a mind to accept the offer you've carried to me from abroad, Richard Hesketh. But before I can affirm it, I've need to consult with my mother, Lady Margaret, the Dowager Countess of Derby. For it's she, after all, who's heir presumptive to the throne, being a direct descendent of Mary Tudor, Henry the Eighth's youngest sister."

"The countess?" Hesketh said, his now dry brow tightly knitting. "But she'd have no support within the realm, my lord, and certainly none abroad. And she's without doubt a—"

"I'm well aware of the arguments, Richard. In any turmoil brought about from my ascending to the throne, her claim might not undermine my own sovereignty, but it could well prove an unnecessary distraction. It would be better to have her consent aforehand, and thereby her promise not to interfere."

"If you say so, my lord."

"I do. What's more, the one I'd choose of credit to carry my answer to Sir William Stanley also lives in London. So, provided you can stay with me these next two weeks or so, you'll be ideally positioned to make a shorter return with him, and so more speedily guide him and my reply." A grin flickered across Hesketh's features, as though he could hardly believe all was going as well as it was.

"I'd be more than content to accompany you, my lord."

"Excellens, Richard. In which case, search out my secretary, Michael Doughtie, and explain you'll be joining our party in the morning. We'll be leaving not long after daybreak. And you may accompany me at times, for I'm sure your tales of foreign lands will prove most entertaining during the tedium of our journey."

"Thank you, my lord. I'd be most honoured. I have, though, as yet been remiss of visiting my wife, or of any of my family, being so set upon delivering the message I've carried. I wonder if my lord might not request of Sir William that he afford me a pen and ink, and some paper, that I may write to them?"

"Of course, Richard. I'll come with you to search him out, but then I must go to bed. There's still much of the long journey ahead of us. And I intend to have a clear head when I take advantage of it to decide upon which families would, in utmost earnestness, support me upon my new course."

"Indeed, my lord. And I'm sure, certainly from within Lancashire and much of Yorkshire, that by it you'll gather to you a Catholic force that, when joined with that of Spain, will mightily affirm your claim to the English throne."

"An overwhelming choice of the righteous within this realm of ours, eh, Richard? And a Stanley where my father always knew a Stanley should sit," he finally rounded off quite quietly to himself.

19   MISFITS

There was a dampness to the air when Ferdinando stepped out of the front door, the morning sun still too low and weak as yet to dispel its chill feel. His company awaited him, all now mounted, Michael Doughtie and William Farington close behind his grey stallion. The horse whickered, snatching up its head against the horse-groom's gentle but unyielding hold.

Ferdinando grinned, but then looked a little way beyond his eager horse, catching sight of the Baron of Newton and Richard Hesketh, and the third man who'd been with them at their arrival. This man, Peter decided, must be Richard Baylye, the trumpeter and Hesketh's man since Canterbury. Although Hesketh and the baron stood close in conversation between their horses, the short and sanguine-looking Baylye remained apart, holding a fine-looking white palfrey.

"I hope the weather holds for you," Sir William said from behind Ferdinando, turning him about. Beside William stood Mary, this morning the lady of the house once again.

"But, Father, the sun always shines upon the righteous," she said with a smile, at which Ferdinando stiffened.

"The righteous?"

It must have been the look on his face, but Mary also stiffened as her eyes grew wide. "I'm sorry, my lord. I meant no ill by my words, just that—"

"No, Mary. Not at all. It… Well, it matters not. But what did I tell you yesterday?"

"Yesterday? Oh, yes. My apologies, *Ferdinando*," and she giggled at the smile that now grew on his face.

"All's now ready for your lordship," Michael Doughtie reported. Ferdinando returned a nod to the man, but then his gaze once more drifted over to Hesketh's group of three, of whom the baron and Baylye were now mounting their horses.

At their small breakfast earlier, the baron had presented himself to Ferdinando, offering what, to Peter, had seemed like quite genuine condolences on his father's death. Peter had wondered how sincere he'd really been, considering Earl Henry had, just a few years before, been pursuing the man on a charge of murder. Then he remembered Sophie's comment from the previous night, how cards in this society were always played close to the chest.

Now, though, the baron and Baylye had started out down the driveway together, leaving Hesketh to lead his horse towards the position he'd no doubt been allotted by Michael Doughtie. They slipped in some four or five horses behind Ferdinando's own, Hesketh soon in the saddle.

"Very well, Michael," Ferdinando at last replied as he went down the steps and mounted his horse. Once settled, he bade William and Mary a fond farewell and led his column off at a walk, the baron and Baylye already well ahead down the driveway.

The two men had turned north at the estate's gatehouse, almost out of sight up the road when Ferdinando's party emerged and headed south. They'd eventually left Brereton far behind when Peter came to comment on how slow their progress again seemed to be.

"They're actually rushing," Sophie said, her voice once more surprising him, and he laughed.

"Rushing? But they never get out of a walk. I thought they'd at least be trotting."

"Their horses are doing an active walk because anything more and they'd not last the distance. It's all about pacing."

"It must take ages to get messages and letters about the country, then."

"Ah, no. Urgent stuff travels fast because messengers can ride a new horse each day if need be, sometimes two or three. Hired from inns along the way. And Ferdinando's only 'rushing' because he's got a valid excuse: his need to sort out his inheritance and to have the Queen confirm his earldom."

"Why should he need an excuse?"

"Because it's considered unseemly for a nobleman to be seen going about the place in any kind of haste. Everything in this period of history is tightly dictated by what's socially acceptable, often backed up by the laws of the land."

"Sounds restrictive."

"It is, and one practical reason why time travel couldn't really work, even if it were possible. Imagine being arrested for wearing the wrong colour clothes in public."

"What? Really? Well, in which case, there'd be no real need for that paradox of yours."

"Ha, you could say that. Speaking of which, what was it you were going to say last night? You said something had struck you about it."

"Uh? Oh, about the paradox. Yeah, that and the butterfly effect."

"What about them?"

"It's just that... Well, if we assume that me knowing something small about the future, like the colour of your hair, could snowball through time to become a big change, then there'd be no way of you knowing if that change had happened."

"Because?"

"Well, let's say that, when you boarded the ghost train from your time, you had a brother. Then I learn of your hair colour and that ripples through to you then having a sister, instead. The brother would never have existed. You'd have only ever grown up with a sister, so you'd be none the wiser."

"Right. I see what you mean. Although, wouldn't *you* know, like if I suddenly wasn't here? Any changes you cause couldn't affect your own present, surely?"

"Ah. Now you have me. Reckon I'm going to have to think that one through a bit more."

Sophie's voice then seemed to soften, gaining an unexpected warmth: "You're pretty good at thinking logically, aren't you?"

"Well, I am a doctor. I've spent most of my adult

life diagnosing ailments, taking all the investigative results and coming to a logical conclusion. Most of them life-or-death."

"And you've coped so remarkably well with everything that's happened to you since seeing that first ghost. Stuff that—as you've so quaintly put it before—would've *freaked* most people out. We have to have loads of training and short-term test runs before we're allowed to do even half of what you've already done. And quite a few never get through it all and have to drop out."

"I don't know why, Sophie. Maybe I'm just a natural."

"Hmm, maybe."

"Or... Or maybe it's because I've never really felt totally connected with my own world."

Sophie didn't answer, a discomforting silence ensuing for a while, then she quietly told him, "I... I know what you mean."

"You do?"

"Pretty well. When I think about it, all those who got through training and are now on the teams don't mix all that easily, either. Not socially inept, you understand, but awkward around people, unable to touch base with them."

"And does that describe you, Sophie?"

"Er, well, I'd better not answer that; butterflies and all that."

"I must admit, you were a bit short with me when we first met."

"I thought you were from my own time. One of the other teams trying to muscle in on my run. I never imagined you'd be from twenty-ten."

Peter fell quiet for a while, just feeling the incessant sway of Ferdinando's horse, the now familiarly reassuring clop of hooves, the creak of leather and the jingle of tack at their back. And against all this, the pleasantly warmer sun bathed his face as a gentle breeze blew in from the west.

Presently, he said, "I wonder if it's because we can only hear each other that we seem to be getting along pretty well now."

"Yah, I suppose. But there's…there's more to it than just hearing, you know."

"What do you mean?"

"Well, I can sort of… Er, like, feel you."

"Feel me? Like how?" but then Peter remembered all those times he'd felt restricted, as though squeezed into a tight space. "Oh, my God. You… You don't mean—"

"I think it's the edges of our minds touching."

"Phew. That's a relief, although I'm not quite sure what I thought I was imagining." But then Peter thought about it for a moment. "That's a bit…well, cliched, isn't it?"

"Yah, sort of," and Sophie laughed. "Maybe it's why I've come to find you so easy to get on with; uniquely easy."

"Uniquely?"

But Sophie refused to be drawn, finally changing the subject by asking why he'd chosen the name Sophie for her.

"Ah. Sophie. Yes," and memories of a hot summer came back to Peter, a summer that had lived on in his hopes, although long since consigned to that "Get Real" box. "Oh, it was just the first name that came to mind, that's all."

"That's all?"

"Well, okay, a bit more than that. It was a friend I had when I was fourteen. The daughter of some American neighbours along the street from where we lived. I think her dad was something big in the City, at an American bank or the like."

"And you liked her?"

"Liked? Yes, I did," and Peter let out a wistful breath. "We used to play together quite a lot, and her parents had a swimming pool, of all things. Imagine that. Although we both preferred getting away, into the woods or the fields, or down by the river. Yes, I did like her, but then I went on holiday with mum and dad, and when we got back she'd gone, just like that. Back to America. Mum said her dad had done something terrible at work and been dismissed."

"And you never saw her again?"

"No. Never."

"And you really missed her?"

"I… I think we got on so well because she too didn't quite connect with her world. England was so different for her. It quite fazed her. She'd never been out of the States until then. And looking back on it, I suppose she found some reassurance in having a friend who could explain all the weird English customs to her."

"So, her need overcame your reticence?"

"I suppose so."

"Two misfits thrown together, eh?"

Peter realised he'd not thought of it like that before, but eventually had to agree.

After this they both remained silent, Peter deep in

thought as the well-made road continued to "hasten" them on southwards. To their next night's stop near Stafford, from what Peter had half heard Ferdinando discussing with Michael.

20 WHAT OF STAFFORDSHIRE?

Presently, Ferdinando called Richard Hesketh up to join him and they rode together for a while. The others of their party respectfully dropped behind a short way. Sophie then urgently called "Silent running", but the nature of the two men's subsequent conversation touched on nothing more controversial than the ways of those in the Low Countries: their habits and outlooks, the wealth or otherwise of their people, and in particular, what theatre they enjoyed.

Peter got the distinct impression that Ferdinando was purposely distracting himself from having to think about Hesketh's offer. Or perhaps he was attempting to judge the man's reliability, delving for any unguarded comments or views that may have helped in his decision. Whatever the aim, Richard Hesketh seemed far more relaxed come the end of their talk than he had hitherto.

Other than this convivial conversation, Ferdinando rode on for most of the rest of the day in silence, clearly consumed by his own thoughts. Even at their midday meal, in a comfortable inn along the way, he contributed little more than pleasantries.

Peter noted covert looks thrown their lord and master's way by Michael Doughtie and William Farington, but he couldn't discern their meaning. He knew they'd not been apprised of Hesketh's offer, so it had to be Ferdinando's unexplained guest and his unusually quiet mood that had unsettled them.

Come late afternoon, their party turned from the main road south and onto a narrow lane. After a mile or so it brought them to the tree-enshrouded gatehouse of a small estate, its entrance opening a gap in its ivy-covered, redbrick boundary wall. One gate stood partway open but no one seemed to be about.

"If you'd allow me," Michael Doughtie said to Ferdinando and spurred his horse past and up to the unsecured gate. He leant from his saddle and thrust it fully open, whereupon it clattered stridently against its latch.

Ferdinando and their party's first few riders had already ridden through when a surly-looking man in nothing more than breeches and boots came out of the gatehouse, hurriedly fastening his waistband about a noticeable paunch.

Something else clearly caught Ferdinando's attention, for he flicked his and Peter's gaze up at a first-floor window of the gatehouse. A figure was looking out, long tousled hair and bare shoulders revealed above a closely-clasped shift. Ferdinando grunted quietly to himself as the figure hastily withdrew, then levelled his narrowed gaze at the approaching man, whose surliness quickly drained from him at the sight of Ferdinando and his large entourage.

"My Lord Strange," he stammered, coming before him and onto one knee. "Please, my lord, forgive me my not noticing your approach. Your lordship wasn't expected this early."

"Expected?" Ferdinando growled. "I come and go at my own pleasure. Without leave of any *supposed* gatekeeper. What's your name, man?" The gatekeeper clearly had problems speaking past the huge dry swallow that now afflicted him.

"Thomas Scrobbes, my Lord Strange," he finally managed.

"Then note this, Thomas Scrobbes, you are now addressing the new Earl of Derby. Something you had better take close heed of, more so by far than you clearly do of other things that distract you from your duty." Ferdinando again glanced up at the still empty first-floor window.

The man's ignored supplications fell behind them as Ferdinando purposefully led his entourage away and up the driveway, out from the trees surrounding the gatehouse and into sight of a rambling timber property. Of this, not one wall matched another in its angle to the ground or the others, the rooflines bowed under their great weight of age and the chimneystacks twisted and bent as though infirm. A stocky and rosy-faced gentleman and two of his servants met them at its ivy-arched entrance, a broad door wide open behind them.

"My Lord Strange;" the gentleman said, "it is, my lord, a great pleasure to greet you once again. I hope your journey's proved uneventful and fair-weathered."

"It has," Ferdinando informed him as he

dismounted, handing his horse's reins to one of the gentleman's servants who'd stepped forward. "Though your gatekeeper's displeased me."

"Thomas has? How so, my lord?" The man's eyes had widened in alarm, the more so as Ferdinando detailed the way they'd been received.

"I'll have severe words with him, Lord Strange. I assure you," but by now his gaze avoided Ferdinando's eyes, his manner clearly flustered.

"And where are your horse-grooms, Sir John? Am I expected to take my own horse to its stabling?"

"Robert, here, will look after him, my lord," and he indicated the servant holding the reins. "And he'll show your party to the stables."

Ferdinando stared up at the ivy about the entrance, wild and overgrown, then out at what could be seen of the once clearly well-laid-out gardens and estate. To Peter, this too looked somewhat untamed. Staring back at Sir John, Ferdinando eventually drew the man's gaze.

"I think, Sir John, you and I will eat apart from your household."

"As you will, my lord," and Sir John bowed his head before offering the way through the entrance and into his home.

By the time Ferdinando and Sir John came to sit together at a table in the half-light of a long and low-ceilinged room, Peter had begun to get used to the disconcerting slants of the walls and floors.

The table, he noticed, had been jacked up on blocks at one end, to level it, which only went to accentuate the crazy angles of everything else. A single candle flickered between them, casting their laden plates with only just enough light by which to eat, despite the still bright early evening light beyond the small leaded light windows.

"I'm surprised," Ferdinando broke the silence between them by saying, having swallowed a mouthful of food. "Although it's my responsibility as your landlord to cover major costs of maintenance, the distinct lack of upkeep to the grounds and estate are due your own dereliction, sir. As you well know."

"Indeed, my lord, but you see—"

"And as for your gatekeeper's…laxity, well…"

"You may remember, my lord, that my own father died last year."

"Yes, of course I do," and Ferdinando's voice faltered a little.

"Unfortunately, I have yet to take receipt of my inheritance, my lord. My father's will is being most unfairly contested by his widow, so my pecuniary state of affairs has become somewhat drawn of late."

"Drawn? Hmm. Well, you have my sympathy, Sir John. The land laws of England are becoming far from simple, benefitting no one but lawyers."

"It is they, my lord, who are steadily draining me of my dwindling wealth. I am afeared I'm drawing close to having to issue deferments against my future inheritance. The uncertainty in such a matter, as you'll appreciate, has greatly unsettled me and complicated the running of this house and its estate."

For a moment, Ferdinando said nothing, only dabbed at his lips with the edge of his napkin. He pushed his plate away a little then rested his hands on the edge of the table.

"Do I take it that your commitment to your

gatekeeper, Thomas Scrobbes, is in arrears?"

"It is, my Lord Strange," and Sir John's gaze dipped to his plate.

"And your horse-grooms?" to which the man summarily nodded.

"You should have given me notice earlier of your predicament, before it got so dire."

"I dared not put upon your most noble self, my lord. You've done greater than I merit in having agreed to a peppercorn rent for my tenure here. I could not find it within me to be so bold as to—"

"Well, Sir John, as it happens, I'm of late more in need of your services here in Staffordshire. So, to this end, and in consideration of your unfortunate legal predicament, I'm prepared to offer you the services of a practiced land lawyer from Stafford. Another retainer of the Stanley family. I'll defer his cost to you for his first year, by which time we should both have a better idea of your likely prospects."

"That's most generous of you, my lord. And I—"

"I'll instruct my secretary to make the arrangements, to be delivered to the said lawyer when we pass through Stafford tomorrow. In the meantime, if you've any pressing need against outstanding debts, then let him have the details before this day's out."

Even in the poor light, Sir John's relief was plain to see.

"And have more candles brought, tapers if you must; I can hardly see what I'm eating," at which Sir John rose, a weight seeming to have been lifted from his shoulders. He soon summoned a servant, sent upon the errand. When Sir John sat down again,

Ferdinando smiled across at him.

"So, now some of your cares have been put aside, what do you have for me since last we talked?"

Sir John pulled out a small fold of papers from his doublet and carefully spread them out before Ferdinando, who now began picking at his meal.

"Peter," Sophie said into Peter's mind, but he was quick to cut her off.

"I know. Silent running."

"Yay, you're getting the hang of this."

Various lists of names and places filled the sheets, none familiar to Peter. Sir John was by now pointing at the first column.

"Significant marriages," he explained, and Ferdinando took his time running his finger down the list of paired names. When he got to the bottom, Sir John commented: "You may not be aware, my lord, but the one between the Phethean and Brough families is particularly significant here in Staffordshire."

Ferdinando raised both his gaze and an eyebrow to Sir John.

"Each has a large affinity in its own right, my lord. So, their joining through marriage creates an even larger alliance. Only a few important in themselves, you understand, but as a whole... Well, certainly something with which to be conversant, my lord."

"Indeed," and Ferdinando mulled it over. "And...how do any of those families stand in regard to The Earl of Essex?"

"Essex? Well, let me see, now," and Sir John leant back in his chair, staring in thought at the ceiling.

"The de Betleys are strident proponents of the Earl, openly displaying his livery. And the Simcocks likewise. Now I consider it, a good many are his retainers. But then, he does display a great deal of favour in his gathering of support, despite Her Majesty keeping him close to her Court. As I believe she's wont to do with those she herself favours."

A knock came at the door and Sir John called in a servant who placed another two lit candlesticks on the table and withdrew.

"There's growing talk of late, my lord, that Essex's promised favours rarely bear fruit, though. Mind you, my lord, despite this, as he's now a member of Her Majesty's Privy Council, it would be fair to say that many are still inclined to hold out better hope of those promises. An optimism, in my view, that his being born of this county goes a long way to explaining. One of their own, as it were, and perhaps why he's so well liked."

"And how many of those families are suspected recusants?"

"Catholics, my lord? Er, well, a few, I suppose. Although one has to be more prudent in such a supposition in regards to this county: they being small in number here compared with your own Lancashire, thereby more secretive in their true inclinations."

Sir John's brows furrowed slightly as he regarded Ferdinando, now once again staring distractedly down at the sheets of paper. Peter noticed, in Ferdinando's peripheral vision, that the man seemed expectant, as though awaiting a reason for this line of questioning, but Ferdinando kept to his own counsel.

In that counsel, however, he let slip a quiet comment: "Few, eh? And largely Essex's own."

"The Earl of Essex, my lord, shows little apparent

regard for religious inclination in those he's happy to culture. As a consequence, his support in the county is now both substantial and loyal."

"Loyal, eh?" and Ferdinando drew in a deep breath, pushing himself away from the lists to level his gaze at Sir John. "I'd like you to make a mark against all those families you believe to be Catholic. But before you do, you can go on to tell me what more you have to report that should demand my attention. Any more I ought to know of this county of Staffordshire that sits so firmly between Lancashire and London."

"Er, well, my lord…" and Sir John gathered his thoughts and lost his frown before going on to detail other but unrelated recent events.

"So," Peter marvelled aloud, "he's clearly seriously considering accepting Hesketh's offer. Oops. Sorry, Sophie. Didn't mean to break our silent running."

"Later," she snapped.

That later came quite quickly, as it turned out. Sir John's report moved on to sufficiently less interesting aspects of Staffordshire life. But all she came back with was "Maybe".

"That's not much help," Peter shot back, disappointed.

"You purposely didn't want me to tell you what was going to happen. You said so right at the beginning, remember?" which Peter couldn't deny.

"Okay, but I reckon he must be seriously considering it, from what he's been asking. I mean, if he does accept Hesketh's offer and eventually makes a bid for the throne, he'd be drawing most of his support from the North. A force swollen considerably by a Spanish army, likely landed on the Lancashire coast. It'd have to be. And by the sound of it, Staffordshire under Essex would form a substantial impediment to any march on the capital. I bet Ferdy was looking to gain Catholic support here, enough disgruntled families to ease his push south, not loyal supporters of Essex set against him. And I take it Essex *is* a firm Protestant."

"He is...and maybe Ferdinando really is considering it...maybe."

"Hmm. I can see this is going to be a bit of a one-sided discussion."

"Do you really want to know?"

Peter took a moment to think, a moment in which he imagined having to endure this imprisonment in Ferdinando's mind knowing full well what was going to happen.

"No," he finally concluded. "No, it'd ruin the intrigue. The best part of which is the speculation."

"So, stop asking me, then."

"Am I warm, though?"

Sophie sighed. "Maybe," she resignedly told him. "But then...maybe not."

21   CHANCE OF A RARE WISDOM

Come their customary midday meal—this time at the Bell Inn in the market town of Leighton Busar, somewhere in Bedfordshire and a full week since setting off from Brereton—Peter and Sophie had grown accustomed to their own shared company. Although still guarding against the butterfly effect, they'd progressively discovered they'd a surprising amount in common.

"This isn't what will one day become Leighton Buzzard, is it?" Peter had asked Sophie as Ferdinando stepped from the inn, out into the sunlit market square. There, his horses and servants dominated the open space.

"I haven't the slightest idea," she admitted. "Not a part of the country I know that well." But then the earl stopped abruptly, staring at a knot of men drinking by a well in one corner of the square. Peter felt a frown furrow Ferdinando's face.

"Michael," he said to his secretary, who'd just

stepped out of the inn behind him, "do any of those men by the well look familiar to you?"

As Michael stared at them, two of the seated figures averted their faces and took swigs from their tankards.

"I don't think so, my lord, although the tall one at the end looks a little like John Golborne, your clerk of the kitchen."

"Hmm," but Ferdinando kept his gaze squarely on the two seemingly hiding their faces. One reached into a bag by his feet and withdrew something, at which both men laughed, the other stealing a covert glance towards the inn. He quickly looked back, words passing between the two.

"The men now rising?" Ferdinando said as they got up, but Michael assured him he didn't recognise either when they briefly gave sight of their faces as they strode from the square.

"I'm sure the shorter one passed us on the road south, not long after leaving Brereton." Ferdinando reckoned, absently tugging at the point of his beard. "Go over there, Michael, and as discreetly as you can, see if they've left anything in their tankards."

When Michael came back, he reported a good third of ale remained in both.

"Is that so?" and Ferdinando stared at the offending tankards for a moment, then at Richard Hesketh as he too came out of the inn, wiping his mouth on the sleeve of his shirt.

"Let's be on our way, then," Ferdinando announced. "We shouldn't be too late arriving at Gaddesden."

He lifted an egg-shaped pendant, worn on a chain about his neck, and flipped it open. Peter had seen this item numerous times during the journey, marvelling on each occasion at the small one-handed clock face it contained. He'd even got the knack of reading it: about a quarter of an hour before noon, he noted.

"Do you think," Sophie asked, "those men were spies of the Earl of Essex?"

"Possibly, though I suppose it's not unlikely they were just travelling the same way and Ferdy's getting paranoid. I mean, all roads lead to London, don't they?"

"Rome."

"You know what I mean."

"Well, I haven't seen anyone acting suspiciously, and I've been checking. But don't forget what Ferdy risks losing were he to accept Hesketh's offer. Traitors of his rank are beheaded."

"Ah, well, yeah. You have a point. But anyway, do you know what's at Gaddesden?"

"I don't, but I'm sure I remember reading that Great Gaddesden was one of the Stanley manors. Although I don't think much more's known than that. It is, however, within a day's striking distance of Windsor Castle. That I do know."

"Windsor? Are you saying that's where they're going next, not straight to London?"

"They won't be going into London at all, Peter. The Court moved out of there to avoid the plague. And I imagine the castle will be where, in the first instance, Ferdy will want to search out Secretary Cecil."

"You 'imagine'?"

"Most of what happened after Brereton is unknown, I'm afraid. Any records ended up being lost. It's believed that Secretary Cecil did a pretty thorough job of eradicating anything that didn't fit in with the history he wanted to leave behind. A very early example of why our Chronoscope team came into being, to recover what's been…"

Sophie sounded a little contrite when she then went on to say, "Well, what's important is that this is the early modern period, the start of a renaissance in Western art and science. An important time in understanding how we got to where we are in our own time."

"Right."

"You really should have taken more interest in History at school, Peter. You really should. The foundations of a lot of our modern thinking were laid down in this period. And why we ended up in the shit we got ourselves… Ah, poo. I really am going to have to watch what I'm saying."

Peter fought the urge to ask what she'd meant to say, but when the wings of the threatened butterfly-effect fluttered in his stomach, he metaphorically bit his tongue. The prospect of Sophie's voice falling ever-silent chilled his blood. And anyway, Ferdinando was now mounted and leading his entourage out of the market square and back onto the road for Gaddesden. No doubt to yet another grand property that awaited them there.

It turned out to be a more modest place than Peter had imagined. The irregular L-shaped timber-framed building lay within pleasant but not extensive gardens in somewhere called Southall, not far beyond Gaddesden. Their reception proved somewhat unusual in that no lord of the manor nor even a squire met them at its door. Rather, it was an ancient and clearly trusted servant who somewhat reservedly greeted Ferdinando, a number of stable-lads and other servants in his attendance.

"Welcome, m'Lord Strange," the man announced. "My thoughts are with you 'pon your recent travails," he added more privately as Ferdinando dismounted. "I trust you're shouldering your burdens well, m'lord."

"Well enough, Robert, to which kind thoughts I give you my thanks," and Ferdinando let one of the horse-grooms take charge of his mount. "But how's your mistress faring? I hope she's the strength to see me."

"At rare times she 'as, m'lord. Perhaps today, and you may even be fortunate in 'er recognising you. But please, m'lord, if I may first invite you most cordially into 'er home. I've a table spread if you've a wish for food n' drink." Then, as though the master of the house, Robert instructed the servants to attend to Ferdinando's party and stood aside for him.

"When you're all done, join me in the hall," Ferdinando told Michael, his secretary, before handing over his sword to a servant and stepping into the cool and dim interior.

The porch into which he'd stepped gave way to a small but airy vestibule, then through into a long and high hall, one wall a filigree of floor to ceiling leaded-light windows. At one end, a broad brick hearth held a smouldering grate. From it, wisps of smoke licked up around an ornate stone lintel and into the room, rising to the lofty, dark-stained beams and boards of the roof.

A handful of hounds lazing on the hearthstone pushed themselves alert at Ferdinando's footsteps on the stone-flagged floor. Growls, threatening barks, then grumbled from their upstretched snouts.

"Back down, curs," was the only bark that arose, coming from Robert in the manner of a lord of this manor. The dogs immediately stilled.

A large table down the centre of the hall groaned under its load, and as Ferdinando indicated the wine, he asked after the mistress's daughters.

"The Lady Susan's been away to the West Country with 'er husband, Sir Edward Lewkenor, these past three weeks, m'lord. So, she'll not know of your visit. But Anne's around, although unfortunately she can't be here to receive you. For which omission she 'umbly beseeches your pardon, m'lord. She was so looking forward to seeing you again, but 'er husband, Thomas Clere, took a fall from his horse this morning and she's rushed to be at his side."

"I'm saddened to hear that, Robert. Do you know how he is?"

"No, m'lord. We're waiting to hear."

"Well, she mustn't fret about not being here for me. I'm sure you'll afford me the same hospitality she would have given me herself, and I'm only here for the one night. Have you someone who could carry my assurances to her?"

"Most gracious of you, m'lord. I'll arrange it in due course. And by it, 'pon God's providence, hope to have our minds put at rest as to 'er husband."

Robert showed Ferdinando to a side room where a ewer of water and a large basin rested on a small table, and where he washed away some of the grime of the road. When he got back to the hall, a glass of wine stood waiting, but as yet no sign of Michael and the others.

Ferdinando took a long draught as he stood before the

table, then removed a kerchief and dabbed at his lips.

"Would it be convenient to attend your mistress now, Robert?"

"One time be no better than another, m'lord. I'll show you up."

Robert led Ferdinando back into the vestibule and up a series of short and tightly twisting flights to a small landing. An open door took them through into an unoccupied bedroom, at the far side of which stood a closed door.

Pausing before it, Robert informed Ferdinando: "It's Helen who's sitting wi' the mistress now, m'lord. I'll have her withdraw to where she can hear if you need assistance, although Mistress Jermyn's been quite placid of late. But 'er hearing's not what it used to be," at which he opened the door.

The darkened room within smelt stuffy, a fire in a small grate lending it both a stifling heat and the tang of woodsmoke. Ferdinando's searching gaze found little more than a simple wooden bed, a large chest between the room's two partially shuttered windows, and a chair beside the bed holding a stout-looking young woman. She rose, putting some darning she'd been doing into the clasp of her hands at her chest as she bowed her head.

"Helen," Ferdinando softly said, to which she lowered her head still further.

"My Lord Strange," she returned in a small voice. "'Tis good to welcome you again, my lord."

Ferdinando's gaze moved to the bed, to the mound of pillows into which a small head lay deeply sunken. A linen bonnet obscured any hair, the drawn-up sheets any neck, but the skin of the face left revealed had a tallow lustre to it. Set within its waxy sheen, the woman's closed eyes somehow lurked mysteriously deep within their darkly ashen pits.

Robert signalled that Helen withdraw and she hastened from the room, pausing only to curtsy briefly to the two men.

"She'll come at your call if need be, m'lord," Robert reminded Ferdinando, then he too was gone, leaving Ferdinando in the close-set silence of the room, staring down at the bedbound woman.

"Mistress Martha?" he softly called after a moment or two. When she seemed not to have heard, he quietly went to Helen's vacated chair and carefully turned it to face the bed. He sat down, the creak of the chair sounding loud in Peter's hearing.

Ferdinando called her name once more, then sought the outline of her arm beneath the layers of blankets and coverlets when she again failed to respond. At the first touch, Martha's eyes shot open and she lifted her head from the pillows and pushed herself up.

"By Saint Gabriel's leave," she yelped, "what fancy is this?" and her eyes myopically darted to and fro.

"It's Ferdinando Stanley, Mistress Martha. Come a-visiting. There's no need for alarm." She seemed to locate his voice and stared roughly in his direction, her body still taut with surprise.

"Edmund! Take not such liberty, husband. 'Tis Sunday: God's own day," but then a grin suffused her lips. "Matter thee hold the heat of thy blood 'til Monday." For a moment she froze, then barked a peremptory laugh before slumping back against the pillows, now seeming to stare at the ceiling off to one side above her bed.

"I'm not Edmund, Mistress—"

"Fah. An ox-plough, I'm sure. No more, no less. Take it or leave it."

When she turned her face further away, Ferdinando pushed himself back in his chair and crossed his legs, absently brushing a feather from his hose. She refused to look his way and so he sat, quietly regarding her presented profile.

After a short while, Ferdinando surprised Peter when he quietly said, "She was a wise woman once," and for the very first time, Peter felt he was being addressed directly by his host.

"A wise woman?" he answered without thinking.

"Indeed," Ferdinando said, a smile suffusing his lips. "There's much wisdom in this world, that I've always known. But now I know that scarcely much of it resides in the minds of men. A king may be a fool, sir, whereas his fool may prove to be a king. Ah, and into such foolishness as this trod our wisest of queens. As Martha, here, has had her wisdom walled in by her infirmity of years, so too has Secretary Cecil, the Earl of Essex and all the rest of her courtly retinue just as firmly immured Our Sovereign Lady's own keen wit.

"But, whereas I could ne'er afford to speak at all openly with Her Majesty, for fear of courtly politics, Martha was one of those rarest of jewels amongst women: a wise one who could keep a confidence."

He let out a short breath of exasperation. "How I'll miss such privy discourse as we two once had. Eh, Mistress Martha?" which he finished saying a little more loudly, and to which she turned her head and stared at him.

"Then what of Lady Alice?" she asked, raising a brow.

"You know me," he marvelled.

"The good Lord Strange, and in my bedchamber after all these years," at which she smiled, thinly.

"How're you faring, Mistress?"

"Betwixt and between, Ferdinando. Sometimes here, more often not. Until my maker calls me unto Him and I leave for ever. Which won't be long; that I know. So, whilst I'm here: what troubles you now, my innocent young man?"

Ferdinando drew his chair closer, resting his hand on the bedcover, and as quietly as Martha's hearing would allow, told her of Richard Hesketh's offer.

When he'd finished, staring expectantly into her cloudy eyes, she only stared back at him, her features unreadable. Then she shook her head, ever so slightly.

"For one so clever, you're sadly in want of wits, my lad," but then a raised voice from below cut in at the window before coming up through the floorboards. Martha's eyes widened and she cast her startled gaze furtively about the room.

"They'll not take my girls' inheritance," she objected in a rising voice of panic.

Despite Ferdinando's attempts to settle her, she was soon screaming, until Helen bustled into the room. Waving Ferdinando away, she took the once wise but now clearly distraught Martha into her ample embrace and set to: softly soothing the poor woman's pitiful anguish.

22 COCKING A SNOOK

When Ferdinando returned to the hall, he found some of his gentleman-servants at the table, who all stood at his entrance. But their stares quickly went back to an out of breath young lad now standing before an imposingly upright Robert.

"I met the son of the smith on errand with a message for you, Master Tidburn" the lad was saying. "Told 'im I'd bring his tidings on for 'im."

Robert nodded for him to proceed.

"Mister Clere, sir: he'll live, but 'is shoulder were put out of joint."

"His shoulder?"

"Bartholomew the smith were on hand and forced it back, Master Tidburn, to much screams of agony from Master Clere, though. Seems he went as white as a foal's teeth, so I were told," and the lad looked a bit wan himself at the thought.

"And Mistress Alice?" Robert prompted.

"Oh, aye. Said to express her gratitude to his

lordship," to whom the lad turned, "for your kind consideration, your lordship. Asks your pardon for her staying on with Master Clere, seeing he's in so much pain, like."

When the lad was dismissed, a flea in his ear for having raised such a racket at his arrival, Ferdinando expressed his relief to Robert that Alice's husband had at least been spared his life. He then discreetly instructed Michael to ask Richard Hesketh to join him outside.

"I'll be in the herb garden. And, Michael, do you think Ela Longespee will have space for the man at William's lodgings in Windsor?"

"I'm doubtful, my lord. With the fair being on, I imagine all her rooms will be taken."

"I want him close by William at all times, so I know where he is."

"There's a truckle bed in the room she always assigns him. I'm sure Mistress Longespee wouldn't mind him bedding down there for a small added fee."

"I'd be much obliged to William, Michael, if you'd inform him. You can settle the increased cost against my own account."

"Very well, my lord," and the man's eyes narrowed a touch.

"I've important business to conclude with him in due course, Michael, so would just prefer he be kept close at hand," to which Michael nodded.

When Ferdinando entered by the gate in its wall, he found the deserted herb garden still held a hint of its summer scents, thin on the early evening air. He wandered along the brick paths between the beds and had bent to examine the blue and pink bell-shaped flowers of a vigorous-looking comfrey when Richard Hesketh came into the garden.

"My lord?" he said as he drew near.

"Richard," Ferdinando replied with a smile. "Is this not a bewitching place? So still and warm within its confining walls. A privier setting I cannot imagine," and he raised his brows a touch, at which Hesketh seemed to brighten.

"It is, my lord. Most secret," and a wary enthusiasm had entered his voice.

"You've been very patient, Richard," Ferdinando said more quietly. "Admirably so. And much have I considered the generous offer you brought me. Greatly so during our journey."

Hesketh appeared to have forgotten to breathe, his gaze intent on Ferdinando's features. Only when another smile blossomed across them did the man then draw in a long breath.

"My greatest worry, though," Ferdinando went on to confide, "rests with Staffordshire. With the paucity of affinity it would afford me amongst its Catholic families."

"Staffordshire, my lord?"

"An impediment to any direct march on London, so one best avoided."

"Avoided, my lord?"

"In the right season, my own Lancashire forces, combined with those of the Spanish landed on our coast, can always cross the Lancashire Hills into Yorkshire. There, we could immediately join with its own Catholic families, instead of awaiting them in the south. In addition, the Great Northern Road that runs through that county can then take us more speedily on to London. And by it, Richard, well to the east of our troublesome Staffordshire."

"You've clearly put much thought to it, my lord. Can I take this as your…as your acceptance of the cardinal's offer?" and Hesketh's tongue briefly licked along his lips.

Ferdinando gazed at the man in silence for a moment. "Once I've spoken with my mother and am assured she will herself be no impediment, as I explained at Brereton."

"Of course, my lord. Forgive me."

"And I still have need to recruit my messenger in London, to accompany you back with my answer. Although it's likely he's moved elsewhere by now, to avoid the plague. So, he'll need searching out. But more immediately, I've an audience with the Queen to seek. There's much to do, Richard Hesketh, and so you must resign yourself to a delay of some few days more at least."

"As you wish, my lord, but I've limited coin with which to defray my keep. It'll last me no more than a—"

"Worry not, Richard. I'm staying at Windsor Castle whilst I await Her Majesty's pleasure. As the town will be packed for its fair, I've asked my secretary to arrange for you to stay with William Farington in his room in his lodgings there, which I've instructed be paid at my own expense. So, you'll be able to save your coin for your return abroad, will you not?"

"Thank you, my lord. Most generous. I'm much obliged."

Once Hesketh had been dismissed, Ferdinando continued his leisurely walk through the herb garden.

He bent often to inspect this leaf or that flower, to take in its scent or regard it for a moment. Occasionally, he'd rub a leaf between his finger and thumb, to draw its scent out and nearer his nose. But throughout all this, his thoughts clearly remained elsewhere.

Peter, however, could hold his peace no longer, although his voice came out almost as a stage whisper.

"Did he... Do you think Ferdy actually heard me back there, Sophie? When we were up with the old woman. Or did I just imagine it?"

"Coincidence, I reckon," she said, but her voice, too, suggested her mind was elsewhere.

"It was spooky, the way he seemed to be talking directly to me."

"What? Oh, yah. I'm pretty sure it was just coincidence. But more to the point: would you say he was genuinely thinking of taking up Hesketh's offer?"

"His offer? Er, well, I'm not sure. Sounds like it. He's certainly put some thought into how to go about it."

"But what about his keenness to have Hesketh kept close, so he knows where he is whilst they're apart?"

"Well, like you said before: he's got a lot to lose, so he's probably just being cautious. I think I'd do the same in his position."

"In which case, you reckon he's going to go for it, then? That he wants to be King of England."

"You know, Sophie, I think he does. And I reckon it's a lot to do with his father."

"His father?"

"Yeah. The man was clearly loved and highly respected, even by his enemies. And the Queen obviously thought highly of him. An illustrious career, you might say. Whereas, I get the impression

Ferdy's always felt he was in his dad's shadow."

"A lot to live up to, eh?"

"Indeed, and although Ferdy strikes me as highly intelligent and forward-thinking, he does seem a bit...well, politically naïve; more the artsy sort."

"What makes you say that?"

"When you told me about his time at Elizabeth's Court, after he'd left Oxford, when he was to be... How did you describe it?"

"To be shaped in good manners."

"That was it. Well, during his five years there, close to the Queen, the only position he had was as a simple squire. I know he was only in his early teens, but you mentioned that she gave others in a similar position—like Essex, for example—far more important duties. It's as though she didn't think that much of him as a political animal. But you said she liked him and enjoyed the poetry he wrote for her."

"I see your point."

"So, it doesn't strike me she'd be that keen on having him as her successor, and Ferdy's bound to have picked up on that. I reckon he knows he doesn't stand a chance of her passing the crown on to him, so his only other option's to take it by force. And what better way of cocking a snook at his father's grand and accomplished legacy than becoming king by right and by his own might?"

"Taking the crown by force, eh? From someone he's known intimately for the greater part of his life. Someone he's always clearly respected. From Elizabeth, his Sovereign Queen?"

"Christ. When you put it like that, it makes you think. This isn't just some cold bit of historical evidence we're discussing, not some dusty old parchment, but a real living man making a damned hard decision that'll put his very real life on the line."

"And his family name, and all failure would bring down on his wife, Alice, and his daughters. All of whom we know he dearly loves."

"Shit," and a lead weight seemed to settle in Peter's stomach. He felt sick at the prospect. "And all to become a Catholic King of England."

"Which he clearly doesn't, though. Does he?"

"No, not unless I missed mention of a King Ferdinando in my History lessons."

Sophie remained silent, leaving Peter racing through what they now knew of Ferdinando as a very real man. As a fallible human being.

"Shit," Peter eventually hissed. "He's going to go for it and get fucked, isn't he, Sophie? He's going to take Hesketh's offer and be exposed by Essex. That bastard really is going to get him caught for treason and executed, just like he and Ferdy's brother, William, planned all along. Right from their meeting aboard that ship."

"*If* what you *dreamt* really did happen."

"Oh, I'm sure it did. Damned sure. And now I'm sure our poor conspired-against fool of a host is going to end up losing his otherwise clever little head. And just when I was getting to like him."

23   A DIFFERENT MOUNTAIN

Despite being overcast the following day, it remained warm now they were further south. Upon that close afternoon air came a familiar and pungent smell. Ahead, along the straight road before them, its likely source lay within view: the first few buildings of the next hamlet or town.

Most prominent amongst them, clear against the grey sky and rising above the surrounding fields and hedgerows, stood an impressive chapel or church of some kind. Around it lay a castellated and chimney-festooned spread of purposeful-looking brick buildings.

"Eton," Sophie informed Peter as Ferdinando's horse led the way onto a narrow wooden bridge over a brook. "Windsor's not far beyond. On the other side of the Thames."

"What, this is Eton School? I didn't realise it was so old. Nor that it was so near Windsor."

"It's already been here for more than a hundred and fifty years, Peter. And the two places are near enough for the school to be called the 'King's College of Our Lady of Eton beside Windsor'."

"Well, it may be Eton, but it's just as smelly as the last place we passed through."

"Slough. And that's probably because there hasn't been enough rain of late to flush their ordure down to the Thames."

"Their what?"

"The shit and other effluent the inhabitants carry out of their hamlets in barrels and dump into nearby streams and brooks, like the one now below us."

"That explains a lot."

Having crossed the bridge, the road again widened. Michael came to ride alongside Ferdinando and laughed as he nodded up ahead.

"My lord; a fool and his money be soon at debate," he quoted, "which after with sorrow, repents him too late."

"Ha," Ferdinando exclaimed, pleasure evident in his voice, and he slapped his secretary on his back. "Indeed, Michael, but far more poignantly: Sweet April showers / Do spring May flowers."

"Ah, but April's still some time off, my lord. Winter's cold days lay twixt us and its promise to come."

"They do, but we can always enjoy it afore then by virtue of Thomas Tusser's fine poetry. Did you know I benefitted from conversation with that very alumnus of this college, not long before he died? The man was a rare jewel, Michael; truly he was. Possessed of an honest wisdom his exemplary command of language never failed to impart."

Soon, the college buildings, and those of the hamlet of Eton they dominated, hemmed in their party, but not before it had been beset by a horde of ragamuffins. As had been the case on entering most sizeable places they'd passed through, these had slipped out like eels from the many alleyways and entries, almost knocking the other inhabitants over in their haste. In a rising competition of offers, they'd promised guidance to where the best pies, strongest ales and the comeliest of the girls could be found. But a few coins tossed amongst them, as on previous occasions, had immediately diverted their nuisance.

At the end of the hamlet, Ferdinando's party came to a junction of three ways and there turned left, towards a long wooden bridge over a broad river—clearly the Thames.

Here, the view south lay open once more, but this time to Peter's stunned gaze. As seen through Ferdinando's own more studied one, it had followed the aim of the bridge to a long and prominent ridge of land on the far side of the Thames. This rose proud of a jumble of less than enticing buildings huddled at its western foot. But along the top of the ridge marched the recognisably imposing walls and towers of Windsor Castle, its outline surprisingly just as in photographs Peter had seen of it in his own time, although the round keep seemed lower than he remembered.

The castle of Lathom House may have impressed Peter, but this royal palace far exceeded it in size and in its more commanding position. It looked impregnable and all-powerful as it stood aloof from the rather pitiable buildings below its formidable walls. It also carried the royal standard, lazily fluttering atop the keep, midway along the castles extensive stretch.

As they crossed the bridge, another horde of youths swarmed out and amassed at the Windsor end, as though they could smell the silver coin in the purses of Ferdinando's party. The ensuing entreaties were dealt with in like manner, leaving only the heavy throng of the townsfolk of Windsor to impede their progress.

"It's already crammed," Ferdinando commented to Michael and William Farington, both now urging their horses ahead of their master's, to part a path through the town's streets.

"Here for Martinmas tomorrow, my lord," William almost had to shout above the growing clamour. "The town will be far more crowded come the start of the fair on Saturday, though."

"Indeed, but I've need to petition the Queen's secretary of state before this day's out. So, press on and make haste as best you can."

Before too long, they came beside those properties that ran at the foot of the castle's steep rampart, its surmounting northern wall towering above their roofs. Presently, they rounded a huge and high tower at the castle's north-western corner and began a gentle climb beside the continuing wall. At the top, they came to a broad junction and bore left, coming almost immediately before a great twin-towered gate. This stood open, unimpeded by people but attended by two liveried guards.

Ferdinando took the lead and urged his horse towards them, the sounds of hooves clattering in his wake on the hard-packed earth and stones of the road.

The guards immediately snapped to attention as Ferdinando approached. They then each stepped across the gateway, barring the way with their crossed halberds. One, however, clearly recognised him.

"Your lordship," he said, then they each raised and rested their weapons and bowed. "My Lord Strange, God give you good day."

Ferdinando, having come to a halt, only nodded in acknowledgement.

"You are expected, my lord, and most welcome," the man went on to say. "I'll send word of your arrival to the Knight Marshal, my lord. I have Sir George's instructions to have you escorted to your apartments, if it would so please your lordship?" Again, Ferdinando nodded, but then smiled down at the man.

"You appear well, Master Algernon. Better so than when last I was here. Is that gout of yours in abeyance at last?"

"It is, my lord. And for which great easing I must give thanks to your own good self. As your lordship sagely advised, I've since quit much of the strong ale I once drank."

When Ferdinando then pushed on through the gateway and into a grassed bailey within, Peter found himself enrapt at the sight of a building on the far side. There rose an enormous chapel made seemingly weightless by its walls of soaring windows.

More liveried men appeared, and Ferdinando undid his sword and passed it to one, the others of his party doing the same with theirs. Then he turned back to Master Algernon.

"Do you know if Her Majesty's Secretary of State is here?"

"I do believe he is, my lord."

"Good. In which case, let's be to my lodgings," whereupon his whole mounted retinue were escorted by the livered company of men across the bailey, away from the gate and towards the Round Tower.

Before long they were in what Sophie told Peter was the middle ward, at the base of the great conical mound on which the tower sat. This they skirted until they came to another gatehouse, where the guards here also gave them leave to enter. Beyond it, they went into the upper ward: a large quadrangle enclosed by extensive and grand-looking buildings. Soon, they were before the entrance to one of these, where it turned out Ferdinando was to be lodged.

He dismounted and handed his horse to one of the livered men. Then, with no command seemingly necessary, Ferdinando's entourage likewise dismounted.

Those with laden horses immediately began unstrapping their burdens. Soon, a snake of men carrying boxes, carefully wrapped packages, small items of furniture, sacks, and long rolls of bedding streamed past and into the building.

"If I may show you to the reception room, my lord," one of the liveried men offered. "Where you may wash whilst you wait for your apartments to be got ready. And where, my lord, the Knight Marshal will attend you at his earliest."

Out of the corner of Ferdinando's eye, Peter noticed Richard Hesketh relinquishing his own mount. He then stood by, out of the way, clutching his bag to his chest, clearly in awe of his surroundings.

Having washed his hands and face in the basin provided in the room to which he was shown, Ferdinando was gazing out of the window into the quadrangle when a knock came at the door.

"Come," he called out.

A slight and curly-haired man entered, his moderately long, ginger-tinged beard somewhat frizzy, but broad when compared with Ferdinando's. The nascent bags under his eyes belied a cunning astuteness, something made more sinister by the hint of a sneer on his full-lipped but narrow mouth. The effect dissolved, though, when his seeking gaze found Ferdinando.

"My Lord Strange," he almost enthused. "How it lightens my heart to have your lordship amongst us again, but how it adds such weight that it be upon this so sorrowful an occasion. We are all truly diminished by the death of your noble father, my lord. The late Earl will be sorely missed."

"Sir George. I value your kind words, sir, and much solace do they bring, for which you have my gratitude. But to be in the presence of one of the Lord Chamberlain's Men's own patrons once more favours me with a deal of recompense. To which matter, how fares your father, Henry, Baron of Hunsdon and Lord Chamberlain of the Royal Household?"

"He's well enough, my Lord Strange, and enjoying the success of his players. Upon which thought, how fares your own company? I hear they're currently performing in Norfolk. You must, quite naturally, miss not being involved of late, what with your present travails…"

For a while they discussed matters touching upon their respective companies of players, in particular bemoaning the plague that had kept their performances from London. They even asked after each other's wives, which surprised Peter until it became apparent they were sisters.

And so, it wasn't long before a genuine if somewhat guarded warmth settled between the two men. Presently, though, Ferdinando brought their current subject to a close.

"As you'll appreciate, Sir George, I've need to speak with Secretary Cecil, to seek an audience with Her Majesty. Is the good Secretary currently in residence?" at which that taint of cunning returned to Sir George's features.

"I'll enquire, my lord. And if so, then I'll endeavour to deliver your request and have its answer despatched to you at your apartments. Now, if there are no other matters, I beg to take my leave, my lord. The sooner to satisfy your wishes."

It was the following morning, Friday, and after morning mass in celebration of Michaelmas, when Secretary Cecil's reply arrived at Ferdinando's apartments. He was sitting at his desk in a rather plain and sparsely furnished room, writing a letter to Alice, when Michael came in.

"My lord, there's a message just arrived from Her Majesty's Secretary of State. He says he'd be obliged if you could attend him at his apartments at ten o'clock." Ferdinando consulted his timepiece.

"Excellens, Michael. Tell the messenger I'll be most pleased to see him then."

Some quarter of an hour before the appointed time, Ferdinando found himself in Secretary Cecil's reception room, awaiting the man's pleasure. The Secretary's aide had gone off to announce his arrival, leaving him with nothing but the silence of the room as company.

Another of this alien and largely unmechanised time's unnerving silences, Peter thought. Silences that seemed to swathe most of the land and much of what happened within it. Silence he was only now beginning to understand.

Ferdinando, all the while, had stood at the window, staring across the corner of the quadrangle at his own apartments, and at the occasional comings and goings elsewhere within sight. A nearby clocktower had long rung out the hour, though, before the door finally opened again. When Ferdinando swung around to see who it was, Peter gasped, audibly enough for Sophie to hear.

"Of all times, Peter," she vehemently warned, "this is the one time for silent running. So don't dare say a word; not a word, do you hear?"

"But—"

"Shush."

"My dearly beloved Lord Strange," the short man with a rather odd gait who'd entered was now saying, as he hurried over to take Ferdinando's hands in his. "It's so sad that such sorrowful hurt attends your coming to the Court this time. Know you that my own heart be most sorely bereft, for the realm has lost an inestimable jewel in your father's death."

"What's *he* doing here?" Peter hissed.

"Eh?" Sophie said, now clearly even more exasperated. "I told you: keep quiet."

"My loving friend and cousin," Ferdinando was now returning. "That you yourself express such sentiments upon mine and my father's behalf does greatly uplift my heart. It gives me such greater hope for the settling of his affairs, and for my furtherance of his good work in Lancashire on behalf of Her Gracious Majesty. To which end, I humbly trust I may presume your valued support, my most respected and beloved Sir Robert."

"See," Peter almost cried out, "Sir Robert. Robert Devereux. The Earl of Essex, for God's sake. What's he doing... Hang on. *Sir* Robert?"

"This, Peter, is Sir Robert *Cecil*, Secretary of State to Her Majesty. The very man on which Ferdinando holds out so much hope for his own and his family's fortunes. I know this for certain because I recognise him from de Critz's excellent portrait."

"In which case, Sophie, if you're really sure of this, then all I can say is 'Shit'; a big, fat mother of a mountain of shit."

"You've lost me, Peter. You really have," Sophie said, as, for the moment, Ferdinando and Secretary Cecil exchanged little more than further cultured pleasantries.

"It's simple, Sophie. The man you see before us now is the very same man I saw in my dream. The man who five years ago sat down aboard that ship with Ferdinando's brother, William, and set in motion this whole damned plot against him. *This* man, Sophie, this Sir Robert Cecil, not Robert Devereux, The Earl of Essex, as we thought all along. The very man poor old Ferdinando trusts above all others. The one who it now turns out has long been planning his untimely death."

24 CONSOLATIONE PHILOSOPHIAE

"**B**ut it can't be," Sophie said. "This man's a short hunchback, and you never mentioned *that* when you told me about the one in your dream."

"But the captain's cabin was dimly lit, and he was sitting down all the time, mostly silhouetted against a window. But this is definitely him. Although, now I can see him better, I'd diagnose congenital scoliosis."

"Yeah, well…whatever. But what makes you so sure it's him?"

"There was enough light to see his face by, but even if there hadn't been, I certainly recognise his voice; very distinctive."

"You're really sure it was him?"

"Absolutely. Without a shadow of a doubt. Which means that the men we saw in the market place in Leighton Busar, one of whom Ferdy reckons he saw when we were leaving Brereton, must've been Secretary Cecil's spies. He's no doubt been getting updates at every step since Hesketh came into the country. Just watching our naïve Ferdy blithely walking into his carefully laid trap. But why? That's what I want to know."

"Later, Peter. I need to listen to this," Sophie hurried to say, and Peter turned his attention to the words now being spoken by Secretary Cecil.

"As to your immediate needs, Lord Strange, I'm afraid Her Majesty's unlikely to grant you an audience at present."

"That would most disquiet my hopes, Secretary Cecil. My father's body awaits my return, that he may be buried at Ormskirk. Lathom's chapel may be chill, but this unseasonably warm weather will bear ill on his mortal remains." Secretary Cecil stared at Ferdinando for a moment, then dared a brief smile.

"I'll see what I can do, my Lord Strange, but you know how headstrong Her Majesty can be. King Henri's reconciliation with the Catholic Church in July has done little to settle her mood. And that Essex adherent the Countess of Pembroke's work on translating King David's Psalms has only added to her frustration."

"Ah, I did wonder how the Countess's furthering of that militant Protestant tract would sit with Her Majesty. Knowing how Our Sovereign Lady has a like mind to ourselves," and here, Ferdinando held Secretary Cecil even closer in his gaze, "I can well imagine she hasn't taken kindly to its implication that it's the Queen's duty to take our fight against the Catholics to countries abroad." Secretary Cecil coughed, politely.

"I couldn't presume to comment, my Lord Strange, other than to say that she's chosen to make a translation herself, although in her case of Boethius's Consolation of Philosophy. Her Majesty began only yesterday, and it will likely consume her for a while yet."

"Ah," Ferdinando exclaimed. "An apt choice indeed. Such an exemplary work on patience and forbearance would serve most admirably as a just riposte to the patronising voices championed by the Countess. It would certainly make it clear to all Her Majesty's subjects that she's not to be pestered into doing what others may expect of her."

"I'm sure, were it to be regarded as such, then you would indeed be right in saying so, my Lord Strange."

Ferdinando fell silent, only staring off to one side of the man before him, as though in distracted thought. It left Secretary Cecil with little more to do than furrow his brow in return.

"Yes," Ferdinando said after a discomforting silence, but more to himself. "Yes, a most apt choice." The Secretary's eyes had all the while been progressively narrowing.

"A work pertaining to human happiness," Ferdinando went on to say, just as quietly, "and how it can be reached in the midst of adversity through the powers of reason and a faith in the natural order of things. What better rebuff to throw at those English reformists who seem so keen to spill English blood abroad."

"My Lord Strange?" Secretary Cecil enquired, uncertainly, looking decidedly worried.

"O grievous hap when wicked sword / To cruel venom joins."

"Do you perhaps ail in some way, my lord?" The

Secretary reached out a tentative hand to Ferdinando.

"Naturally, I too possess a copy of the work in its Latin form. But a translation I myself made of some of its lines—in instruction of one I suspected of being a recusant—now comes to mind. To my now most chastened mind," Ferdinando finished saying as though alone with his thoughts. "I should have turned to the wisdom of Boethius afore now," he even more softly told himself, then went on to recite:

"He in holy peace doth hold
The bounded peoples' pact,
And links sacred wedlock
With chaste goodwill,
Who laws, his own, to true associates gives.
O happy humankind,
If Love your minds—
The same, that heaven doth rule, might guide."

"I'm sure it's been a trying time for you of late, my…my greatly esteemed Ferdinando. So, if I might make to suggest—"

"My most beloved cousin and trusted friend," Ferdinando now more volubly said with a hitherto missing sense of resolve. "Her Majesty's grant of an audience is of less concern when set against the matter I must now place before you. A matter demanding more urgent redress. A matter that pertains, in short, to a sovereign threat upon our most gracious and rightful Majesty."

But all Secretary Cecil now seemed able to say in return was a rather open-mouthed and knowing "Ah".

25 SETTING WHEELS IN MOTION

"**A**nd you never thought to have this Hesketh arrested whilst at Brereton?" Secretary Cecil aimed at Ferdinando once he'd finished his revelation, to which Ferdinando at first hesitated.

"I didn't wish to delay my attendance upon Her Majesty. It would have taken another day, Sir Robert, to summon the sheriff. Maybe longer. And of course, I've yet to be granted the Lord-Lieutenancy of Lancashire and Cheshire, so have no authority as yet to arrest him myself. Besides, Hesketh's a large man, Secretary Cecil, one keen of cunning; I couldn't countenance his escaping and so returning abroad...beyond your remit."

"So, it seems you chose instead to welcome him into your company with open arms."

"Upon the subterfuge, as I've already explained, that I needed to consult with my mother before I could give him my answer."

The Secretary closely eyed Ferdinando, a silence

descending between them, until he asked, "Could you not at least have sent a message of warning ahead of you? So I could have prepared a more secure reception."

"I didn't wish to arouse any suspicion in the man, Secretary Cecil. My only thought was to keep him close until I could safely deliver him up to you."

"But as it is, he may very well have already made his escape, seeing you thought fit not to apprise your servants of any of this...or so you say. So, where should he be at this moment?"

"With my gentleman-servant William Farington, at Ela Longespee's lodging house in Peascod Street."

"Unless they've followed their noses to any one of a number of inns nearby...or more likely the stew down that way."

"They'll be easy enough to find if they have, Secretary Cecil, for, as I've already said, Hesketh's a large man, with a distinctive head of yellow hair."

"Well, we'll just have to see, won't we?" Secretary Cecil almost growled. Then he barked out for his aide, startling Peter.

"Sir Robert?" the man responded, having opened the door almost immediately.

"Have Sir George, the Knight Marshal, and the castle's bailiff attend me."

"Of course, Sir Robert. Immediately," and the man was gone in an instant.

The Secretary regarded Ferdinando for a moment, then asked, "What of Sir William Brereton in all this? Did you make him aware of what treasonous matters were being conducted under his very own roof?"

"Er, no, Secretary Cecil. I thought it best to involve as few people as possible."

"And only Hesketh approached you? He had no accomplice with him?"

"Only a man of his. A servant he'd taken to his service on his way from Canterbury. I'm sure he knew nothing of Hesketh's design, though."

"Do you, Lord Strange? Do you indeed? So, what name did this servant go by?"

"Richard Baylye, Secretary Cecil. A trumpeter late of Francis More's service unto the Earl of Essex."

"And he didn't come with you, as another *guest* of your party?"

"No, Sir Robert. Hesketh dismissed him to return to Lancashire."

A knock came at the door, and Secretary Cecil admitted Sir George Carey and another man, one Peter didn't recognise. Both, though, seemed to bring a chill to the room.

"Secretary Cecil?" Sir George said, an apprehensive glance sent Ferdinando's way.

"You're to arrest a man named Richard Hesketh, of Lancashire," Secretary Cecil instructed. "For treason against Her Majesty. He should currently be in company of one of Lord Strange's gentleman-servants, lodging at Ela Longespee's in Peascod Street."

"I know it well, Sir Robert," Sir George affirmed.

"He'll be with William Farington, Sir George," Ferdinando added, "with whom I believe you're already acquainted."

"Indeed, Lord Strange," and the look he turned to Ferdinando seemed one of genuine relief.

"Very well, then, Sir George," Secretary Cecil concluded. "Let's be having you. The sooner the man's detained, the better. Oh, and send word to

Mister Waad to prepare to attend Hesketh at Sutton Park, where you'll take him from here at first light tomorrow for interrogation."

"As you wish, Sir Robert."

"That's all for now. And have your report ready for me upon your return."

Sir George nodded and swept the bailiff with him as he withdrew, the two men falling to close discussion once they were beyond the room.

This time, it was Secretary Cecil's turn to stare out of the window. Clearly, Ferdinando had sensibly chosen to remain silent, patiently watching the man's back, as though it spoke of his thoughts.

"And when were you intending a visit to your mother, Lady Margaret Stanley, my Lord Strange?" the Secretary finally and now more levelly asked.

"I had no genuine intention of doing so, Secretary Cecil. It was but a ruse. An excuse for keeping Hesketh close."

"Indeed? I am, of course, aware of the understandable antipathy that existed between your mother and your late father. But it would seem somewhat uncivil, particularly in the eyes of others, not to afford Lady Margaret such a common decency upon her widowed state. Would you not agree? And I'm sure the Queen would look less than favourably upon such a slight made to her beloved cousin." He turned from the window, the glint of his eyes leaping from his silhouetted face.

"I… Naturally, I demur to your wisdom on the matter, my most trusted Sir Robert. I shall make arrangements anon."

"I suggest you not leave it too long. It would be a

most politic decision, my Lord Strange. And as for this current matter, you may leave it entirely in my own hands, it now being a matter of State."

Before Ferdinando could answer, and without further word, Secretary Cecil hastened from the room, leaving the door pointedly wide open behind him.

26   AN ARRESTING THOUGHT

"**A**nd there we leave behind a well and truly pissed off Sir Robert Cecil," Peter commented to Sophie as Ferdinando stepped out into the quadrangle and turned towards his apartments.

"But I reckon it was only because Ferdy hadn't sent a warning ahead, that's all. That Secretary Cecil hadn't been able to prepare Hesketh's arrest in advance. He was thought to be a bit obsessive in that respect."

"Nah. I'm sure as Hell it's because his long-standing plot's been scuppered. But we still don't know why he planned it all in the first place."

"Well, given that Secretary Cecil eventually becomes instrumental in supporting James the Sixth of Scotland's claim to the throne, I think it's safe to say he's not at all keen on Ferdy becoming King."

"But I thought the incumbent sovereign chose their own successor."

"Usually, but Elizabeth used her refusal to name someone as a political tool, to keep her Court factions in line. A refusal she maintained right up to her death."

Ferdinando was now entering his apartments, where he called out for his secretary, Michael Doughtie, who hurried from a side room and accompanied him into the solar. Here, Ferdinando stood before its window and looked out through its leaded lights onto the quadrangle below.

He remained motionless, keeping his back to his secretary as he told him, "I've had cause to keep a matter of some import concerning Mister Hesketh from all in my service."

"Indeed, my lord?" but Michael didn't sound at all surprised.

"Indeed I have, Michael," at which Ferdinando cleared his throat. "My need has been, as any true lord must acquit to those under his protection, to guard you all against any mortal hurt or besmirching of your names."

Michael silently waited as Ferdinando clasped one hand in the other behind his back, his free one slowly opening and closing as he rocked back and forth on his heels. Presently, he took a deep breath, his explanation carried out upon its release and the many that followed.

Carefully, he apprised Michael of much of the same matters as he'd disclosed to Secretary Cecil, but as though availing himself of the opportunity to refine his story.

It seemed to Peter that he was also, in some measure, appeasing a hurt he expected his secretary to have felt at having been excluded. But that Ferdinando was being no more candid with his own personal secretary disappointed Peter, for he suspected he was even now keeping far removed from the whole truth.

"But if Hesketh puts up a fight, my lord, might not William risk getting hurt in the arrest?"

"Which is why I want you to search them out yourself. If you come upon them before Hesketh's taken, keep your distance, unless William should need your aid; although I have made his innocence in this matter known to the Knight Marshal. And if possible, return to me here with William once Hesketh's in custody. I've particular interest in what the man may protest at his arrest."

Having instructed Michael to make William aware of all he himself had now learnt, Ferdinando sent him off, suggesting he first try the lodgings in Peascod Street. He then returned to staring unseeingly out of the window, his hands all the while again tightly clasped behind his back.

Peter, not for the first time, dearly wished he could listen in on their host's most inner thoughts.

"Sophie?" he asked after a while.

"Hmm?"

"What was all that about Boethius's Consolation of Philosophy? I got that something about it appeared to swing Ferdy against accepting Hesketh's offer, and so pushing him into turning the man in, but what, exactly?"

"Ah, Boethius. Well, some thousand years before Ferdy's time he was a powerful man in Rome. He was brought down, though, by treachery and ended up spending a year in prison, awaiting his trial and eventual execution."

"Treachery, eh?" and Peter wondered what Ferdinando really suspected of Secretary Cecil. "And he'd written a philosophy?"

"Whilst in prison, yes. His time there had made him rethink things."

"Things?"

"The work he wrote is his imagined conversation with Lady Philosophy on all manner of things, the transitory nature of fame and wealth being just one. 'No man can ever truly be secure until he has been forsaken by Fortune' was the way she put it to him, and what Ferdy was probably reminded of. That 'The one true good', as she had again put it, is in truth the ultimate superiority of things of the mind."

"Like the writing and performing of plays?"

"That and poetry, and the natural sciences, and a whole raft of other virtuous stuff this Renaissance period was rapidly bringing about that Ferdy had a passion for."

"More so than leading armies against his Queen."

"Precisely. And a queen who wanted essentially the same as him for the future of her realm."

"That's even more amazing when you consider how mired she must have been in her own politics."

"She was a very wise and great monarch, Peter. One who was well versed in the lessons of history. A truly renaissance queen."

Peter thought about what Sophie had said, then told her, "You know, Sophie, I reckon I've missed out on a lot of important lessons in life through my single-minded focus on medicine."

"Hmm, and probably not helped by all that wellbeing poo that was being peddled in your time, and the damage done by the subsequent Western Cultural Revolution."

"Wellbeing? Cultural Revolution? I think that must have passed me by, as well."

"Eh? Oh, yah; that'll be a bit after your time, when everything started... Anyway, the thing is: it's history that teaches us the most about how best to live our lives, not platitudes, especially when...when things start falling apart," on which haunted note she fell ominously silent.

It was sometime towards late afternoon when Michael returned, William Farington in tow and looking somewhat flustered. Ferdinando had been sitting at a table, a half-empty glass of wine before him. Once the two men had been admitted and had bowed to Ferdinando, he nodded towards a couple of unused glasses and a bottle of wine standing at the centre of the table.

"You look as though you would benefit," Ferdinando said to William, a rather sheepish grin lamely suffusing his features.

"Thank you, my lord," William said and charged both glasses, passing one to Michael before swiftly quaffing the whole of his own. Ferdinando waved indulgently at the bottle, from which William recharged his glass.

"Sit yourselves down, gentlemen," Ferdinando allowed and leant forward, resting his elbows on the table as they took their seats opposite. "You are unhurt, I take it, William?"

"I am, my lord. Hesketh went as meekly as a lamb."

"I thought so," Ferdinando affirmed, rather too emphatically. "I rightly took him to be a gentle giant, though a lewd fellow, all the same. I'm glad he afforded you no great threat of injury in his taking. But tell me:

what had he to say for himself at his apprehending?"

"Nothing, my lord," William informed him. "It was all over at a trice. Hesketh but cast me a hurtful look, full in my face, before hanging his head and being mutely led away."

"Did he, indeed? Good. And where were you when this happened?"

"At the White Hart, my lord; enjoying a particularly robust claret," at which he took another swig of Ferdinando's own offering.

"Ela Longespee directed me there, my lord," Michael furthered, "not long after she'd told the same, apparently, to the Knight Marshal and his bailiff."

"I imagine the whole affair will be common knowledge by now," Ferdinando lamented.

"Without doubt, my lord," was William's view. "The White Hart was crowded with those here for the fair."

"Speaking of which," Ferdinando said, a weariness entering his voice, "what consequence do you think it'll likely have on us hiring a barge to take us on to Clerkenwell? I've decided I ought to visit my mother whilst we're only a day's journey from there."

"I'll enquire, my lord," Michael offered, clearly intrigued. "When you feel you can spare me. But I'll be surprised if one can be got before the fair's out, not at such short notice."

"Oh, and I mustn't forget my good lady's need of dried figs. So, as you're probably right about the barge, Michael, I say we attend the fair tomorrow and leave Clerkenwell until Sunday at the earliest. Although…" and Ferdinando cupped his chin in his hand, thoughtfully toying with his neatly-trimmed beard.

"Perhaps…" he slowly mused, his eyes narrowing

a touch. "Perhaps I ought first to seek an audience with Her Majesty before presenting myself to my mother's incautious and somewhat hard-of-hearing scrutiny. Yes, perhaps that would be wiser."

He flashed a look of resolve at Michael. "Monday should be enough forewarning to find a barge, should it not?"

"I imagine so, my lord."

"In which case, seek to engage one to leave here mid-morning, returning early the next day. And in the meantime, I'll seek an audience with the Queen for Sunday. Then, God willing and if all goes well, we might find ourselves back on the road to Lathom come the middle of the week, and all this lamentable affair behind us."

"Well, my lord," Michael said, downing the last of his wine, "the sooner I find a bargeman, the more chance one can be got for the Monday," and he stood.

Ferdinando waved his dismissal, at which Michael bowed and retreated from the room, leaving Ferdinando closely regarding William, now well down his second glass of wine.

"William?" and the man looked across the rim of his glass at Ferdinando.

"My lord?"

"I offer you my regret for a wrong done unto you, my faithful servant."

"Nay, my lord, you've no need to—"

"Hear me out, William. I've wronged you, for which I'm truly sorry."

Ferdinando rose and placed his glass on the table, William immediately scrambling to his own feet.

"The lesser of two evils, I'm afraid, my good sir,"

Ferdinando went on to say with great dignity, before he stepped around the table and stood before William. Taking him firmly by his shoulders, Ferdinando leant in and kissed him once on each cheek before stepping back at arms' length.

William curtly bowed his head then raised his gaze to his lord's, the pride in his face seeming almost to outshine the slant of fitful sunlight currently streaming in at the window.

"My Lord Stanley, you...you do honour me beyond any merit of my actions. I assure you, my lord: Sir George, the Knight Marshal, was attended by six of his stoutest fellows. I was in no genuine danger. And Sir George was quick to impress upon me his knowledge of my innocence, for which it is I who should owe you my own great gratitude."

"But I ought to have shown due regard to your having felt obliged to protect any and all guests of mine."

"In all truth, my lord, Michael and I already had our suspicions about the man. We have, after all, both served long in yours and your father's service. So, the Knight Marshal's intervention hardly came as a great surprise."

"Ha. Yes, I should have realised. All the same, you've done me good service, William. Take the wine with you and consider yourself at liberty for the rest of the..."

A thought suddenly crashed in on Peter, obscuring the men's conversation: the way Sophie had so abruptly broken off what she'd been saying earlier and how he'd not heard from her since. His metaphorical blood rapidly chilled.

What had she been saying just before then?

Something about when things start falling apart—
things in her own time, clearly. Things yet to come
in Peter's future, and which he feared she shouldn't
have disclosed to anyone from her past.

The chill in his blood now froze to ice, ice that
reflected the fluttering wings of a butterfly that he
suspected had since flown free upon its future-
changing course.

"Sophie?" he ventured, but no reply came back at
him.

"Shit," he hissed at himself. Then, more loudly
implored, "Answer me, Sophie; Answer me, for
Christ's sake. Tell me you still exist!"

At her continued silence, he screamed her name at the
top of his imagined lungs, and still there was no answer.

Panic erupted from the darkest depths of his mind,
engulfing him. A mind only half aware that
Ferdinando had started at his urgent cry, and who'd
then darted his gaze questioningly about the room.

"Did you hear someone call just then?" he shot at
William as the man was about to leave, but
Ferdinando's gentleman-servant only cocked his ear
for a moment.

"No, my lord. No, I'm afraid I didn't," he finally
answered. "I heard nothing; nothing at all."

27 HOPE DASHED

"**W**hat demon are you that haunts my thoughts?" Ferdinando said softly to himself, but now shockingly loud in Peter's hearing.

As he watched William again bow and this time retreat from the room, Peter pressed himself up against something firm yet yielding at his back. That he somehow now felt nakedly exposed cowed him into silence, a silence seemingly filled with a hubbub of everyday sounds.

"What are you?" Ferdinando growled more volubly, his words palpably pummelling Peter.

Into the muted swirl of disjointed refrains and snatches of speech left in the wake of those words, through the burbling of streams and the clop of horses' hooves, came a stunning realisation: Peter was now listening to Ferdinando's very thoughts and memories.

Somewhere amongst them all, a barely discernible but familiar voice strained to be heard. Peter drew himself short of excitedly calling out

"Sophie" and listened harder.

Muffled words were coming from behind him, through whatever pressed against his back. And then he heard his name, of that he was sure.

For the first time since embarking upon these "dreams", he sensed he had something of a body. A back and arms and hands at least, a hand now feeling along the pliant divide that kept him here.

Just as Ferdinando was asking "Sophia? What's this *wisdom* you speak of, demon?" Peter's fingers slipped into a softly yielding fold and he seemed to slide through and tumble back into a womblike silence.

Those recently discovered hands and arms now found themselves about the warmth of a closely pressed body, Sophie's tremulous voice yet more intimate still.

"Dei be thanked; I thought I'd lost you," she said and hugged him tighter. "Where on Earth have you been?"

"Lost *me*?" Peter could hardly get out, his own voice shaky. "I thought it was you who I'd lost; that I'd somehow destroyed you. I really did," at which he could no longer hold back his sobs.

"But you can plainly hear you haven't, Peter," she soothed. "I'm talking to you now, so you can't have."

A wave of rational relief finally washed over him. Then he forced back his tears and marvelled, "And… And *holding* me so intimately close."

"Holding you?" and he felt her tense, then felt her arms hurriedly slip from around him. "I…"

He kept his own arms around her, though, even as he asked, "You haven't been totally honest with me, have you?" He could feel her shake her head. "But then, nor have I with you."

"I... I had the advantage over you, Peter: I knew what it felt like to be in a...to be *alone* in a target's mind. I knew you were here as soon as you joined me. As soon as I felt you press in against me. So I... So I kept my mind and my...and my body still, till I could work out who or what you were. What harm you might threaten. I just never imagined..."

"Imagined what, Sophie?"

"That I... Nothing; it doesn't matter. It's not important. So, what is it you've kept from *me*, then?"

"Kept from you? No. If I'm honest, kept from myself. The shock at thinking I'd lost you brought home to me just how...just how much...how much you...you mean to me."

Nothing but the sound of Ferdinando getting to his feet and going to the open window invaded the silence that now fell between them. Nothing but the twitter of birds flying past outside, and the crunch of footfall below in the quadrangle.

Such a quiet world, Peter once more noted, but not as quiet as Sophie had now become.

"Don't worry me again, Sophie. Please. At least reassure me you're still here."

Voices from below marked a greeting, a few more quiet words passing before the footsteps hastened away, still out of sight along the edge of the quadrangle immediately beneath the window. Presently, at the sound of someone approaching the door to the room, Sophie lightly coughed.

"Yes," she said, quietly, "I'm still here," but then a knock came at the door.

"Come," Ferdinando called out as he shook his head, as though to dislodge an irritating thought, and he turned from the window.

Michael entered, something in his hand.

"My lord, I was just on my way to search out a bargeman when I bumped into a messenger delivering a letter for you." which he passed into Ferdinando's hand.

"Ah, from our good Secretary Cecil," and Ferdinando prised off its seal and opened it out to read.

Despite his pressing need to hear Sophie's voice, though dreading what she might say, Peter couldn't help but follow Ferdinando's gaze as it passed over the Secretary's words. It availed him little, though, for the letter's hand proved all but indecipherable to his unpractised eye.

"It's but confirmation that Hesketh's now held captive within the castle," Ferdinando presently made light to say. "And that he's already admitted his guilt in the matter. Thankfully, it's now out of my hands entirely." He quickly folded the letter and slipped it into his doublet.

"So, let me not delay you, Michael. All God's speed in your finding us a passage for Monday."

Michael bowed and retreated, closing the door once he was beyond the room. At the sound of his footsteps along the passage, Ferdinando retrieved the letter and read it again, but this time more carefully. Even during the protracted silence that followed, Sophie said not a word.

In his now more settled state of mind, Peter began to regret the candour he'd shown, not only to her but to himself.

What madness had made him think that anything could possibly have come from such a confession, nor of his feelings towards her that he now had to accept were very real.

They lived in separate times, he and Sophie, never—except as disembodied voices in this last shared dream—to be anything other than eternally apart. And at this thought, a heaviness stubbornly settled about his heart.

From below came the crunch of Michael's feet as the man hurried beneath the window, away on his search for a bargeman who would be free and willing to carry them on to Clerkenwell.

28   "BUTTERFLY ATTACK"

On the table lay Secretary Cecil's letter before which Ferdinando had been sitting for some few minutes. Although it clearly occupied him greatly, for Peter the scrawl of handwriting offered only a spidery backdrop to his self-recrimination.

He'd created an awkward situation, he realised that now, and one neither he nor Sophie could escape. For the remainder of their time together he would have to live with the embarrassment of his outburst, but also be mindful that she didn't feel threatened by it in any way. And the shame of it was that their enforced company had proven so easy and pleasant until now, sharing a similar sense of humour, a surprisingly common outlook on life.

Mentally, he kicked himself.

"I'm sorry, Sophie. For what I said earlier. It was well out of order. I realise that now. I just got myself into a bit of a state, that's all, thinking I'd been the cause of your never having existed, if you see what I mean. It made me a bit thoughtless, to say the least."

"I don't want to talk about it, Peter. Please. Just leave it, eh?"

"Of course. But—"

"We've another three weeks to get through before we'll," her voice hitched, "before we'll be saying our final goodbyes. We… We have to put it behind us, otherwise we'll always be—"

"It's all right, Sophie; I understand. Consider it well and truly put-behind-us," but Peter couldn't deny having heard a certain wistfulness in her voice, or had it just been his own wishful thinking?

"What's… What's more important now," she hurried to say, "is where the Hell you went to. And how you got there."

"Well, the first is sort of easy: I reckon it must have been another part of Ferdy's mind, but a part where I could actually hear his thoughts and memories."

"You what? Hear them? And could he hear you?"

"Er, unfortunately, yes. Thought I was some sort of demon. Heard me call your name. Though I think he confused it with something else; asked me why I'd shouted 'Wisdom' at him."

"Wisdom? Well, whatever. That's beside the point now. If he heard you, then you've gone and done it again."

"Done what?"

"Broken the friggin' time travel paradox. You're making a damned habit of it, for Dei's sake."

"Eh? Oh, right. Yeah, I suppose I must have; spoken to someone from my own past."

"*Our* past, Peter. This time you've put both our existences at risk."

"Shit. In which case, I'd better not go there again."

"How did you, though? Go there, I mean."

Peter thought hard to remember exactly what had happened, but much of it seemed a blur. He told Sophie how her protracted silence had eventually worried him, more so when she'd not answered his query. How he'd panicked when he'd fruitlessly called out more urgently, and then... Then what?

Then, he now vaguely remembered, he'd found himself blindly pushing out in search of her, pushing with his hands against something soft and yielding.

"Why have I only now felt I have a body, Sophie? Why haven't I been aware of it all along?"

"Because the association with the body you're inhabiting, the one you're feeling through Ferdy, swamps out any sense of your own. It took us a while before we realised we kind of retained one; a sort of phantom body. It sounds like your panic pushed Ferdy's genuine one far enough from your awareness for you to discover it."

"So, it's not real?"

"Not really, no, but it clearly gave impetus to your mind to strike out into another part of Ferdy's, which is totally new to me. Imagine if we could develop a technique for doing it at will. We'd be able to listen in on any target's thoughts, to learn what they were thinking. It'd take all the interpretation out of our work."

Peter was sure he could feel his phantom eyes narrowing. "What *is* your work, Sophie? Why are you really here?"

She didn't answer at first, raising a shade of his recent despair that even now remained so raw in his mind. So much so that he fervently prayed she wouldn't tell him.

"Butterflies and all that," she finally said, a hint of amusement in her voice, and Peter let out a mental sigh. "And I'd appreciate it if you'd consign your newfound sense of us having bodies to a box labelled 'For no further use', if you wouldn't mind. Can I trust you on that?"

Peter agreed, trying not to note how that weight about his heart had got just that little bit heavier.

"But why didn't you answer me when I first called out?"

"Ah, right. Well, it was just that I was in the middle of sorting out my records, getting to grips with a tricky mnemonic, so I wasn't really listening. Sorry, but how was I to know you were going to get yourself into such a state?"

"Maybe we should have a trigger word or phrase for such occasions."

"What, like 'Butterfly Attack! Get your tin hats on and man the ack-ack guns'?"

"That's not funny, Sophie; believe me."

"No, no it's not. Sorry. Just a bit on edge at the moment. But maybe 'Butterfly Attack' isn't such a bad idea. At least it's unambiguous."

"Okay. 'Butterfly Attack' it is, then. But tin hats and ack-ack were well before my time, you know. I'm not *that* old. Only thirty-one."

"Thirty-one? Is that all? But… But yes, I know. Second World War and all that. Although you do come over as a bit older, what with all your quaint ways. Sort of homely and comforting and safe…well, comfortable I suppose I meant."

"I'll take that as a compliment, however

backhanded," and it seemed to Peter that an unspoken understanding had been reached, one that might return some of that easy-going companionship that had been steadily growing between them. But then Ferdinando muttered to himself as he pushed the letter away and sat back.

"Wisdom, eh? Well, perhaps it was an angel and not a demon." Ferdinando took in a deep breath and let it out slowly before barking out a single laugh. "But then, perhaps it was my own dearest 'new Minerva', lauding from afar the wisdom of my decision," although he then gently thumped his fist on the table top a couple of times.

"How I've missed your always sage advice, my beloved wife. Would that Mistress Fortune hadn't denied me your company upon this so trying a journey. And so, my cherished Alice, I'll try my hardest to find you the finest of figs tomorrow. That I promise, for I know how dearly you love them."

He raised his glass and drained the last of its charge before carefully placing it back down. This time he sat back and closed his eyes as he slowly drummed his fingers on the arm of his chair.

29 AN INNOCENT SPY

"**I**'m afraid the only barge to be got, my lord, won't take the horses," Michael explained after they'd greeted one another in his lordship's garderobe on the Saturday morning. "If your lordship still wishes to see Lady Margaret on Monday, then the cost of their stabling will have to be borne here, I'm afraid. Then there'll be the hire of palfreys when we disembark at Brid Well."

Ferdinando let out an exasperated breath as Michael took an item of clothing from a travelling chest, one that looked little different from the long nightshirt Ferdinando was now removing. The hem of this Michael then presented to his master's lowered head and slid the garment onto him.

"Well, if it has to be, it has to be, I suppose," Ferdinando said, somewhat muffled from within the linen shirt. "Not getting to see Her Majesty tomorrow may very well delay our return," he said as his head popped out through the neckline, "but I've no wish to be the cause of it myself."

"As you wish, my lord," and Michael helped him get his arms into the sleeves of the shirt before taking down his doublet and its own sleeves from their hooks and helping him into them. He tied the sleeves to the body but was soon fussing at them.

"Is that comfortable, my lord, or do they need to be tighter."

"They'll suffice, Michael. Come on, now, get my lower stocks on; I need you to write me a reply to Secretary Cecil before we leave for the fair."

"Of course, my lord."

Michael hurried to remove what to Peter looked like a pair of white silk stockings from the chest. He knelt before Ferdinando, placing one on his knee before rolling back the opening of the other for Ferdinando to slip his foot in. Ferdinando steadied himself with a hand on Michael's head as the hose was rolled up his leg. Soon, the other was in place, the two swiftly tied together around his waist, his manhood dangling free from where they failed to meet.

It was a good fifteen minutes before Ferdinando was fully dressed, his modesty by then maintained by what Michael had referred to as "upper stocks", but which to Peter looked like a short ballooning skirt gathered to the thighs.

Finally, the two men went through to the solar, where Michael sat before his lordship's travelling desk and opened a small box that stood upon it.

Inside were two inlaid jars, and beside the box lay a number of quills. Michael took one up and expertly pared away at it with a blade he'd taken from the box. Once satisfied, he took a clean sheet of paper from a drawer and laid it out on the table before him.

"My lord?" he finally said, removing a stopper from one of the jars and carefully loading the quill's nib with black ink.

Ferdinando coughed in preparation and then dictated: "I have received your kind letter…" at which he paused whilst Michael scratched away at the paper then reinked his quill's nib, "and am glad to hear that the lewd fellow hath shown himself…" and again he waited, "as base in mind as he is bad in manners…" and in like manner he carried on: "because Her Majesty may see I have said nothing but truth. I wish that such vile men may never have more strength to stand against the truth, and will pray that all men may ever carry like faith as myself, to her whom I prize above myself."

Ferdinando leant closer over Michael's shoulder, reading the script back to himself.

"Excellens, Michael. Now, carry on with: I will by the grace of God be at the Court to-morrow morning, for I cannot see my mother until Monday night, and therefore wish that I may see her Highness, holding myself the happier… No, make that: may see her Highness, when she shall please, holding myself the happier the more I see her. It is my exceeding comfort if I have done anything that may content her, for in that I joy most."

Again, he read through what his secretary had proven to have faithfully penned.

"Very good, Michael. In which case, finish with 'Your loving friend and cousin', and have it declare this day's date, the thirteenth day of October."

Once complete, Michael took out the as yet unused

jar from the box and sprinkled fine sand onto the paper, clearly to dry the ink, and then blew it clear.

Ferdinando took the offered pen and signed "The L. Strange" in a flourished manner, after which Michael again dusted the paper.

"Address it to 'Sir Robert Cecil, Secretary of State to Her Majesty, Queen Elizabeth' and have it delivered without delay. Then we can put this all behind us and get ourselves off to the fair, and so to more enjoyable matters, eh?"

The Lower Ward, when they eventually passed through, proved busy enough, but it paled against the press of people that met Ferdinando's gaze when he and his small entourage of gentleman-servants went out through the castle gate. Not only was Windsor's High Street packed with stalls and their high-spirited customers, but the same scene presented itself along the many streets that led from it, as far as the eye could see.

For once, Peter felt a hint of his own noisy times, for here were stallholders shouting out their wares, wandering pie and oyster sellers promising their most healthy and filling delights, jugglers and acrobats playing for thrown coins, and every conceivable language, dialect and accent swelling in and amongst it all.

Ferdinando was soon just a part of the throng, his status seeming to offer little advantage in his pursuit of figs for Alice. It was also likely why, as Peter had noticed earlier, Michael had slipped the purse he carried deep into his doublet. However, he and the other servants, some of whom carried large hessian bags, kept as protectively close as they could to their lord and master.

Before Peter's fascinated gaze soon passed the usual fare he'd become familiar with, that of plump geese, suckling pigs, capons, hens, and rabbits. Along with these, though, came a whole host of produce he'd not as yet seen in Ferdinando's time: oranges, a great many forms of sugar, dates and almonds, aniseed and liquorice.

Then Ferdinando exclaimed "Ah" before pushing his way through to a particular stall. Here, he at last found what he'd clearly been seeking: small barrels packed with dried figs.

Drawing his knife, he prised away at the uppermost layer, peering in at those below.

"Hmm," he grunted as he withdrew his knife and before the stallholder could press him to buy. "I think we'll try elsewhere," he told Michael.

In the shade beneath the raised guildhall further along the high street he found another stall selling figs and again inspected them. This time he nodded agreeably and beckoned the stallholder.

"What's the price of your figs, coster?"

"Ah, well, those, my lordship, are the best you'll find in Berkshire, I assure you. And only a shilling and fourpence a pound."

Michael whispered, "That's a little costly," into Ferdinando's ear.

"If I were to take four pounds, then what price would you ask?" to which the stallholder bit his lip and narrowed one eye.

"Fourteen pennies, if you would, my lord. I can't go lower, not and still make it worth my while." Michael gave a slight nod, at which Ferdinando beamed at the stallholder.

"Make it a shilling a pound and I'll take six in weight, provided they're packed well enough for a long journey." The man regarded Ferdinando closely for a moment before letting out a small sigh.

"Very well, a shilling it is, my lord," and he reached down to a barrel beside him on the ground.

"But only if..." Ferdinando interrupted, tapping the barrel he'd just inspected, "they're taken from this one."

"As you wish, my lord," and the man's enthusiasm appeared to wane somewhat, the more so as Ferdinando stood over him as he drew out and weighed the figs into a small wooden crate.

As Michael removed his purse and counted out the coins into the coster's hand, Ferdinando's gaze happened to settle on a man loitering nearby.

"Master Algernon? Is that you?" he called to him, and the man stepped forward through the crush and attempted to bow low before Ferdinando.

"My most esteemed Lord—" he began, but his backside collided with a woman behind him and he nearly tumbled to the ground.

"Never mind, Master Algernon; I note your intended respect. But tell me, have you been given leave of your castle duties, or are you here upon its own business?"

Peter suspected that the small bag Algernon carried suggested the former.

"Seeking but my own pleasure, my good Lord Strange, thank you for asking. Sir George has kindly allowed us each in turn a little time to enjoy the fair."

"And I trust your own will be spent well away from any strong ale, eh, Master Algernon?"

"Indeed, Lord Strange, as was your sage advice, which it'd be remiss of me to ignore." At this, though, the cat seemed to have got Algernon's tongue, for he stood there looking a little lost. Ferdinando smiled benevolently down upon him.

"I'm glad to hear that. But as your time's so precious, you needn't tarry upon my pleasure. I'll say God grant you a good day, Master Algernon," and Ferdinando waved his leave as he turned to check that his crate of figs had been safely vested with one of his servants.

As he did so, Peter noticed, out of the corner of Ferdinando's eye, that Algernon hadn't moved on. Indeed, he seemed to have been edging himself closer to William Farington, who'd been chatting with two pretty young lasses. But then, Ferdinando became intent on other things and Peter lost sight of the man.

A good few hours were then spent looking at everything else on offer, stopping only to find seats in the White Hart Inn for a leisurely meal. The hessian bags of Ferdinando's servants had steadily filled all the while, until, by early afternoon, Ferdinando finally announced he'd had enough and they made their way back towards the castle.

As they approached its gate, and within earshot of Ferdinando, Michael asked William what it had been that Algernon the gatekeeper had passed to him.

"Oh, that," William replied. "It was just a small favour he'd asked of me. Seems his mother's long been unwell and he'd bought her some medicines from an apothecary here at the fair. As she lives in Blackfriars, he wondered if I might take them with me to The Swan Inn in Brid Well; where we'll likely be hiring palfreys and where one of his brothers works as a horse-groom." By now they'd reached the gatehouse, where Ferdinando brought them to a halt and turned on William.

"And how, in God's good name, did he know we were going to be travelling that way?"

"But, my lord, you asked us to make it known at large that you intended visiting your mother, so we've none of us kept it a secret."

"That we were going to Clerkenwell, yes, and by barge could be guessed, but not that the barge would be insufficient to take our horses, and that we'd then have need to hire some at Brid Well. I only learnt of it myself this morning. Did the gatekeeper not say anything of how he knew this?"

"He mentioned he'd overheard Sir George talking about it with a messenger. Here at this gate. One he'd been sending out on an errand. Do you wish me to find the gatekeeper again to learn more, my lord?"

Ferdinando glanced about them, then shook his head.

"No, William. I think I've learned enough. We'll say no more on the matter, not where the walls clearly have ears. In which case, you may return to your lodgings now, or to whatever else you had in mind."

"Thank you, my lord," and William turned to leave but then stopped and patted the bag that hung from his shoulder.

"My lord? The medicines for the gatekeeper's mother? Have I your leave to discharge my promise to him?"

"You have, William. A fair payment, it seems to

me, for the warning he's unknowingly given me. And in good time, before my likely audience with the Queen tomorrow."

At this, Ferdinando summarily swept Michael, and those servants carrying his many purchases, back with him into the supposedly safe confines of the castle.

30   AUDIENCE WITH THE QUEEN

The morning had dawned grey and misty, a salutary reminder of that year's overdue Autumn. It had also felt decidedly cooler, almost chill, as Michael had dressed Ferdinando by candlelight.

The mist, though, had lifted and a promise of warm sunshine seemed to have lightened Ferdinando's footsteps when they came to walk down to the lower ward and to the Sabbath service in St. George's chapel. By the time they'd left and returned to the upper ward, the sun had long broken free, bathing the castle in a now thinner light, more befitting an October day.

As they entered the quadrangle, Ferdinando parted company with Michael and turned towards the main entrance to the Royal Lodgings. There, he presented himself to an extravagantly liveried man who conducted him through elegantly impressive halls and chambers until they came to one containing only benches set against its wood-panelled walls.

Here sat a number of people already, each standing and bowing at Ferdinando's passing. He himself was finally seated upon a bench beside a firmly closed door, and where he clearly settled himself in, as though for a likely long wait.

Time did indeed drag by, doggedly, and all against little more than a soporific murmur of conversation punctuated by an occasional stifled yawn.

After what seemed like an age, the door beside Ferdinando did finally open, jolting him fully awake. A courtier stepped through and approached him, bowing low as Ferdinando got to his feet.

"My Lord Strange, if I may conduct you into Her Majesty's presence?"

Ferdinando dipped his head in acknowledgement and accompanied the courtier through the doorway and into a small room beyond. From here, voices could be heard drifting in through an opening in the far wall, to where the courtier led Ferdinando. Halting just inside the room beyond, the man formally announced, "Ferdinando Stanley, The Lord Strange of Knockyn."

When the man then stepped aside, it was to reveal a moderately sized but sumptuous room, its walls decorated in patterns of greenery and brightly coloured flowers. Knots of gentlemen and nobles stood here and there in conversation, although they all faced but one way: towards the quite literally majestic figure of the Queen of England.

Flanked by ladies-in-waiting, attended by a tall, dapper-looking nobleman with a distinct air of confidence, and standing a little away from a scarlet-coloured throne, Her Majesty easily outshone them all. Her sumptuously ornate, creped and lustrous white gown flared voluminously from the dagger point waist of her bodice, the sleeves of which were heavily puffed to close-fitting cuffs.

As Ferdinando dropped to one knee at the threshold of the room, the gaze he kept on His Sovereign Lady allowed Peter to note that she gave no indication of having noticed his entrance. Without looking his way, she only leant in closer to the nobleman at her side, continued quiet words passing between them.

Ferdinando rose and strode to the centre of the room and there again sank to one knee, his gaze all the while held captive upon his Queen. After a moment or two, he again rose but only to sink once more to his knee, where he then remained, motionless and seemingly forgotten.

Now they were that much closer, Peter's initial awe gave leave for him to take in more intimate detail of the Queen's appearance: the band of huge pearls surmounted by a steepling confection of blood-red and night-blue gems that delicately crowned her tightly curled ginger hair, suspiciously abundant and richly coloured; her pale and expansive forehead, etched with the thinnest of roundly arched brows spanning the shaded wells of her large brown eyes; the glassy blackness of their pupils, revealing the keen and astute intensity of the penetrating gaze they held.

Although a sharp laugh from her companion abruptly rang out about the room, Ferdinando remained deferentially on one knee, his face carefully held passive, his gaze persistently attentive upon his Queen.

A queen whose noble countenance entirely enthralled Peter: a long and sharply narrow nose, a stern bud of a mouth within an oval frame of powder-masked age lines, all set against an extravagantly fanned high collar of stiffened silvery-white lace. Within the window of lead-white skin framed by this collar's parting and the low straight neckline of her bodice hung a richly bejewelled gold pendant brooch. The shimmer of its flawless stones and single pendant pearl matched those of her crown, as they did the further pearls that hung in a long string from about her heavily powdered throat.

This was certainly a mature woman, Peter noted to himself. Sixty years of age, he remembered Sophie telling him. A grand old age in this much harsher world, but he knew she'd another ten years yet before death would finally claim her. Then her eyes flicked momentarily Ferdinando's way before she cast an almost imperceptible nod to a gentleman who stood at a respectful distance to one side behind her.

The gentleman came forward and stood before Ferdinando, where he bowed his head before informing him, "My lord, Her Majesty wishes your lordship's immediate presence." He stepped to one side as Ferdinando rose, revealing the Queen to be still engaged in close conversation with her noble companion.

Only a few steps across the room and Ferdinando finally stood but feet from England's Virgin Queen, his presence still unacknowledged, his gaze again held subserviently upon her face.

Leisurely, she finished what she was saying and turned her now studiedly gracious face towards Ferdinando, her gaze searching deep into his eyes.

Peter felt somehow exposed, as though she were seeing through to where he lay hidden within Ferdinando's mind.

"It's good to have you once more at our Court, our too-long-absent Lord Strange," she said in a confidential tone that clearly carried to every ear present. "Your presence amongst us has been sorely missed."

Only when she raised an eyebrow did Ferdinando reply: "An absence, your most gracious Majesty, felt all too keenly upon my own behalf. For my father's late ailing has unavoidably kept the balm of the inestimable beauty of your fair countenance from enrapturing my gaze."

The Queen arched a brow as she regarded him, a smile threatening to unfurl the tight bud of her rose-stained lips.

"You are, as ever, Lord Strange, entertainingly honey-tongued. That and your close resemblance to your now dead father does raise great regret in our heart at his passing, for he too did much to lighten our mood and hone our purpose when first we came to the throne. Would that his health had allowed him one last attendance upon our person, but God, in His infinite wisdom, plainly thought otherwise." She turned to the nobleman beside her.

"We feel certain you'll excuse our absence, Lord Devereaux," at which name Peter gasped. "But our translation of Boethius's excellent work has left little time today for exercise, so we're in pressing need of a walk along the North Terrace. Where we may also talk more privily with our most loyal servant Lord Strange."

She paused, but the Earl of Essex uttered not a word.

"Naturally, there's the consequences of the late Earl of Derby's death to address, but also the little matter of our crouchback pygmy's recent report; the one, if you remember, sir, that touches upon a certain treasonous act perpetrated of late within this, our Realm."

The Queen now held her challenging gaze unfalteringly upon the Earl of Essex.

"Something of which you yourself, despite your boasts, lamentably seemed to have been unaware."

The Earl hesitated, but then slowly bowed low to Her Majesty and stepped back a few paces.

"As you will, Your Grace." But his eyes narrowed momentarily towards Ferdinando. "I shall hold the matter of our conversation in abeyance, for it will keep."

"Whether it will or no," was all the Queen said before she swept from the room, Ferdinando drawn dutifully into her wake. Her ladies-in-waiting and her gentleman usher came up at their rear, soon leaving behind a throne room of silently genuflecting courtiers.

When they presently came out of the Royal Lodgings, it was on the north side of the castle, onto an enclosed terrace running a considerable distance along the broad top of its defensive wall. It overlooked gardens laid out on the steep slope below and offered a wonderful view over the Thames in the near distance, and of Eton beyond.

Peter only had the chance of a glimpse before Ferdinando hurried to keep up with the Queen's determined pace, his gaze soon held upon Her Majesty.

"Come, walk at our side," she commanded, at which her attendants fell discretely behind.

"Our crouchback Secretary of State," Her Majesty went on to say, "has made it known that our

Chancery has your father's inquisition post-mortem well in hand." Ferdinando remained silent, although Peter felt his jaw tighten.

"It should, therefore, not be long before our Exchequer knows what will then be owed it. And as we're content for his earldom to descend upon your own good self, as of right of heredity, then the amount of the fine for his title's relief shouldn't be overly long in coming."

Peter felt Ferdinando's jaw now relax, although he still said nothing.

"You've oft excused your absence at our Court, Ferdinando, upon urgent matters of your family's estates, which industry we're reliably informed has borne it great fortune. So, as we foresee no pecuniary impediment to the fine's prompt payment—in full, mind—we're therefore content for you to assume rightful use of your inherited title. And rightful use as of this day, we are yet further content to add."

By now they were drawing to the end of the terrace, where the Queen turned about and retraced her steps. They came between her attendants, who'd already stepped aside to make way.

"It does, of course," she went on to say a little more lightly, "beg you consider a new name for your band of players, your Lord Strange's Men. Perhaps 'Derby's Men', hmm? What say you, Ferdinando, our now newly ennobled *Earl of Derby*?"

"By... By all means, as you wish, your Majesty."

"We have in the past so enjoyed their plays at our Court. Perhaps as Derby's Men they may one day find such similar favour of royal command. Perhaps more so if that 'Upstart crow' William Shakespeare, as we're told Robert Greene has called him, were still to be one of their number."

At the Queen's slight lifting of her brow, Ferdinando expressed his like hope that it would be so, then added, "And in the matter of the title, Your Grace, I'm profoundly indebted. A beneficence that does truly reward this, her loyal servant. An act wholly in keeping with the largesse for which your Majesty is so rightly lauded throughout her realm," and he bowed as low as their brisk walk would allow.

"Ha. Is that so, Ferdinando? Well, it does greatly please our heart to hear it. But we fear that not all currently within our realm share such a sentiment," and again she raised a brow.

"Your Majesty?"

"It seems we owe you a debt of gratitude for the deliverance of one solely intent upon pursuing treason against our royal person."

"Ah, yes. Indeed, Your Grace. Although I did little more than would any true servant of your Majesty."

"However, it has to be said: the manner in which you set about your duty does appear to have soured the mood of our diligent Secretary of State." The Queen slowed her pace and cocked her head to one side.

"And, we must also say: that you failed to send word ahead could, by some, be construed as somewhat suspicious."

"But I assure you, your Majesty, that—"

"Take care, Ferdinando; we have not yet given you leave to speak." This time it was the muscles in Ferdinando's neck that tensed. "We'll say no more on the matter," and the Queen picked up her pace, keeping her own counsel for a while.

As they drew nearer where they'd begun their terrace walk, the Queen at last spoke again, but this time noticeably softer.

"And what of your good lady wife? How is the Lady Alice keeping?" but Ferdinando held his tongue until she'd turned a clearly enquiring look his way.

"My beloved wife is in good health, Your Grace, though saddened at having to remain at Lathom and thereby far from your person. But she's taken it upon herself to ensure that all funerary matters are... Oh, and yes; it'd woe betide me were I not to deliver her letter," at which he reached into his doublet.

The Queen slowed to a halt and beckoned her usher to draw near, into whose hand Ferdinando placed Alice's letter.

"We'll look forward to hearing her news from your northern lands, Ferdinando. Her company at our Court has, for too long a time now, been sorely missed. Although, despite our own loss at her betrothing to you, we did find generosity in our heart at the time to declare how, in her doing so, it seemed Dame Fortune had smiled down upon you. But take care, our Earl of Derby, that you keep a hand at your table for that oft fickle card."

No leave to answer came from the Queen as she closely regarded Ferdinando's countenance, one Peter felt he struggled hard to keep passive.

"And make sure you convey our fondest love to our most valued Alice," she again softened her voice to say.

After this, with only a dismissive wave of her hand, Ferdinando soon found himself alone on the terrace, now distractedly chewing at his lip.

31   ST. JAMES'S, CLERKENWELL

Taking only Michael and William, and four others of his gentleman-servants, Ferdinando's party had boarded a small barge at the wharf in Windsor. Its complement of six young oarsmen seemed hard put to make headway against an unusually brisk and often rain-laden easterly. And so, when they'd come ashore late in the morning for a meal at Staines, it had been unusually hurried for fear of arriving at Brid Well after dark.

The afternoon had then brought with it an ominously lowering sky. Against this, the steadily more sodden and steaming oarsmen determinedly pushed the barge on through the river traffic, ever nearer London.

When it at long last thumped against the wharf at Brid Well, the crew jumped ashore only to find themselves skittering about on a thin scattering of hailstones, defiantly glistening beneath a now bruised and sullen late afternoon sky.

"Seems winter's stolen a march on Autumn, my lord," Michael commented, once the barge had been secured and they'd been helped across to the quayside.

"Let's hope not, for the sake of the roads we've yet to take," Ferdinando bemoaned, in a subdued manner he'd carried with him since his previous day's audience with the Queen. He glanced up and narrowed his eyes. "At least we've missed the recent hail they've had here," and he absently kicked at its evidence littering the ground. "Come on, Michael, better we were in The Swan Inn if more's loosed upon us."

The hostelry was only a few minutes' walk away, where he and Michael were soon ensconced in its parlour, a flask of wine between them. William and the other servants meanwhile had gone off to arrange the hire of palfreys and pack horses, the latter led back to the barge to be loaded.

When William eventually strolled into the parlour to join them, rubbing his hands against their chill, Ferdinando asked if he'd remembered to deliver the medicine for the gatekeeper's mother.

"I did, my lord. His brother was most lavish with his praise."

"And did he seem genuinely surprised?"

"Er, he did, my lord; most surprised."

"Good," Ferdinando said, almost as a sigh, then cupped his chin in his hand and stared off into the distance.

"There's also been no reports of plague hereabouts, my lord," which did at least brighten Ferdinando's expression a little, drawing him to look up at William.

"Even better," he allowed, but his voice sounded weary.

"And the horses are now ready, my lord. Added to which, the sky's brightening somewhat to the east. So, maybe the last of the hail's passed us by."

When they eventually left the inn, only a grainy slush remained in the gutter that ran down the centre of the street, and the wind had dropped. By the time they'd mounted and were riding northwards through the noticeably busier streets, a vestige of afternoon daylight had begun to glare from the cobbles passing beneath the horses' hooves.

Presently, they turned east, along a wide but this time muddy road. It aimed Ferdinando's gaze directly towards a massive church in the distance, its square tower rising hugely above the roofs about it. A slant of sunlight then cut through a rent in the clouds and struck its flanks, and that of its enormous west front. From this stared back a great round window, like some suddenly startled cyclops.

"That must be the old Saint Paul's," Peter guessed, for its sheer size spoke of it being nothing less than a cathedral. Then he noticed that a tall, solid wall and its gatehouse cut across the far end of the road, what must have been the city walls beyond which raged London's plague. But then they turned north again, the view quickly lost behind the close and often tightly packed buildings that lined their further way.

Soon, they entered a broad and open area of land between more substantial buildings, prompting Michael to break the silence that had accompanied them since leaving the inn.

"It's fortunate we're here on a Monday, my lord, so we're not pushing our way through the press of

Smyth Field's market."

"And nor will we have to on our return tomorrow, Michael. We should, I trust, be on the road back to Lathom come Friday, when this place descends into its weekly noisome hell. Which is why I didn't have you bring me a pomander," at which Ferdinando cracked his first smile since his attendance at the Court.

"But there's Saint John's Gate," he then said, looking ahead. "Not far now to Saint James's," but the thin and fleeting joy that had been in his voice had already flown free into the cold October air.

Not long after, they passed a small church and came into a square around which stood a number of respectable properties. Through the arched gateway of one of these and down its side, Ferdinando led them into a stable yard. A couple of grooms rushed out to meet them, soon helping Ferdinando's servants tend to the horses and the loads some of them carried.

As Ferdinando approached the property's rear door, it opened and a well-dressed gentleman stepped out to invite him in.

"My good Lord Strange," the man said, a sombre smile upon his face, "welcome to Isleworth House. I hope your journey down's proved comfortable enough, my lord."

"Passable, Mister Hickman. I've been fortunate enough to miss the worst of today's weather."

"And may I offer you my gravest sympathies upon the late Earl's death, may his soul soon rest in Heaven."

Thank you, Richard. It is, I must say, very strange without him. But how have you been since last we met? What must be some time ago now."

"Oh, still possessed of life and limb, my Lord Strange. Can't grumble, not in all honesty."

"That's good to hear. Oh, and you may wish to note that Her Majesty has now given me leave to assume my father's title, in advance of its relief."

"Indeed, my…my Lord Stanley. That *is* good news. But if I may show you in. Lady Margaret awaits you in the hall, where she's taken to sitting by the fire, it being so suddenly cold these past two days."

Mr Hickman conducted Ferdinando down a short, dark passage and into a narrow but lighter room, its tall, south-facing window looking out onto the square. Here, though, he stopped and asked if Ferdinando had received his last letter, the one listing those known to the family who'd lately died of the plague.

"I did, Richard, and thank you for that. It made for grim reading. Which reminds me, if you'd see Michael Doughtie; he's got some letters to send on to those sadly affected. Oh, and I've every intention of keeping you on in my service, if you wish to remain with the Stanley family. You've long been a loyal servant to my late father. There may, I'm afraid, be a short delay in your payments, though, until the estate's been settled in my favour."

"I would consider it an honour, my lord, and all in your own good time, naturally. I'm not yet poverty stricken, my lord, thank God in His divine benevolence."

Ferdinando made to carry on towards the hall but Mr Hickman held back. "I asked about the letter, my Lord Stanley, because the innkeeper at the White Lion, just up the road in Islington, expressed some concern about its safe arrival."

"Some concern, Richard?"

"He'd sent word to us that there was a gentleman staying with him who was bound for Lancashire, to see your father, the late Earl, and wondered if we'd any letters we might want him to take with him. So, I finished off the one I was then writing and sent it with my lad John Waterworth."

"The letter I did indeed receive."

"The very one, my lord. It was just that, after talking with the gentleman that evening, the innkeeper formed the opinion that something wasn't quite right about him; that he seemed somewhat evasive. I just wanted to put my mind at rest that...now, what was the gentleman's name? Ah, yes, one Mister Hesketh, I do believe. That Mister Hesketh had indeed been true to his word, that was all. But clearly he had, so all's well that ends well, is it not, my lord?" and he smiled his evident satisfaction.

Ferdinando paused for a moment, seemingly scrutinising Mr Hickman's apparently innocent features, as though lost to a thought. But then he snapped out of it.

"Indeed, it is, Richard. Indeed, we must hope it to be so," and after a furtive glance through the window, he continued on.

They came into a high-ceilinged hall, a long dining table on one side and settles and chairs arranged about a large fireplace on the other.

In one of the chairs sat a figure swathed in a shawl, its back towards them, a plain velvet cap drawn down over its pinned grey hair.

"My Lady Stanley," Mr Hickman loudly announced. "Ferdinando Stanley, the now Earl of Derby, is here to see you, my lady," and the woman's head jerked stiffly in surprise.

Slowly, she turned her face towards Ferdinando as he stepped between the chairs and came beside her. With a somewhat myopic stare, she studiously looked him up and down before her eyes widened in recognition.

"Ah," she croaked, then cleared her throat. "Ferdinando, eh? I did wonder," and this time she peered more closely at his face. "Ha, so it is you. One of my sons at last deigns to visit once more." With a small puff of her breath, she relaxed her stare, her gaze swinging back to the hearth's warmly flickering flames.

"Well, sit yourself down," she offered. "Deliver the condolence you've so clearly wished to bring. But I'll not grieve, son of mine. I will not grieve."

Ferdinando gingerly sat in the chair beside her and regarded her features for a short while.

"Has Richard offered you something to eat or drink?" she asked before he could speak.

"No, Lady Margaret. No, he hasn't."

"Well, he should've done. Richard?" she almost barked.

"My apologies, my lady, but... I'm sorry, my lord, but do excuse my previous adherence to etiquette; clearly, I should now have enquired at your arrival. But could I offer you anything? Some wine, perhaps. A bite to eat?" and the man's eyes narrowed as he stared at the back of Lady Margaret's head.

Having requested a little wine, and as Richard left upon the errand, Ferdinando sat back a bit further in his chair, again closely regarding his mother.

"You may as well," she told him, "save yourself any consoling words on matters pertaining to my late husband, your father. Unless—by some act of God's own mercy—he's left me a substantial allowance in his will. Something to hold at bay my many creditors."

"In which case, Lady Margaret, if that is indeed your wish, then may I ask after your own health?"

"My health? My health's of no consequence. I get by. But it seems your own fortunes are faring far better. By the sound of it, my cousin's already given you dispensation to bear your father's title."

"She has. Only yesterday."

"Well, would that she could see her way to dispensing such largesse in regard to the unfairly prolonged imprisonment she's imposed upon me. 'Tis so unjust in light of my innocence in the matter, as all right-thinking people must surely see. And as to my poor maligned William Randall: no sorcerer he. Purely my physician, as I did oft protest but to no avail. He didn't deserve such a death, Ferdinando. And what aches and pains I've had to suffer since in his absence. It's most trying, I tell you."

Ferdinando didn't answer.

"Perhaps, in your newly elevated position, your own entreaties upon my behalf might be heard by my cousin the Queen, where Sir Francis Walsingham's certainly weren't. I would so cherish gaining her love again, and of course, being received at the Court once more."

Again, Ferdinando refrained from answering, a quiet sigh escaping him.

"But then," Lady Margaret concluded, resignation entering her voice, "your little foray into entertaining traitors has no doubt put paid to that prospect," at which Ferdinando jerked upright and stared open-mouthed at his mother. He was soon peering nervously about the hall.

"How… How did you come to hear?"

"Oh, it's the talk of London, or so my maid assures me."

"So quickly? But then," he quietly said to himself, "Richard gave no intimation of knowing it."

"So it's true, then? You did bring a Catholic plotter to the Court? Into Her Majesty's presence, of all things?"

"No. No, that's not what I did at all. How the gossipmongers embellish and dissemble."

"Did Elizabeth teach you nothing in your five years at her Court, Ferdinando?" but at this point, his gaze alighted on a small slit of an opening, high up in the wall above the fireplace.

Peter was sure he too had noticed movement there. But then Richard returned with a glass of wine, bringing a small table over on which to rest it beside Ferdinando.

"Is there anything else, my lady?" Richard sought, in answer to which she only cursorily dismissed him.

In a restrained voice, Ferdinando then assured his mother that the traitor he'd delivered up to justice had got no nearer the Queen than a very brief dalliance outside his apartments in Windsor Castle.

"But why bring him with you at all? What those you call gossipmongers must surely want to know is why you didn't have the man arrested yourself, whilst still in the North. Or, as they'd no doubt ask in the privacy of their own bedchambers, just tell him to take himself off, back to the Continent; the less said the better. Why make an already dangerous situation even more so? Unless…unless you harboured a genuine desire to…"

Ferdinando's mouth dropped open, but then he

gathered it up and spluttered, "I…" before once more glancing up at the small opening far above the fireplace.

"I thought it… Thought it an opportunity to please Her Majesty, and…and so to raise myself in her estimation. With… With an eye to her seeing fit to award me what should be mine by right of heredity: the Lord-Lieutenancy of Lancashire and Cheshire."

"Ha, did you indeed?" his mother barked. "And you never thought of all the hostility such a foolhardy course would bring in its wake once the traitor was hung, drawn and quartered? Which he most certainly will be, without a shadow of a doubt. The Hesketh family, Ferdinando, are not without some power, enough for one or two of them to do more than just bear you a grudge."

Clearly lost for words, Ferdinando merely gawped.

"Well, if you didn't, as seems the case from the look on your face, then you're considerably less of the man your father once was."

Ferdinando shot to his feet and glared impotently at Lady Margaret, his words still refusing him as he clenched his fists at his side.

"And I thought you the clever one," she wearily chided as she ignored him and looked back into the flames of the hearth, and from where the brief sound of logs settling softly spilled out into the hall.

Or, Peter thought as Ferdinando yet again glanced up at the opening, had that noise really come from somewhere else, and from something other than the inanimate yielding of burning logs?

32   A ROCK AND A HARD PLACE

Not until the day after they'd got back from Clerkenwell, the Wednesday afternoon, did Ferdinando get to speak with Sir George Carey, the Knight Marshal. He told him he was going back to Lathom early the following day, unless either the Queen or her Secretary of State wished anything further of him. He wondered if he might be required to make a deposition regarding Hesketh, which Sir George promised he'd find out.

Peter had thought Ferdinando a little subdued before going to visit his mother, but now he seemed decidedly withdrawn. If Lady Margaret proved right about the Heskeths bearing more than a grudge, then Ferdinando's path would undoubtedly take him between a rock and a hard place.

For most of the time since that visit, Peter had said little to Sophie, and she to him. On Peter's part it had started out as reticence, a wariness arising out of his rash revelation. But something else had steadily come to usurp it.

As Ferdinando sat morosely alone in his apartments, Peter suddenly blurted out, "I can't do it any longer, Sophie."

"Do what?"

"I'm afraid I've got to accept it: I've been so close to Ferdy for so long, I can no longer see his plight as that of just a character in a story. The prospect of what might happen to him feels like it might happen to me. He's become like my second-self, as though the boundary between us has almost dissolved away. And I think it's because I see something in him that painfully reflects the person I've been myself, all along."

"The person *you've* been?"

"His preoccupation with the arts, with poetry and plays; it's made me see how much I've concentrated on little but my own fascination with medicine. Just as he seems blind to the machinations going on in his own world, so too have I been blind to my emotions. Both, in our own ways, hamstrung by our weaknesses."

"Don't you think you're being a bit harsh on yourself, Peter? On both of you?"

"Harsh?" Peter stared at the truth he'd uncovered within himself. "No harsher than life can be when left to its own unthinking judgement. So, whatever I said before about not spoiling the intrigue of his story, well, now I really do want to know what's going to happen to him."

"Sorry, Peter, but no can do."

"But why not?"

"Not now I know you've the ability to speak with Ferdy, to warn him about his future. I can't risk you giving away anything that could end up changing the course of history."

"But I wouldn't do that. Honestly, I wouldn't. I know how serious it would be. I just need to—"

"It doesn't matter whether you would or you wouldn't. As the potential's there, that makes it a definite no-no. You can beg till you're blue in the face, Peter, but it'll make no difference."

Peter's heart sank, despite the sobering knowledge that Sophie was undeniably right.

"And whatever you do, don't stray into that part of Ferdy's mind again. If you do, accidentally, then don't say a word to him. Not a word, Peter. Not a single word, do you hear?"

"Yes. I hear you. And of course I understand."

Silence fell between them for a few moments, until Sophie said, in a softer tone: "I should have thought to warn you. We're trained to avoid getting personally involved, mainly to keep our observations objective. If I had done, it might have headed this problem off. Sorry. I should really have thought. And maybe I should've thought to take better note myself."

"Yourself?" but she wouldn't be drawn, only once more falling into a protracted silence.

Sir George returned to Ferdinando later in the day, assuring him that he was no longer required at the Court and was free to leave. So, the Thursday morning saw Ferdinando's entourage this time making easier progress through the streets of Windsor. Once over the bridge and into Eton, they carried on northwards, towards Lancashire.

It was at their first night, back in Southall, near Gaddesden, that Sophie happened to say, "You know, Peter, what you were saying about Ferdy being hamstrung by his political naivety; it's got me wondering if he's twigged yet that Secretary Cecil's behind it all."

"What, because it was him who encouraged Ferdy to go and see his mother?"

"That and Ferdy's clear suspicion that someone at the squint was eavesdropping on their conversation. Surely, he has to have put two and two together."

"The squint?"

"Eh? Oh, the slit opening above the fireplace in the hall. I thought I'd said: what was built into most houses of the sort, so they could keep an eye on the goings-on in their halls. I mean, he certainly kept looking up at it."

"Yeah. At Lady Margaret's maid, I reckon. Committing everything they said to memory for reporting back to Secretary Cecil. No doubt through that agent the gatekeeper said Sir George had dispatched from Windsor."

"You think so?"

"It'd make sense of a few things. Just stop to think: the Secretary's plan's fallen apart, delivering not a traitor in Ferdy, but the very one to reveal the existence of a plot against the Queen. Secretary Cecil will be working like mad to recover something from the disaster. Dirt to smear on Ferdy."

"And Ferdy did seem suddenly keen to get his audience with the Queen over with *before* seeing his mother. Probably to avoid the Queen being primed with anything either of them might let slip during their conversation."

"And why he was so careful to make his excuse for delaying Hesketh's arrest sound as plausible as possible: this business of the lord-lieutenancy he's after securing."

"Which, I grant you, is a big thing for the Stanleys. A mark of their importance and power."

"Something else the Queen carefully avoided mentioning."

"True. But it's all supposition, Peter. As far as Ferdy's concerned, there's nothing to say it isn't the Earl of Essex who's behind it all. That Secretary Cecil encouraging Ferdy to see his mum was nothing more than well-meant advice. Both men, after all, are at the Court, and each clearly has the Queen's ear."

"And they both have it in for Ferdy."

"Seems so. But either way, it's now out of his hands. The Court's clearly excluding him from Hesketh's arraignment, which must be really peeing Ferdy off if not greatly worrying him."

"You know, Sophie, once he gets back to Lathom, I reckon he's going to be in a whole load of trouble with Alice. If she'd been with him at Brereton, she'd have said the same as his mother: just pack Richard Hesketh back off to the Continent and say nothing about it."

"Well, whatever he should or shouldn't have done, it's all water under the bridge now. What will happen will happen, as long as you keep from interfering."

Their journey back up to Lancashire proved more protracted and arduous than the one down, the days being that bit shorter, the weather less favourable. But by the eleventh day from leaving Windsor, the walls and towers of Lathom House at long last came into view as they emerged from the woods.

The day had been wet, though the rain had abated by the time they arrived at the outer gate. Tired and somewhat bedraggled, they filed in to the outer bailey and snaked towards the inner gate.

As some of Ferdinando's household servants came out to welcome them, he sighed and drew his horse to a halt. Stiffly, he dismounted, a couple of servants hurrying across towards him.

"My Lord Strange, is all well?" the first to reach him warily asked.

"Well enough, Thomas. A backside I've long forgotten the feel of, but otherwise just in need of a last short walk to stretch my legs."

As Ferdinando led his horse and his party towards the gatehouse, Sophie's close and earnest voice surprised Peter.

"I just wanted to…" but her breath hitched just as Ferdinando stepped onto the cobbled approach to the gateway. Her lips then pressed firmly against Peter's, her brief but intense kiss completely disarming him, stealing his breath away.

"However much I'd promised myself I wouldn't," she hurried to say, "I can't bear the thought of saying goodbye without you knowing how much of my heart you've stolen."

"Goodbye?"

"I shouldn't say this, I know, but I have to," and again her lips pressed against his, although she soon drew away.

"I love you, too," she barely choked out. "Goodbye, my love. Goodbye for ever," then the shadow of the gatehouse somehow darkened the more, and Peter was wrenched away.

A tumble of lights, a searing pain across his forehead, and there stood Beryl, the sofa between them. She held her expectant gaze fast to Peter's startled eyes. But eyes now brimmed with tears, tears that soon fell free down his pitifully distraught face.

33 OF THE HEART, NOT THE HEAD

The traffic on the A59 out of Preston towards Longton was particularly light for a Monday evening. Even the bit of drizzle, periodically swept from the windscreen by the car's intermittent wipe, brought Peter the reward of a low sun's partial rainbow. It arced almost upliftingly over the Lancashire countryside that silently rushed by beyond the rain-flecked driver's window. As had been the case over the weekend just gone, Peter's eyes again threatened to overflow.

The music from the car radio had given way to the news, which he only half took in: "*A snowstorm and avalanche in the Nepalese Himalayas, triggered by the remnants of Cyclone Hudhud, has killed an estimated forty-three people.*"

Peter took the roundabout near the Anchor Inn and carried on down Liverpool Road. "*There's been suggestions from some in the science community that this is a possible symptom of global warming.*"

251

Peter's ears pricked up. *"However, a spokesman for the IPCC warns that individual events like this cannot be directly attributed to Climate Change."* But another item followed on, and so Peter went back to concentrating on the road ahead.

Beside him on the passenger seat lay a bouquet of flowers his secretary had nipped out to get him, from the florist's across from the hospital. Water had pooled on the leather around the cut stems. Peter fumbled for a tissue in the door pocket and dropped it onto the seat, to soak up the water.

Looking back at the road, he saw he'd nearly missed the entrance to Beryl's drive. Braking hard, he swung the car across the road and in though the open gate. At the crunch of the tyres on the gravel, Peter drew in a deep breath and glanced at the front door, before pulling in beside Beryl's Range Rover.

By the time he came to stand before the door, a trickle of the bouquet's water had run down beneath his watchstrap. He again took a deep breath and finally pressed the doorbell.

"Peter," Beryl said, a little too enthusiastically, when she opened the door, her gaze scrutinising his features before darting to the flowers. "For me?" and her forced smile took on a legitimacy all its own.

"Just a little thank-you," he told her, sheepishly passing them into her hand. "And thanks for letting me drop by at such short notice."

"You're more than welcome, Peter. You know you are; or should do. How are you now? But first, come on in. The coffee machine's on specially, so I hope you're up for a cup."

She showed him through to the kitchen and into

its welcoming, coffee-rich aroma. Peter stood a little lamely, dabbing at his wet wrist with his handkerchief.

"These *are* beautiful," Beryl said as she put the flowers on the drainer. "Protea and roses, two of my favourites. You shouldn't have."

"It seemed the least I could do, after the scene I made on Friday. I feel so guilty, making such a fool of myself."

"It was perfectly understandable, Peter, after what you'd been through. And you didn't make a fool of yourself. Honestly, you didn't. But you haven't answered my question: how are you? Really?"

"Not brilliant, if I'm honest. Better, but, well…"

"Come on, let me put these in water and then get us those coffees, then we can take them through to the lounge and you can tell me there. I've been so worried about you."

The flowers in water, she soon handed him his coffee and led him back out into the entrance hall and through to a spacious and airy room. Beyond expensive-looking armchairs and a large sofa, the completely glazed far wall gave out onto a large and seemingly obsessively manicured garden.

"Take a seat," Beryl offered. "Get yourself comfortable and tell me how you really feel now. And how your first day at work's been."

"Better than I thought," he told her, once he'd sat in one of the armchairs. "There's nothing like the plight of others far worse off than yourself to put your own problems into perspective."

"You're going to be feeling tender still, Peter. Naturally, you are. It's only been three days." Beryl sat on the sofa facing him, her blond hair lustrous against the garden's greenery seen through the window behind her.

"I know," and Peter let out a soft breath. "But it just makes the thought of all those to come seem that much more daunting."

"Well, if there's anything I or Derek can do to help, you know you've only to ask. Even if it's just keeping you company. Speaking of whom, Derek shouldn't be long getting home now."

Peter put his coffee down on a coaster on a table beside his chair and inspected his hands. They seemed like someone else's, someone he'd once known but now barely recognised.

"I'm not giving up on Sophie, Beryl. I'm not," he quietly said, not daring to look at her. "I've thought long and hard over the weekend, and if nothing else has come of it, it's that I'm determined to see her again."

"But if she's—"

"I know it sounds crazy. It is, Beryl, my head tells me it is. But I can't let the only woman I've ever felt such strong…such strong *emotions* for slip through my fingers. Whatever it takes, for however short a time we can be together again, I have to try."

The fluttering wings of a goldfinch caught his eye, the brightly-coloured bird settling on an ornate array of feeders on a post not far beyond the window. He'd have seen the creature's presence as being as fleeting as he knew Sophie to be, had his obdurate determination not said otherwise.

"Ferdinando's story isn't over yet," he more told himself than Beryl. "There's more to it than I've witnessed so far. There has to be."

"You… You didn't tell me much on Friday morning, Peter. Not about Ferdinando, anyway. Do you think it'd help to do so now? To get it all—"

"She'll travel back there again, Beryl. I know she will. To find out what happens to him. She'll go back to pick up from where we left off, like last time. And I'm going to be ready and waiting for when she does. To jump aboard that express ghost train as it once more passes through my lounge."

A warm but doubtful-looking grin grew on Beryl's face. "But how will you know when to catch it?"

"Simple," he affirmed, smiling for the first time in days. "You remember, at my previous visit, the one Derek was there for, that the two days I spent with Ferdinando ran ahead of our own time here?" Beryl nodded. "Well, this last time, I spent a whole month there."

"A month? Jeez. You never said it'd been that long. And again, all over in an instant!"

"Thirty days, Beryl. Which'll put the passing of that next ghost train sometime during the early hours of Sunday, the seventh of November."

"And today's the…the eleventh of October."

"I know it's grabbing at straws, Beryl. I know it is. But it's a straw I'm determined to hang on to with all my might. A straw that might well carry me back into the arms of the only woman I've ever truly loved. And who, I now know with certainty, loves *me*."

34   HOPE SPRINGS ETERNAL

Like approaching Christmases when he was a child, Peter's days dragged by ever slower as the seventh of November drew nearer and nearer. Only the demands of his pressured profession gave him any real respite, as he willingly submerged himself in the frenetic and seemingly shorter hours that came with hospital life. He found himself spending more and more time there, time not spent at Beryl and Derek's going over and over the detail of his latest visit to the sixteenth century.

Right at the beginning, though, before he'd tell them anything, Peter had impressed upon them both not to reveal a thing of what would subsequently happen. He'd asked them to wait for his story to spell out why, and so, dutifully, they'd only listened. When he got to where he'd slipped into another part of Ferdinando's mind, his explanation of Sophie's subsequent alarm finally brought home the overwhelming need for their utmost caution.

"That's a bit of a bummer," Beryl had said at the time, "because I've been doing loads of research," at which she'd bit her lip and stared at him intently. But she, like Derek, had then promised to keep him completely in the dark.

In the little spare time these diversions gave him, he couldn't help but think of Sophie. Even in the few days since their parting, Peter's longing for her had grown immeasurably. That they'd never actually seen each other, and had only had the most fleeting of phantom contact, did, though, seem to beggar the intensity of his feelings.

Then he thought of those stories he'd heard of people falling in love over the internet, separated by thousands of miles and different cultures. But at least *they'd* been able to jump on a plane and finally get to meet each other in the very real flesh. The only opportunity Peter had was the outlandish ghost train and its guesswork timetable that ran through his lounge.

Eventually, the early morning when that train was once more due to appear finally arrived. On the Saturday night of the sixth of November, he, Derek and Beryl all sat sipping at their teas in Peter's lounge. And when his mock-Victorian longcase clock roundly chimed midnight, that seemingly unreachable Sunday morning at last began in earnest.

"Are you sure you're all set for this, Peter?" Derek asked.

Peter drew in a long and hopefully settling breath. "As I ever will be," he said, a slight tremble to his voice that didn't help.

"Sometime mid-afternoon, you reckon?" Beryl asked as she peered at the notes in her lap, as though to settle her own nerves.

"As best I can guess. His retainer's manor house in Newton-le-Willows, where Ferdy stayed that last night of the journey, was only about fifteen miles away. Some five hours' journey. As we'd started out late, he'd have returned here, at the inner gate, sometime around three or four o'clock. Three or four o'clock this morning, when you add in the twelve-hour difference."

"And where he'll come to pass," Derek said, "though the same space from where you started out with him."

"But...in which case," Beryl drew out, "if your theory's right, that a dream only ends when Ferdy next passes through that same space, then why didn't it end when he left here to visit that parcel of land he was buying? Or when they left on the journey down to Windsor?"

"Yeah, that bugged me for a while", Peter confessed. "Then I remembered he was on horseback on each of those occasions." He raised his gaze nearer the ceiling. "A saddle height above where I'd joined him when he'd been hurrying in on foot."

"Ah, I see. So, not the same space at all. But he did pass through the same space after his horse had gone lame and he'd walked it back, and the last time when he'd dismounted to stretch his legs."

"Exactly."

"But if that's the case, what if he never again walks through here but always rides?"

"I'm assuming that's what Sophie meant when she said they 'targeted' the hosts. There'd be no way they'd send her there without knowing she could get back."

Beryl's face dropped. "I damn well hope not, Peter. You don't want to be stuck there when... Well, stuck there for...for too long," and she avoided his eyes by again looking down at her notes.

As it got nearer the expected time, Peter remained in the room in readiness. Derek and Beryl occasionally left to make them all drinks, or Beryl to have a cigarette. But Peter knew he'd feel it when the ghost of Ferdinando was about to appear, for he remembered how the room had each time gone still just before, how the air had gained a sharpness to it.

But as it turned out, neither of those two things happened as first three o'clock rolled by, then four. By the time the clock had whirred and chimed five times, Peter's suspense had wound him as tight as one of the clock's springs. It was beginning to appear that Sophie's ghost train had, for some inexplicable reason, failed to sweep silently through his lounge once more.

When a first smudge of dawn light presently began to lift silhouettes of trees from the previously inky-black view through the windows, Peter finally took a deep breath and noisily exhaled.

"Looks like I was wrong, folks," he flatly announced, his resignation failing to unwind him. Beryl wearily lifted herself from her armchair and slumped down beside him on the sofa.

"I'm sorry, Peter," and she took his hand in hers. "And you'd pinned so much hope on it; it's not fair, I know. But we doublechecked we'd got the right date, and it's now way beyond the expected time. So, I'm afraid I have to agree. Clearly, Sophie didn't intend going back, after all."

"Clearly not," Peter glumly concurred, but then he shot her a suddenly buoyant look. "Not this time she didn't, no, but she has to at some point. Ferdy's story's not yet over; I can feel it. Secretary Cecil didn't strike me as the sort to give up so easily, and the look the Earl of Essex shot Ferdy in the throne room, well…" and Peter at last felt himself unwind.

He leaned away from Beryl, his gaze now darting back and forth between her eyes.

"But you know that already, don't you, Beryl? You've been digging into it; you said so yourself."

"I…"

"It's all right. You needn't tell me *what* happens, but you can answer me some general questions. Like: is there really more to Ferdy's story? Something that'd take Sophie back there to investigate."

Beryl slowly nodded.

"Something big?"

Again, she nodded.

Peter slumped back against the sofa and stared unseeingly across at Derek, at which the poor man clasped his hands together, nervously.

"And when does this…this *big thing* happen?" he asked, not moving his gaze from Derek.

"April. During April of the following year, fifteen-ninety-four, which ties in with something Sophie herself said."

"Sophie?"

"You said you'd asked her how old Ferdy's daughter Lady Elizabeth was, and that Sophie had told you 'seven years, four months and twenty-one days next April'. But then you said she'd brought herself up short, before she could say any more."

"Yes. That's why I made a point of remembering exactly what she'd said. April, eh? Early or late?"

"The first half; by their calendar. Latter half by ours. Do you want the exact dates I know about?"

"No. No, that should be enough."

"Enough for what, though?" Derek asked, and Peter started, as though he'd only just noticed him. But a smile soon steadily spread across Peter's face in reply, one that narrowed his eyes.

"I reckon they wouldn't subject Sophie to much more than the month we spent there last time," he told Derek. "So, if I can work in a month's leave of absence at the hospital, I can stake out my lounge from mid-March and be pretty sure of being here when the next ghost train passes through. I'll just need to be patient and watchful."

"And never leave this room," Derek suggested, a degree of incredulity in his voice that came over as sarcasm.

"We could help with that, though," Beryl was quick to say. "We could keep you supplied with food and whatnot. Keep you company for some of the time."

When Peter returned his gaze to her, the sparkle in her eyes gave him that last bit of confidence he needed. "You sure you wouldn't mind doing that for me? It's a lot to ask." Beryl's grin now carried the light from her eyes to the rest of her face.

"Of course not, Peter. Of course, we wouldn't," and she darted a brief but stern look at Derek. "We'd be more than happy to help. Wouldn't we, Derek?" at which her husband dutifully nodded.

35   A LETTER IN EVIDENCE

It soon became a rather restricted life for Peter. Despite the likely time for the reappearance of the ghost train being months off, when at home he found himself sticking to the lounge as much as possible. Just in case one came along earlier. And there he'd sit in his favourite armchair, watching television, half an eye on the far corner of the room.

Beryl and Derek periodically visited, sometimes just her. They tended to go over the record she'd kept of Peter's dreams, correcting or expanding as he thought back over what had happened. Beryl had kept on with her research, only mentioning things from Ferdinando's time once they'd safely passed in the corresponding march of their own.

Little seemed to be of any great significance to Ferdinando's future; his father's impressively grand funeral on the fourth of December being the most notable. But then Beryl mentioned something that took Peter aback.

"Only a few days before that, though," she guardedly told him, "Richard Hesketh was finally executed at St. Albans."

"Executed?" Peter whispered.

"And when on the scaffold, he named Sir William Stanley and others—although not Ferdinando himself—cursing the time he'd ever known any of them."

Peter stared at her for a good long while, then said, "The poor fool," before slowly shaking his head.

At another visit, a few days before Christmas and over a sample of some sloe-gin she'd put to steep in the Autumn especially for the festive period, Beryl mentioned a letter she'd recently come across. One from Ferdinando to the Earl of Essex.

Peter's ears had pricked up.

"You remember that land purchase at Woodvale near Parbold you said Ferdy had gone to see? Well, it seems it brought with it a bit of bad blood between Ferdy and some of his retainers living nearby."

"That doesn't surprise me. But why the letter to Essex?"

She passed him a sheet of paper. "That's what Ferdy wrote. It's clearly his reply to a previous letter from Essex. One I've not yet come across."

When he'd finished reading, Peter looked questioningly across at Beryl.

"I know it's not easy to follow," she said, "but it looks like Essex must have been standing up for the disgruntled retainers. They argued that the land had long been held in common, and that Ferdy's bailiff shouldn't have barred them from going on to hunt and hawk."

"But why would Essex want to support them?"

"Because they'd transferred their allegiance to him, that's why. They'd become *his* retainers, no longer Ferdy's."

"Ah, I see. Poor old Ferdy. That would've been a bit embarrassing for him."

"Reading between the lines and the highly cultured language, I think he was ticking Essex off for interfering in his own back yard."

"But again, why should he want to?"

"I don't know, and I'm having problems digging up anything else that touches on the incident. But at least that letter's some proof that Essex was gunning for Ferdy. Oh, and you may have also noted that Ferdy touches on the Queen having awarded him the Chamberlainship of Cheshire; as though Essex's earlier letter had implied it should have gone to him."

"Yeah, I noticed that."

"Salt rubbed into a wound still tender from when Ferdy told Cecil how Essex's literary group had been critical of the Queen."

"But awarding Ferdy the chamberlainship doesn't sound like the action of a queen who's pissed off with her new Earl of Derby."

"It went through the House of Lords only a few days after his dad's death, before Hesketh had even got to speaking of treason with him."

"Okay. So, so far it seems it's only Essex trying to make life difficult for Ferdy, unless you've uncovered any dirt on Secretary Cecil."

Beryl shook her head. "No, but I wouldn't read too much into that. I think it's just that Secretary Cecil was more thorough in sanitising the historical records. Helped, of course, by his being around a lot longer than Essex, which... Oh," and her eyes widened. "Sorry. I shouldn't really have said that, should I?"

"No, not really; I'll forget you did. But as to the two men: I know retainers were important back then—the men a lord could call upon to form his own private army when needed—but Cecil's concerns seem far weightier: worries about the succession and a possible Spanish invasion. Plus, knowing he's already attempted to set Ferdy up with a charge of treason, I'm still convinced it's got to be him behind whatever happens this coming April." Beryl looked as though she was going to say something in connection with this, but then clearly thought otherwise.

"True," she chose to say. "Unless Essex really did have an eye to forcibly taking the throne himself. There are hints of it here and there in the records, but nothing definitive." When Peter failed to respond, she tipped her head to one side and closely regarded him, her features clouding.

"I know Sophie's going to be on your mind a lot, Peter. She's bound to be."

He stared through her and sucked in his lips. "She is, Beryl," he eventually admitted. "Always. But it's what's keeping me going. It's what'll see me through my confinement here when it starts for real. Speaking of which, I can't get free until the beginning of the last week in March. I just hope that's not going to be too late."

"Hmm. Might be cutting it a bit fine, but then I've nothing really concrete to go on, so it's all guesswork, anyway. You can always keep an eye out beforehand, mind, during the evenings and your weekends off."

"Ha," and Peter raised his brows. "I'm finding it hard enough leaving the apartment, as it is. I'm like someone with OCD; I keep having to make a last check in here for ghosts." Beryl's face froze for a moment as she scoured his own for clues, but when he grinned, she laughed.

"As long as you don't go doublechecking that you've turned off the gas, as well," and Beryl's own grin pushed at the corners of her mouth.

Peter felt that same feeling he'd had before with Beryl, of there being a particular easiness between them. It held his gaze a little too long on her eyes. When she looked down at her hands, Peter coughed lightly.

"This sloe-gin's definitely got a kick to it," he said, putting his glass down. "So it should go down a real treat with your Christmas guests."

She angled a look at him through her lowered brows and smiled.

"Family?" he asked. "Friends? Both, I suppose. Have you a large—"

"There's quite a tribe on my side," she said, raising her gaze, "but not that many on Derek's. Why don't you join us on Christmas Day? Unless you've got—"

"Oh, I didn't mean it that way. I assure you. I wasn't angling to gate-crash. Honestly, I wasn't. And anyway, there's my newly developed OCD to consider. I might never be able to get out of the door by then."

"But I suppose you'll have your own family to see."

"Yes. Yes, I will. There's...er, a cousin or two and their families. And aunts and uncles, naturally.

And…er…"

Beryl's face softened. "You don't have anyone at all, do you, Peter?"

"Er… No, not really; not who're still in this country, anyway. Not that I've seen in recent years."

"Well, why don't you come along, then. We can always cater for another mouth," and her eyes fair danced enticingly before his lightened gaze. But then Peter ran that gaze past Beryl's expensive curls and into the corner of the lounge.

"Thanks. I appreciate the thought, but…" and he nodded that way.

"Well," Beryl said, not pushing it, "if you change your mind, the offer's always there," and she looked at her watch. "Is that the time? Derek'll be pilfering biscuits by now. I'd better get back; his cooking's atrocious."

When Peter came to show her out, she suggested she and Derek should arrange to see him on another day over Christmas, that she'd bring mince pies and crackers. And with that, she crunched her way across the gravel drive and towards the car park.

When he returned to the lounge, the apartment suddenly seemed very empty, his only company the singular scent of Beryl's perfume hanging hauntingly on the air.

36   STIR-CRAZY

Beryl and Derek spent most of the day after Boxing Day with Peter, beginning with a pleasant walk. It had been cold over Christmas, very cold, the coldest in over a hundred years, the Met Office had said, but a thaw seemed to be setting in. The surrounding fields and woodland lay dormant, patches of snow persisting against the drystone walls and in other places where the ground had been denied the sun.

Beryl had indeed come armed with mince pies and a box of crackers, and even better, a couple of bottles of good Champagne. Peter had found surprising pleasure in choosing the local supermarket's finest organic turkey, and had carved it with the skill of a surgeon. So, they'd spent the remainder of the day and the evening in the convivial warmth of his apartment.

Although they frequently spoke on the phone, it wasn't until the end of that milder February's first week that Beryl once more appeared at his door. It had been a brief call on her way to lunch with some of her girlfriends, but before she'd even got inside, her excitement was already bubbling over.

"Guess what?" she enthused as she removed her coat. "I might not have turned up Essex's first letter to Ferdy, but I've come across his subsequent reply to the one of Ferdinando's I showed you before Christmas."

"That's great," Peter said, hanging up her coat. "What's it say?" and they went into the kitchen, where he offered her coffee.

"Thanks, but I can't stay that long," she told him, sitting down at the counter. "But this letter I've found: it was sent on the seventeenth of January, and other than the usual feigned pleasantries, basically says: freemen are free to choose their own lords. He then goes on to opine that, seeing Ferdy's retainers were so pissed off with him and his father, it's hardly surprising they'd wanted to come over to him."

"He said that?"

"Not in so many words, no, but that's the general gist. Essex concludes by assuring Ferdy that, if he can reconcile himself to his lost retainers, then he'd be more than happy to butt out."

"Believing Ferdy could never do that, I assume."

"Actually, I don't think he really did. I reckon he was getting to the point where he hoped they actually *would* be reconciled."

"Oh. What makes you say that?"

"Well, I found this latest letter in the Talbot collection, currently held in the Lambeth Palace Library. And you'd never believe what else—"

"You've not been all the way down there, have you?" and Peter looked aghast.

"No, silly. They've been putting their stuff online.

But the thing is: they had some other interesting papers that belonged to the Earl of Shrewsbury."

"Hang on. What's the Earl of Shrewsbury got to do with it?"

"Essex sent a letter to his friend Gilbert Talbot, the seventh Earl of Shrewsbury—probably the most powerful earl in the country—asking him to adjudicate on who was in the right over this land issue, him or Ferdy. Essex enclosed copies of both letters for him to assess, hence why they got into his collection."

"And what did he decide?"

"Don't know. I couldn't find any more on it, but I did come across two things that might indicate the way it went: firstly, incredibly warm correspondence between him and Ferdy, the exchange of valuable gifts and the like; and secondly, evidence of a spat that soon ensued between him and Essex over an alleged traitor in Shrewsbury's own service. So, I shouldn't imagine it went Essex's way."

"But you don't know that for certain?"

"No. True. But having now read tons about Essex, it seems he was considered a bit impetuous, quick to take the side of those who considered themselves wronged or slighted in some way."

"Especially if it offered a way to get back at someone."

"Especially then. It's as though he thrived on being popular, regardless of the long-term cost to himself."

"So, you think Essex jumped in at the first opportunity? When he was either petitioned or after making it clear he'd be amenable to helping out, then found himself in a pickle over it?"

"The long and short of it: yes."

"Impetuous, you say. Whereas, we know Secretary Cecil to have been subtle, meticulous and incredibly astute. One who certainly played the long game. A game he'd be more than willing and able to see through into this coming April."

"Can't argue with that. But look, I have to get on. Can't have the girls waiting," and she got up, pecked him on the cheek and was soon gone.

In the weeks that followed, they tended to talk on the phone every few days, unless either Beryl or Derek could find time to visit. But at the start of the last week in March—the beginning of Peter's stake-out—she made a point of going with him on his weekly Saturday shop.

At first, she only made notes of his preferences, but was soon tut-tutting and making suggestions for a far healthier diet. Peter let himself be gently coerced, all too keenly aware of how much she would soon be putting herself out on his account.

By the time they got to his apartment and were unloading, the reality of his pending hermit existence had finally begun to hit home with Peter. Even Beryl seemed anxious, her usually sanguine manner veering towards irritability. This soon became more than apparent when she snagged her fingernail whilst taking one of the boxes from the boot of the car.

"Damn," she growled, shooting daggers at her torn nail, its normally immaculate manicure now ruined.

"Here," Peter said, "I'll take them in. Here's my keys; you open up and sort your nail out, as best you can," at which she snatched the keys from him and stormed off towards his apartment.

Once he'd got everything from the car to the

kitchen, Peter went looking for Beryl. They bumped into each other in the hall as she, still filing her one short nail, came out of the lounge.

"My God, Peter. It's like a student bedsit in there," and she laughed.

"I was aiming more for premier hotel room. You know, bed, brewing facilities and breakfast-in-bed. Although a toaster's the nearest I got to that last one."

"You've even got a minibar!"

"The drinks cabinet? It's always been in there."

"Oh. I've never noticed."

"I must've just left the cabinet doors open," at which he suggested they go back in.

"Though I must say, your bed doesn't look at all comfortable," she said as they did so, indicating the now largely duvet-obscured sofa. "Have you tried it yet?"

"Last night, and it was actually quite comfortable."

"You're not going to tell me you've a commode hidden in here somewhere, as well, are you?"

"Of course. En suite bathroom. Only the best of hotel rooms." Beryl's eyes grew wide. "Ha; only joking. Seeing as I can sense when a ghost's about to appear, I reckoned I could make it from the bathroom in time, even if my pants had to be around my ankles."

Beryl smirked and looked down that way.

"I take it you've managed to rescue that fingernail of yours, then?" he said to her distant grin.

"Hmm? Oh, no, not really, but it'll last until… Ah. Right. Sorry. About the strop, I mean. But I hate breaking a fingernail."

"I gathered," and he smiled in a way he hoped would convey a degree of understanding.

"You know, Peter," she said, angling her head this

way and that, "I could start envying Sophie." She leant nearer and kissed him lightly on his cheek. "Derek only ever offers me Superglue, never sympathy," and she laughed as she took a cigarette from its packet, waved it in way of explanation, winked, and slipped out to the yard.

When it came time for Beryl to leave, she stood in the lounge, amidst Peter's carefully arranged clutter. "Well, if you think you've got everything you need, Peter, I'll be off."

"I'm pretty sure I have. And thanks again, Beryl. For all your help."

"You're welcome, Peter. I just hope you don't go stir-crazy in here."

"There's the telly, the radio, books, and the magazines you brought. I think I'll be all right."

Beryl's brows briefly lofted. "Okay. In which case, I'll see you next Saturday with another week's supplies. But if I get a chance, I might pop over during the week. I'll see how things pan out."

"I'd appreciate that, but don't go putting yourself out. You're doing more than enough for me, as it is."

She smiled. "I'm actually enjoying it, and all this preparation does seem to have lifted your spirits. I hope it works out and you get to be with Sophie again."

After a peck on his cheek and a brief hug, she made for the door. "I'll see myself out. Oh, and your keys are on the mantelpiece. See you—"

"Just a minute, Beryl. I nearly forgot. Here," and he went and picked up the keys. "You'd best take these. They're my spare set." He held them out to her. "You can then let yourself in whenever."

"If… If you're sure," she said, gingerly taking

them in her hand.

"Means I won't have to leave this room to answer the door to you."

"Okay, then. Makes sense. Well, take care of yourself, Peter. And if it happens before I see you again, say 'Hi' to Sophie for me."

Peter nodded and put a brave face on it. "I've a better feeling about it this time."

For a moment, they stared at each other, then Beryl wrapped her arms about him, his own hesitantly doing the same about her.

She squeezed him, reassuringly, and whispered "Good luck" in his ear, then she was gone, the front door soon closing behind her.

His first week of captivity passed uneventfully and not at all unpleasantly. He soon found the radio his best companion, for, unlike reading or the television, it left him freer to watch out for his hoped-for next haunting.

Saturday saw Beryl once more at his apartment, wearing gloves this time as she brought in his supplies. When she took them off, he noticed all her fingernails now appeared immaculate.

She called again the following Tuesday, as they'd arranged on the Saturday, but her appearance three days later, on the Friday night, came out of the blue.

"I was just on my way home," she explained, having let herself in, "and thought I'd bob in and see you were okay."

"Bored," he admitted. "So, it's lovely to see you. You know, I've always been happy enough with my own company, but even I'm now getting hacked off with myself," and he laughed. "You've arrived just in time to stop me from beating myself up."

"Aw. Poor you," she mocked. "How about we raid your minibar for a snifter or two, eh? Ward off this damp, cold night's air."

"Brilliant idea," and Peter started sorting out their drinks. "It is the eighth of April today, isn't it? I'm beginning to lose track."

"It is. And a Friday—all day—so I'll be seeing you again tomorrow, as planned. By the way, last Saturday's order was okay for you, wasn't it? Nothing wrong or missing? Anything extra you've discovered you now need?"

Peter passed Beryl the particular whiskey he knew she liked. "No. Everything was perfect, thanks."

She took a large sip. "Ah, that hits the spot," and she swirled the spirit around in its tumbler. "I take it you've not yet been back to the sixteenth century." Peter resignedly drew in a deep breath, slowly letting it out through his partially closed lips.

"Nope. No sign of Sophie yet. But if it's the eighth of April now, then this coming Sunday's going to be the thirty-first of March, the start of Easter week, back in Ferdy's time. So, we're nearly into their first week of April, when your 'big thing' is due to happen."

"Try to be realistic, though, Peter. I'm worried you're getting your hopes up for something that may never happen. You don't know that Sophie's going to be going back for it; not really. And you don't really know why she has in the past. It's not that I'm…" but Peter's spine had begun to tingle, the air suddenly feeling still and sharp to his nose.

He peered over Beryl's shoulder, at the far corner of the lounge, seeing only shadows.

"Peter? Are you listening? You seem a bit…"

Then the hairs on the back of Peter's neck stood on end, and he peered more intently into the corner.

"Peter? Sophie's ghost train isn't about to…" but Beryl's eyes suddenly grew large and wild. "Behind you, Peter," she urged. "Behind you," and she spun him around before darting out of the way.

As he came to a stop, a face loomed startlingly large in Peter's vision. A flash immediately obscured it, a short, sharp pain shooting across his brow. Then the bailey of Lathom House lay before him, its great wall seemingly growing ever larger as he was swiftly carried outwards towards its gatehouse.

37   AN ILL WIND

"Sophie?" Peter called out in his mind, feverishly trying to sense her presence. "Are you here, Sophie?"

"Peter? How in the hell did you... I... I can't believe..."

By now, they'd already been carried well across the bailey, clouds scudding quickly across the sky above its great outer wall and gatehouse, which they were rapidly approaching. To either side of the stony track, the gusting wind scythed the long grass and buffeted their headlong dash.

"I knew you'd have to come back," Peter told her, but they'd now reached the gatehouse, the archway at the far end of its passage framing their shared vision.

Beyond it and to one side was an extraordinary sight. Suspended some four or five feet above the planks of the outer drawbridge thrashed all four hooves of a horse. Its terrified whinnying echoed down the passage towards them, freezing Peter's blood as they came to an abrupt halt.

"What the…" Sophie exclaimed, clearly just as stupefied.

Behind the horse, they could see a wagon lying at a slant down the short bank of the moat, its wheels and axles visible and resting against the edge of the bridge from where it had clearly slid, its shafts angled skywards. From these hung the panicked horse, its chest foam-flecked, its body twisted and grotesquely suspended from its straining harness like a broken marionette.

Cautiously now, Peter was carried into the shadow of the passage and through to its end.

A group of agitated men were gathered on the far side of the bridge, a pool of water spreading out from between their feet. Then Peter found himself on the exposed bridge itself, a gust of wind catching him as he was ducked clear of the thrashing hooves, past the perilously positioned wagon and on towards the men.

"What in God's good name's happened here?" a young man's voice sought, completely surprising Peter by seeming to come from between his own lips.

"Ah, Master Wardell," one of the men said as the group parted, revealing a short, stout and bedraggled man, his sodden hair and clothes streaked with slimy weeds.

"The miller, here," continued the speaker as he nodded at the dripping man, "says his horse shied at something in the moat as they were coming onto the bridge."

"Probably t'weeds, sir, blowing in t'wind," the miller spluttered, before coughing and spitting foul water into the pool at his feet. "This gale's gone and made 'er a bit skittish, like."

"But why haven't you been trying to get the poor creature down?" Master Wardell demanded, glancing up at the horse.

Seeing the whites of its eyes, stark against its dun-coloured face, dragged Peter's heart all the way down to Master Wardell's boots.

"We've only just managed to fish the miller out the moat, Master Wardell," another man proffered. "He were almost drowned by the time we got here, sir."

This drew Master Wardell's gaze to the moat, to its milky white stain now seeping out from the disgorged sacks littered about the upended and partly submerged wagon. As his gaze swung back to the men, it caught sight of two horsemen approaching at a gallop from out of the woods towards Newparke.

"Ah, thank the Almighty," he gasped; "Mister Doughtie'll know what to do."

The men all turned to look as another gust buffeted them and swung the haunches of the already distressed horse against the wagon. Most of the poor beast's plaintive whinnying was fortuitously swept away on the wind, through the rustling clatter of bulrushes at the edge of the moat.

"What's going on here, Simon?" the first of the riders to arrive called out, at which Master Wardell's voice shook with relief as he relayed what he'd only just learnt himself.

"In which case, come and take charge of my horse," the man instructed as the second rider drew up beside him. "I need a closer look."

"Watch you don't get crushed, Robert," his companion warned. "That wagon looks precarious."

"That I will, Mister Farington. Fear not." As Simon grabbed the bridle, Robert swiftly dismounted.

From Simon's mention of Mister Doughtie, Peter had been expecting one of the riders to have been

Michael, but clearly neither were.

"Whatever you do, keep yourself clear of that horse's hooves, lad," this Robert Doughtie whispered as he handed Simon the reins of his own.

Simon nodded. "I will, Mister Doughtie," but another gust blew, raising the tail of Robert's horse. Simon turned it about, muzzle into the wind, and nervously stroked its neck.

Mister Doughtie was soon issuing commands, for a drawing harness, lengths of rope and long, stout poles. A number of the men edged past the suspended horse and hurried through the gateway, swiftly about their errands.

"You're doing well," Robert quietly told Simon as he came beside him. "She can be a bit spirited, so keep her calm," and he raised the saddle-flap and undid the girth, smoothly lifting the saddle clear.

The man who'd been sent for the drawing harness soon returned past the wagon's now flagging horse, its constricted chest irregularly heaving as it fought to breathe. Before long, the harness was on Robert's mare, a rope strung between it and the wagon, about which men armed with long poles were now carefully positioned.

"Right," Robert said to Simon, "I'll take the reins now. You get yourself clear."

With the mare and the rope blocking his way off the bridge, Simon backed up towards the gateway, ducking beneath the suspended horse. But as Robert urged the mare forward and the rope went taut, rocking the wagon, a loud crack rang out.

Simon looked up.

A shaft had splintered, snapping as he watched in

horror. The unfortunate horse dropped a foot or so nearer Simon, then swung beneath the remaining shaft, its legs again thrashing out in panic.

Instinctively, Simon stepped back, but a gust of wind caught him and pushed him forward.

At a dull thud, loud in his ears, his neck jarred to one side. Then the world tumbled dizzyingly, a nauseating pain searing through his jaw as his cheek struck dirt-strewn timber, his breath forced from him.

For the briefest of moments as he lay there, Peter's world seemed suddenly calm and peaceful, until he gently slid from it into an all-enfolding darkness.

38   IN THE DARK

Only slowly did the utter blackness lift, and only faint and flickering the blood-coloured light that replaced it in Peter's vision. Sounds came, too: the bellow and whine of wind gusting across the head of a chimney stack; the roar it brought from the insistent crackle of a fire, mimicking the dull pain that throbbed proud of the burning sting he felt at Simon's neck.

Then Peter remembered.

"Sophie?"

Groggily, she answered, her words indistinct.

"Wake up, Sophie. Tell me what happened."

"I... I don't know, Peter. And, where are we? I can't see a thing," at which Peter felt her shift uncomfortably, but then still. "How... How did you know when to catch the ghost train, Peter?"

"I didn't, not exactly, and if it hadn't been for Beryl, I wouldn't have."

"Beryl?"

"Oh, the…wife of a colleague of mine. She was with me when…when Simon's ghost came through my lounge. Who is Simon, Sophie? Why aren't we in Ferdinando's mind?"

"Simon? Ah, yes. The target."

"Well?"

"He's the only one we could track with any certainty who'd enable me to get back again. We'd no name, just his movements."

"So you knew he'd get kicked by that damned horse?"

"No. No, I wish we had. It might've prepared me for the… Oh, Peter, that was ghastly. The poor thing. I wonder how it is."

"I'd be more concerned about Simon. You sure he does get back to the inner gate? So we can safely get away from here?"

"Positive. I've already told you: we tracked his movements, but only his passing through the gate. It's as far as we can see. But, Peter, I'm going to have to assume you can talk with him like you did with Ferdy, so I can't afford to tell you much."

The man himself then groaned, softly, and began to stir, but a hand gently yet firmly pressed against his chest.

"Try to keep still," came a voice as a shadow darkened Simon's closed eyelids. "You don't want to disturb that poultice wise-woman Agnes has diligently crafted for your neck."

"Poultice?" Simon groggily queried, then Peter realised the other voice had been that of Robert Doughtie, although noticeably softer and more solicitous than it had been at the drawbridge.

"You were lucky she was at the castle," he went

on to say. "She was just coming from tending to Mister Dudley's ague when we carried you in."

"Carried me?" and although Simon's eyelids flickered, they remained closed.

"You took a nasty kick from the miller's horse, Simon. To that softly silken neck of yours. Then you knocked yourself out when you fell. We must be thankful for God's providence that you didn't tumble from the bridge; the moat's deep at that point."

"I… I don't…don't remember," and Simon's eyes finally fluttered open.

Above him was Robert Doughtie's face, his worry barely masked by reassurance. Then Peter at last saw what had always been there, the family resemblance: a slightly younger version of Ferdinando's personal secretary, Michael Doughtie.

His expression, though, suddenly changed, chagrin darkening his features as he slowly shook his head.

"You foolish boy, Simon. Why didn't you get out of the way? Why did you have to stop beneath that damned horse?" but then his mouth set to a firm line. "Why didn't I think?" he berated himself. "How did I let my haste deafen me to my heart's own caution?"

He lowered his mouth to Simon's cheek, across which he delicately trailed kisses, until his lips fell full upon Simon's own.

An insistence, seemingly borne of relief, impressed a shared fervour into their kiss, one Robert soon fought to resist. Reluctantly, he drew away, composing himself as he sat more upright on the bedside stool.

Peter felt a smile suffuse Simon's face, his pain magically banished, at least for the moment. In a small voice of wonder, Simon mused, "That a tongue that can be so harsh at times, can be so tender against my own."

A hint of a grin ruffled Robert's once more carefully composed features.

"Will I live of my injury, Robert?" Simon stoically sought, slipping his hand from beneath the coverlet and warily touching the fabric of the poultice at his neck.

"You will, my treasure, for I've faith in Mistress Agnes's healing skills. You're too precious to me to believe otherwise."

"As he is to us both. Is he not, Mister Doughtie?" a man's voice said from the doorway, cutting its way to their ears through the dimly daylit room. Robert and Simon both snapped their gazes that way.

The cloaked figure of a substantial man stepped into the room, his boots clomping on its bare boards.

"Mister Halsall," Robert acknowledged. "I trust you're in good health, sir?"

"As I, too, wish of yourself, Mister Doughtie. And what I do so earnestly hope may soon truthfully be said of your valet. How is he?"

"No bones broken, sir, for which we must give thanks to our Lord."

"Indeed, we must. But having only just returned to Lathom, I was late hearing about the, er…the unfortunate incident at the gate."

Robert explained how Simon had been fortunate himself in only receiving the sharp edge of the horse's hoof, not the full force of its kick; that now he was awake, the concussion he'd taken from his fall had clearly left him with no lasting ill effect.

"He should be up and about in a day or so," Robert concluded.

"Good. I am relieved," Mister Halsall assured him, then told Simon, "We can't have you sent to stand before your maker's judgement in an untimely manner. Now can we, Mister Doughtie?" at whom he pointedly aimed a decidedly thin smile.

"Hopefully," Robert hastened to say, "it'll be in time for our move to the hunting lodge at Knowsley come Sunday. His lordship's already said how much he's looking forward to the sport to be had in the park there over the Easter week."

"During which your services to him will, I have no doubt, be most eagerly sought. To which matter, Mister Doughtie, my return brings with it some timely success. If you can bring yourself to forsake this fortunate lad, I'd like to discuss some matters with you in the privacy of my room."

Without further word, he strode out, the clomp of his boots echoing away down the passage.

Robert stared unseeingly at Simon for a while, his eyes narrowed, his fingers drumming silently on the coverlet beside Simon's thigh. When he began to bite at his lip, Simon tried to lift his head, to look Robert more in the eye.

"What business have you with Mister Halsall, Robert?" but he received nothing but a rebuke for having displaced his poultice.

"Come here, let me settle it back in place. We don't want that wound of yours going foul."

When Simon continued to stare at him, he dismissed his business with Mister Halsall as nothing more than routine household matters.

"Nothing for you to worry about, but I'd best go see him. Will you be safe on your own? You're not going to move and upset this poultice again, are you?"

Simon made to shake his head, but then answered that he'd keep as still as the ice on a winter's pond.

"Good. And make sure you do." Robert rose, a brief smile afforded Simon, then he was gone.

As Simon carefully settled his head into his pillow, Peter asked, "So, Sophie, what've these two to do with Ferdy's future?"

"I haven't the faintest idea about Simon. He's a total unknown. And there's not much I know about Robert Doughtie, other than he might've been a younger brother to Michael Doughtie, Ferdy's principal personal secretary."

"You're not just being wary of butterflies in what you're telling me, are you?"

"No. I'm being straight with you. It's just that there's so little known."

"But the Stanleys were an important family."

"Indeed they were, but all their household accounts for this period were supposedly destroyed during the Civil War, some fifty-years on from now. When Lathom House fell to the Parliamentarians."

"*Supposedly* destroyed?"

"If you ask me, I reckon it's more likely that Secretary Cecil was behind their destruction before then."

"Sounds like him. What about Halsall? Anything known about him?"

"Again, very little, and what there is doesn't really stack up. But as to the whys and wherefores, you can blame a butterfly if I don't say any more."

"I still find it hard to believe there's so little's known

about those in Ferdy's service. What about records kept outside the family papers?" and here, Peter thought back to Beryl's discovery of the Talbot collection.

"You've got to remember, Peter: there were about six hundred people in his service, a good number following him as he moved about between his various properties during the year. Only the really important ones got into any form of record. Most, like Simon, wouldn't even have warranted a footnote."

"Okay. I get the picture."

"Plus, we're entering an episode of Ferdy's history that's a real mess of competing viewpoints, shot through with misinformation and skulduggery. For which we're going to have to keep our wits about us if we're to see through to the truth."

"The truth? The truth about what...exactly?"

"About... About what's really going to happen over the next three weeks. What else?" at which Peter remembered something Beryl had said when she'd warned him not to get his hopes up: that he'd no real idea why Sophie should be investigating Ferdinando's life. Peter's thoughts then seemed to veer off of their own accord, disturbingly along avenues they'd never before trod.

39   SALUTARY REFLECTION

A lad of some sixteen years turned up not much later, telling Simon that Mister Doughtie had sent him to sit with him until he could get back. Simon clearly knew the youth, whose principal interest seemed to lie in what had happened at the gate that morning.

"Heard the miller's horse got clean away once they'd cut it free of the wagon," the lad told Simon. "Ran straight into the forest in fright, it did. Despite Mister Farington chasing after it on his own horse."

Peter heard Sophie let out a sigh of relief.

"I'm glad to hear it came through the ordeal unharmed, Thomas," Simon said.

"That's charitable of you, what with the kicking it gave you," and Thomas choked back a laugh.

"Did the miller manage to catch it?"

"Not the last I heard, although Mister Farington sent half a dozen to assist him. Though I don't think they've got back yet. Hey, but you're going to have to keep still; that poultice of yours has slipped."

Whilst Thomas rescued it, Simon asked, "You don't happen to know where Mister Halsall's been, do you?"

"Mister Halsall? No. Why? Has he been away?"

"Got back today. He was here earlier, wanting to speak with Mister Doughtie. It's just that he seemed concerned about *me*."

"About you?"

"Hmm."

"He's not usually concerned about anyone but his lordship, especially not us lower servants. Here, just lift your head a bit; I need to tuck this in. It's a pity I can't tie it round your neck."

"What? Like a hangman's noose?" at which they both laughed.

When their conversation presently drifted into more mundane matters, Sophie very quietly said, "Peter?"

"Yes, Sophie?" he replied as quietly, wary of her tone.

"You know when we parted last time? When I… When I said I…I loved you?"

Peter could find neither the courage nor the words to answer.

"Well, it was wrong of me. I shouldn't have," and he felt the strings binding his hopes together begin to unravel.

"Because… Because you didn't really love me?" he finally managed. "Is that it, Sophie?"

"No. No, I… I did… I do. What I meant was that it wasn't fair to tell you; wasn't fair on either of us. We've no future together, Peter. You can see that, surely? Once these three weeks are over, I won't be coming back. Not this way. We're moving on to new sources. This is my last journey through your lounge, so we can't ever be together again, Peter. Not ever."

Although despair urged him to deny it, Peter knew full well she was right. He'd known it all along, but that stubbornness of his insisted he held out hope. But what hope, he couldn't begin to imagine.

"But…we have these three weeks at least, Sophie. Isn't that worth—"

"It'd only make it worse in the end, Peter. It would; I know it would. And that'd be too hard to take. Don't you see? Fate's ruled it out, and Fate can't be argued with."

"But you still love me?"

Sophie didn't answer at first, although Peter could sense her nearness, as though she yearned to touch, perhaps to console him; or herself.

"I understand, Sophie," it broke his heart to say. "I understand. But it won't lessen my love for you."

"Don't, Peter. Please. Don't."

"I'm sorry, but I can't lie. Not to you, Sophie. However kind it might be to us both, I still can't deny it. I'll always love you, come what may."

It was late in the day, long after Simon and Thomas had exhausted their chitchat and gossip, that Robert returned with a young boy bearing a platter laden with food.

Thomas shot to his feet.

"Put it on the coverlet," Robert instructed the boy before going to stand over Simon. "You may go now, Thomas," he said, before silently gazing down on Simon until they were alone at last.

"How are you?" he asked, a distance to his voice.

Simon searched Robert's features before

answering that he felt much better. "Well enough to go with you to the Knowsley hunting lodge on Sunday," he told him, a hopefulness in his voice.

"Yes," Robert seemed to say more to himself than Simon. "Yes, better you're close by. Well," he then said, lightening his voice, "you'd best get stuck in to this food," at which he moved the platter onto Simon's lap once he'd shuffled himself more upright.

"I see your poultice is staying put," Robert noted. "Must be scabbing, which is a good sign."

After a few mouthfuls, and with Robert remaining motionless over him, Simon swallowed hard.

"I'll… I'll get out of your bed, Robert, if you wish to sleep now. I can eat this on the stool." Robert seemed startled, as though he'd been miles away.

"Oh, no, Simon. You stay where you are. It's easier to tend to you there. When I'm ready to put my head down, I'll use your truckle bed."

"But—"

"And I'll have no argument. Your need is greater; your care more important at present." He went around the bed to the stool, where he sat and silently watched Simon eat.

"You could always slip in later, when all's gone quiet," Simon presently and tentatively suggested. "Like I've often done with you," and an inviting smile spread across his lips. Although Robert's eyes appeared hollow, he too smiled, but it soon slipped from his face.

"It's bad enough keeping that poultice in place when it's just you in the bed, so… No, the truckle bed will be comfortable enough, I'm sure. Now, you get that meal into you. It'll do you good."

Whilst Simon spooned more of the food into his mouth, Peter noticed Robert hunch forward on his stool, his hand slipping surreptitiously into his jacket.

He half-removed something that glinted in the dying daylight that was now fast draining from the room, about which Robert's gaze then flitted. It finally came to rest on an unlit candle standing on a small, simple table under the window. His hand then slipped back inside his jacket and he slapped his thigh, commenting on how quickly the daylight was fading.

"I'll go light the candle," he said, and went to pick it up. "Try get some sleep when you've eaten. If you do, I'll be careful not to wake you when I get back."

By the time Robert returned with the lit candle, Simon was lying down again, his eyes closed. That Peter could see the candlelight flickering across Simon's eyelids, and hear Robert quietly moving about in the room, suggested he was only feigning sleep. Indeed, when the truncated scrape of a table leg briefly filled the room, Simon half-opened one eye.

At first, Peter couldn't work out what he was seeing, then realised the candle, once more on the table, lit Robert's arched back beneath it. Knelt beside the table, his form obscured whatever it was he was doing.

"Robert?" Simon quietly asked, startling Robert's head up against the edge of the table.

"What… What is it, Simon?"

"Why are you—"

"I've just dropped something. And I can't see a damned thing in this light. Never mind. I'll find it in the morning," and after a few long moments of delay, he got to his feet.

"I'd hoped not to wake you," he said. "You go back to sleep. I just need to undress, then I can do the same myself."

"But you'll need someone to undress you. You can't do it yourself."

"I can do most of it, Simon. You stay in bed. I'll come over to you when I need to."

When it came to undoing the sleeves of his shirt, Robert sat on the edge of the bed whilst Simon untied the bows. As the last one came free and Robert was about to stand, Simon slipped his hand to Robert's neck, kneading what looked like knots in the muscles there.

"Is all well, Robert? It's just that you seem a bit cold since you got back from seeing Mister Halsall."

At first, Robert only stared at the candle, his profile picked out by its mellow light. Then he lowered his head for a moment before raising his gaze to Simon.

"It's what happened to you this morning. What nearly...nearly came of it. Something that doesn't bear thinking about. What's made me realise how much you really mean to me, that's all," and Robert drew his lips to a reassuring smile.

"It's why I insist you stay in my bed tonight, my sweetest one. To make sure you heal properly. For I now know I'd do anything, anything at all, to keep you from coming to harm."

In the ensuing silence, they gazed at each other, Robert's mouth all the while steadily firming to a more resolute smile.

40   PALM SUNDAY

The following day, the Saturday, saw Simon more intent on getting out of bed. Before going about his own business for the day, though, Robert forbade him to get up until Mistress Agnes had been to assess his wound.

She came mid-morning, her face lighting up at what she found.

"Ay, but the vigour of youth," she exclaimed as she peered at his neck, and then she chortled to herself. "I'll just mix up some lotion to stop the scab breaking, which you'll apply every three hours; you hear? And no forgetting, otherwise it'll weep. And who knows what nastiness'll get into it then."

"If I promise, can I then get back to my duties, Mistress Agnes?" She puckered her lips and stared at him.

"Nothing strenuous, mind. No heavy lifting," to which he enthusiastically nodded. "Then I don't see why not," and he beamed a huge smile at her.

When, not long after, he reported to Mister

Farington, the man looked decidedly sceptical and refused him any work that day.

"Why don't you go get everything you can ready for tomorrow for Mister Doughtie? In your present state, Master Wardell, I reckon it'd be better done today, and thereby in less haste."

Lathom House seemed busy as Simon returned to his shared rooms, where he reluctantly remained until the evening meal in the great hall. Sitting some way down one of the lower tables, he only got distant sight of Robert. The man sat at the far end and nearest the high table, where Ferdinando and his extended family had earlier been seated with their guests for the evening.

The food was Lenten in its plainness and comprised fewer courses. But the merriment and conviviality seemed just the same, Simon sitting amongst friends and enjoying their good humour; although much was made of his injury and how it had come about.

At the end of the meal, he couldn't help but join in with the other kitchen servants: clearing the trestle tables and mopping them down. But when it came to folding and stacking them against the wall, Mister Farington came over and told him off.

Bowing his head in deference, when he raised his gaze, it was Robert who stood before him. He looked somewhat displeased, though he said nothing, other than to take a lit candle to their rooms.

"Seeing we've to be up early for the Palm Sunday service in the chapel, it's best we get an early night," he said, before going off in search of Mister Farington, now talking with his lord and ladyship.

Simon took down a candle from a wooden box beside the great fireplace and lit it from the hearth, shielding its flame as he returned to their rooms. There, he applied some more of Agnes's lotion. But as he did so, his gaze absently fell on the table beneath the window. He put the lotion aside, wiping his hands on his hose, and went over, soon on his hands and knees.

He found nothing on the floor, however much he peered and groped, although some dust and flakes of stone lay in a small pile beneath a gap in the wall at the back. Simon was just reaching to poke a finger in when the door opened.

"I found it this morning, Simon," Robert told him.

"Ah. Good," Simon shot back, his voice rather muffled from where he knelt.

"You can undress me now, before I wash. Then I'll reclaim my bed, seeing you're so clearly back to your usual rude health."

And so it went, Simon presently rolling out the truckle bed from beneath Robert's, in which, after snuffing out the candle, he was soon wrapped against the cooler night air.

Sunday morning, before the sun had yet struck even the highest roofs and towers of Lathom House, found Simon quietly following Robert through its convoluted passages to the chapel. Once down its steps and inside, Peter recognised it as where Ferdinando's father had been laid out not six months before.

Now, though, it blazed in the light of dozens of candles. It was also crammed with gentry and their wives and children, seated on pews towards the front, many of whom Peter recognised. Behind them and even more close-pressed sat the Stanley family gentleman-servants, their own personal servants making up the rear, and where Simon went and sat.

At the far end of the chapel, clergymen stood attendant before a branch-adorned altar, on which the crucifix stood draped in a purple cloth. The clerics waited patiently, long after seemingly the last of the congregation had entered and were all finally gathered together in reverent silence.

Eventually, they drew themselves more upright, their eyes now intent upon their lord, the fifth Earl of Derby, as he and his close family solemnly entered the chapel. Amongst them, for Peter, were some familiar faces: Alice, of course, and her three daughters, Uncle Edward, and the elderly Jane Halsall and her own son and daughters.

For the first time, Peter found himself near enough to the Earl for a shiver to run down his spine. From all the time he'd spent within the man's mind, almost as the man himself, seeing him from the outside felt decidedly unreal.

As the Earl's party passed between the congregation, it gave Peter a brief opportunity to appraise him properly. Framed by wavy, shoulder-length auburn hair and a high-styled quiff, his narrow, softly featured face was on the pretty side of handsome. His broad-set eyes seemed warmer than their grey colour might have suggested, his easy gaze looking out from beneath roundly-arched brows. A narrow, noble nose shaded a goatee beard, neatly trimmed to a sharp point, and his almost pursed lips glistened, plump and naturally red. A dark mole on the forehead above his left eye finally marked him out.

Upon the Earl's arm came his wife, Countess Alice, short and pretty, dark-haired and formally dressed. Behind them stepped their three daughters, each in diminutive versions of their mother's adult finery. Long-legged Uncle Edward came next, his dead brother's commonly accepted mistress, Jane, leaning heavily upon her own son's arm, her daughters in their stately wake.

Then they'd passed, without a single sideways glance, only a nod of acknowledgement to their vicar as they made their way to the front pews. Once the party had settled themselves in, and with little further delay, that day's Palm Sunday service at last began— all two hours of it.

At its end, Simon rushed back to their rooms. There, he hurriedly put together the last of his and Robert's personal effects, soon packed and taken down to the inner bailey. They were loaded onto one of a dozen or so waiting packhorses.

Back in their rooms, he packed the few items they'd need on the journey into a shoulder bag, and sometime later and wearing a travelling cloak, was once more in the inner bailey, bag in hand.

A different line of horses met him this time, held at the head of which was what Peter recognised as Ferdinando's unmounted dapple-grey stallion. Mounted on a horse just behind sat Robert's brother, Michael Doughtie, Robert himself much further down the line.

Silently, Simon stood and waited to be noticed, for beside Robert and likewise mounted, another gentleman was in the middle of telling him about the damage the storm had left behind.

"That big tree by the smithy in Newburgh came down, so Joseph was telling me. Says it went clean through its roof."

"Aye, I'd heard," Robert said. "And Mister Farington told me last night that one had come down across the Ormskirk road, halfway down Greetby Hill. And of a wall that had collapsed in Westhead."

"Not heard of anyone being hurt yet, though, thank the good Lord Jesus. But let's pray there's nothing blocking our road to Knowsley, eh?" At this point, Robert at last acknowledged Simon's presence.

"Ah, Master Wardell. Everything tended to, I trust?"

"It is, Mister Doughtie. I've all you'll need on the way, here in my…" but Simon's gaze had been drawn to Robert's hand, which the gentleman had leant towards and briefly touched, to draw his attention.

"By the way, Mister Doughtie," the man quietly said, ignoring Simon, "have you heard the rumour?"

"Rumour?"

"That Lady Alice," he said, yet more quietly, "may be with child again?" to which Robert only shrugged.

The gentleman laughed. "I must commend you for your loyal discretion, Mister Doughtie; for I know your privileged position must have afforded you some better knowledge, certainly more so than any amount of hearsay."

"Well," he said more loudly when Robert didn't respond, "I sincerely hope it's true, and that they're favoured with a boy-child at long last. A strong and healthy one, eh?"

"Please. Mister Doughtie?" Simon at last steeled himself to interrupt.

"Hmm? What is it, Master Wardell?"

"Your ring, sir. His lordship's gift?" and Robert looked down at his hand.

"Ah. How remiss of me," he said, a seeming absence of surprise in his voice. "I took it off to scrub away a stubborn ink stain. But it wouldn't do to have his lordship think I'm eschewing his noble token of trust; now, would it? It's only in my rooms. I won't be long," and he dismounted, handing his horse's reins to Simon. "I'll hazard our lord will be delayed a while longer yet by her ladyship," at which the other gentleman raised an eyebrow.

"I'll run and get it for you, Mister Doughtie," Simon offered.

"There's no need. A stretch of the legs won't go amiss before our journey. And anyway, I put it in a place of safekeeping, somewhere you won't know about, which is why it was overlooked." Robert pressed the reins more firmly into Simon's hand and made his way back into the house.

It wasn't long before he returned. Simon handed him his horse's reins and was dismissed to carry on down the line. Near the back, he came to a young horse-groom, patiently waiting with a finely-boned piebald mare. Once in the saddle, Simon just happened to look down the line of horses when he caught sight of the arm of Robert's riding jacket, at which his eyes narrowed to slits as he frowned.

Even Peter noticed the stain: a smudge of dust, its hue not unlike the pile Simon had come across whilst groping beneath the table.

But just then, Ferdinando came down the steps from the house and across to his mount. Upon his arm he carried a hooded hawk, its wings outstretched then fluttering to keep its balance. Once settled in his saddle and the bird now calm, he spoke to the same officious-looking man Peter remembered having been there at their departure for Windsor.

The stiff-backed man stepped back and diligently surveyed the line of riders, nodding in response to the raising of hands. He then bowed his head to the Earl, who urged his horse forward at a leisurely walk. And with this, their party departed upon that early spring day, snaking its way out from the castle and south towards Knowsley.

41   A WEEPING WOUND

Their journey proved unhindered by the aftermath of
the high winds, getting them to a westward turn off
from the highway by early-afternoon.

Here, they passed through an arched stone
entrance and into the extensive spread of what was
clearly wooded parkland. It gave an eerie stillness to
the final leg of their ride, during which they met not
another soul.

Within half an hour, they'd come to a low rise
amidst the park's largely flat land, upon which stood
a substantial two-storey, red-stone manor house
surmounted by tall, twisting chimneys. To the north
of this and higher up the rise, rose a tall but narrow
connected chapel, its soaring Gothic east window
staring down upon their approach. Beyond these, two
spire-topped towers could just be seen standing
proud at the rear. But when it became clear that this
was their journey's end, it surprised Peter.

For a hunting lodge, he'd been expecting something

considerably smaller. From the number of windows, he reckoned the house must have had a good dozen rooms to the front alone. And when they eventually came to the rear, he guessed at probably more there, all looking down onto a courtyard surrounded by stabling and the wing from which the two towers rose.

In contrast to their peaceful ride through the park, the place soon became a purposed melee of men, of their own party and those already at the house. In amongst it all, Simon had only just reached for a pannier to take in when Robert intervened.

"You can carry the shoulder bag, but that's your lot, Master Wardell. Mistress Agnes told me all about your promise."

"Very well, Mister Doughtie. As you wish."

"See Mister Farington for where we're to bed down," which Simon did, soon directed to one of the second storey rooms at the rear. There he came across a young man of roughly his own age, arranging panniers against a wall.

"Mister Doughtie asked me to bring yours up," he told Simon, pointing to two of them.

"I'm bound by ties of gratitude, Randle, though I'd have preferred to have done it myself if they'd have let me."

"In which case, Simon, you're indebted to me."

"Duly noted. So, we're to share with you and Mister Smith, then," but here, he looked around at the small bare room. "There's no one else, is there?"

"No. Just the four of us, not that we'll spend much time in here, not now his lordship's out of sight of the Church. It won't be just the hunting and hawking he'll be enjoying in his privacy, you mark my words;

Lent or no Lent. Have you seen how much wine we've brought down with us?"

"Aye, we've all noticed how his lordship's taken to drinking a bit more since becoming Earl, but I don't think Mister Doughtie'll be overly enthusiastic. He's not a big drinker."

"What? His lordship's waiting-gentleman and cupbearer doesn't himself imbibe?"

"He'll take a little, but not to excess. He likes to keep his wits about him."

"Sometimes, I wish Mister Smith was the same. Getting him undressed when he's in his cups ain't easy, I can tell you," and the two young men laughed.

The remainder of the day was spent settling in: pallets on which to sleep stuffed with clean straw and brought in to the bedchambers, covered with sheets and coverlets, and the kitchens geared up for the now swollen household numbers.

It seemed the Earl had spared little time in starting on the wine they'd brought, for Robert was only infrequently seen. Simon would sometimes catch sight of him carrying bottles from the cellars, where they'd earlier been lain, up to his lordship's apartments at the front of the house. Simon and Randle—whose own master, Mister Smith, was also with their lordship—could therefore both relax. They found themselves at rare leisure, until the next mealtime at least.

"Well, it is the beginning of Easter Week, is it not, Simon?" Randle had said as he'd looked out onto the courtyard below.

"The end of the week, and Lent will be over," Simon had returned. "Oh, indeed; and I can't say how fed up I am of dried fish and dry bread," at which they'd both heavily sighed.

The following morning, first thing and not long after sunrise, the Earl had taken a small band of his gentleman-servants out into the park to go hawking. With Robert being one, Simon had made his way to the kitchen, where he'd cautiously joined Randle in its various menial tasks.

He'd earlier carefully applied Mistress Agnes's lotion to his neck, pleased the scab had remained unbroken. But after an hour or so, Peter felt something trickling down Simon's neck, which he hoped was sweat. Simon's dab at it revealed blood on his fingertips, evidence the Master of the Kitchen happened to notice and which justified him chasing Simon from his domain.

Having mopped his wound and applied more lotion, Simon wandered out to the front of the house and leant on the wall of its terrace, from where he scanned the parkland below. Although a little overcast, a hazy sun suggested to Peter that their midday meal shouldn't be that far off. Just as he was thinking this, Simon's gaze found what it must have been looking for.

In the near distance, above open grassland between two arms of woodland, a hawk hung hovering—but not for long. It plummeted like a stone, straight towards the bounding form of an unsuspecting hare, the creature's ears angling to and fro as it darted this way and that. Then it vanished beneath a tent of outstretched wings, into which the hawk's head repeatedly stabbed.

Horses appeared from the woodland, the Earl's

dapple-grey stallion galloping ahead, his lordship bent over its head, urging it on. Soon they were about the hawk and its enfolded prey, the Earl leaping from the saddle and swiftly intervening.

Once the bird had been hooded and was back on the Earl's arm, the dead hare dropped into a servant's shoulder bag, the hawking party remounted and set off towards the house. Before long they'd climbed the rise and had come before its door. The Earl dismounted, patted his horse's neck and handed its reins to one of his servants. Robert and the other gentleman-servants did likewise, all following his lordship into the house.

As grooms led the horses away to the stables, Simon stared back out across the park towards the far distant Pennine Hills. After a while, he heard footsteps determinedly approaching from behind. When he turned and straightened, he found Robert bearing down on him, still in his hunting clothes, a face like thunder.

"What did you promise?" he growled, his face now flushed. "What do you mean by setting yourself to toil in the kitchen? Eh, Master Wardell? When you'd expressly told me you wouldn't—"

"But, Mister—"

"And what did I tell you earlier about saving that neck of yours?"

"Saving… Saving my neck?" Simon queried, his eyes widening in alarm. Mister Doughtie stepped back a pace, his mouth dropping open.

"What?" he stammered, then shook his head. "No, I didn't mean… I meant to say: saving that wound of yours."

"Oh. I see," and Simon let out a long-held breath. But Mister Doughtie stepped forward, lowering his voice, menacingly.

"The Master of the Kitchens has just told me you were in there doing all manner of tasks for him. You're not about to deny it, are you?"

"No, Mister Doughtie. I did... I did do a little light work for—"

"Which brought a bleed to your wound, did it not? What *were* you thinking? The neck, Simon, as you well know, is not a good place for foulness to...to find...find a...find a home," he finally spluttered before his voice was stolen from him.

"I'm truly sorry, Mister Doughtie," Simon said in a small voice, seemingly impaled by Robert's intense stare. "I... I won't do it again. I promise. It's just that I hate...hate being...being idle..." but Robert's eyes were now glazed over with tears.

When some of those tears broke free, and when Simon raised his hand to brush them away, Robert shuddered, as though someone had walked over his grave. He then averted his face, his whole body seeming to stiffen, before he turned on his heel and stormed back towards the house.

"What the..." Simon barely breathed as he stared after Mister Doughtie's fast retreating back.

42   THE SUPERIOR WEAPON

"**A**h, so here you are," Randle said as he burst into their shared room, startling Simon from gazing out of the window. For some time, he'd been watching a horse being groomed, down in the courtyard. "Are you all right? You look a bit… Well, lost."

"Eh? Oh. Er, no. No, I'm quite content, Randle."

"It's not your wound, is it?"

"No, that's… Well, maybe a little. Its throbbing's a bit wearing, that's all," which intrigued Peter, for now it hardly seemed noticeable.

"Here; let's have a look," at which Simon reluctantly held his collar away from his neck.

"Well, it doesn't look angry. I suppose all you can do is rest it the best you can, although maybe you ought to find something to take your mind off it. Anyway, I've only popped back for my knife," which item he took from a bag beside his pallet, tossing it into the air and expertly catching it by its handle. "I'll have to get back to the kitchen. See you later."

When he got to the door, though, he stopped. "Is… Is Mister Doughtie all right?"

"Er, yes. As far as I know. Why?"

"It's just that Mister Smith sought me out in the kitchen earlier and said he seemed a bit tetchy and wondered if I might know why."

"No. He's been no different with me. Maybe Mister Smith's annoyed him somehow," at which Simon hastily went back to looking down into the courtyard, this time chewing at his lip.

"That's what Mister Smith wondered, but he can't for the life of him think of anything he's done." When Simon didn't respond, Randle concluded, "Oh, well. Given your…*closeness*, it's likely just him fretting about your wound," and then he was gone.

Earlier, the Earl had embarked upon an afternoon of hunting, clearly enjoyed so much that it was almost dark by the time they returned. Simon happened to be passing through the entrance hall when they came in. He bowed his head as his lord swept by without a word. But as for Mister Doughtie, Simon fixed him with an imploring look.

Robert faltered in his stride, a surreptitious glance at the others as he stood aside and let them carry on. When they were alone, Robert briefly lowered his gaze to the floor.

"Have you something for me, Master Wardell?" Simon waited until Robert had lifted his gaze once more.

"Only my apologies, Mister Doughtie. Disregarding your wishes was entirely unforgiveable. I should have—"

"Simon," Robert barely said above a whisper, checking to see they were still alone, "it's not you

310

who should apologise. You must forgive me my earlier outburst. It wasn't fair. But…" He glanced after where the others had gone. "I can't delay. His lordship will be crying out for a drink. We'll talk when we can, eh?" but his tentative smile quickly slipped from his face as he hurried on down the hall.

For a split-second, Simon stared at the empty space where Robert had just been, then swung his stare to follow him. Peter was sure his attention centred on the Earl's gift of a ring. Previously, it alone had adorned Robert's hand, but now it had an equally large and ornate companion.

That evening, as on the previous, Simon's injury had kept him from waiting on the table in the great hall. He'd eaten his meal with the other servants, after the Earl and his gentleman-servants had finished theirs. So, he didn't see Robert again until going up with him to undress him for bed. Unfortunately, Mister Smith and Randle went up at the same time, leaving them no privacy at all.

The next three days were spent in much the same way. On the Thursday, though, Simon did get to be in Robert's presence, if only as one of those waiting on his lordship's table in the evening. Now considered well enough, he stood with the others for much of the time, off to one side.

"Did you see how cleanly I brought down that last deer?" the Earl boasted at one point, his voice a little slurred. "The arrow clean through its chest to its heart," at which he sat back in his chair at the head of the table, goblet in hand, and peered rather uncertainly at the dozen or so men before him.

"I've not seen better, my lord," Mister Smith

rejoined, his ruddy face beaming. "Not in all my hunts. Patent mastery of the bow, I'd say." The others slapped their hands on the table in agreement. "Though... I still contend better can be achieved with a musket," to which they all groaned.

"Tell him again, Michael," the Earl said in exasperation. "Tell him why the bow remains superior; as if you haven't had cause to a hundred times already," and he slowly but unsteadily shook his head. Michael Doughtie raised his eyes to the heavens as he drew in a deep breath.

"Because, Mister Smith—"

"I'm well aware of your argument, sir; and yours with respect, my noble lord; but I still contend it's wiser to bring a beast down in one fell swoop than risk having to chase it once it's injured; especially a boar. And especially if you don't want the meat disfiguring."

"And have all the game within earshot of its powder sent scattered at large?" Michael challenged. "The hunt then becoming nothing but a drawn-out chase after fleeing game for the next hour?"

"Nay," Mister Smith persisted, then launched into an argument with which they each seemed all too familiar. During this, the Earl caught Robert's eye, indicating his wine goblet.

"There's still some of the same bottle, my lord," Robert explained as he rose. "Or would something sweeter be more to your liking now? There's the Earl of Shrewsbury's gift from Christmas."

"Hmm," the Earl scowled. "I must say: the Queen giving Essex the monopoly on the duty of such wines after Leicester's death in eighty-eight has somewhat soured my taste for them."

A hint of a smile came to Robert's lips, which the Earl clearly read, a grin growing on his own.

"A foolishness on my own part, I know, Robert; cutting off my own nose. But I do object to adding any more revenue to that man's coffers."

When the argument amongst the others briefly flared up, distracting the Earl, Robert stared across at Simon, the tip of his tongue between his now tightly drawn lips.

Simon couldn't help but smile coyly back, but when the furore subsided, Robert turned once more to the Earl.

"But, my lord, on this occasion it's already been paid by the Earl of Shrewsbury, so it's well beyond your own coffers now. Is it not?" The Earl's grin grew broader, then he clapped Robert's arm.

"Your tongue, my dear fellow, has shown itself likely as sweet, if not sweeter, than the wine may prove itself to be. So yes; uncork one and be damned, I say," at which he pushed his goblet towards Robert.

"In which case, my lord, I'll firstly clean this of its previous charge, the better to savour the next."

As Robert took the goblet to a sideboard, the Earl commanded silence before asking the table, "So, has the man seen sense yet, eh? Well, has he? Has Mister Smith finally accepted the rightness of bow over musket?" and in emphasis, he slapped his hand on the table, catching the edge of a bowl that spilled messily to the floor.

Simon and the other waiting servants rushed to assist, the Earl heartily swearing as he shook remnants of food from his hand. In all the kerfuffle, no one it seemed but Peter noticed Robert calmly but carefully carry the goblet back, where he stood with it until it could be safely placed on the table before the Earl.

As Simon dried his lordship's hand, having just washed it clean, the Earl reached out his other to the goblet. He took it up and swiftly swallowed most of its sweet contents. Then he turned to Simon, holding the young man's gaze a little waveringly in his own.

"Without question," Ferdinando assured him, taking his hand from within the towel and unsteadily holding his finger up in front of Simon's nose, "for the kill, young sir, the bow's the superior weapon. By far." Then he drank down the remainder of his wine.

43   GOOD FRIDAY

The Good Friday service in the chapel at Knowsley the following morning seemed twice as long as the one on Palm Sunday at Lathom. Being of no faith, Peter found it most trying, his time spent picking out the exquisite architectural detail of the building and its ornate decoration; along with the small private foibles of the packed congregation nearest. The discreet picking of noses and scratching seemed to be the most common practice.

Simon and Randle stood amongst the other lower orders at the back of the nave. From there, Peter could see little of the Earl, or of Robert and the other gentleman-servants, seated in the few rows of pews at the end nearest the raised altar.

When the service at long last drew to a close, the Earl rose and spoke briefly with the vicar before returning down the aisle and between the parting congregation. In his brief passing, Peter thought he looked somewhat worse for wear. Clearly, the previous evening's drinking had taken its toll.

He'd looked a little better during the plain midday meal sometime later, when Simon had again been one of those waiting on his table in the great hall. When, unlike his gentleman-servants and the vicar and his clerics, he refused wine, preferring an infusion of agrimony, Peter knew he had to be hungover. So, it didn't surprise him when Ferdinando retired to his apartments before the meal had run its course. He took with him one of his secretaries, John Golborne, the Clerk of the Kitchens.

This brought about the sharing of looks amongst those left at the table. Peter overheard a comment to the effect that the Earl would no doubt be blaming his being out-of-sorts on the previous evening's meal.

After Simon and the other servants had finished theirs, he returned to his duties in the busy kitchen. He was scouring a large metal pan with sand sometime later when one of the Earl's pages hurried in. He looked a little worried and breathlessly demanded another infusion of agrimony for his lord.

"Leave that," the Master of the Kitchens told Simon, "and sort this out for his lordship." Before long, the white-faced page was gingerly taking the steaming hot mug from Simon, hurrying as carefully as he could from the kitchen.

Later still, and in a rare break from his tasks, Simon had gone to the one small window the kitchen afforded, cooling himself in the gentle late afternoon breeze that blew in at its opening. It looked down onto a small enclosed yard stacked with barrels. Beside these stood Michael Doughtie, tall and poised and a little hunched, and his younger brother Robert, handsome but stockier, both in close conversation.

"But we all ate of the same dishes," Michael was in the middle of saying, "and no one else is feeling ill. Are you sure that nothing of what he alone drank was soured? You know he'd never have noticed, not in the state he was in."

"I assure you, brother, I tasted all he was served, as I always do and what would have been noticed had I not, and I'm as right as rain."

"Well, his lordship isn't; bad enough for Mister Golborne to have sought my opinion."

"It'll be the quantity of wine he downed. You'll see," but even at that distance, Peter could see sweat glistening in the dying daylight on Robert's brow. He also noticed that his hand now boasted only the one ring: the one gifted to him by Ferdinando.

"Master Wardell?" the Master of the Kitchen called over, and Simon hurried from the window to find out what further duties lay ahead of him now.

When the evening drew in and Simon was again waiting on at the table, he ran his glance over the gathering men. Peter recognised a quietness to them, their talk subdued even once they were seated. And all the while, Ferdinando's place remained ominously empty, as did Mister Golborne's.

As Simon passed along the places, serving fish from a platter, he overheard Mister Smith quietly saying to those close by, "It doesn't bode well for his lordship to have spewed *that* many times. Thrice, you say, and with a foulness to it?" to which Michael Doughtie nodded. "What do *you* think?" Mister Smith then directed at Robert.

"What?" Robert said, as though he'd been miles

away, a startled look in his eyes. "Oh, er, well…in his lordship's wisdom, he has had something of a surfeit of wine this past week, as I well know. And on top of that, there's his vehement exercise hunting. It doesn't surprise me his body's taken so badly to it all."

"Hmm," Mister Smith said, sagely nodding. "Provided he rests, I'm sure he'll soon throw it off. After all, he's been stoutly robust and of very good health all his life." He raised his cup of wine before him in salute, the others joining in, their toast to his speedy recovery briefly lifting their spirits.

The remainder of the evening continued to be a subdued affair, as was the time Simon and the other three men spent preparing for sleep once they were back in their room. The more so, it seemed to Peter, where Robert was concerned. When he wasn't off in a world of his own, he was surreptitiously lending an eye to Simon, a strangely resigned look on his face.

Although having been back to his full duties and his wound no longer bothering him, sleep didn't immediately claim Simon. He lay awake in the dark for a while, listening to Robert twist and turn on his pallet and to his incoherent mumbling as he fitfully slept.

Hope grew anew the following day when the Earl appeared for their midday meal, but his demeanour and faintly jaundiced look tempered their joy. Although he ate some bread, his appetite was clearly dulled. Nor did he speak much, which suppressed the conversation. So much so that the air felt brittle by the time he suddenly pushed himself upright in his chair.

"Mister Golborne," he said, a strained resolve in his voice, "and you, Michael," at which he looked at Robert's brother.

"We'll return to Lathom early. This afternoon indeed, if you'd make the arrangements between you." Before anyone could speak, the Earl pushed himself to his feet and left the hall.

For a moment, Mister Golborne and Michael Doughtie stared at each other across the table. Then, pushing their plates away, they rose, a succession of instructions from each galvanising those about them.

Rapidly, a clamour of activity cut to every corner of Knowsley Hall as their preparations to leave were urgently pushed on apace.

44 HOLY SATURDAY

The thud and crack of the axe biting into and splitting dry wood echoed about the timber structure of the barn, fragments sent skittering across its stone floor. Simon placed another lump of tree trunk on the cutting block before him. A swing of the axe and he repeated his strike, again and again, until this last lump, too, was reduced to a pile of firewood at his feet.

"That should be enough," he panted as he dusted off the blade and returned the axe to its place on the wall. Wiping sweat from his forehead, he scooped the firewood into a broad and shallow basket before slipping his arm through its handle.

Facing the open side of the barn, a rear wing of Lathom House rose within its own shadow, its high battlements silhouetted against a clear-blue, early evening sky. Simon returned beneath its wall to a door through which he'd earlier rushed out upon his errand. As he approached, it swung open. Holding it back was a gnarled old man in a leather apron.

"For 'is lordship, I take it, sir, by tha's haste?" the man said. "Heard he took ill while away."

"It is; and he did," Simon allowed as he squeezed past and hurried on down the dark passage beyond.

At its end, he came out into the great hall and across to the staircase. Before long, he stood at the open doorway to his lordship's apartments, seemingly stunned to a standstill by the opulence of what he saw within.

"Ah, Master Wardell," Mister Halsall called as he stepped through a door at the far side. "Is that the firewood I asked Mister Doughtie to have brought?"

"It is, sir."

"Well, don't just stand there. Bring it through," and he stood aside.

Simon passed into a bedchamber, its warmth nearly knocking him over as he came to an abrupt halt just inside the doorway. As Mister Halsall closed the door behind them, Simon's gaze darted between those present: Mister Golborne by one of the windows, speaking quietly with Robert's older brother, Michael Doughtie; Mistress Agnes on a stool by the hearth, stirring a small pot she held in her hand; the Earl in his shirt sleeves, his chest exposed, sitting on the edge of a large fourposter; Lady Alice standing before her husband, her palm pressed against his brow.

"You should have thought to send for Doctor Case before leaving Knowsley," she admonished him. "It'll be fortunate from here, at this late hour, if our messenger gets through to Chester before tomorrow morning's out. Unless by chance it stays clear and God grants him a good moon," then she noticed

Simon and his basket.

"Ah. About time," she called across. "And don't just stand there. Get some of that wood on the fire, for pity's sake." Simon's legs unfroze, hurrying him to kneel beside Mistress Agnes, from where he stacked the fire with fresh wood.

Seeming to summon his strength, his lordship protested, "You say that, my lady, but when it came time to leave, I'd begun to feel much better. So much so, I had second thoughts about returning."

"Well, by the look of you now, and the heat in your brow, it's a good thing you did. I should have gone with you, though. I really should," at which her hand came to rest on her stomach. "If nothing but to keep you from debauching yourself, as I gather was the case."

Seemingly oblivious to their exchange, Mistress Agnes quietly commented to Simon, "That wound of yours looks to be doing well. Still using my lotion?"

"Er…"

"When you remember, eh?" and Simon's face flushed, although it could have been the renewed heat of the fire.

Once he'd stacked the unused wood in an alcove beside the hearth, his gaze searched out Mister Halsall. He was now talking quietly with her ladyship, but Mistress Agnes shook her spoon dry towards the hearth, distracting Simon.

"That should do," she said. "Once I've got this inside his lordship, I'll have a look at that wound of yours," and she gave him a brief smile.

Whilst she went off to administer her concoction, Simon remained by the fire, clearly forgotten. As he waited, he couldn't help but overhear Mister Golborne telling Mister Doughtie about the message he'd written to Doctor Case.

"I suggested he collect Doctor Canon on the way, for his own learned opinion, seeing we've no real idea what afflicts his lordship."

"I hope," Michael Doughtie softly said, "that it is just the amount he drank whilst at Knowsley."

"That, let's not forget," Mister Halsall quietly added as he joined them by the window, "and his lordship overexerting himself. Had I been there myself, I'd have cautioned against it," he assured them. "Especially so soon after his inactivity over the winter."

"But he's never suffered like this before," Mister Golborne challenged, looking down his nose at Mister Halsall.

"No. True. But then…" Mister Halsall glanced towards his lordship, lowering his voice still further. Simon now had to strain to hear. "But then, he's never enjoyed his wine quite as much as he has these past six months," which brought Mister Golborne to clamp his lips to a silent pout. "Which is perhaps understandable, what with the Queen still not having awarded him the Lieutenantship of Lancashire and Cheshire. Added to that, there was all that business with the Earl of Essex."

"Indeed," Mister Doughtie concurred, "and that embarrassing admission he had to make to Secretary Cecil that the Baron of Newton had been with Richard Hesketh at Brereton. And the lawyer Sir Thomas Hesketh, damn the man; what was *he* thinking? Crossing our lordship, the way he did. It wouldn't surprise me if his malice didn't have some

Catholic purpose behind it."

"Nay," Mister Halsall objected, "but he's a well-respected Protestant; likely the only one of those Heskeths. You've only got to look at his prosecution of Catholics to see that. And don't forget, Richard Hesketh *was* his blood brother. So, he was bound to have felt some hurt when he heard his lordship had been behind his arrest."

"I'm not so sure. What about all that talk of Richard Hesketh threatening his lordship with Catholic retribution if he didn't—"

"Just tittle-tattle, Mister Doughtie. Nothing more. His lordship told me himself the man had never once made any such threat. Nothing more than the stirring up of trouble amongst disaffected recusants, you mark my words. And God himself knows we've enough of those here in—"

An almighty groan filled the room, all eyes turning towards their lordship, now doubled-over on the edge of his bed. The gentlemen at the window rushed across, crowding around him and the two women. Peter hoped Simon would join them, so he could get a better look at Ferdinando. Not only had he great sympathy for his onetime host, but his professional intrigue had again been piqued.

But Simon didn't move. He only stared helplessly at what he could see of Ferdinando as his lordship slowly sat up straight once more. Although obscured by those about him, Peter did at least catch a glimpse of his slightly puffy and now clearly jaundiced face. Before long, the Earl had been undressed and helped into a nightshirt, then under the sheets, his back propped against a mound of pillows.

The door opening distracted Simon. William Farington and Sir Edward, Ferdinando's uncle, stepped through. Mister Farington's gaze first locked onto Simon then darted towards those still gathered around the Earl's bed. Soon joining them, they asked after his lordship, at which Lady Alice requested they all leave, excepting Mister Golborne, Mister Halsall and Mistress Agnes.

"His lordship's greatest need now is rest and quiet," she insisted. "I'm sure you'll understand," she then directed at Sir Edward. "Mister Halsall will keep you all informed." At this, the gentlemen withdrew, leaving Simon still unnoticed and waiting by the fire for further instructions.

As Mister Halsall was taken aside by Lady Alice, he must have remembered him.

"My lady, a moment," he begged, and came over.

"Master Wardell, as you're clearly now well recovered, you can go and wait in the passage outside. I'll have need of someone to run me errands."

"As you wish, Mister Halsall," and there Simon went and stood in the gloomy silence, waiting on the gentleman's pleasure. And there, too, Peter bided his time, idly wondering what Robert Doughtie had been up to since sending Simon off to chop firewood for Mister Halsall.

45 THE COLOUR OF RUSTY IRON

The first message Simon had to convey took him to the kitchens, to have food brought up to his lordship's apartments for Lady Alice, Mister Golborne, Mister Halsall, and himself. Mistress Agnes had earlier joined those in the great hall for the communal evening meal, returning with a chicken broth for his lordship, the preparation of which she'd overseen herself. Not long after, two young servants turned up with trays of food, laid out on the table in the outer room.

Mister Halsall took a selection into the bedchamber to her ladyship, returning with Mister Golborne to eat their own at the table, urging Simon to do likewise.

After a while, Mister Halsall commented to Simon that Lady Alice wouldn't leave the Earl's side, so great was her worry. Not until his lordship was clearly on the mend.

"Which means, Master Wardell, that this room

will go largely unused. So, you may as well wait upon me in here. After all, we can't have that cold passage being the death of you; now, can we?"

"I'm much obliged, Mister Halsall."

"And you're going to have to get some sleep at some point, so I'll need someone else to share your duties with you."

"If it'd please you, sir, Master Hopkirk is most trustworthy," at which Peter noticed Mister Golborne nod, approvingly.

"Mister Smith's lad?" Mister Halsall asked.

"Yes, sir."

"Provided Mister Smith agrees, but he'll need to bring some bedding, as you yourself will. You can take turns on the settle by the door. At least you'll be off the floor," after saying which, they went on to finish their meals in silence.

Simon went first to get his own things, rushing in to find Robert standing by the small table in the rooms they shared.

"What is it?" he snapped, snatching up something from the candlelit, paper-strewn table and bringing Simon up with a start. "Have I been summoned?"

"N...No, Mister Doughtie; you haven't," and Simon hurriedly explained why he was there.

"Ah. I see." Robert's shoulders slumped as he let out a ragged breath. "Very well, then. Be quick about it," and he gathered up the papers and rolled them loosely together.

"Before I do, and although I haven't much time, can we talk, Robert? Please? You... You said we would; when we got the chance."

Robert tied a ribbon around the papers and stared

at Simon for a moment. "How's his lordship?"

"His… Well, he's in some pain."

"Has he vomited again?"

"Not that I know of," and for a moment, Simon's gaze flitted about Robert's features. "I'm afraid I can't stay long, Robert, but… Why were you so angry with me? That day my wound—"

"So, Mister Halsall reckons he'll need the two of you, does he?" and Robert let out a short but mirthless laugh. "He must think he'll be needing your services for a while longer, then. Did he say for how long?"

"Er, no. No, he didn't. But, Robert… It was so unlike you: to be that harsh with me. It hurt me so. It really did. The thought I may have lost your love has played so much upon my mind since. So," and here, Simon desperately grabbed Robert's arm, "please, Robert, please, can we just—"

"Simon?" Robert said, softly, placing his hand on Simon's own, but Simon only gazed at him, tears blossoming in his eyes, blurring his vision.

"You want to know how much I love you? Is that it, Simon?"

"I…" but all Simon could do now was wipe away his tears.

"With all my heart, Simon; that's how much," and Robert smiled. "With all my heart. A heart that'll always be yours, come what may. Remember that, Simon, my sweetest one. Keep that at the forefront of that precious mind of yours."

"But—"

"In time, Simon. All in good time. But for now, you've your duty to Mister Halsall to consider," and he waved his dismissal as he turned away, staring down at the candle.

Simon stood and stared at Robert's profile, until he turned his back on him. But as Simon then made to move, Robert added, "And remember, my treasure: a true love's stalwart companion is always unquestioning trust."

This held Simon for a moment, until he quietly answered, "A companion that my own true love for you could never deny; I assure you, my beloved Robert."

When Robert didn't move, Simon carried on through to their bedchamber, soon gathering what he needed and returning. Robert had gone, the table now bare of all but the candle.

A little later, Simon returned to his lordship's apartments with Randle at his side, the lad clearly as awed as Simon had been earlier. They soon settled in, though, their bedding tidily arranged at either end of the long settle.

As the two idly chatted together, little happened for the rest of that Saturday evening, other than the restocking of the firewood. That neither seemed inclined to sleep until well into the early hours of the following morning, Peter put down to the novelty of their new duties and their imposing surroundings.

It had been Simon who'd first climbed under his blanket and nodded off, leaving Randle with instructions to wake him if he felt the need to sleep himself. It had still been dark, the room lit by candlelight, when Simon awoke to his shoulder being shaken.

"What… What is it?" he mumbled, prising his eyes open. Then he heard it himself: the sickening sound of retching.

He rubbed the sleep from his eyes, but a

protracted groan from beyond the door to the bedchamber quickly got him to his feet. He and Randle went over and stood by it, listening closely.

Her ladyship's soothing voice could be heard, then her more abrupt asides to one of the gentlemen, before she distinctly said, "Here, Ferdinando, drink a little more of Mistress Agnes's infusion. It did so much to ease your pain before." Then the door opened and Mister Halsall stood before Simon and Randle, clearly startled to find them there.

"One of you," he swiftly recovered himself to say, "run and see if there's any sign of the doctors. Her ladyship's getting most anxious."

"I'll go," Randle offered, "seeing you've only just woken up, Simon," and off he hurried.

As the door closed behind Randle, Ferdinando let out a blood-chilling cry of pain, and Mister Halsall hurried back, leaving the door to the bedchamber open. Horribly fascinated, Simon stepped in a few paces.

Lady Alice sat beside the bed, Mistress Agnes at the other side, Mister Golborne standing close by. Mister Halsall had only got halfway across the room, though, when Ferdinando doubled over. He heaved once or twice before a great flow of fluid issued from his mouth, splashing noisily into a silver bowl he held in his lap.

Lady Alice shot to her feet and stepped back a pace.

"My God," Peter thought. "Blood! It's coloured by blood," and his doctor's mind tumbled through diagnoses. Then the stench hit Simon and he recoiled, turning away, his arm across his nose and mouth.

"Oh, for Dei's sake," Sophie exclaimed. "Poor old Ferdinando."

An icy silence seemed to have frozen the air of the room, slowing the return of Simon's gaze back towards the bed.

Ferdinando remained hunched over the bowl and into which he stared, wide-eyed. Then, almost imperceptibly, he lifted his head away before slumping back against his pillows, a long breath of relief escaping him.

Like horrified statues, Lady Alice and Mistress Agnes stared down at what lay within the bowl.

Mister Halsall was the first to move. With his mouth clamped shut and a strained look on his face, he removed the silver bowl from Ferdinando's lap and gingerly carried it over to Simon. At that moment, Randle appeared at Simon's side, the words he was about to say lost to the sight and stench of what Mister Halsall held in his hands.

Trying to speak without breathing, Mister Halsall told Randle to bring the cloth from the washstand and to cover the bowl, and then for Simon to dispose of it well away from the house.

"Once the bowl's been cleaned, bring it back, but with some more cloths. Ones soaked in water this time."

Simon only nodded as he took the surprisingly heavy bowl in his hands, its contents now even plainer to see: fatty and the colour of rusty iron. His stomach churned and he looked away, until Randle had lain the cloth across it.

Peter initially cursed the missed chance of his own longer professional inspection, until relief for Sophie's sake flooded through him. In its wake came an intense longing to reach out and comfort her, but then, sadly, he remembered his promise.

46   BLACK-SWATHED GENTLEMEN

However hard Simon scrubbed and scoured, the silver bowl refused to give up its bark-coloured stain. The Master of the Kitchen came out to the yard, and in the thin dawn light, scowled at the results.

"It doesn't look as though that's ever going to come out, Master Wardell" and he gave Simon a rather puzzled look. "But here are the towels you asked for." He handed Simon half-a-dozen well-soaked items.

When Simon got back upstairs, Randle told him all had been quiet since his lordship had been washed and got into a fresh nightshirt. Sure enough, as Simon put the wet towels aside, nothing could be heard from beyond the closed door.

Dozing in turns, Simon happened to be the one awake when, later in the morning, the peace and quiet again became ripped apart by the sound of vomiting. This time, some minutes passed before Mister Halsall opened the bedchamber door. The bowl he handed Simon felt heavier than the last.

Towards midday, Mister Halsall sent Randle to find his lordship's lawyer, Sir Richard Shuttleworth, with instructions for him to come equipped to prepare his lordship's cautionary last will and testament. He then gave Simon a pile of letters to have despatched, the uppermost clearly addressed to "Bishop Wm. Chaderton of Chester".

Over the course of that Easter Sunday, either Simon or Randle had cause to empty the bowls on another five occasions between them, each seeming lighter. What grew weightier, though, was Ferdinando's moans and groans, increasingly punctuated by hiccoughs and agony-laden oaths. Despite this, he seemingly laboured on at his will, for his lawyer was with him, on and off, for most of that day.

Come the early evening, Mister Halsall brought his lordship's chamberpot out to be emptied. Whereas his water had previously looked and smelt like anyone else's, now it was hard to tell apart from the contents of his bowls.

Peter drew in a sharp breath and willed Simon to take a good sniff and a closer look, which of course he didn't.

"So?" Sophie asked.

"So," Peter considered. "I'd have said kidney infection—which would certainly explain his pain— if it wasn't for the fatty deposits and his hiccups. To be honest, they've got me a bit stumped. And where's his doctors? for crying out loud. I could do with knowing what their hands-on examination's going to reveal."

"If it's an infection, then they've no antibiotics to

call on, Peter, nor blues-and-twos to get his doctors here quickly. We're a good twelve hours from Chester, maybe nine at a push."

A little later and after the lawyer had finally withdrawn, and for maybe half an hour, Lady Alice was absent from her husband's side, visiting their daughters. But what she could have told them, Peter couldn't imagine, other than carefully contrived reassurances.

Shortly after she'd got back, Randle was sent to replenish the water jug. He came rushing back, slopping its contents onto the floor in his haste, keen to let them know he'd seen two gentlemen arrive who were now being shown up.

Peter felt a growing anticipation. He was likely about to meet two colleagues from the very advent of his own medical age, two doctors from a time when superstition and science lay together as such easy bedfellows.

As Simon knocked on the bedchamber door, Peter heard their footsteps hurrying down the passage.

"We think the doctors are here," was all Simon got out when Mister Halsall opened the door and before Michael Doughtie swept in.

Behind him came two black-swathed gentlemen, their mud-spattered travelling cloaks bringing in vestiges of the damp and cooler night air. In their wake came their servants, both equally dark and mud-caked but each carrying two large panniers.

"Doctor Case," Mister Halsall addressed the taller gentleman. "How overjoyed I am to see you, sir. And you, Doctor Canon. Welcome both. You are, Gentlemen, truly a sight for sore eyes."

"My dear Mister Halsall," returned the sharp-featured Doctor Case as he took Mister Halsall's arm in both his hands. "All the way here, I've been praying to God that we'd end up having a wasted journey," but then his voice dropped to a sombre whisper: "Although I see from your face that my prayers may not have been heard."

As Mister Halsall invited them in to the bedchamber, all he would say was, "I think you'll find it evident that his lordship's in dire need of your consummate knowledge and skills, Gentlemen." He then stood aside, stale air wafting past him from within.

Before moving, Doctor Case instructed the servants to put their panniers by the table, then he, Mister Doughtie and Doctor Canon filed in. As the door closed behind them, Simon and Randle stared at each other before they both sighed their relief.

Once the doctors' servants had removed their cloaks and stood by the fire in the outer room, stretching their legs and rubbing their backsides, Simon and Randle introduced themselves. Before long, they'd learnt of the tiring journey from Chester to Wigan, and finally on to Lathom, but how God had favoured them with clear skies and the light of a half-decent moon.

"I can't help thinking, though," Randle glumly said at one point, "that us all missing our Easter Sunday services can't bode well. Not at all. I'd liked to have gone to say my prayers for his lordship's speedy recovery," to which they all said their Amens.

Not long after, the bedchamber door opened and Doctor Case leant through, instructing his servant to bring him some items from his pannier.

Other than that, it was perhaps an hour later, long after they'd seated themselves around the table, that the bedchamber door opened again. This time, both doctors came through, Mister Golborne behind them. He held a cloth-covered chamberpot, which he soon passed to Simon.

As he did so, Doctor Case quietly said, "Oh, and don't forget, Doctor Canon, we must endeavour to make an even more particular record of what we do, and of his lordship's indications."

Doctor Canon nodded, knowingly.

"But I must say: I'm a little more hopeful, now we've administered the clyster. That it's done his lordship some good at last."

"He does seem to be at some better ease now," Doctor Canon observed.

"Well, let's hope it's drawn the course of his humors downwards, which is the best we can hope for at this stage." Doctor Case then turned his inclined head to Mister Golborne, raising an eyebrow.

"If you'd follow me," Mister Golborne offered, "I'll take your good selves and your servants down to the great hall, where a meal awaits. Then, whenever it may suit, I'll show you to your rooms."

To the scrape of benches, the two servants rose, offering their nods to Simon and Randle before enthusiastically joining their masters. As the group followed Mister Golborne out, one of the doctors made mention of the size of his lordship's spleen. Their ensuing discussion of this, though, was soon swallowed by their retreat down the passage.

As Simon and Randle fell to discussing what they'd understood of it all, Peter quickly but cautiously saw it as further evidence of an infection.

"But what kind of infection?" he asked himself,

"when it's accompanied by hiccups. Although I have to say, his jaundiced appearance does suggest ARLD."

"What's AR…whatever you said?" Sophie asked.

"Alcohol Related Liver Disease; but then, it's highly unlikely after only six months of increased consumption. That's just too soon," and mentally, he shook his head.

"And what's a clyster?"

"A… Oh, yes, that. It's, er, what we'd know as an enema."

"Oh. Right. I wish I'd not asked."

"But no, it can't be ARLD. It doesn't add up. So, it has to be cholera, or possibly… No, the vomiting wouldn't be as severe with typhoid. But it has to be some pathogen or other, something endemic to the insanitary third-world conditions of this time."

"I'm not one of your medical colleagues, Peter."

"What?"

"Although I think I get your drift."

"Oh. Yeah. Sorry."

"I take it you mean no flush toilets, and all that?"

"The long and short of it."

"Right. Okay, if that's what you think it is."

"Don't you?"

"I'm hardly in a position to say."

"What? But you already know, surely? And Ferdy's condition must be well beyond us having to worry about butterflies anymore. So, why can't you just tell me what—"

"All I'll say is: remember the times they live in, and not just their lack of flush toilets. Theirs may have had third-world hygiene, but it was also a harsh world in other ways; all so unlike your own, Peter," she finished with a seeming tinge of envy.

But beyond this, she wouldn't be drawn, which left Peter not only stumped but maddeningly intrigued— the word itself then leaping into his thoughts.

"Intrigue?" he mulled over as he thought back over his previous "dreams", all those months before. "Intrigue," he repeated to himself, and then things slowly began to fall into place, rather like a sinister jigsaw puzzle.

47   "IMAGE OF WAXE"

His lordship's apartments soon became busy, sometimes overwhelmingly so. Simon and Randle were kept on their toes, running errands, carrying messages and accompanying the doctors' servants in their searches for herbs and minerals.

On occasion, Sir Edward would arrive to update his lordship on matters concerning the household, and no doubt to find out with his own eyes how he was doing. And of course, the doctors themselves were constantly in and out of Ferdinando's bedchamber, consulting the great mass of large books and papers that had been laid out on the table.

During a rare quiet period, when no one else happened to be in the room, Simon's curiosity took him over to have a look.

Peter recognised some of what he saw: astrology charts and tables, herbals, surprisingly accurate diagrams of the body's internal organs, but much of the rest was wholly mysterious.

From the many conversations the doctors had had, it seemed their initial concerns lay with exactly when his lordship had felt this, done that, and ingested or expelled the other, down to the very hour. They applied this precise and detailed diary to the various charts and lists, methodically arriving at diagnoses and remedies that more often than not completely flummoxed Peter.

What did strike him as very familiar was the way in which they took their detailed observations. It was usually Doctor Canon, spectacles perched on his nose, who'd sit at the table and enter into Ferdinando's growing "case notes" what his colleague dictated. The whole thing felt reminiscent of those protracted cases of Peter's own, where narrowing down the site of a primary cancer had proved so elusive, despite extensive investigations and voluminous notes.

What was clearly dissimilar was how far off the mark most of their conclusions were, which brought Peter to comment, "It makes you realise how fortunate we are in our own times, doesn't it, Sophie?"

"In yours, maybe," Sophie let slip but then quickly changed the subject: "If only I'd met you back in your time. Before all the years came between us."

"But they haven't, have they? Not really. We're together now, aren't we? In a shared past, granted, but one that's at least given us a couple of weeks still to savour something of the love we have for each other."

"But only two weeks."

"Two weeks with you, Sophie, even against all that's happening here, would be worth more than a lifetime with anyone else. Don't you see? We shouldn't waste it. We should value it for what it is, not lament its brevity."

Sophie fell silent for a while, then, in a small voice, admitted, "I'm afraid, Peter. Afraid that, if we do live in the moment, the pain at our parting will be all the more unbearable. I don't think I could take that."

"But at least we'd have something of our love to remember, not regret."

"I don't know, Peter. I honestly don't," to which Peter somehow knew he shouldn't push it any more. Not now, perhaps. Not yet.

During the following day, the Monday, Doctor Case ordered his lordship be given an infusion of rhubarb and manna in chicken broth, the latter kindly brought up from the kitchens by Mistress Agnes. What this was supposed to have achieved, Peter couldn't imagine, but the doctors seemed pleased when, over the course of the day, his lordship vomited no less than nine times. But when it had been Simon's turn to dispose of the results, Peter could see no lessening of its rusty stain. If anything, it had seemed even darker.

On the Tuesday, Doctor Canon urged that they should bleed his lordship, to try and reduce the amount of blood he was vomiting. But Ferdinando had clearly had more than enough by then. He flatly refused, and so fomentation, oils and plasters for external use were made up and applied instead.

The tormented man must have seen something of his fate, for he no longer seemed willing to bear the doctors' more unpleasant remedies, not on top of his already intolerable suffering. Either way, for the rest of that day, Simon and Randle found themselves emptying his silver bowls no more often than before.

During the afternoon, the Bishop of Chester arrived. He was invited into the bedchamber, to sit with Ferdinando and Lady Alice whilst all those then present retired to the outer chamber. After an hour or so, her ladyship came out, to give the two men some spiritual privacy.

By then, other worried-faced gentlemen had swelled the numbers waiting there, friends and close associates of the Earl who'd been anxious to attend his lordship. Simon and Randle found themselves edged into a corner, their presence unnoticed.

From the subdued greetings and general talk Peter overheard, it seemed most of them were from notable local, and some more distant, families who'd answered Mister Golborne's solicitous letters.

When the Bishop finally made way for them, these other gentlemen went in, one by one, to sit with his lordship; unless his strength failed him or the doctors needed to administer some remedy or other, or he'd cause to use one of the silver bowls again.

The next day—the Wednesday and last day of Easter— as Simon was returning from one of these errands, he met Mistress Agnes on her way down from the apartments. Clearly not at all happy, her face seemed distinctly put out of joint. She didn't even acknowledge him as they passed on the stairs.

Once back in the outer room, the explanation soon became apparent.

"I think the doctors' frustrations are beginning to show," Randle told Simon as he sat down beside him, his candour fuelled by their now being unusually alone.

"Mistress Agnes, I take it? I've just passed her on the stairs."

"Aye, well, she'd a face like thunder when she came out. Spitting criticisms into thin air, she was. Clutching her bag to her chest, as though it might be stolen from her." Simon absently felt the wound at his neck, sliding his fingertips over its smoothly-healed skin.

"Well, they don't seem to be doing any better than she did," and to mark the point, the sound of retching again came from the bedchamber.

"I take it the doctors are still in there, then?" Simon asked, as though to block out the sound.

"Yes, although Mister Halsall went off somewhere about an hour ago. I think he went to report to Mister Farington and the others. Though what good he'll have to tell them, I don't know."

A little later, the doctors and Mister Golborne left, leaving only her ladyship with her husband, although nothing could be heard of her or, thankfully, from him. It seemed unnaturally quiet after the past few days of hectic comings and goings. Simon had begun to nod off in the pleasant warmth coming in at the window from the bright spring day outside when the outer door opened.

Mister Halsall stepped in, a quick look around the room and then a brief nod at Simon and Randle before he passed through and into the bedchamber. His and her ladyship's voices could soon be heard, softly discussing something. Peter was certain he heard the name Anne, then Lady Alice herself appeared at the door.

Peter was shocked by how drawn she looked; her eyes hollow, her lips almost non-existent, her hair hanging loose in places. As though in a dream, she

343

crossed the room without a sideways glance and slipped out through the open outer door, her footsteps dwindling away down the passage.

That stark image of the suffering wife made Peter's heart feel leaden.

Simon and Randle must have sensed the same, for they sat silently avoiding each other's eyes, until Mister Smith appeared in the doorway.

"Ah, Randle," he softly said, a wariness about him. "Is Mister Halsall about? He left word for me."

"In with his lordship, sir."

"Very good," and he went and quietly knocked, the door presently opening.

"Mister Halsall, I believe you—"

"Come in, Mister Smith, but quietly now. His lordship's at last found some ease to sleep," and in he stepped, the door gently closing behind him.

It wasn't long before his initially quiet voice began to rise, loud enough for Peter to hear him exclaim, "A waxen image? Of his lordship? Are you sure, Mister Halsall?" the reply to which was too soft to hear.

"Then where is it? Show me," by which time, Simon had risen and now stood by the door, his ear cocked, his hand cupped behind it.

"I threw it on the fire, of course," Mister Halsall emphatically returned. "The sooner to relieve his lordship of its witchcraft, and to burn the witch that's been so cruelly tormenting him with its curse."

"And it was behind his lordship's headboard, you say?"

"Indeed, and with some of his hair threaded through it, belly to groin."

"But who, in God's good name, would wish to…"

but after this, both their voices dropped so low neither could be made out.

"Witchcraft?" Peter marvelled.

"Don't underestimate it, Peter," Sophie assured him. "It was a serious matter at this time. In less than twenty years from now, there'll be the Lancashire and Pendle witch trials."

"But for such educated men as these to believe in such a thing!"

"Everyone did at this time, Peter. It was just an everyday part of their lives."

Peter wondered if Mistress Agnes's precipitate departure had anything to do with this revelation. And again, it came home to him how little he really understood of the lives of these people, despite how long he'd now spent amongst them.

The Thursday morning broke wet and windy, the light so poor the candles were left burning. Both doctors arrived not much later, earnestly discussing, as they passed through the outer room, a purge they intended giving his lordship, to cleanse his bowels. It clearly worked very well, for Simon lost count of the number of times he and Randle had to go and empty his chamberpot.

About mid-morning, the day still dark and overcast, Doctor Canon came in on his own and rifled through one of the panniers, pulling out a stumpy bottle. He peered at its contents against the light of the candle, shaking his head and drawing in air through his teeth.

"This diascordium's getting low," he mumbled to himself, then carried it through to the bedchamber.

"Dare I ask?" Sophie warily ventured.

"I think it's an old medicine along the lines of kaolin and morphine. But I'm pretty sure that at this time it was opium they would have used, and quite a lot of it."

"Phew. Well, at least that should take him out of it for a while, the poor man."

And indeed, his lordship soon seemed much more at ease, from the little Peter could subsequently hear, as though perhaps he'd escaped his torment this time through a more peaceful slumber.

Doctor Case turned up not much later, along with Mister Golborne, Mister Smith and Michael Doughtie, all of whom passed without word into the bedchamber. There was a muffled but earnest discussion for a while, then the two doctors came back out. In their dour-faced preoccupation, they seemed oblivious of Simon and Randle, sitting together at the other side of the room.

"Well," Doctor Case confidentially let out on a long breath as they came to a halt before the fire, "where do we go from here? Especially in the light of Mister Halsall's revelation."

When Doctor Canon said nothing, plainly at a loss, Doctor Case, his face pale and drawn, went on to say, "I think we have to accept we're now in need of further opinions. Perhaps of those more acquainted with maleficium and its dark ways."

Doctor Canon stared at the floor for a moment, his lips pressed firmly together. Then he raised a somewhat brighter eye to his colleague.

"There's always Doctor Joynar. He doesn't live far from here."

"Joynar, eh? I know of him."

"Then you'll know he's learned in some of the

more foreign practices. Ah, and of course, there's Doctor Bate. Now, he definitely does have experience of treating those who've been bewitched. They're both in Lancashire, too, so could easily be got within the day."

"Hmm," Doctor Case pondered, fingering his beard. "It's certainly worth a try, seeing we're now so lamentably at a loss."

"Well, at least we'll be showing due diligence. And you never know, one of them may uncover something that's so far eluded us."

"Not merely due diligence, my good Doctor Canon, but for the fear of failing a beloved friend of many years. A man whose life I've always cherished, no more so than now," at which Doctor Case hung his head for a moment, as though to hide the wetness about his eyes."

"I know, my dear Doctor Case. I know," but then Doctor Case held his chin up high and placed his hand on his colleague's arm.

"A decision," he resolutely stated, "made of my love for my lord and friend: it's time we informed her ladyship of our dour despair. But a despair at least tempered by a new hope borne of Doctors Joynar and Bate; may God grant them success where He's only graced us with failure."

Resignedly, they returned to Ferdinando's sickbed, and so to the mounting despair they knew they were about to bring to his devoted and beloved wife, the Lady Alice.

48   A DIFFERENT PERSPECTIVE

Early that afternoon, carefully carrying a polished-wood box under his arm, a short, slight and stooping gentleman came into the outer room, where Mister Halsall had been speaking with Simon and Randle. He stood there before them, silently mouthing words, his slightly opposed eyes like those of a hare that's just been startled awake.

"Ah, Mister Ellis," Mister Halsall greeted him.

"Sent for. By…by her…her ladyship. A letter."

"Indeed you were; some time ago, if I remember. Well, you may as well go straight in. Lady Alice is with his lordship and Mister Golborne," and he opened his arm towards the bedchamber door. Without a further word, the man went straight in without knocking.

A few minutes later, Mister Golborne came out, looking none too pleased.

"If it weren't for her ladyship's liking of that man," he acidly commented to Mister Halsall, "which for the life of me I'll never understand, I'd have had that uncivil jack-o'-knaves…" but then he seemed to notice Simon and Randle for the first time.

"He does seem to be a law unto himself," Mister Halsall allowed. "How long ago was it her ladyship had us send for him?"

"Long enough that she could have written her letter herself by now."

"Mind you, that the man can hardly string a sentence of conversation together and has barely a friend to call his own must make him the most discreet of aides, wouldn't you say?"

"I wonder," Peter couldn't help but blurt out to Sophie, "what it is she wants him to write for her," but Mister Golborne was speaking again.

"More importantly, his lordship's instructed that he's to be given no more potions to relieve his pain. Not until his last will and testament's been signed. He's hoping it'll be ready no later than tomorrow."

"But he's still in such pain. Would that be at all wise?"

"The only pains he's worried about now are those he wishes to take, to make sure—if the worse comes to the worst—that his will can't possibly be contested; that he'll be wholly and irrefutably of sound mind when it comes to him signing it. For the sake of Lady Alice and their daughters, of course. You know what little trust his lordship places in his brother, William. Who, it's looking increasingly likely and heaven forfend, could very well be the next earl, remember," at which he fixed Mister Halsall with an all too knowing look.

"Very well. I'll make sure the doctors are told."

"And one of you," Mister Golborne then said, turning to Simon and Randle, "can go and find his lordship's chaplain, Mister Lee."

Randle leapt at the chance, leaving Simon with the two gentlemen, whose talk then fell to the more mundane.

"Actually, Peter," Sophie finally took the opportunity to reply, "I can tell you exactly what she'll be dictating, given a record of it even came down through history to my own time. And with regards to butterflies: given you were far more likely to have come across it in your own."

"More likely?"

"It's a letter to Secretary Cecil, one that'll say:" and here Sophie mechanically recounted, "Bear with me to my using a secretary, for my senses are overcome with sorrow. It hath pleased God to visit my lord with sickness, that there is little hope of recovery except in His mercy. And therefore, I must entreat your favour and assistance, both of yourself and of my lord your father, on behalf of me and my poor children. And that as you were dear unto my lord in love and friendship, so you would be pleased to continue it for the furtherance of me and mine in the justice of our causes."

Peter took a moment for its meaning to sink in, then gasped, "Blimey. And she's writing this to the very man I still reckon set the whole Hesketh conspiracy in motion in the first place. Back on that ship, when he met with Ferdy's brother, William."

"The letter will be signed as being from Lathom, on the eleventh of April, fifteen-ninety-four, which is today and where we are. So, there you have it,

Peter. Aren't you impressed by my recall? Not bad for a late-middle-aged woman, eh?"

"Well, you are a mnemonist, so you wouldn't really expect me to…" but then Peter paused for a moment, before carefully asking, "How late is 'late'?"

"What? Ah. Bugger. I shouldn't have let that slip," but however much Peter tried, he could draw nothing more from her.

Things otherwise carried on for the rest of the day in much the same way as before: short visits to his lordship by various gentlemen, by his chaplain, long quiet periods with her ladyship. All the while, he fought his worsening pain, nausea and continuing violent hiccoughs. He had a wretched night, and by the Friday afternoon, Sir Richard—Ferdinando's lawyer—the Bishop of Chester, and a number of the other gentlemen who'd been around over the past few days went in together. The door was firmly closed behind them.

In the meantime, his doctors waited in the outer room. Doctor Canon had his bottle of diascordium at the ready, for when, as he put it, "his lordship's finally put his signature to his will and may once again find some release from his pain in prolonged sleep".

"If only we could devise something to bolster his strength and balance his humors," Doctor Case ruefully commented. "He's become so drawn and starkly jaundiced. I fear his reserves are deserting him," and the doctor ran his hand down his face in despair.

At long last, the door to the bedchamber opened and the gentlemen were soon clattering their way down the passage. The two doctors went back in, Doctor Canon clutching his bottle.

The abrupt stillness left behind as the door closed rang loudly in Peter's hearing, only the sounds of birds flitting about the eaves outside and the crackle of the fire's embers to disturb the two young men left behind. Simon had stepped towards the fire to rebuild it when the sound of feet out in the passage distracted him.

Mister Farington swept in, two dusty gentlemen in riding cloaks in his wake.

"Where are the doctors?" he asked Randle.

"In with his lordship, sir."

Mister Farington rapped on the bedchamber door.

"Doctor Joynar and Doctor Bate are here," he said when it opened.

Doctor Case came out and welcomed the two new arrivals. He took them in to see his lordship, explaining the situation so far as he did so. The afternoon then wore on until Simon happened to glance at the fire.

"Oh no, I forgot. We need some more firewood," he told Randle.

"I'll go and get it," Randle offered, but before he could leave, he closely scrutinised Simon's face.

"You look as tired as a dog after a long chase," he told him.

"It's all this broken sleep."

"Well, why don't you get your head down? It's quiet now. I think I'll try and find Mister Smith. After all, those new doctors are going to be ages prodding and poking his lordship, no doubt arguing over their diagnoses all over again." A wearied grin crept over his face.

Once Randle had gone, Simon lay on the settle and wrapped himself in his blanket, pulling it up over his head to block out the daylight. He must have nodded straight off, for the next thing Peter knew there were voices close by. As the veil of sleep slipped from his mind, he recognised one of them as that of Doctor Case.

"Doctor Joynar, if you would," he was saying, deliberately, "please tell Doctor Canon what you were telling me a moment ago," at which Simon slowed and quietened his breathing.

"Well, I can't be sure, of course, but his lordship's symptoms do remind me of some of the cases I came across whilst abroad, particularly in the Italian city states."

"Abroad?" Doctor Canon queried.

"Yes, my learned colleague. I've journeyed far and wide upon the Continent, you know. In my continued search for a better understanding of—"

"Please, Doctor Joynar: please tell him what you told me."

"Oh, yes. Er, by all means, Doctor Case."

"Well, then?"

"Indeed," and the good Doctor Joynar coughed, to clear his throat. "Poison," he stated. "In my humble opinion, his lordship may very well have been poisoned."

49   ON EAGLE'S WINGS

"**W**hat?" Doctor Bate and Doctor Canon said, clearly shocked.

"Are you sure?"

"No. Not entirely," Doctor Joynar admitted, "for that's the very nature of arsenic; it's such a deceptive mimic of many common sicknesses. Cholera in particular."

"Arsenic?" asked Doctor Canon.

"I for one, I must say," Doctor Case declared, "have never come across arsenic poisoning before, not of such wilful vehemence as we see with his lordship. Not in all my years as a physick."

"That's hardly surprising," Doctor Joynar told him. "Its malicious use is rarely seen in England, although it's common enough in Italy, where they call it the *inheritor's powder*."

"Nothing would surprise me of such a Catholic country," Doctor Bate wearily dismissed.

"If it *had* been used on his lordship," Doctor Case

sought, "how do you think it might have been administered?"

"In its strongest form, only a small amount would be needed. Most easily dissolved in a—"

"What on Earth's all this talk of poison?" Mister Halsall challenged from the doorway, startling them to silence. Doctor Case was the first to recover his voice.

"We have to consider all possibilities, Mister Halsall."

"What? When the clear cause has already been found, close to his lordship's very person? Hidden there behind the headboard of his bed."

"But—"

"Witchcraft, my good Doctor. That's what's behind my beloved lord's perilous condition. Why look any further than those whose evil ways his lordship has always set himself against: witches and warlocks? Who else would wish him such a fate?"

"It's not our place to judge intent, Mister Halsall, only to heal his lordship; from whatever it may be that ails him."

"Which would be sooner done by treating his bewitchment. After all, you yourself told me you've been giving his lordship Bezars stone and unicorn's horn as a matter of course. If he had been poisoned, surely they would have slaked it from his body and he'd now be improving?"

Doctor Case turned to Doctor Bate. "Of us all, you're best placed to judge on the matter of bewitchment. What do you think?"

"Well, I must say," the doctor carefully considered, "there is merit in the charge. Although such strong bewitchment is uncommon in my experience, for his lordship to be vomiting so cruelly. But then… A waxen image of his lordship, you say?"

"Riven through with hair from his very own head," Mister Halsall impressed upon the doctor.

"Indeed so," Doctor Case allowed, "or so it would seem."

"Then it could be so, that the spell could bring forth the very fluids of his lordship's body. But it'd take a powerful witch to cast such a spell; an unusually powerful witch."

"Or more than one, perhaps," Mister Halsall seemed knowingly to suggest, which again brought silence to the room, then Simon's leg began to cramp.

Unmoving beneath his blanket, he suffered its pain to grow as the silence continued to hold the room. Finally, though, Doctor Case drew in a deep breath.

"The weight of evidence does appear to tip the balance towards witchcraft," he resignedly announced. "For as you say, Mister Halsall, our usual precaution against poisoning has indeed brought no relief for his lordship. We must, therefore, be guided by your better knowledge in this matter, Doctor Bate."

"If that's your wish, Doctor Case, then so be it," Doctor Bate concurred.

Their footsteps could soon be heard returning to the bedchamber, leaving Simon to throw off the blanket before quietly groaning himself upright as he rubbed his leg.

"Poison?" he whispered very quietly to himself. "And only a small amount. I wonder how small."

When Randle returned a little later, he asked Simon if he'd recently seen his master, Mister Doughtie.

"No," Simon said. "I've not had a chance. Why?"

"It's just that Mister Smith was asking after him. Said he'd not seen him in a while and wondered if his lordship's illness might not have lowered his spirits."

"Are you staying here? I might go to our rooms and find out."

When Simon got there, he found them empty, although one of Robert's shirts hung on the back of a chair. He tidied it away then stared at the table beneath the window. Cocking his ear, he knelt beneath it.

Poking a couple of fingers into the hole in the wall at the back, he felt something soft and pliable. Before long, he'd teased out a small cloth bag, its neck drawn together by a cord. He listened out again, then undid the tie and upended the bag into his hand. A ring fell out, its gold and gems glittering in his palm.

"The one I saw Robert wearing at Knowsley," he quietly told himself as he gingerly picked it up and looked at it closely.

To Peter, it seemed rather ugly, its thick band and bulky setting hardly appealing. But then it struck him how light it felt, for something that looked so substantial.

The same thought must have crossed Simon's mind, for he tapped it with his fingernail. Its setting sounded hollow. But just then, footsteps came from the passage and Simon quickly returned the ring in its bag to its hiding place.

Scrambling to his feet, he faced the door, but the footsteps passed on by, further down the passage until they faded to silence. Simon took a deep breath.

"No," he gasped into the room's still air. "Surely not. I must be wrong," but Peter felt Simon's stomach turn suddenly leaden.

Peter felt inclined to agree with Simon's gut reaction. Although he'd never seen arsenic poisoning himself, from what he knew of it, it seemed too good a fit to be ignored. Indeed, the more he considered it, the more likely it seemed.

Simon didn't come across Robert on his way back to his lordship's apartments, where he found Randle still waiting. Before they'd a chance to speak, though, Doctor Case and Doctor Joynar came out from the bedchamber. This time, when they updated his lordship's case notes, it became clear they were now greatly worried that his waters had stopped.

Over the next few days, despite the doctors' best efforts, that remained the case. Each day, the poor man's cries of agony did lessen, although only because he was now falling more and more into long trances.

It may have been his quieter state that prompted Lady Alice to bring their daughters in to sit with him for an hour or so. But when their mother eventually shepherded them out, they looked saddened and withdrawn.

That they were such very young girls drew Peter up short. Their confused suffering placed his own feelings for Sophie in a starkly real light. Any hope he'd started out with for their shared love now seemed crass, unworthy of mention against the great weight of sadness being heaped upon the Stanley household. And so, as the outer chamber fell silent at their leaving, Peter finally let his hopes slip through his fingers. He'd find support in Sophie's presence, certainly, but would seek no more in the time they'd have left.

The next day, the Monday, Doctor Case asked Randle to go and find his servant. He then rummaged through the panniers beside the table.

"Can I help, Doctor Case?" Simon asked. The doctor peered at him for a moment.

"Actually, you can. Go and fetch me some boiled water. Enough for my servant to clean this," at which he took something from a cloth and held it up.

To Peter, it looked remarkably like a catheter, one the doctor then rewrapped and placed on the table.

When Simon got back with the water, it was to find the doctor's servant chatting with Randle, the catheter lying unwrapped on the table beside him. After thoroughly cleaning it, the young man took the instrument through to the doctor.

"What's that thing for, then?" Simon asked Randle.

"Seems they're going to try drawing his waters out," Randle told him. Simon clearly took a moment to think this through, then groaned as a shiver ran up his back.

About an hour later, the doctor's servant reappeared, his expression no more encouraging than when he'd gone in. It seemed his lordship's waters had remained elusive.

"Is that bad?" Simon asked. The servant stared at him for a moment, as though at an imbecile, then clearly relented.

"As his lordship's been kept well sated with drinking water, if it's not gone to his bladder, then where has it gone?"

Simon only stared at him, his mouth slowly hanging open.

During the early afternoon of the following day, Tuesday the sixteenth of April, those gentlemen who'd been staying at the castle over the past week or so again attended his lordship's sickbed. Swelling their numbers were other, newly arrived gentlemen, along with Ferdinando's personal staff, and the clerics Chaplain Lee and Bishop Chaderton. There was, though, no sign of Robert Doughtie, Ferdinando's waiting-gentleman and cupbearer.

The press of people in the bedchamber was such that the door was left open, just inside of which Simon and Randle surreptitiously positioned themselves.

The knots of dark-clothed figures about the room—whispering their close conversations whilst they kept their grave faces turned towards their recumbent lord—reminded Peter of his shocked first arrival at Lathom House. Only six months earlier, the previous September, he'd stood beside this same fourposter bed. It was clearly and lamentably yet again set to become the deathbed of an Earl of Derby.

As with the father, now with the son, Peter sadly reflected, even down to the same day of the week, a Tuesday.

Whereas then Jane Halsall had been attentive to the grey and sunken face of her common-law-husband, Henry, now it was Alice who sat silently staring at the mottled and jaundiced face of his son, her husband. Behind her stood Jane Halsall and Ferdinando's uncle, Sir Edward, their own faces disfigured by foreboding looks of wretched sadness.

From what Peter could tell, Ferdinando seemed to spend much of the time in the supposed sanctuary of his trances. But occasionally, the murmur of his voice would rise, only to reach those nearest to him.

Towards the middle of the afternoon, as though rallying his strength, Ferdinando's voice once more became clear for all to hear.

He told Alice, "I'm resolved presently to die, my beloved wife, and to take away with me only one part of my coat-of-arms. I mean the eagle's wings, so I will fly swiftly into the bosom of Christ my only saviour."

For the first time within Peter's hearing, Alice quietly wept, her head bowing down and so out of sight. No doubt she'd bent to kiss her husband farewell, for those in the room likewise lowered their own heads. The soft intoning of prayers then gently filled the air as the Bishop of Chester stepped nearer, offering his final comfort to his old friend the Earl.

At five o'clock, the sunlight streaming in at the windows casting long shadows across the room, Ferdinando Stanley, the fifth Earl of Derby, putative King of England, departed this life. He'd spoken just the once more, to assure Alice of his profound love for her and their daughters.

Only Alice's quiet sobs now filled the room, until the Bishop's cracked voice finally led the prayers for all those gathered there in their tearful sorrow.

And there, too, within Simon's downcast head, Peter and Sophie wept for the departed soul of the man they'd both come to regard as so intimately a part of themselves. A gentle and thoughtful man he'd been, a man whose fate had clearly cast him as one of harsh history's most unfortunate victims.

50   THE LESSER OF TWO EVILS

The prayer over with, Simon raised his head. Peter
noticed that Jane Halsall had now taken a comforting
hold of Alice. But it wasn't long before the lady lifted
her gaze from her now peacefully stilled husband, a
steeliness in her eyes. She took a deep and purposeful
breath and lifted her chin, seeking out someone from
those around her.

"Mister Halsall, if you would?" she requested, at
which Jane slipped her hands from Alice's arms, as
though they'd been shrugged off. Mister Halsall
dipped his head and retreated from the room,
sweeping Simon with him as he turned at the door.

"Find your master," he quietly instructed. "Inform
him that his lordship no longer draws breath." Simon
nodded. "And, Master Wardell, you've well acquitted
your service to his lordship and myself over these past
two weeks, for which I'm indebted. So, you can,
thereafter, consider yourself released from it," at which
he dismissed Simon and returned to the bedchamber.

Simon stood for a moment, staring after him, his hands slowly gripping into fists at his side. Then, under his breath, he asked himself, "Why Robert? Why him first?" Feeling lightheaded, he snapped to, turned about and resolutely left the apartments.

When he came into the great hall, the man himself was there, quietly talking with another gentleman. At a discreet distance away, Simon aimed his scrutiny squarely at Robert, shifting from foot to foot as he waited to be noticed.

"Ah," Robert said to the gentleman as he turned in Simon's direction, a heavy foreboding in his voice, "I've a dark feeling we're just about to find out. The darker, I'd wager, by the look on your face, Master Wardell," at which he waved Simon nearer.

"Mister Doughtie, Mister Holcrofte," Simon gritted out between his teeth, briefly dipping his head. "Mister Halsall has sent me with a message, Mister Doughtie."

Robert's shoulders slumped as he beckoned Simon to speak.

"I'm to inform you, sir, that his lordship no longer…no longer draws breath." Peter felt a tear well in the corner of Simon's eye, his teeth soon clamped together to steady his jaw.

"And so it is," Robert said, as though the ghost of Ferdinando now stood accusingly before him, "the dark foreboding gains solid form. And with it, weighs my heart most painfully low as it casts its shadow upon my soul." Robert's eyes had dulled, his skin drained of its colour.

"A dark day, indeed, Mister Doughtie," Mister Holcrofte lowered his head to say, incredulity hollowing out his voice. "A most sad and shocking day for Lathom," at which the gentleman seemed close to tears.

"A sad day for the whole of Lancashire, sir, but in particular for her ladyship and her poor unfortunate daughters; to which urgent end I must take my leave." He nodded to the gentleman, then addressed Simon directly, but with his voice, not his eyes.

"If you're free to attend me now, Master Wardell?" although he didn't wait for an answer before stepping out towards their apartments.

Clothes were scattered about the room when they got there. As Simon closed the door behind them, he also noticed two panniers set against the wall.

"Are you... Are you off somewhere, Mister Doughtie?"

"I can't delay, Simon. I must be on the road as soon as possible; to take advantage of what's left of the daylight."

"But... But where are you going? And why? And...and why so late in the day?"

"I'm to speed the news of his lordship's death to the Court in London," Robert hurriedly told him, as though distracting himself with practicalities. "Her ladyship's now trusting to Secretary Cecil to protect her interests, so the sooner he knows, the better."

"But surely I should go with you?" Simon carefully said. "As your valet," and by now, his every muscle had drawn as tight as a bowstring.

"Not this time, Simon. No. You're to stay here. Mister Farington will assign you your duties whilst I'm gone." All the while, Robert had refused to look Simon in the eye, which seemed to course the blood more loudly in Simon's ears.

With his hands now bunched painfully into fists, Simon tersely demanded, "So, why you, Robert?"

"What?"

"Why're you being sent? Why not a usual messenger?"

Despite Simon's intense stare, Robert closely scrutinised his valet's features, his eyes narrowing, his shoulders square and tense.

"Mister Halsall," he warily said, "wanted someone of note for the weight of the tidings. Someone he could trust to deliver a...a true report. I've a fair copy of the doctors' notes to take with me, and Mister Halsall's own report, both of which—"

"You say *true* report," Simon challenged, to which Robert only stared at him, his mouth agape. "That his lordship died of witchcraft, I take it?" Simon went on to say in a menacingly precise voice. "That no mention's to be made of *poison*, perhaps?" by which time his intense stare had become an outright glare.

"P...Poison? Why should—"

"I see you're no longer wearing your new ring, *Robert*."

Robert glanced down at his hand, then towards the table beneath the window, his jaw set firm when he again faced Simon.

"I assume you've carefully packed the evidence away in one of your panniers."

"How did... Who... Who told... Has Mister Halsall said something?"

"How could you?" Simon spat at him, shuddering. "And why? Against our own good lord and master. A lord and master who's always treated us with nothing but kindness and understanding."

"How could I?" The face Robert now presented looked close to tears. "How could… I *couldn't*; not of my own free will," and anguish suddenly broke free across his face. "I'd gladly have suffered death myself as a reward for my refusal, had that very same free will itself not denied me such a loyal and honourable course."

"Denied you?"

"I asked you to trust me, Simon. To put your trust in my love for you." Robert stretched out to take Simon's arm but he drew back, out of reach, a shiver running up his back.

"Your love for me?" Simon barely whispered. "Love? I'm no longer sure what love is; whether I can still love a man who…who… Oh, why, Robert? Why did you murder our beloved lord? And so cruelly so?"

Robert winced. "I… I was told it would take him swiftly. God damn them! You must believe me, Simon: I never wanted him to suffer as he did, nor for you to be there to witness it."

"Damn who, Robert? Who put you up to it, and in God's good name, why? Why, Robert? Why would anyone want his lordship dead?"

Robert appeared to stare through Simon for what seemed an age. But then he only shook his head, his lips pressed firmly together.

Simon's breathing had now become dizzyingly shallow, his voice quavering: "Tell me something, Robert; something other than of blind trust; something to make right that I should hold my tongue. Something to stop me from running straight to Mister Golborne and telling him all, and where the proof of it lies," at which he thrust his arm out towards the panniers.

"You… You can't. You mustn't, Simon. But… But not for my own pitiful sake. No, not for mine."

"For whose, then?" Simon barked back. "Mister Halsall's? For he's plainly got a hand in it."

"No, Simon. No. Neither he nor I. Neither of us are that important."

His words left an iciness hanging in the air, through which Simon now stared at Robert. Stared as though the answers he sought were somehow written on the face of the man Peter suspected he still loved far too much. Then that face crumpled under a weight Robert could clearly no longer bear.

"It was for your own sweet sake, Simon," he finally blurted out through his tears. "*Yours* alone. For I couldn't bear the thought of…"

"Bear… Bear the thought of what, Robert? For Christ's sake, what couldn't you bear?"

Robert's tears ran freely now. "Had I not agreed to the vile act, someone close to Her Majesty, in Her Majesty's own Government, would have had us…had us both…arrested."

"*Arrested*?"

"Ours, Simon, is a love deemed unlawful against Church and State. Its penalty: to hang by the neck."

Simon stared mutely at Robert, open-mouthed, the force that had steeled his body quickly leaching away.

"Cruelly, they promised me my own clemency. Only mine, mind. So, how could I possibly deny them? Tell me that, Simon. How could I choose to send the only man I've ever truly loved to the gallows? How, in sweet Heaven's name, could I possibly have suffered that for the rest of my miserable life? How, Simon? How could I?"

51   A STALWART COMPANION

As though he'd been hewn from stone, Simon's stare seemed to go straight through Robert's tearstained face, not a breath passing between his parted lips. Then his legs gave way.

Robert caught him, enfolding him in his arms, taking his weight from the legs he could no longer feel. As Robert held him close, Simon let out a ragged breath and slowly summoned the strength to return his lover's embrace. He shuddered, the hot tears stinging his face soon mingling with Robert's own.

"I'm sorry, my love," Robert breathed into Simon's ear. "I'm so sorry. If only I could have kept it from you; for your own sake. But I should've realised you'd suspect me; I've barely recognised myself these past three weeks."

"I…" Simon waveringly began, only to bury his face in Robert's neck. They stood this way for a while, until Simon choked back his tears and mumbled, "I… I hope I'm the only one who has."

"Another reason for me to get away soon, Simon, and why Mister Halsall insisted I kept myself to myself. But once I've returned the ring, there'll be nothing concrete to link me to his lordship's death, whatever suspicions might arise. And there's only Mister Halsall and his real masters who know of my part in it." Simon blenched at the stark use of the word "death".

"And now me," he said, in a small voice.

"And now you, Simon. Now you."

"But… But why Mister Halsall, of all people? Why him? I always thought him such a faithful servant of this house; a friend to his lordship, not his downfall. I… I can't believe it."

"Things are… Things are always more mired than we'd want them to be, Simon. But all you need know now is that you can trust him with your life."

"My life?" Simon quietly marvelled, then drew his head away, to look Robert in the eyes. "The thing that's brought you so cruelly to murder the man we vowed to protect and serve. The one we truly loved and who's given us no cause for such treachery."

"Simon, listen to me. Please. It was my own choice; mine alone, do you hear? You're not to blame for my being forced into choosing between you, and for choosing your life over his."

"But mine's worthless against any nobleman's, Robert, never mind our own—"

"To me, Simon, you're everything; all that matters; all that will ever matter. A rare ray of sunshine in what would otherwise be a dark world."

Simon slowly began shaking his head, but Robert stilled it between his hands, holding Simon's gaze in his own.

"Our lord's days were numbered anyway, Simon, whether by my hand or another's. He blotted his copy-book at the outset, when he didn't immediately refuse Richard Hesketh's traitorous offer."

"How could you possibly know that?"

"Mister Halsall deemed it might ease my qualms if he told me. He also told me of his lordship's final damning error: his denial of the Baron of Newton's presence with Hesketh at Brereton, where the offer was first made. Something that was already known to those close to Her Majesty."

"But I can't believe our lord would have seriously considered—"

"It doesn't matter what he intended, Simon. It's what he did, his actions, that counted. And what's since set the whole Court against him. His lordship lost a stalwart companion from both the Court and Her Majesty: their trust. And what with his strong claim to the crown, such a mistake was bound, eventually, to prove fatal."

"But, however foolhardy his lordship may have been, for it to have been by our *own* hands, Robert!"

"It's done now, Simon. There's nothing to be had by anyone knowing of my part in it, only much hurt, hurt neither of us need suffer. Or for me, to suffer beyond the heinous sin I've already committed against God, whose forgiveness I'll implore for the rest of my life."

Simon silently stared at Robert, clearly torn. Presently, though, he slowly began to nod, his shoulders slumping in acceptance.

"How safe will we be, Robert? We two who know too much of the matter."

"No one but me knows you know, and as for Mister Halsall: your continued safety is his guarantee that his own part in it will never come to light. So, Simon, for your sake and mine, you must now solemnly swear you'll never reveal anything of it. Do you understand? Not a word to anyone, ever."

Simon froze for a moment, then finally resolved, "I will, Robert, but only if you tell me why Mister Halsall can come to hold his position here when he's clearly got no honest oath of allegiance to the Earls of Derby. How I can be content to hold my tongue against his duplicitous presence amongst us."

"Ah, yes. Mister Halsall's part. Well, Simon, all I can tell you is what I suspect, for I don't really know. But has it never struck you how the old Earl lived so openly with Jane Halsall, as his common-law wife, when he was still legally wed to the Lady Margaret? How he could then go on to bestow the Stanley name on one of his illegitimate sons by her, without prejudice from Her Majesty or anyone of her Government?" Simon stared at Robert for a moment, then let out a knowing breath.

"Ah, a blind eye turned for services rendered, I take it? The Halsall family's privileged position left unchallenged, in payment for one of theirs being a continual government spy and agent in the Stanley household?"

"I suspect so, Simon. But as to whether Jane's aware of this herself, well, I don't suppose we'll ever know."

"Clearly, nothing's as it seems. That's plain now, which shows how naïve I've been." Simon drew in an affirming breath. "Very well, I'll say nothing. I'll keep my respect for Mister Halsall's position, however much it might stick in my craw."

Robert clearly relaxed, his expression lightening, until Simon narrowed his eyes at him.

"You keep mentioning love's stalwart companion, Robert. Well, now *you* must trust *me*, starting with what else you've to do for Mister Halsall, once you're away from Lathom."

"What else I've to… No, you're right, Simon: we must trust each other completely from now on. What I should have done from the very beginning. And yes, there's much I've yet to do, but none of it, thank the good Lord, as evil as my last deed." Robert glanced out of the window.

"I'll have to be brief, though, Simon; time's slipping by."

He drew away from their embrace and nearer the window, looking out without seeing for a moment before telling Simon, "Her Majesty's Government wants to avoid any Catholic unrest in this handful of England. But after what happened to Richard Hesketh, people will naturally assume his lordship's unusual death to be their retribution on him for his part in it."

"I've already heard such talk."

"Already, eh? Well, that's my next task: to help put the blame fairly and squarely at the door of witchcraft. To tell anyone who'll listen on my way to London of what I've supposedly witnessed here. Stories of his lordship upsetting a witch by refusing her offer of advancement in his causes, by means of divination and the like; of a strange apparition that came to him the day before he fell ill; and others."

"All false, I take it."

"All no more true than the waxen image Mister Halsall said he'd found."

"I thought it very strange that no one else saw it before he threw it on the fire."

"Before long, through mine and the efforts of others, the whole of England will be convinced that witchcraft's to blame for his lordship's death. Not disaffected Catholics…nor any hint of involvement by Her Majesty's Government."

"And once that's done, and you've delivered the news of his lordship's death, you'll come straight back to me here? Unharmed?"

"As soon as I safely can, Simon, yes, I will. I promise. Until then, you're to trust to Mister Halsall to look after your interests."

"There's still one thing you haven't answered."

"Hmm? And what's that?"

"Who actually ordered the death of our lord, and why."

Robert at first only stared at Simon, but then told him, "Trust, Simon, is a hard thing to yield to any man, evidenced by what little Mister Halsall's afforded me. The plain truth of it is that I don't know, but he did carefully instruct me to deliver my message directly into the hand of only one man—that of Her Majesty's Secretary of State, Sir Robert Cecil. Make of that what you will."

"Sir Robert? But I thought he'd always been a good friend to our lord, as he was to his father," to which Robert gave out a hollow laugh.

"As I see it, he's the new kingmaker. And kingmakers have no real friends, Simon. This one certainly not, for he clearly saw no place for our unfortunate lord's claim to the throne in his plans for England's wholly Protestant future."

"But why would—"

"I'm sorry, Simon, but time's moving on, and that's everything I know, or am ever likely to. So, my sweetest heart," and he opened his arms wide, "if you're recovered enough now, give me your best farewell. To soften the blow of having to leave you behind. Then I really must go."

Simon faltered for a moment, but then rushed into his arms, their lips pressed urgently to a fervent kiss, each holding tight to the other in their reaffirmed love. When, at long last, Robert drew apart, his face beamed a reassuring promise that all would be well. Enough for Simon to steal a final fleeting kiss.

Before long, Simon had dressed him in a riding cloak and stout leather boots, wrapped and shod and ready to take to the road. When Robert picked up his panniers, Simon held the door open for him. Robert, though, just stood there, drinking in the sight of him. Slowly, a cautious smile suffused his now plainly relieved face.

"Keep well and safe, Simon. I'll be back as soon as it's deemed wise, then maybe we can start to put this all behind us. Certainly, once his lordship's brother, William, arrives; our next lord and master, and before long the sixth Earl of Derby," at which he spat at the floor.

Without a further word, he was out in the passage, a lingering last look at Simon before he hurried away towards the stables.

Exhausted, Simon went to the window and slumped down on its deep sill. He looked out, down onto an alleyway below, and waited. After a short while, Robert's cloaked figure hurried past, soon vanishing from sight when he turned at the far end of the alley.

In the heavy silence that now swaddled him, Simon softly wept, rocking gently to and fro on the windowsill. He'd just taken out his kerchief, to mop his eyes, when an idea clearly struck him.

"A keepsake," he exclaimed. "He should have a keepsake. If I rush, I can give him this to take with him, to kiss each night before he falls asleep."

He was soon off the windowsill, out of the room and flying along the passage, leaping down the steps to the great hall. Here, he slowed as he made his way through and out into the bailey. From across it came the clop of hooves, towards which Simon then raced, hell for leather. And there, in the distance, Robert's mounted figure slipped from sight at a walk into the gatehouse passageway.

"Oh, shit," Peter let out, panic surging up from his guts. "Sophie?" and to his relief she answered with a startled yelp.

"I'll not get caught out again," he told her, and not only could he now once more feel his own phantom body but also Sophie's, hurriedly drawn into his urgent embrace.

Before she could protest, he kissed her, although her lips soon yielded to his. Her mouth tasted sweet, her scent intoxicating, her soft murmur far too seductive. But then he saw how close Simon had got to the gatehouse, hot on Robert's heels.

"Come what may, Sophie, my only love," he rushed to say as Simon came into its ominous shadow,

"I'll love you for ever and a day. I truly will."

Now within the passageway, Robert in sight ahead of them in the outer bailey, Peter tensed at seeing the very place from where he knew he'd soon be torn from her.

"He was right," he exclaimed. "Robert was right, Sophie," but then Simon stepped onto the cobbles beyond the gatehouse and Peter's vision began to dim.

"Our own stalwart companion," he blurted out. "Put your trust in me, Sophie, for I'm far too stubborn to be—" but then that familiar sharp pain shot across his brow and everything blinked to blackness.

The mundane sight of the alcove beside the chimneybreast in his apartment's lounge appeared before him, although a groan from behind made him turn around.

"Has it worked? Did you get to meet up with Sophie again?" Beryl asked, hopefully, as she got to her feet from the floor. Peter vaguely remembered it was where she'd fallen after spinning him around to face Simon's ghost.

"Yes, Beryl," he distantly told her, feeling strangely numb. "I did. But for the last time, apparently. As Sophie was all too often at pains to tell me. 'For the very last time,' she'd say," but Beryl only stared at him, the hope that had been on her face now replaced by puzzlement.

"But you've no need to worry about me, Beryl. No need at all," and a resolve settled into Peter's stubborn heart. A resolve he knew would keep his tears at bay through the empty years ahead.

52   FOR A GRACEFUL CHILD'S DAY

Wearing a broad-brimmed waxed hat, and a sweat-soaked T-shirt and shorts under his long Barbour jacket—one that had long since seen better days—Peter trudged on through the torrential January rain. The humid air he breathed in came thick in his throat as his sandal-shod feet splashed through the gritty puddles and pools, and his backpack's straps dug deep into his shoulders.

Coming towards him, through the spray thrown up from the wide road's old broken tarmac, rode three mounted men. Their own broad-brimmed hats proudly displayed recognisable if somewhat bedraggled plumes.

"Constables," Peter mumbled under his breath and quietly cursed as he surreptitiously felt in the lining of his jacket for his long knife. Before long, they drew near.

"So, what do we have here, then?" the foremost of the three men called. "A face I certainly don't know.

Either of you?" he asked his companions as the rain sluiced from their long capes, the kind that stretched back over the haunches of their horses.

"Not from these parts, I'd say," one of them reckoned, hunching forward to get a better view of Peter's face as they came to a halt before him, blocking his way.

"Outsider," the other asserted, dismissively.

"I trust you've a Lancashire Barons' Court passport about your *foreign* person?" the first enquired.

As the horses whinnied and snickered and snatched at their bits, Peter slowly slipped his arms from his backpack. Keeping half an eye on the men, he swung it around to his chest, sheltering its opening beneath the brim of his hat.

He passed a worn leather wallet up to the constable, who sheltered it beneath his own hat as he removed a document. After peering at it closely for a while, he lifted an eyebrow at Peter.

"Doctor, eh?" He shot a mischievous look at one of his companions. "Better 'ave you take a look at me colleague here's bad breath, then," and he barked a cruel laugh, although he soon sobered. "Well, this all looks in order, though you're a long ways from Norfolk. But a healthy enough place, I suppose; what I hear's still left above water these days."

The constable inclined his head, enquiringly, tipping rainwater from his hat's brim to his shoulder.

"If I might ask what business you 'ave here, Doctor Buchanan?" and he leaned forward to return Peter's wallet.

"I'm looking for a man," Peter said, putting his passport safely away and slipping his backpack back on. "I've been told he lives in Westhead. Artificer Jameson, if you know him?" The constable raised the other brow.

"Ai, happ'n I do. Like I do most hereabouts. Friend of yours, or summat else?" Peter angled a forced smile up at him, bringing a warm trickle of rainwater to slip down his neck. He hunched his shoulders, to soak it up in his T-shirt.

"I used to live near here."

"Oh, ai. You don't sound like you ever did…if you don't mind me saying, *sir*."

"It was a long time ago, Constable."

"It must've been. Well, you'll find 'im at t'smithy, not far past t'Old Prince Albert. Pop into t'pub; they'll tell you where it is."

"Is it far?"

"Nah; about a mile and a half, so you'll be there well before t'curfew," at which he tapped his finger against the brim of his hat. "Stay out o' trouble n' you'll stay out of our way," he advised and jabbed his heels into his horse's flanks.

Peter stepped smartly aside.

The Old Prince Albert, unlike most of the properties he'd passed on his way through the largely deserted village, looked spruce and occupied, its walls newly whitewashed, its windows clean, its front door latched wide open. Peter went in.

The slap of his sandals on the flagged floor brought a head to appear above the bar that ran along the wall opposite. A curly-haired man of about forty straightened up, finally standing a good foot taller than Peter as he peered down at him, his hair brushing the rafters. His gaze then dropped lower, to the rainwater Peter had brought in with him, now pooling about his feet.

The man tutted. "I've not long mopped that floor," at which Peter apologised. But at the sound of his foreign accent, the landlord stiffened, his hand slipping out of sight beneath the bar.

"You after a drink?" he cautiously asked. "Just that we ain't set up for owt but barter."

"No. Just after directions," Peter assured him. "Looking for the smithy. Constables told me it was near here."

"Constables, eh? They seen ya, then?" to which Peter smiled, disarmingly.

"On the road into here. Checked my passport if that's what's worrying you."

"Ah, right," and the landlord clearly relaxed a little, planting both palms on the countertop. "Who you after at t'smithy, if I might ask?"

"Artificer Jameson."

"Right. And 'e knows yer coming?"

"No, but we knew each other in the old days."

"Hmm," and the man stared hard at Peter for a moment. "Best go with you," at which he hollered through an opening behind him: "Just goin' out, Vicky. Won't be long, chuck," to which a voice from somewhere in the depths of the pub acknowledged him.

He leant through the opening, retrieving a cloak and hat and putting them on as he came out from behind the bar.

"Right, this way," and he led Peter back out into the rain.

"Just a couple o' roads down on t'left," he said as they headed east, away from the centre of the village and skirting a flooded section of the road. "House n' outbuildings on t'corner," but the man said nothing more, not until they'd arrived at a sideroad bearing the nameplate "Forge Close".

"This is it," he told Peter. "Yard on t'right, up there, but I'll show you which door."

He took Peter a short way up Forge Close to what looked like a stone-flagged mews entrance. Around the yard it led to stood a variety of old farm buildings. Each had, at some time in the past, been expensively converted into bijou individual dwellings, although they were now making a good stab at returning to something nearer their original use.

The landlord led Peter to the first of the buildings, pointing out a door in the gable end of its lean-to.

"There you are," he said, and Peter went over and knocked.

Footsteps could be heard from within, then the door cracked open for a moment before flying wide.

"I don't believe it," the woman now standing in the doorway gasped, her hand shooting to her long brown, grey-streaked hair. She stared at Peter, her other hand clasping at the plain apron she wore. Peter paused, momentarily taken aback.

"Hello, Beryl. You remember me, then?"

"Derek," she yelled. "Just come and see what the cat's brought home."

"She bringing in bloody rats again?" came Derek's voice from somewhere within. "We're going to have to... Oh, my God," he let out as he came up behind Beryl, his white hair stark against the gloom of what looked like a cloakroom behind him.

"Derek!" Beryl quietly admonished, and growled,

"Not when the world and its dog can hear," at which she gave half an eye to The Old Prince Albert's waiting landlord. "But by Dei," she then enthused more loudly, "you're a sight for sore eyes, Peter Buchanan."

The landlord coughed. "I take it everything's cool, then? If so, I'll get mesen back."

"Never better," Beryl assured him, a sparkle in her eyes, then she thanked him before almost pulling Peter inside and closing the door against the rain.

"Get yourself out of those wet things," she insisted, "so I can give you a proper hug." Her face beamed in the half-light as her gaze flitted about Peter's overjoyed features, and as Derek leant past her to shake his hand.

"Oh, I can't tell you how good it is to see you both again," Peter himself now enthused. "You don't know how much."

"Well, knock me over with a feather, but you're the last person I expected," Derek told him, his grin threatening to split his face. "But you're more than welcome, Peter. More than welcome, my friend. But how long has it been now? It's got to have been…what? Ten years, at least?"

Peter got out of his wet things, which Beryl then took away to dry.

"Nearly fifteen since my contract ended and I left The Royal Preston for the Hellesdon in Norwich," Peter said. "But when did you and Beryl move from Longton?"

"Must be coming up to eight years now. We saw the way it was going back in twenty-four and knew we were too near Preston. Skem's just down the road, I know, but its population wasn't anywhere near the same size. And here, I'm a local lad, having grown up in the village."

Beryl rushed back and threw her arms around Peter.

"Oh, it's so good to know you're alive and well," her muffled voice enthused against his neck as he hugged her back, but then she held him at arm's length. "Wet through to the skin, though. I'll get you a towel."

"It really is wonderful seeing you two again, it really is. And thanks, Beryl, but there's no need for a towel. I'll dry off quickly enough in this heat."

"Have you eaten?" she asked. "Are you hungry?"

"Not since this morning. And yes, ravenous."

"Then come on through. We've plenty of rice and some mutton, well, mainly rice; but it'll fill you up."

She stopped and shook her head.

"I still can't believe it," but then she bustled him through to a kitchen dominated by an Aga range and a long pine table. She offered him a seat then asked how long he'd been in Lancashire, and how on Earth he'd got in.

"Doctors are in short supply and in huge demand everywhere these days."

"Tell us about it," Derek groaned. "Our nearest's in Mawdesley, a good five miles away. You wouldn't be planning on staying, would you? There are plenty of properties still in good nick in the village."

"I can't think of anywhere better, for the time being, anyway."

"What? Really? In perpetually sodden Lancashire?"

"Preferable to the insufferable heat of a three-year-drought-stricken and fast threatening-to-be-an-island Norfolk."

"Still, it seems a long way to come to spend your days getting drenched. Surely there are better places?"

"I've actually been here over a year now, Derek. So, I've had plenty of time to grow a set of gills."

"A year?"

"Earning my leave-to-stay by serving as a border guard medic, over on the coast. Been stationed on the Scarisbrick headland, opposite Formby Island. From where I came this afternoon."

"So, you've not been that far from us for the past year," Derek marvelled.

"Nope. Just a couple of hours' walk. But it was only by chance I knew you were here. Your name came up in the mess, a couple of weeks ago. A conscript from here."

"That'd be Phillip Ashby."

"That's him. Until then, I'd assumed you'd not come through it all, what with you living so close to a biggish city like Preston; the cholera and the rest."

"Here you are," Beryl said, putting a bowl down on the table. "Get yourself outside that."

Derek sat across the table from Peter, watching him eat whilst Beryl went off to get their guest some water from the well.

After Peter had got a good few mouthfuls of rice into him, Derek quietly ventured, "You were coming here anyway, weren't you, Peter? Or hereabouts."

Peter only lifted his gaze from his meal and stared back, his head cocked to one side.

"I mean, it must've been a long and arduous journey from Norwich; not to mention dangerous. More than—now, don't take this the wrong way, Peter—but more than having once had close friends up here would warrant. Ones who in all likelihood wouldn't have survived anyway. Unless you're going to tell me it was the plentiful supply of warm Atlantic rain that's what's really drawn you back." A grin slowly spread across Peter's face.

"What I've always valued in you, Derek: your directness...and your insight."

"So?"

"So what?" Beryl asked as she came back in and placed a mug of water beside Peter's bowl of rice.

"Derek's just asked me for the real reason I've come back," Peter told her.

"I did wonder myself. So? Why have you, Peter? beyond the pleasure of catching up with us, of course."

Peter took a long swig of his water and sighed.

"You know," he said, a satisfied look on his face. "I don't think I'll ever take Lancashire water for granted." But as he thoughtfully placed the mug down, he cocked an eye Derek's way.

"It's a bit of a long shot, but it's all to do with Tuesdays," he said, but before the threat of his grin could take hold, he tucked back into his rice.

53   BIT OF A LONG SHOT

"It's been pitch black since we lost the daylight, Peter," Derek complained.

"Shush. Not so loud."

"But," he now whispered, "there's no one around to hear us. We'd have seen lights by now, surely?"

"Maybe, but then, maybe not," and Peter took another look out of the window of the rusted old Transit van in which they'd chosen to hide. He strained to see anything of the dilapidated Lathom House, his old apartment's ground floor windows barely forty feet away.

"You said yourself it might not be this year," Derek again whispered. "And this van's sweltering."

"There's still plenty of water in my backpack," and then Peter saw a few stars twinkling through gaps in the cloud cover. "At least it's stopped raining."

"Hmm. I wouldn't hold your breath."

"We humans have certainly put the kybosh on the term 'April showers'. It's the eighth, and this is the first time it's stopped raining since March."

"But if you're wrong, and it's not this year, when was it you said the next opportunity would be?"

"Twenty-forty-two; eleven years off. The next to have its dates on the same days of the week as in Ferdy's time. When I'll be sixty-two, for Dei's sake. And damn the Beatles for making it sound so old."

"It was sixty-four."

"What was?"

"When I'm sixty-*four*," Derek quietly sang.

"Oh, well, that's all right, then; make that two years before I'll be past it."

Peter rummaged in his backpack, finally finding what he was after. The inside of the van briefly and faintly glowed a pale green.

"What you got there?" Derek asked.

"It's half-nine. There should be something going on by now."

"You've got a watch? You must've hung on to a fair few batteries for that."

"Solar powered. Digital; so there's no moving parts to wear out. Been keeping it safe for tonight."

"I'll give you ten out of ten for planning."

"Come on; we need to get closer. We're going to have to go inside. Clouds have cleared a bit more. I reckon we've just enough starlight to see by."

"Well, don't lose me. I didn't know the place like you did," and they scrambled about in the van as quietly as they could until they found the back doors and clambered out.

The gravel of the driveway sounded loud in Peter's ears, then Derek grabbed hold of him. Peter directed his grip to the tail of his jacket. Together, they inched their way towards the faint outline of the house, trying not to crunch the gravel too much beneath their feet.

"We'll go round the back," Peter whispered. "If we can get in through the French window, we'll be straight into my old bedroom."

It seemed to take an age before they'd even reached the front wall of the house, then another before they'd rounded its gable end, their feet by now bruised by debris and clogged with soil. Peter found the path into the rear carpark and made surer progress to the low wall of his old apartment's backyard. He then felt his way to the French window and tested its handle.

"Poo," he whispered. "Real poo bad," and he shook his head, the disappointment almost shattering his long-frayed nerves.

"What is it?" Derek whispered.

"It's locked."

"Doesn't matter."

"Why?"

Derek quietly chortled. "There won't be any glass in the frames, that's why."

"No glass?"

"Haven't you noticed? We're standing on shards of the stuff."

Peter shuffled his feet, realising Derek was right, then slipped his hand from the handle to feel within the frames. It glanced the sharp edge of a remnant of a pane.

"Ow," he fought to let out quietly, then tasted the edge of his hand. "I've bloody well cut myself."

"Well, that was a daft thing to do."

Once they'd cautiously stepped inside, their feet crunched more broken glass into what was now the squelching sound of sodden carpet. Making as little noise as they could, they fumbled their way around the room and onto quieter and drier carpet, Derek still holding onto Peter's jacket. By the time he'd found the door, Peter had his ear cocked.

"Can you hear something?"

Derek was silent for a few seconds. "Sort of."

Pressing his ear to the doorframe, Peter could just make out a fast, regular but low thumping noise. He got Derek to do the same.

"If I'm not mistaken," Peter whispered, his heart now in his throat, "I'd say that's a diesel engine."

"Oh, yeah. Does sound a bit like one, well muffled or some way off. Not heard one of those in donkey's."

Peter cracked open the door, the hallway beyond seeming even blacker.

He was just stepping through when he was sure he heard a voice coming from the lounge, low and indistinct. Before he could make out any words, though, its door swung open, a shock of bright light and the muted thump of a diesel generator flooding out into that end of the hallway.

Much to Peter's surprise, the glare of the light revealed it had recently been refurbished, the spare bedroom door beyond the kitchen wide open, presenting a glimpse of the recreated comforts of the old days when Peter had lived here. But then, two women emerged from the lounge.

Peter's heart almost hitched into his mouth at the sight of the second, her tightly-curled black hair reminding him of something Sophie had long ago let slip. In the gloom at their own end of the hallway, Peter froze, despite Derek nudging him from behind, keen to know what was going on.

"You go through to Debrief, Lynda," the first woman was now sympathetically urging, "and I'll bring you in a nice warm drink whilst you get yourself comfy. I've never seen you this upset before."

"But I feel so wretched," Lynda strained to say, her face drawn, then she sobbed, "Oh, Tina, how am I ever going to get over losing—"

"Sophie?" Peter softly blurted out, his thin voice surprising him. "That is you, isn't it, Sophie?" Both women jerked and swung their startled faces his way, peering into the gloom at his end of the hall.

"Who's there?" Tina growled against the blinding glare of the light from the lounge. "Who are you?"

"No. No, it can't be," Lynda uttered as she took a step forward, out of the light, her hand on Tina's arm. "It can't possibly… That voice can't be… Oh, by Dei, it is, isn't it? It really is you," and she took another step, slowly shaking her head as she peered, open-mouthed and wide-eyed, at Peter.

"It is, my love," Peter heard himself say, his face strangely numb, his limbs frozen, his mind whirling. "Here to make happy that wretched heart of yours. As my stubbornness promised I would before we were so painfully torn from each other, just…just a few of your own short minutes ago."

All that now moved in his old apartment's hallway were the tears that trickled down his cheeks, tears of relief, tears of joy, until Lynda's face—no, until Sophie's face—suddenly lit up. She rushed into his arms, her voice soon sobbing close against his neck.

"I should've believed you, Peter. Trusted you really meant it. Trusted I'd… But, wow, I can't get my head around it: that you've waited *all* those long years of your own to be with me again. But this time, in the very real flesh and blood," at which she hugged him tighter, as though not daring to believe it was anything other than a dream.

"Trusted I'd get to taste your lips for real," she finally marvelled, before pressing her own to his.

The taste was everything Peter could ever have wished for. The simplest and profoundest of things: the genuine touch of a lover; something so cruelly denied them both until now. Until trust had conquered time and brought their two worlds together. And with it, the chance of a shared future, one at long last free from the ripples of any butterfly's wings.

54   A LANCASHIRE RENAISSANCE

The hallway suddenly seemed crammed with people, a tall and angular man pushing his way through to Peter and Sophie.

"What's going on? And who're these two?" he demanded, flicking a dismissive finger at Peter and Derek. That Sophie and Peter were in each other's arms then clearly took him aback.

"This is Peter," Sophie said, drawing apart from him, wonder still in her voice. "Doctor Peter Buchanan."

"Peter Bu…" then his mystification gave way to utter amazement, the hallway behind him now jammed with faces jostling to see past each other.

"Everyone back to their tasks," he commanded over his shoulder, "and you three: into the kitchen; now." He stood aside, Sophie, Peter and Derek slipping past him, shuffling towards the kitchen door against the tight squeeze of people returning to the lounge.

Peter was shocked to find the lamplit kitchen still recognisable from when he'd last laid eyes upon it, although some of the units had been removed, the old fireplace they'd hidden now exposed, embers smouldering in its grate. A stack of barrels hid most of the now bricked-up window, some rough crates stacked in front of them.

Sophie, a wondering smile still on her face, set out to convince the man that Peter was indeed the person who'd joined her on her visits to the sixteenth century. He seemed doubtful, until Peter had told him enough of what had happened to him over the past twenty-one years, including Derek and Beryl's parts. The man had listened, finally staring, wide-eyed, at Peter.

"Oh, and Peter, this is Tom Leyton," Sophie said. "Assistant to the Barons' Court Council Chronoscope Administrator, the man who in turn reports directly to the Baron Lieutenant of Lancashire and Westmorland, Stan Bickerstaff."

"What?" Peter said. "The Stan Bickerstaff I pledged my oath to when I was conscripted into the border guard? King Stan, as everyone called him?" Sophie nodded. "In which case," and he turned to Tom. "How do you do?" and he smiled and held out his hand.

"Surprised," Tom presently told him, and lamely shook his hand. But then he abruptly withdrew his own and narrowed his eyes at Peter.

"There's nothing for it. You'll have to come with me. Both of you," he said, glancing between Peter and Derek. "First thing in the morning. Back to Hoghton Tower. This is all well beyond my remit. And you, Sophie, you'd best get off to Debrief." He stood aside, his arm outstretched towards the doorway.

Sophie stole a glance at Peter, a quick reassuring smile and she was gone, leaving Peter feeling bereft.

"But I need to get back to Westhead," Derek protested. "I've work to do tomorrow, and Beryl will go out of her mind, wondering where I've got to."

"It can't be helped. You're both now Barons' Court wards. You'll stay in *this* room until we leave in the morning."

"You can't do this," Derek said. "I can't be away from—"

"You've no choice in the matter, Artificer Jameson. And if you give me any trouble, I'll arrest you."

"Arrest me? For what? Visiting an old derelict property?"

"For breaking the curfew, for one thing."

"Ah," Derek said on a long outward breath. "Right. Well, I suppose the village will look after her until I get back. It won't be long, though, will it?" but Tom Leyton just bustled out, leaving them to themselves.

A few moments later and a young, stocky-looking man positioned himself by the doorway, clearly there to keep them from escaping.

"I'm sorry, Derek," Peter said. "I shouldn't have got you involved. I hope Beryl doesn't—"

"Don't worry about it, Peter. It was my own fault. I shouldn't have insisted on coming with you."

"I was glad you did, but now, well, now I'm not at all sure I should've let you. But anyway, there's nothing for it, we're just going to have to settle ourselves down here for the night, as best we can."

Come the morning, Sophie was conspicuous by her absence, likely asleep after her night's debriefing. Peter kept a hopeful eye out for her whilst he sat around with Derek, digesting the meagre breakfast they'd had and waiting for Tom Leyton to finish issuing orders. There seemed to be a lot of packing going on in the lounge, the rustle of straw and the hammering of crates being sealed shut.

They finally left Lathom House mid-morning, Peter, Derek, Tom Leyton, and the stout young man no doubt along as their guard. Unusually, the sky cleared as the morning wore on, bright April sunshine streaming down to scorch their backs as they trudged north-eastwards. Other than lunch at a pub on the way, they pressed on without stopping, finally mounting the long drive up to the manor house of Hoghton Tower towards late afternoon.

One look at the place told Peter why this had clearly become one of Lancashire's new seats of power, despite—but then, perhaps because of—its ancient origins; its intact and substantial defensive walls, its commanding hilltop position, its central location, its remove from any cities or towns, its essentially simple construction in wood and stone.

The sentries manning its imposing gatehouse hurriedly gave way to Tom Leyton's confident if somewhat weary entry. He soon deposited Peter and Derek in an anteroom that looked out onto an inner courtyard. And for the first time all day, even here in its bright interior, Peter felt cool, its large awnings shading the expansive leaded-light windows from the worst of the sun's heat.

After they'd been there an hour or so, sitting on a bench against the cool stones of its wall, the inner door opened. A man in sandals and a long, lightweight cotton tunic strode out. Derek and Peter promptly got to their feet.

"Which one of you's Doctor Buchanan?"

"That's me," Peter said, stepping forward.

"I'm Alan Stevens, the Barons' Court Council Chronoscope Administrator. And you must be Artificer Jameson," he then said to Derek, who nodded. "Well, you'll have to wait here whilst I speak with Doctor Buchanan." He stretched his arm out towards the door. "If you would, Doctor."

Peter went through into a room that looked out onto the outer courtyard and, beyond the gatehouse and its broad defensive wall, down the long slope of the hill to a pastoral spread of fields and woodland below. A large, somewhat cluttered desk stood before the window, an imposingly ornate, high-backed chair behind it. A simpler one stood before it, to which the Administrator nodded.

"Please, Doctor Buchanan. Take a seat," and once he'd sat down himself, he cleared his throat.

"Well, I won't deny I'm surprised. Greatly so. Your shenanigans have caused us no end of trouble; do you know that, Doctor Buchanan? No end of trouble. Or, to be more accurate, caused our poor scientists no end of trouble."

"How do you do it?" Peter bluntly asked, to which the Administrator seemed taken aback, but then grinned.

"I take it you mean, how do we see back through time?"

Peter nodded, at which the man steepled his fingers before him.

"Back in the good old days, before the Great Tipping Point, I was an administrator at Lancaster University. Back when life was so easy for so many."

He looked off into the distance, as though reliving it in his thoughts.

"But now, you see," he went on to say, "we've cast ourselves back in time in a much more immediate way, back to a version of the Middle Ages—*late* Middle Ages, I'm reliably informed. Although Dark Ages would be more accurate."

"Dark Ages?"

"We've lost so much, Doctor Buchanan, as you're well aware. So much across the board; from the simple to the complex. Firstly, through the collapse of the internet; then the loss of those who curated our knowledge, what was left after the Western Cultural Revolution got into its destructive swing and eradicated anything it found distressing, or that offended it. How much we've suffered from the steady denigration of authoritative facts."

"Tell me about it. I'm still looking for a copy of Culpeper's Complete Herbal, not that there'd be that many of the species he refers to still around these days."

"No, but thank Dei, our Baron Lieutenant Bickerstaff, in his wisdom and immense enthusiasm, had a vision for this new world of ours. But one, unfortunately, that would've taken generations to fulfil."

"A vision?"

"Of a New Renaissance, Doctor Buchanan. Not an English one, as in the seventeenth century, no, naturally not, but of a new Lancashire Renaissance."

"Ah," Peter sighed, "and one for which he'd need all those lost skills and knowledge, and all pretty damn fast. Stuff we could more rapidly pick up if only we could see back into the past, eh?"

"Exactly, and that's where I came in. My

university had been doing some research for the CCFE. You might remember them? The Culham Centre for Fusion Energy, down near Oxford?"

"Rings a bell."

"One of the pinnacles of human endeavour, in my view: to create and safely hold a miniature sun in the lab; the promise of eternal energy without the need to resort to using any of the Earth's polluting resources. And now we're hard pressed to find enough wood to cook with. What a come-down, eh?" An exasperated breath escaped him and he shook his head.

"What my university was doing for them back then was research into novel ways of containing plasma. But they had a bit of an accident, you see, a few years before everything went tits-up. A technician got hit by the freak escape of a super-thin sheet of the stuff, as best I understood it at the time."

"And, I take it, he found himself in the past?"

"Long and short of it, though it took them a few years to pin down how it had happened, what the physics behind it all was."

"And how it could be replicated?"

"Hmm," and the Administrator stared at Peter, his head cocked to one side. "They would have done, had they had time. But then the world went pear-shaped around them."

"But it works now. Clearly it does."

"I ended up serving the newly created Barons' Court Council and mentioned it to the Baron Lieutenant himself when I heard about his vision for the future. I can still vividly remember the way his eyes lit up."

"And the rest's history, as they say."

"Two of the lead scientists had survived, plus a technician—the one who'd got hit, as it happened. Enough of the original equipment was salvaged, along with generators and the like. Facilities provided as best we could, and a Barons' Council exemption granted for their use of fossil fuels; to power the generators."

"And they finally made time travel a reality."

"Not only a reality but mobile, just about. So we'd have a far wider reach. So we could go anywhere in Lancashire and Westmorland to target key people from the past, and the myriad lost skills we're crying out to relearn."

"But why did you target Ferdinando Stanley? Why him?"

"Ah, yes. The fifth Earl of Derby. Well, what better place than Lathom House to learn how to govern a land that's now become so alike their own. And what better tale to teach us about the dark inner workings of such a society, of its alliances, its enmities, its strengths and weaknesses. Of what must be done or guarded against in once more building a strong Lancashire powerbase."

"So, why are you telling me all this? The one who's caused you no end of trouble. It can't be just to satisfy my curiosity."

"No. Indeed not, Doctor Buchanan. If only life nowadays could afford such altruism."

"So?"

"It's all to do with that no-end-of-trouble you've caused us."

"I'm not with you."

"You wait till the scientists find out their

troublemaker's now so close at hand, in the here and now."

"Why? What're they going to do?"

"Peter—may I call you Peter?"

Peter cautiously nodded.

"With all your innocent breaking of some of the fundamental laws of physics, you've pushed their knowledge into new areas. Given them new avenues to investigate."

"I have?"

The man laughed. "And Lynda—or should I say Sophie?—reckons you're clearly an adept time traveller. The best she's seen, despite you having had no training."

"She does?"

"So, whilst they set up the equipment in its new location, I'm going to suggest you and Sophie take a break."

"A break?"

"All at the expense of the Barons' Court Council, of course. Enjoy yourselves for a couple of weeks. Take it easy."

"Easy? Why?"

"Then you'll both feel fully refreshed, won't you? For your next trip together...when you can both once more step into the past and give us a clearer view through the mists of time."

HISTORICAL NOTES

Introduction

Although this book is a work of fiction, it may interest some readers to know what parts of it draw upon real and recorded events from the period and what is conjecture, and how reasonable that conjecture may be. The historical events covered have huge gaps in their record, which of course is where the creativity of the author comes in. However, great care has been taken at all times to keep this fictional content in keeping with what over two years of extensive research has shown those involved to have been as very real people, and the lives they led.

Wherever possible, primary sources have been used, to avoid the perennial problem of the promulgation of erroneous facts, a problem encountered time and again. Care has also been taken in the sensitive interpretation of these primary sources, for people in the past were no more inclined to be open and honest than they are now. Judicious reading between the lines has not only served to tease out fresh understanding, but has also added immeasurably to bringing people alive in the author's mind.

As for accurately identifying many of those people, especially the less well known, great diligence was put into matching them with their respective spouses and parents. The practice of using the same few—particularly male—forenames in every generation can cause great confusion for posterity.

This postscript separates out the known fact from the author's fictional conjecture, often presenting the reasoning behind the creative infill. It does so more or less in the order the reader will come across them during his or her reading of this story, beginning with the significance of the location of Peter's apartment.

As with any historical research, there may have been sources that never came to light, and which may invalidate some of the assumptions made by the author. If this is the case, then the author humbly seeks the reader's forgiveness and will always stand to be corrected. Regardless, it's hoped you, the reader, will have found this tale from one of England's most fascinating periods of history otherwise most enjoyable and thought-provoking.

Clive S. Johnson
Manchester, England, February 2019

Notes on the Narrative

It's not known if the remaining wing of the C18th Lathom House, in which Peter Buchanan's apartment has been placed, does in fact stand where the approach to the inner bailey gatehouse of the castle once stood. Little has been excavated, even the precise location of the castle itself still being largely conjectural.

There is no record of any meeting between Secretary Cecil (1563-1612) and Ferdinando's younger brother, William (1561-1642), on any ship anchored outside a Continental harbour. This event is entirely fictitious, but not beyond the realms of possibility, its creation used to set the plot in motion.

Ferdinando's brother William Stanley was at the Court of King Henry III. of France until 1586, as part of the embassy of Queen Elizabeth I. After that, he spent the following three years in "private travels" on the Continent, of which little if anything is reliably known—not unusual for a younger son. So, any clandestine meeting during 1587 would have to have been held on the Continent.

The soldier Sir William Stanley (1548-1630), a relative of Ferdinando, was educated at Lathom House and brought up in the Catholic faith. After school, he entered the service of his kinsman, Edward Stanley, Ferdinando's grandfather, 3rd Earl of Derby (c.1508–1572). He then served in the Netherlands and Ireland until his surrender of Deventer in 1587, when he became a traitor to Queen Elizabeth I., thereafter serving the Catholic Spanish Crown in the Netherlands.

Ferdinando's claim to the throne came through his mother, Lady Margaret Stanley (nee Clifford), Countess of Derby (1540-1596), heir presumptive to Queen Elizabeth I. through the will and Third Succession Act of Henry VIII. At the death of her mother, she became 7th in line. However, both her cousins Lady Jane Grey and Lady Mary Grey died without issue and their sister, Lady Catherine Grey, died without legitimacy of her two sons being proven. This placed Margaret Clifford first in line, but she died (1596) before the death of Elizabeth I. in 1603.

There was great suspicion about Ferdinando's religious leanings, some believing him a secret Catholic, others that he was a less than staunch Protestant, and yet others that he was in effect an atheist. Given his keen interest in the burgeoning science of the time and the lack of any definitive documented evidence to the contrary, the author has assumed him to be of the latter persuasion: a closet atheist.

The "Hesketh Plot", as it became known, is quite well documented, largely through the record of Richard Hesketh's interrogation, and various other associated records held in the Cecil Papers in Hatfield House. This work has adhered to the known facts and their timeline without exception.

The history of Lathom House and the "Stanley Myth" of the eagle and child, narrated by Derek in chapter 3, is as the facts are known.

Ferdinando's father, the fourth Earl of Derby, probably died at Newparke, not Lathom House. The castle was chosen for his death scene for dramatic and plotline purposes. The two properties were only a mile or so apart, Newparke standing in the castle's extensive parkland estate.

Jane Halsall of Knowsley (c. 1535 – c. 1594), Henry, fourth Earl of Derby's, common-law wife and distant cousin, was the daughter of Sir Thomas Halsall, High Sheriff of Chester. She and her two daughters and a son did well from the fourth Earl's will, and the son,

Thomas, did indeed take the Stanley name, despite being illegitimate.

Henry's legal wife, Margaret Stanley, Countess of Derby—Ferdinando's mother—was held in house arrest, largely at Isleworth House in St. James in the parish of Clerkenwell, from 1579 until her death in 1596. Her crime was to seek to predict the death of the Queen, a capital offence at the time, so her house arrest was a lenient commutation. Her doctor and adviser William Randall was executed in 1580 for his part in this.

The C17th historian Camden says {Hist. Queen Eliz., p. 529) that Margaret, Lady Derby, had "a womanish curiosity" in prying into the future, "consulting with wizzards and cunning men," and hints that she aspired to the crown, her mother being the first cousin of queen Elizabeth, and after the execution of the queen of Scots, she and James I. were in an equal degree the descendants of the two daughters of Henry VII.

Richard Hickman, her receiver-general, was her longstanding servant at Isleworth House.

William Chaderton, Bishop of Chester, (1540-1608) was a longstanding close friend of Ferdinando's father, Henry, and a friend and spiritual guardian to Ferdinando himself. His quoting, in chapter 6, of Ferdinando's letters to him provides the title for this book, in its old spelling: "An Handfull of England", in reference to the heavily Catholic county of Lancashire.

There seems to be some confusion regarding the Richard Hesketh of the "Hesketh Plot", brought about by there having been at least two men alive at that time in Lancashire, of the same generation, with the same name. It's commonly believed that the plot's Richard Hesketh was of Rufford, son of a well-known soldier Sir Thomas Hesketh, the more prominent branch of the family. However, the author's own research has established that he was in fact of the lesser Aughton branch, son of one Gabriel Hesketh.

Richard was a common name in the Hesketh family, like many other families where the same few Christian names tended to re-appear in each successive generation. Over the centuries, these two Richards appear to have been conflated—possibly from the Heralds' Hesketh Pedigrees visitations of 1613, 1664, etc..

Even at the time of the Hesketh Plot, confusion existed as to who had actually been arrested, as the prisoner himself had to clarify in a letter to his gaoler, William Waad, dated 5th of November, 1593, the pertinent parts of which say:

"As concerning that Mr. Hesketh which is with the Cardinal, you shall understand that he is the son of one William Hesketh the elder, now so termed, of Little Pulton in Lancashire, a continual recusant, which William married the sister of Cardinal Alane and by her had that son and divers others. This William and I came of two brethren between which brethren there was long suit for my grandfather's lands, and there hath not been any great familarity a[mong] us. And I do think you did take me the other day either for he [William, or for William] the father,

the recusant who cannot be found, although great search have been made for him as I heard. [William] Hesketh his son who is with the Cardinal in [Prague or possibly *Rome] who for anything I know is not acquainted [with the] matter."* … *"I now feel the old grudge in the Cardinal to my father is now bestowed upon me; for he might have sent that Hesketh, but being his nephew he spared him and hath made me the 'enffant perdue' as I wrote to the Cardinal I thought I should prove."*

The point here is that William Waad, Hesketh's gaoler and interrogator, seems at first to have thought he was dealing with the nephew of Cardinal Allen, the major Catholic agent provocateur on the Continent.

What a political coup that might have been if this had indeed been the man who had been trying to persuade Ferdinando to stake his claim to the throne! However, Richard Hesketh (1562-1593) makes it clear in this statement that it was he, Richard of Aughton, who was chosen to carry out the mission, not the Cardinal's nephew—William Hesketh. The Aughton Richard may have been chosen by the Cardinal as the "fall guy of least worth", but nevertheless, he was the guilty party and was subsequently executed as such at St. Albans on 29th of November, 1593.

A Lord Lieutenant was the Sovereign's personal representative in a county, usually invested in a trusted nobleman only during times of unrest and subsequently revoked. The principal responsibility was in organising and often funding the raising of a militia within the county. The Earls of Derby were unusual in holding this office as an hereditary entitlement, although by custom not legislation. This meant they were very much beholden to the monarch's largesse. It carried with it not only great power of law but also prestige and honour, and so was highly valued by the Earls. It also kept what was in effect an almost equally powerful Northern Court at heel to the Royal Court of the sovereign's in the south.

The "Essex adherents" were a group of likeminded people linked with Robert Dudley, Earl of Leicester, Sir Francis Walsingham and Sir Philip Sidney until their deaths in the 1580's, and with the Areopagitae of English poets that used to meet at Leicester House (later Essex House), and included, amongst many over the years of its existence: Robert Devereux, 2nd Earl of Essex; Ferdinando Stanley, Baron Strange, 5th Earl of Derby; his brother William Stanley, 6th Earl of Derby; Frances Walsingham, Countess of Essex, Essex's wife, daughter of Sir Francis Walsingham and widow of Sir Philip Sidney.

Ferdinando was an adherent in the early years, but no evidence has been discovered to support his later attendance, which the author has, rightly or wrongly, taken to be an indication that there was a parting of the ways. Ferdinando's entirely fictional objection to their beliefs and views serves not only as a plot device but also to illustrate the collision between the old and new schools of thought that was evolving during this period.

"The Crow is White": The "Battle of Lea Hall", 1589: In that year, a dispute between Thomas Howghton and

Thomasine Singleton, over cattle, led to the notorious "Affray at Lea". Thomas Langton Lord of Walton (1561-1605)—known as the Baron of Newton—was convinced of the justice of her case, and with others took part in an attempt to repossess the animals from the Howghton's manor house at Lea.

A force including Langton and Thomasine, on the 20th of November at 11 at night, assembled on Preston Marsh and agreed to "go and drive away the cattle". Thomas Howghton had got word of these warlike preparations, and mustered a force of about 30 men, which lay in ambush in one of the outbuildings. When the two forces met, a great affray began, Thomas Langton's company using the password "The crow is white", and Thomas Howghton's "Black, black". Amidst the profusion of heads broken in the dark, Thomas Howghton and another had been killed, whilst Thomas Langton "Being sore wounded…was presently apprehended lying in his bed at Broughton tower".

Three years later, the affair still hadn't been settled between the families, and Henry, the 4th Earl of Derby and Ferdinando's father, wrote to Lord Burghley warning him of the danger of the dispute, urging pardons be granted to "The poorer sorte". There was a real danger of the dispute escalating amongst the gentry involved, for the "Better sorte are great in kindred and affynitie, and soe stoared with friendes, as yf they should be burnte in the hande, I feare it will fall oute to be a ceasles and most dangerous quarrel".

Langton was eventually tried by the Star Chamber, and although he'd merited the death penalty, "frumgild" was substituted, requiring a substantial payment be made to the deceased's wife. This settlement saw the Baron of Newton's heavily mortgaged Walton estate and its Walton Hall, situated on the banks of the Ribble near Preston, eventually having to be sold to cover his mounting debts.

Specifically, the "Woodvale land near Parbold" and its purchase are entirely fictitious, although Ferdinando and his father, the fourth Earl, did have problems with local families over the exclusive use of Stanley land, which did flare up into acrimony resulting in the shifting of some allegiances to the Earl of Essex. Little if any real detail is now known, hence the fictional episode is used to illustrate its general nature.

Sir Thomas Gerrard's visit to view the fourth Earl's remains in the chapel at Lathom House is likewise fictitious, although the man and his circumstances described are historically accurate.

The animosity between Henry the fourth Earl of Derby and his wife, Margaret, is well recorded. Neither Henry nor his son, Ferdinando, made any provision for her in their wills.

Exactly which of his servants accompanied Ferdinando to the Court in Windsor is not recorded, so the author has made best guess assumptions. It's worth noting that the responsibilities of gentleman-servants varied and didn't always correspond to their titles. Such positions as Clerk of the Kitchens were more honorific than functional. To modern ears, this title sounds like some sort of lowly catering role—but it was actually more in the nature of a senior business manager, with considerable authority and responsibility.

The distance from Lathom House to Brereton was at the extreme edge of what such a large party could comfortably cover in a day. This suggested to the author that there was at Brereton something to make such a long day's push worthwhile, and a close friendship between Sir William Brereton and Ferdinando seemed more than plausible, although uncorroborated by any records. Such a relationship would then have provided a believable reason for Ferdinando's failure, at his friend Sir William's request, to mention during his later meetings with Secretary Cecil that the Baron of Newton had been present with Richard Hesketh at Brereton Hall.

Ferdinando had, at a later date, to reply to the Secretary's pointed enquiry regarding this omission with his explanation that he'd at first forgotten to mention the Baron had been there, then that he'd assumed it unimportant against Richard Hesketh's assurance that the man knew nothing of the plot. Even reading that letter now, it does seem a particularly lame excuse in this author's eyes.

Sir William Brereton's bereavement at the time is historically accurate, although his recusant sister-in-law's staying after the funeral of his wife, to help console his daughter, Mary, is again fictional.

Richard Hesketh's revelation of the plot to Ferdinando closely follows the carefully penned text supposedly discovered on him at his arrest. Its rather, for the modern ear, convoluted and archaic period form has been followed to an extent in Hesketh's delivery of the offer in chapter 17, when a more modern form of speech has been used elsewhere. This was in order to convey a sense of its gravitas and momentous implications.

Sir John's property in Staffordshire, where Ferdinando stayed after Brereton, is entirely fictional, including Sir John himself and those alliance families referred to, although their names were recorded as being families dwelling in that county at the time. This fictional interlude was included purely to give a glimpse into Ferdinando's possible thinking in regards to the offer he'd been made by Hesketh. No record has been found as to where Ferdinando's party did stay during the long journey between Brereton and Windsor.

As with their stay in Staffordshire, the one at the manor house of Southall near Gaddesden, although the property and its inhabitants are historically correct, is also fictional, serving a similar literary purpose to his fictional stay in Staffordshire. There is evidence that the Stanley family owned the manor there, and there are plaques commemorating the Stanleys in the local church. It may be of interest to note that the frail Mistress Martha Jermyn, widow of Edmund Jermyn, died not long after Ferdinando's fictional visit, late in 1593.

The second of Windsor's biannual fairs did take place on the Michaelmas weekend after Ferdinando's arrival at Windsor Castle, although the exact date of his arrival is not recorded but has been estimated from the expected progress a party such as his would make at the time, and the known records of his activities whilst at the castle, such as his letter to Secretary Cecil.

Master Algernon, the Windsor Castle gatekeeper, is entirely fictional, although Sir George Carey was the Knight Marshall at that time, and his wife, Elizabeth Spencer, was Ferdinando's sister-in-law.

Queen Elizabeth I. had, the day before Ferdinando's assumed arrival date, begun her translation from the original Latin into English of the Consolatione Philosophiae. At that time, Tudor society did not allow ladies to write any creative pieces, so the translation of chosen Latin texts, in particular, and some limited writing of poetry, were the only avenues open to them to express publicly their own views. In like manner, the Countess of Pembroke (a member of the Essex adherents) had, sometime earlier, started her own translation of King David's Psalms, although her completion of it lay a number of years in the future. All these translations were intentionally widely disseminated.

The precise time and location of Richard Hesketh's arrest seems not to have come down to us in the records, so this event is in this respect fictional. Hesketh was, though, taken to Sutton Park, where he remained during his interrogation. He was clearly cooperative, for he was never taken to the Tower of London, where more persuasive techniques could otherwise have been employed.

Ferdinando's use of his desire to be awarded the position of Lieutenant of Lancashire and Cheshire, as a justification for his not having Hesketh immediately arrested whilst still in the North, is a plausible construct of the author's.

Whether Ferdinando originally intended visiting his mother, Margaret Stanley, in Clerkenwell is unknown, although his intention to do so is documented in a letter to Secretary Cecil written whilst at Windsor Castle. Secretary Cecil's suggestion that he do so is entirely fictional, although quite feasible, and is used as a plot device to implicate, as the author sees it, the Secretary's likely close involvement in the proceedings.

Ferdinando's visit to the Michaelmas market in Windsor is entirely fictional, although highly likely. Annual fairs were opportunities not to be missed at the time, the only events where rare commodities could be obtained. His letter to Secretary Cecil, regarding visiting his mother and his wishes for an audience with the Queen, however, was written and has been presented verbatim.

The author could find no record of Ferdinando's audience with Queen Elizabeth I., although it almost certainly happened, so the event presented is entirely fictional. The etiquette described is, however, an accurate depiction of such an event. Queen Elizabeth was known to have nicknames for many of her courtiers, most of them hardly complimentary, which she'd use quite casually within clear earshot of all at the Court. She was in the habit of calling Secretary Cecil "my crouchback pygmy", in cruel reference to his short stature and hunchback.

There is some uncertainty as to exactly where Margaret Stanley resided at the time, but the author is confident, from the circumstantial evidence, that it was indeed at the newly built Isleworth House in St. James in the parish of Clerkenwell. The meeting between Margaret and her son Ferdinando is entirely fictional, though again, highly plausible from the evidence surrounding the lady and her predicament.

No records could be found covering Ferdinando's return to Lathom House, so all dates are conjectural, but again, perfectly feasible.

Ferdinando was indeed excluded from the arraignment of Richard Hesketh, much to his chagrin. This is further evidence of the distrust he was seen in by the Royal Court.

The letters discovered in the Earl of Shrewsbury's Talbot collection in the Lambeth Palace Library are real but, as mentioned by Sophie, rare pieces of evidence to support the confrontation between Ferdinando and Essex over the disputed land.

The accident involving the miller's horse and wagon at the entrance to Lathom House is entirely fictional. As is Simon Wardell, although both Doughtie brothers, Michael and Robert, are historical characters. Little is indeed known about Robert, other than intimations directed to Secretary Cecil that he may know something of Ferdinando's death, and mentions elsewhere that Ferdinando's "Master of the Horses" had been seen hurriedly leaving Lathom House shortly after Ferdinando's death.

The author has made Robert Doughtie Ferdinando's Waiting Gentleman and Cupbearer for plot purposes, although he's only referred to in the few mentions of him in the records as "Yeoman Waiter". That he could have been conflated with the Master of the Horses, or those reports of the fleeing servant made in error as to his actual title, is not unreasonable.

His sexual orientation is entirely fictitious, although, despite homosexuality being illegal at the time, not uncommon and in certain circles possibly tolerated in Tudor times. It's worth keeping in mind that of the 600 or so in service to Ferdinando, only a small handful were women. This made the Stanley "Northern Court", like many aristocratic houses, a predominantly male enclave, not unlike a boys' public school. The occurrence of such relationships can, therefore, hardly be regarded as a rarity.

Mister Halsall is an historical character, although not a great deal is known about him. He is mentioned in John Stowe's Annals of England 1603 (more later) as having been present during Ferdinando's two weeks of illness leading up to his death. There, he's described as having been the one to discover the waxen image in his lordship's bedchamber.

His exact family relationship to Jane Halsall has

not been determined, so Robert Doughtie's suggested explanation of the reasons for Mister Halsall's involvement is entirely fictitious.

Ferdinando did go to Knowsley for the Easter week, for the hunting and hawking, and did fall ill there.

That Robert Doughtie was responsible for administering arsenic to Ferdinando in a glass of sweet wine is entirely fictitious, as is the poison having been furnished by Mister Halsall.

That Simon would have been chopping firewood for Mister Halsall is not unreasonable. Being in service to the nobility at that time was considered a great honour, even the most menial of tasks willingly carried out as a mark of respect for the lord and master. Further, responsibilities were not rigidly demarcated but tended to be fluid, so work in the kitchens could be followed by tending fireplaces, serving food, and the like. The only area where servants tended to be dedicated was in the laundry, and where, if any, the few women of the household would have worked, other than those in personal service to the lady of the household, such as maids of honour, etc..

This book's timeline for Ferdinando's illness has been kept strictly to that reported in John Stowe's Annals of England 1603, where the doctors' report is presented. Notably, no mention in this likely authentically reproduced record makes any mention of poisoning. The only hint is in its introduction, where Bezars stone and unicorn's horn are detailed as having been administered—standard treatments at the time for poisoning.

However, it would seem a reasonable assumption that these would have been used simply as a matter of course when treating any nobleman. The author has assumed that, certainly initially, the doctors had no genuine suspicions that Ferdinando had been poisoned.

As to the part played by witchcraft, Stowe's book includes this as an afterword to the doctors' report (although quite an extensive one), couched in terms in its introduction that suggest Stowe had little confidence in its veracity. More significantly, in this author's eyes at least, the first two lines, stating: "*A true report of such reasons and conjectures, as caused many learned men to suppose him to be bewitched.*" have been centred on the page. This formatting could not be found anywhere else in Stowe's book, as though he intended it as a clue to his readership of his own scepticism. The author suspects Stowe was pressed into including the bewitchment text by agents of Secretary Cecil, as part of their "fake news" drive.

Stowe names the four doctors in attendance, but does not allude to when any of them arrived at Lathom House. The author has played free with this on the reasonable assumption that it would have been unlikely for more than two to have been summoned initially, and that the extra two were subsequently called in at Ferdinando's worsening condition.

The incident regarding the lawyer (and later MP) Sir Thomas Hesketh, Richard Hesketh's brother and most powerful of the Aughton Heskeths, did occur. However, the exact nature of how he upset Ferdinando, as the Earl described to Cecil in his appeal to him as: *"going about in malice as he doth, to draw the government from me to himself"*, could not be discovered. Ferdinando sought Secretary Cecil's admonishment and censure of the lawyer, but whether Cecil did so or not is unrecorded, although he did seek the opinion of Sir T. Heneage, Vice-Chamberlain, who sided with Thomas Hesketh.

That the Government, and in particular Secretary Cecil, wished to keep the lid on Catholic unrest in Lancashire is well attested in the records. The county was seen as a hotbed of Catholics, from where a very real threat of a Spanish invasion could come (the failed but still terrifying Spanish Armada had happened only 5 years earlier).

To this end, Secretary Cecil kept a map of Lancashire (inherited from his father, Sir William Cecil, Lord Burghley) on which all the notable families were marked as either being of the Protestant or Catholic persuasion, so he would know who to trust in the event of an invasion along its coast. He'd even marked the most likely part of that coast for where the landing of a sizeable Spanish force might occur.

The course of Ferdinando's illness, his symptoms and treatment, is commensurate with the doctors' notes presented in Stowe, although the more horrific aspects have been only obliquely described, to make the reading more palatable.

Alice did write to Secretary Cecil from Lathom House, informing him of Ferdinando's likely fatal illness and hoping she could trust in him for his subsequent support.

Ferdinando's last will and testament was signed on the 12th of April, 1594, four days before his death, which was not an uncommon practice at the time.

Nothing definitive has come down to us through history as to who was ultimately behind the death of Ferdinando—if, indeed, anyone was. Nor whether he died of a "surfeit of wine and strenuous exercise", poison or witchcraft. There appear to be later stories that Ferdinando was "poisoned by the Jesuits" in revenge for not falling in with their plot, but there seems little evidence of this story at the time. The narrative presented is the one that made the most sense to the author of what can be inferred from the records about the characters, their natures and motives, and the known events and politics of the time.

William Stanley, Ferdinando's brother, did indeed become the sixth Earl of Derby, and interestingly, married Secretary Cecil's half-niece, Alice de Vere, the following year, 1595. A case of reward for services rendered, perhaps, but certainly a way of keeping the Earldom of Derby close within Cecil's influence.

There followed some ten years of legal wrangles between William and Alice and her daughters over the inheritance of the Stanley estates. Alice and her daughters' case was no doubt furthered by Alice marrying her legal advisor, the Solicitor General, Lord Keeper and Lord Chancellor Thomas Egerton, the Viscount Brackley.

It appears that, despite successfully retaining some sizeable portion of the estate, and despite his marriage into the prestigious Cecil family, William's Earldom was not a happy one. He retired from public life in his later years to a modest property in Chester, on an annuity of £1,000, where he eventually died. The author has read into this a nagging sense of guilt about his part in his brother, Ferdinando's, downfall, although there are no records explicitly supporting this conjecture.

And finally, the Lady Alice, Countess of Derby's, suspected pregnancy came to nothing. It's possible she miscarried sometime after Ferdinando's death, if she had really been pregnant to begin with. Or, as has been suggested, she maintained the fiction of her pregnancy to forestall the legal process she knew her brother-in-law, William, would embark upon to regain the Stanley estates bequeathed to her and her daughters. This would have posited, in the subsequent birth of a male heir, the scuppering of any hopes William would otherwise have had of becoming the sixth Earl and therefore of having the need to win such a case. As it turned out, in the ultimate absence of any male heir, the case dragged on for some ten years after Ferdinando's death, an equitable settlement finally being arrived at between the parties.

ABOUT THE AUTHOR

Clive Johnson was born in the mid-1950's in Bradford, in what was then the West Riding of the English county of Yorkshire. Mid-way through the 1970s, he found himself lured away by the bright lights of Manchester to attend Salford University.

In addition to getting a degree in electronics, he also had the good fortune of meeting Maureen Medley—his subsequent partner and editor. Manchester retained its lure and has thereafter been his hometown.

Torn between the arts—a natural and easy artist—and the sciences—struggled with maths, youthful rationality favoured science as a living, leaving art as a pastime pleasure. Consequently, after graduation, twenty years were spent implementing technologies for mainframe computer design and manufacture, and being a Group IT Manager for an international print company.

The catalyst of a corporate takeover led to a change of career, and the opportunity to return to the arts. The unearthing of a late seventies manuscript—during loft improvements—resurrected an interest in storytelling, and one thing led to another. A naïve and inexpert seed finally received benefit of mature loam and from it his first novel, Leiyatel's Embrace, soon blossomed.

Find my website at http://www.flyingferrets.com

Connect with Me:

Follow me on Facebook:
https://www.facebook.com/profile.php?id=100003080526007

Subscribe to my blog:
https://www.goodreads.com/author/show/
5333506.Clive_S_Johnson/blog

Printed in Great Britain
by Amazon

253